D0112159

THE COLLECTED
GHOST STORIES OF
MRS. J. H. RIDDELL

THE COLLECTED
GHOST STORIES OF
MRS. J. H. RIDDELL

SELECTED AND INTRODUCED BY

E. F. BLEILER

DOVER PUBLICATIONS, INC.
NEW YORK

Published in Canada by General Publishing Company,
Ltd., 30 Lesmill Road, Don Mills, Toronto, Ontario.
Published in the United Kingdom by Constable and
Company, Ltd., 10 Orange Street, London WC2H 7EG.

The Collected Ghost Stories of Mrs. J. H. Riddell is a new
collection of 14 unabridged stories taken from the sources
indicated on page 345. The selection was made by E. F.
Bleiler, who also wrote the Introduction.

International Standard Book Number: 0-486-23430-4
Library of Congress Catalog Card Number: 76-10907

Manufactured in the United States of America
Dover Publications, Inc.
180 Varick Street
New York, N.Y. 10014

CONTENTS

MRS. RIDDELL, MID-VICTORIAN GHOSTS, AND CHRISTMAS ANNUALS

I

MANY authors wrote ghost stories for the Victorian public. To list them is to list the popular authors of the day: Charles Dickens, for "The Signal-man" and others, although not *A Christmas Carol*, which is properly an allegory; Miss Braddon, author of *Lady Audley's Secret*; Mrs. Ellen Wood, author of *East Lynne*; Miss Rhoda Broughton, author of *Cometh up as a Flower*; Florence Marryat; Amelia Edwards, later of the Egypt Exploration Fund; Mrs. Riddell; Mrs. Molesworth, Arthur Conan Doyle, J. S. LeFanu, James Grant and many others.

Women were predominant in this field, both quantitatively and qualitatively. "One of the chief features of the modern fiction is that it is largely produced by women; probably much more than half of the novels of the day are written by women, and the proportion is constantly increasing" (*Church Review Quarterly*, 1875). This may simply represent business conditions: most of the fiction periodicals had a strong feminist slant, were edited by women, and were aimed at the new, moneyed, educated middle-class wives of the large cities.

Preeminent among these female authors was Mrs. J. H. Riddell, who was the best distaff writer of ghost stories and also came closest to being a specialist in the form. Since it is now almost fifty years ago that S. M. Ellis, in his *Wilkie Collins, LeFanu and Others* (London, 1931) wrote the only biographical essay about Mrs. Riddell, it might be well to give some detail about her life and her works. Since Ellis's day, a little more information has become available and critical positions have changed.

Charlotte Elizabeth Lawson Cowan (1832–1906), later Mrs. J. H. Riddell (pronounced "riddle"), was born in Carrickfergus, a small town near Belfast, of mixed Irish, Scottish and English ancestry. Her father was High Sheriff for County Antrim, and her family was well to do. Her early childhood was spent in a fairly luxurious Italianate villa with extensive grounds, and much of her later life was an attempt to regain this life-style. She never succeeded.

James Cowan, her father, is a shadowy figure, and all that can be said about him is that he had a breakdown of some sort, became invalid or semiinvalid, and lost all his money. The family was reduced to near poverty. But during his lifetime, before his collapse, young Charlotte Cowan followed the path of precocious Victorian girls in reading omnivorously, writing poetry, and finishing a full novel at age fifteen.

At about the time Charlotte Cowan turned twenty-one, her father died. She and her mother tried to live in reduced circumstances in a small village, but without success. They then decided to betake themselves to London, where Charlotte—brave, optimistic, willing to work hard—hoped to follow a literary career. They arrived in London in January 1855, during a winter reported to be unusually severe, and the future Mrs. Riddell used to reflect on the shivering days when she trod the windy streets, trying to place her work with editors and publishers, and the colder nights when she wrote for long hours in draughty rooms heated only by candle.

Mrs. Riddell incorporated many of her own experiences around the Strand in her fourth novel, *The Rich Husband* (1858). In this work Mrs. Judith Mazingford, having quarreled with her sadistic, miserly husband, runs away from home and makes her living for a time by writing fiction.

> Mrs. Mazingford knew little of life—that is, literary life—or she never would have gone in her carriage to ask payment for a novel.
>
> Rich authors are considered, in publishing circles, able to afford the risks attendant on bringing out a new work themselves. Justly, or unjustly, as the reader may please to consider it, they are compelled, except in very rare instances, to pay for their whistle.
>
> Her shrewd sense, however, soon told her what the eminent firm of Noxley and Mobelle were driving at. They talked of per-centages—but Mrs. Mazingford shook her head; of subscribing a hundred and fifty copies among her acquaintances—on which suggestion Judith at once put a somewhat peremptory veto; of clearing expenses—a plan, the lady said, was not to be thought of; and then the polite publishers, being at their wits' end, held their tongues.
>
> "I really do not see what we can do, madam," remarked Mr. Noxley, after a dreary pause, during the continuance of which he had vainly waited for Judith to speak. "Can you think of any plan, Mr. Mobelle?"
>
> Mr. Mobelle was unable to aid his partner's imagination.

"Publishing, you see, is a very uncertain affair," remarked Mr. Noxley, sententiously; "and therefore, in a general way, we do not care to take the entire risk of a new work, by an author as yet unknown to fame" (here Mr. Noxley bowed politely). "We like to be secured against any great amount of loss by a well-known name—that is, a name which will sell a book; or else by a certain number of copies being taken by the writer. Now, amongst your extensive connection, madam—"

"Excuse me, sir," interrupted the lady, haughtily, "but I do not choose to take my book begging about the world. I would rather go and ask each of my acquaintances to give me thirty shillings at once . . . I think I can bring this matter to a point at once. I wish to receive remuneration for my work. . . . I should like you, if you would not consider me too troublesome, to read over my manuscript, and then say whether you can offer me anything for it or not. . . . Will you oblige me by looking at the book?"

Messrs. Noxley and Mobelle were willing to do anything except pay money, and according, after bowing the lady out, they placed the manuscript in the hands of their "reader"—as literary advisers are called—who laid it aside for two months. At the expiration of which time he condescended to listen to various hints, uncomplimentary to his punctuality, and went through it in an evening.

"We regret, madam, that the result is unfavourable," remarked Mr. Noxley, with that unvarying urbanity which is enough to drive a rejected author out of his senses.

As Miss Cowan's experience with Noxley (probably Bentley) shows, book publishing in London in the mid-Victorian period was somewhat different from American publishing of today. There were many small publishers, often men who owned bookshops, who might venture on printing a small edition of a book. Sometimes an author sold a book outright to such a small publisher, but more common was some arrangement to protect the publisher in the case of unknown authors: the author might advance payment of costs and then own the edition, or the author might accept a percentage of profit after and above printing costs. It may have been some arrangement of this sort that resulted in the publication of Mrs. Riddell's first novel, *Zuriel's Grandchild*, under a pseudonym in 1856.

Although very little is known about Mrs. Riddell's personal life, her early years in London must have been very difficult. She had little money and little prospect of immediate success. Her mother did not survive the transplant to England long, and died of cancer; young

Charlotte had to nurse her in addition to writing and "traversing most of the back streets and lanes which literature affects in London—trying to dispose of manuscripts to editors and publishers—asking for interviews with all sorts of people, as if she were striving for variety in rebuffs, refusals, cold civility and constrained politeness" (*The Rich Husband*). Then in 1857, not too long after her mother's death, Charlotte Cowan married Joseph Hadley Riddell, a civil engineer.

Riddell was a disaster, although, as with Charlotte's father, who may have pursued a similar path, no precise information is available. Rumors, however, offer hints if not accuracy. "I believe her husband, through some queer way in business, was resting somewhere at his country's expense," said Harry Furniss, the cartoonist, about an interview with Mrs. Riddell in the early 1870's. Furniss, however, is probably not entirely correct, since there is no evidence that Riddell went to prison. Riddell was a would-be inventor and would-be entrepreneur who totally lacked business sense and was a very poor judge of his fellow man. As Mrs. Riddell wrote of him, years after his death, he was a charming and intelligent man, but completely unsuited to a life of business.

Part of Riddell's downfall was worked into the novel *Mortomley's Estate* (1874). Mortomley is amiable, intellectually brilliant, but overtrusting and a man of poor judgment. After he has a physical and nervous breakdown, his wife becomes entangled with dishonest lawyers and accountants, and eventually must operate the family dye works herself. The situation behind this novel was the Bankruptcy Act of 1866, which could cause great hardship in permitting a bankrupt to go into permanent receivership, without hope of release, while his creditors went without payment. The inferences are that Riddell went through some such situation. (One wonders how Riddell felt about this subliminal pillorying.)

The significance of Joseph H. Riddell to Charlotte Riddell was double. Due to his flaws or misfortunes she was forced to become the breadwinner for both—they remained childless—and she was driven into schedules and a type of writing that prevented her from doing her best work. She spent many years of hard toil liquidating his debts. Her biographer, S. M. Ellis, makes the point that she was almost quixotic in her high sense of business honor, and eventually rendered herself almost penniless.

Riddell's second significance was that he helped his wife with her writing. He contributed technical information to her stories that dealt with mechanical or business matters, and aided her with the intricacies of City folkways. In this respect Riddell was very important to her, for much of her contemporary success and the present interest in her writing is due to her skilful pioneering in these areas.

It is not known whether Riddell went beyond contributing facts and actually wrote part of the texts. But sometimes, as in *City and Suburb* (1861), interspersed with accounts of inventions and labor disputes, there are passages about worthless husbands and domineering wives, and a reader wonders whether this is Riddell emergent, and whether a fair amount of hatred was not intermingled with the devotion, despite Mrs. Riddell's protestations to the contrary.

All this exemplifies the syndrome of the Victorian female author who wrote to support an ineffectual husband. Miss Braddon (Mrs. Maxwell) and Mrs. Oliphant are the two best-known instances. What really happened? Did a trusting girl marry a plausible young man, and then learn that she must undo his follies and create income as well as manage a household? Or did a dominant woman find a weak male, marry him, support him in his follies, while emasculating him by holding up to him his inferiority? Unfortunately, we cannot answer: even less known than the Victorian bedroom is the Victorian breakfast chamber.

By about 1860 Mrs. Riddell had acquired some reputation, and could be considered a professional writer. Success, however, came in 1864 with the novel *George Geith of Fen Court*. The first important novel to point out the romance of commercial life in the City of London, it went through several editions, and in the 1870's was dramatized. It remained on the stage through the 1880's at least, in Great Britain, America, and Australia. It was often played by the Macklins. A later reminiscence by Mrs. Riddell conveys some hint of its significance:

> In those early days he—Mr. Newby—was good enough to take a book of mine. Of course he only knew me by my maiden name, because after my mother's death Welbeck Street lay quite out of my way, and I fear I ungratefully forgot the cheerful fire, and the talks about authors which were once so pleasant.
>
> For this reason he knew nothing of my doings. The years came and

the years went, till after the crash came in our affairs; when I was looking about me for every five-pound note I could get I bethought me of this and another old book, which I can never sufficiently regret republishing. Well, I found I could sell both of them, and forthwith repaired, after all that time, to Mr. Newby's, where nothing looked much changed, and no one seemed much older, except myself, who had lived many lives in the interval.

Of course both Mr. Newby and Miss Springett had a vague memory of me, when I reminded the former that he had published "Zuriel's Grandchild." What I wanted was a copy of the book. He feared he had not one, but promised to ascertain. I can see them both now in that warm, comfortable back room, into which, as a girl, I had often gone shivering.

He took a seat on the one side of a large table, she on the other. I sat facing Mr. Newby—a most anxious woman, yet amused.

"Have you," he said delicately, "gone on at all with literature?"

"Oh, yes," I answered.

"Have you—published anything?" with great caution, so as not to hurt my feelings.

"Several books," I replied.

"Indeed!!!" *amazed.* "Might I ask the names?"—tentatively.

"Well, amongst others, 'George Geith.'"

A dead silence ensued, during which I had the comfort of feeling that they both felt sure I was saying what was not true. I sat quite quiet, and so did they. If I had not been so burdened with care I must have laughed out loud. . . . and then this came from Mr. Newby, while the ribbons on Miss Springett's cap were tremulous:

"*If*—you *really* wrote 'George Geith,' *then* indeed you have achieved a success." (*Notable Woman Authors of the Day* by Helen C. Black, Glasgow, 1893)

While none of Mrs. Riddell's works ever attained to the fantastic popularity of *Lady Audley's Secret* or *East Lynne*, Mrs. Riddell was a solid, dependable author whose work sold well at least up into the 1880's. She wrote extensively for the better fiction magazines—*London Society, Temple Bar, Once a Week*—and saw many of her stories published in book form. For a time—the exact dates are not known, except that they fall in part at least in the 1860's—she edited *Home Magazine* and *St. James's Magazine*; she also is said to have edited less important magazines under pseudonyms now not identified.

In 1880 Joseph H. Riddell died, and a new series of debts was uncovered for Mrs. Riddell to settle. She paid them, but found herself almost penniless. The remainder of her life became increasingly difficult as changes in literary fashion, loss of income, illness, and old age beset her. In the 1890's her work could no longer compete with that of the younger generation, and her last years were spent in poverty, with some assistance from the Society of Authors. She died of cancer in 1906.

In person Mrs. Riddell was tall, slender in her youth, but she became in her later years what the Victorians termed "a fine woman." Her facial features were strong, and revealed her ready Irish wit and kindly good humor. She was amiable, generous and goodhearted, and often went out of her way to help younger, struggling authors and artists. She had a strong mind of her own in critical and literary matters, and in native intelligence was probably much superior to most of her female writing contemporaries.

Mrs. Riddell wrote slowly as Victorian authors went, normally spending about two years on a novel. Unlike Wilkie Collins, who worked with an extremely detailed scenario, or Dickens, who let his unconscious mind do his plotting for him, Mrs. Riddell would work out her entire novel mentally, down to individual conversations, before starting to set it down on paper. She is said to have plotted from the ending forwards, although I suspect that this was not always true. Some of her subject matter was taken consciously from her life and from things she had witnessed or heard about, but she also spent time in free reverie, between sleep and waking, letting ideas and personalities emerge. As for her actual writing process:

> In those Victorian days most of the poetesses and authoresses affected the long flowing black velvet gown, low cut bodices, lace and jewellery. Even such a practical authoress as Mrs. Riddell was so attired. On her writing-table an ordinary cup and saucer answered the purpose of an ink-stand, the cup was half full of ink and half a dozen feather pens lay diagonally across the saucer. (*Some Notable Women* by Harry Furniss, London, 1923)

II

DURING her long literary life Mrs. Riddell wrote at least forty-six novels and forty-one short stories, as well as some miscellaneous material. This count is certainly not complete, however, for much of her work was published anonymously. She did not keep records, and toward the close of her life, when she was questioned by S. M. Ellis, she had lost account of much that she had written. Unlike LeFanu, who also published much anonymously, Mrs. Riddell did not invoke a consistent imaginary geography or repeat name tags for the convenience of the reader. As a result of this a modern reader may examine many of the Christmas annuals of her day and have a suspicion that individual unsigned stories are by Mrs. Riddell, but no certainty.

There is no need to detail Mrs. Riddell's varied work, which ranges in date from *Zuriel's Grandchild* (1856) to *Poor Fellow!* (1902). Let us simply point out a few high points in her non-supernatural fiction.

Mrs. Riddell's earliest work is best forgiven, apart from an occasional felicity of place description, which she always handled well. Her first work of modern interest is *George Geith of Fen Court* (1864), which novel made her fame and fortune, such as they were. Although it is ultimately rooted in a neo-Gothic alienation plot, it describes City life and personalities so aptly that it is still enjoyable reading. *Maxwell Drewitt* (1865), set in Ireland, has moments of melodrama, but well-drawn minor characters and a fine, long description of a riotous Parliamentary election.

Home, Sweet Home (1873) is, in my opinion, Mrs. Riddell's best non-supernatural novel. It is the first-person narrative of a vapid country girl of lowly birth who has remarkable musical ability. Her childhood among unsympathetic relatives, her dilemma at being caught between two sets of standards, her experiences in the family of a German voice-coach and musician, and her problems on the concert circuit are all set forth in a wealth of realistic detail that outweighs a very weak ending. *Mortomley's Estate* (1874) has already been mentioned in connection with the Riddell finances. It analyzes a situation in business law, plus social repercussions, quite well.

The Mystery in Palace Gardens (1880) should be mentioned in passing, not because it is remarkably successful, but because its title has misled many into thinking it is a detective story. It is not. It is a story of social-climbing and adultery. Similarly, the reader should be warned about *A Life's Assize* (1871), which has been misleadingly described as a murder mystery. It is about a clergyman who accidentally kills a man in self-defense, stands trial with a verdict of Not Proven, and languishes under an assumed identity for the remainder of his life. Mrs. Riddell is better at realism.

Miss Gascoyne (1887) quite possibly dips into Mrs. Riddell's life for motivations. An older woman falls desperately in love with a very young man, and tries to buy his love. This novel was written at the time that Mrs. Riddell was associated with A. H. Norway, the young man with whom she made the foot tour of the Black Forest described in her travel book, *A Mad Tour*.

The Nun's Curse (1888) ranks second among Mrs. Riddell's realistic novels. There are supernatural implications in the background, it is true, but it is questionable how these are to be interpreted. During Reformation times a nun who had been hunted like an animal placed a curse on the Connors: No Connor son shall ever succeed his father to the estate, and there shall be perpetual war between father and son. The curse has always been fulfilled, even to the present middle nineteenth-century situation. But Mrs. Riddell also makes the point that all the Connors have been highly irresponsible, and that this was the real curse. Her portrayal of the present Connor, who is a fool; his fiancée, who is a selfish, cold snob; and a host of very fine minor characters make this novel well worth reading.

The Head of the Firm (1892) is based on two themes, the downfall of an amiable, intelligent attorney who turns embezzler, and the sudden acquisition of a fortune by a young female greengrocer. The greengrocer, like Eliza Doolittle, must undergo instruction in speech and deportment to make her fit for her new life. Her situation is created in excellent detail.

Three themes permeate Mrs. Riddell's non-supernatural fiction: London, business or commerce, and social rank. These were probably areas of great importance for her readership.

London is a living force in her work to an extent unmatched by any other novelist of her day. No one else has so savored the old courts and odd passages, and charted the walks and rides of his or her characters with such precision, enthusiasm, and almost compulsion. Often after describing astonishing medieval or renaissance survivals she will make the melancholy comment, "Or, so it was some twenty years ago, where the railroad now is situated." She knew the suburbs well, too, the roads leading to them, the pre-railroad transportation, their social evolution from outlying village to developed suburb to semislum, the classes that inhabited each, the small businesses and farms.

The largest overt theme in her work is business or commerce, and in her lifetime she was known as the Novelist of the City. Through her husband she knew many businessmen, and she seems to have been the first to recognize that business life had a dynamics and glamor of its own. Many of her business novels follow out a topic: *George Geith of Fen Court* is concerned with a man of family who simply finds accounting fascinating; *Austin Friars* is devoted to a financial swindler; *Mortomley's Estate* involves bankruptcy; and *The Race for Wealth* and *Alaric Spenceley* cover business opportunism, greed, and unscrupulousness. Some of Mrs. Riddell's characters are consulting engineers who perform actual tasks; others are inventors and manufacturers; others are lawyers, accountants, or simply speculators. Mrs. Riddell may offer technical information lightly about dyeing in *Mortomley's Estate*, the adulteration industry in *The Race for Wealth*, loan sharking in *The Nun's Curse*, and scientific farming in *Maxwell Drewitt*. In *The Head of the Firm* we learn how a fruiterer obtains supplies from a jobber, who loads the cart, and how much money is likely to be made. This concreteness lends her work a peculiar substantiality that goes some distance toward removing the limitations of circumscribed plots.

Difference of rank, too, is one of Mrs. Riddell's concerns. If the reigning county family betrays its social duty toward a family of the yeoman class, as in *Home, Sweet Home*, what will happen? What is to be the fate of the exceptional person; should she try to escape from the strict social structuring of the countryside, or should she remain in her birth-lot? What is the domestic result of a mesalliance when a young man of family runs off with a handsome farm girl, as in *The Mystery in Palace Gardens*? Will the marriage be stable? How does a City merchant of position, wealth and education, as in *City and Suburb*, relate to an impoverished member of the older landed aristocracy?

These three themes—the social geography of London, the ethnology of business, the dynamics of social mobility in a period of change—were treated seriously by Mrs. Riddell, even though she apparently made concessions in other areas of writing. They interest us today, and they obviously interested the female readership of the better periodicals. Such readers were comfortable urbanites interested in their husband's livelihood and sensitive about their own spirit-position on the British totempole. Mrs. Riddell's concept of limited democracy probably pleased them.

Sensationalism, of course, was the call of the day in fiction, and Mrs. Riddell made half-hearted attempts to be sensational, but this area was not her forte, and sensational elements usually give the appearance of being afterthoughts to her leisurely, detailed, realistic development. One can guess that husbands who meet their prostituted wives, as in *Daisies and Buttercups*; or bigamistic ladies who consort with murderers, as in *The Moors and the Fens*; or adultresses who suppress correspondence from their supposedly dead husbands, to maintain their position, as in *The Mystery in Palace Gardens*; or squires who substitute corpses for their own children, in order to gain control of an inheritance, as in *The Ruling Passion*, were sops to the prevailing trends.

Despite her role as a popular novelist feeding the periodical mind, Mrs. Riddell was in a certain sense a tragic moralist, not in the cosmic sense of Hardy, whose writing career nearly paralleled hers in time, but in a realistic, psychological sense. Many of her leading characters are posited as beings with character flaws; stories develop out of their reactions in certain situations, and they come to bad ends. Engineer Ruthven in *City and Suburb*, for example, is possessed of a ridiculously aggressive family pride, which will not permit him to associate with lesser mortals. When a strike emerges at his plant Ruthven's hauteur restrains him from even speaking to his workers. The brilliant young doctor in *The Rich Man's Daughter* is money-mad, ambitious to make guineas, as he says, instead of shillings. He marries a girl for her money, then discovers that he cannot tap it. The goodhearted lawyer, Edward Desbourne, in *The Head of the Firm*, is estimable in most ways, but he cannot say no, to his wife, to his friends, to supplicants, and his fall is pitiable. Weakness, bad heredity, crookedness, temper, greed, overweening ambition all drag their possessors down, simply as a law of human inevitability. Fate, for Mrs. Riddell, always lurks behind the weed or the rose.

If one considers Mrs. Riddell's non-supernatural fiction as a body, one characteristic is outstanding: its unevenness, both from one work to another, and even within the single work. One can find pages of nicely written concise prose, and one can find pages of inflated gush riddled with stylistic affectations. One can read through several hundred pages of fine development and characterization, to come upon a sentimental ending that almost spoils everything that went before. The reason for these flaws, probably, was her writing circumstance: she wrote out of desperation most of the time and bent to the editor. Hardy, it will be remembered, found his earliest work rejected because it was not sensational enough, and also tried to oblige.

Because of the flaws in her work, Mrs. Riddell is not to be numbered among the giants of general Victorian literature. But this does not mean that she is to be discarded. At her best she had a touch which permits her to enter the company of the great. She need yield to few in evocation of landscape or setting, and she is excellent in situations that call for the invention of consistent life detail. Her second strength lies in the creation of minor characters, many of whom can stand comparison with the work of her greatest contemporaries. They remain with the reader long after the plots and the major characters are forgotten. On the other hand, she had more difficulty with major personalities, perhaps because these had perforce to act in sentimental or melodramatic situations.

All in all, once one has read a large quantity of Mrs. Riddell's non-supernatural work, one emerges with the recognition that she was not a negligible writer, even though many of her novels fall below standard and she seldom realized her potential. Even in her weakest work there is always an interesting personal element.

III

MRS. RIDDELL's corpus of supernatural fiction includes four novels, *Fairy Water* (1873), *The Uninhabited House* (1874), *The Haunted River* (1877) and *The Disappearance of Mr. Jeremiah Redworth* (1878).* Each of these appeared in Routledge's *Christmas Annuals,* and despite their present extreme rarity they were widely circulated in their time. They are successful examples of one of the most difficult literary forms, the long supernatural story.

* *Fairy Water* is reprinted under the title *The Haunted House at Latchford* in *Three Supernatural Novels of the Victorian Period,* edited by E. F. Bleiler (Dover, 1975), and *The Uninhabited House* in *Five Victorian Ghost Novels,* edited by E. F. Bleiler (Dover, 1971).

Fourteen or fifteen (depending on interpretation) short supernatural stories can also be definitely attributed to Mrs. Riddell. These were probably first printed in periodicals, although for most, at present, only the later book publication is known. The six stories that Mrs. Riddell apparently considered her best were gathered up for the exceedingly rare volume, *Weird Stories*, which appeared in 1882. These are "Walnut-Tree House," "The Open Door," "Nut Bush Farm," "The Old House in Vauxhall Walk," "Sandy the Tinker" and "Old Mrs. Jones." Her other supernatural fiction is scattered through periodicals and her short story collections.

The ideas in Mrs. Riddell's ghost stories were not novel; they were shared by most of her contemporaries who wrote such fiction. Whether by Charles Dickens, Wilkie Collins, Amelia B. Edwards, Rhoda Broughton, George Sala, Edmund Yates, Mary Braddon, Mrs. Ellen Wood, or Mrs. Riddell, a ghost story of this period was likely to be very constricted in technique and ideas.*

Above all else the writer of a ghost story in the mid-Victorian era demanded very little suspension of disbelief. There should be only one breach of reality, and this supernaturalism should not grow naturally out of a fantastic background but should be obtrusive in a realistic world. Some authors may have been aware of these principles; others may simply have imitated stories in which they were manifested.

In Dickens's short story "To Be Taken with a Grain of Salt," for example, the setting is a trial for murder. A ghost appears to the defendant-murderer, as the thirteenth man on a jury. The ghost thus doubles as a conscience symbol. Or, in Mrs. Riddell's novel *The Uninhabited House*, a young lady in distressed financial circumstances is forced to rent a neglected house. Her feuds with her unscrupulous, miserly landlord form a setting for the supernatural, which suddenly bursts open for a moment and changes lives.

All this is very different from the supernatural techniques of the preceding, Romantic period, where the prevailing theory seems to have been that the whole work should form a single field of fantasy, with background, personalities, multiple supernaturalisms extended to form an ecstasy beyond daily life.

---

* In this introduction no reference is intended to J. S. LeFanu, whose work was quite different from that of the other Victorians, and did not suffer from the same limitations.

The themes used by Mrs. Riddell and the other mid-Victorians were very few in number and not highly charged with fantasy. In fact, my first impression on tabulating these motives was that they might well mirror living beliefs in her day. These themes were not, for the most part, devils, witches, vampires, black magic, monsters or demons, but they were the equivalent of stories that might have been passed around by word of mouth, from friend to friend. They concerned the strange dream that Aunt Matilda had, that eventuated a few days later; the odd figure that Squire Acres wasn't quite sure if he saw looming in the dark. Perhaps the Victorian writer selected his/her ideas to match contemporary folk belief?

Was there any way to compare story themes with what people actually believed in middle nineteenth-century England? This proved to be quite easy.

The last quarter of the nineteenth century seems to have been the single era in human history when a serious, systematic attempt was made to census the supernatural. This was the work of the psychical research societies. In Great Britain there was the Society for Psychical Research, and in America the American Society for Psychical Research. Both groups were staffed by men of stature, the American including Charles S. Peirce, Josiah Royce, and William James.

In the 1880's the British society placed advertisements in newspapers and periodicals, asking readers to send in reports of paranormal experiences that could be authenticated. These reports were then checked if they looked promising, coordinated by committees, and possibly published. The societies, however, were concerned with the validity or lack of validity of the psychic experience. We are concerned with the results solely as folklore: what was believed and its varied manifestation.

There was another source, too, for factual ghost stories during this period. This was the printed literature of the supernatural, or serious collections of experiences: deathbed visitations, haunted places, revelations from beyond the grave, prophetic dreams, and similar material. Some of these were serious books which attempted to set up a phenomenology and rationale for the supernatural.

Several books of this sort were widely circulated and closely read in Great Britain and America, and formed the background for the supernatural culture of the period. These were Catherine Crowe's

Night-side of Nature, a classified collection of anecdotes, heavily indebted to German sources; *Footfalls on the Boundary of Another World* by Robert Dale Owen, the best of these books; the Rev. Frederick Lee's *Glimpses of the Supernatural*; and John H. Ingram's *Haunted Homes and Family Traditions of Great Britain*, which is somewhat more traditional than the others. Each of these books went through many editions. (It should be added that these books are not the literature of Spiritualism, which had its own sources, nor of magic or occultism, which looked for other enticements.)

A startling coincidence of ideas is to be seen if the factual ghost stories from these two sources are compared with the ghost stories of fiction. In the factual literature there are only three important themes: the supernormal dream, the deathbed apparition, and the haunted house. These three themes are equally important in mid-Victorian fiction, which adds a fourth, a ghost who seeks justice.

To show clearly what is meant by these themes, let me cite brief, clear extracts from the factual literature. These include two kinds of haunted house, involving a poltergeist and an irrational ghost.

A prophetic dream:

> The following still more remarkable dream is given by Dr. Abercrombie as entirely authentic: "A lady dreamt that an aged female relative had been murdered by a servant, and the dream occurred more than once. She was then so impressed by it, that she went to the house of the lady to whom it related, and prevailed upon a gentleman to watch in an adjoining room the following night. About three o'clock in the morning, the gentleman, hearing footsteps on the stair, left his place of conceal-ment, and met the servant carrying up a quantity of coals. Being questioned as to where he was going, he replied, in a confused and hurried manner, that he was going to mend his mistress's fire—which, at three o'clock in the morning, in the middle of the summer, was evidently impossible; and on further investigation, a strong knife was found concealed beneath the coals." (*The Spectre; or, News from the Invisible World . . .*, compiled by T. Ottway, London, 1836)

A deathbed apparition:

> During the celebrated Peninsular campaign, as a lady, whose son, a French officer in Spain, was seated in her room, she was astonished to perceive the folding doors at the bottom of the apartment slowly open, and disclose to her eyes *her son*. He begged her not to be alarmed, and

informed her that he had just been killed by a grapeshot, and even showed her the wound in his side; the doors closed again, and she saw no more. In a few days she received a letter, which informed her that her son had fallen, after distinguishing himself in a most gallant manner, and mentioning the time of his death, which happened at precisely the same moment the apparition was seen by her! And when I add that the lady was not at all addicted to superstition, the strangeness of the occurrence is considerably increased. (*The Spectre; or, News from the Invisible World . . .*, compiled by T. Ottway, London, 1836)

A poltergeist:

[In Edinburgh] Captain Molesworth took the house of a Mr. Webster, who resided in the adjoining one, in May or June, 1835; and when he had been in it about two months, he began to complain of sundry extraordinary noises, which finding it impossible to account for, he took it into his head were made by Mr. Webster. The latter naturally represented that it was not possible he should desire to damage the reputation of his own house, and drive his tenant out of it, and retorted the accusation. Still, as these noises and knockings continued, Captain Molesworth not only lifted the boards in the room most infected, but actually made holes in the walls . . . Do what they would, the thing went on just the same: footsteps of invisible feet, knockings, and scratchings, and rustlings. . . . The beds, too, were occasionally heaved up, as if somebody were underneath . . . (*The Night-side of Nature* by Catherine Crowe, London, n.d.)

A haunting without purpose:

[At the haunted house at Willington, near Newcastle-on-Tyne, in the 1820's] the following more recent case of an apparition seen in the window of the same house from the outside, by four credible witnesses, who had the opportunity of scrutinizing it for more than ten minutes, is given on most unquestionable authority. One of these witnesses is a young lady, a near connection of the family, who, for obvious reasons, did not sleep in the house; another, a respectable man, who has been many years employed in, and is foreman of the manufactory; his daughter, aged about seventeen; and his wife, who first saw the object and called out the others to view it. The appearance presented was that of a bareheaded man, in a flowing robe like a surplice, who glided backward and forward about three feet from the floor, or level with the bottom of the second story window, seeming to enter the wall on each side, and thus present a side view in passing. It then stood still in the window, and a part of the body came through both the blind, which was closed down, and the window. . . . It was semi-transparent, and as bright as a star, diffusing a radiance all around . . . (*The Night-side of Nature* by Catherine Crowe, London, n.d.)

Supernormal dreams and deathbed apparitions were the special interest of the Society for Psychical Research, since this material, they thought, stood a chance of clinical verification. Old Mrs. Torpor, for example, might be visited by the spirit of her nephew in Shanghai, announcing his death. Let Mrs. Torpor make a note of the incident and tell her friends, who also make notes of the story and the time it took place. When the official letter comes three months later, announcing the death, there might be something of evidential value.

The committee on haunted houses of the Society for Psychical Research had this to say of ghosts in its second report:

In the magazine ghost stories, which appear in such numbers every Christmas, the ghost is a fearsome being, dressed in a sweeping sheet or shroud, carrying a lighted candle, and squeaking dreadful words from fleshless lips. It enters at the stroke of midnight, through the sliding panel, just by the blood stain on the floor, which no effort ever could remove. Or it may be only a clinking of chains, a tread as of armed men, heard whilst the candles burn blue, and the dogs howl. These are the ghosts of fiction, and we do not deny that now and then we receive, apparently on good authority, accounts of apparitions which are stated to exhibit some features of a sensational type. Such cases, however, are very rare, and must for the present be dismissed as exceptional. (*Report of the Society for Psychical Research, Volume Two,* London, 1884)

This opinion, however, is as wrong as it could be, for most of the ghosts that appear in fiction written from roughly 1860 to 1885 did not clank chains or inhabit houses with indelible blood stains. There were other, more subtle differences between fact and fiction where haunted houses were concerned.

In fiction, for example, houses haunted by poltergeists are not common, yet in folkloristic ghost lore they appear frequently. Three of the most famous hauntings in British history, indeed, belonged in this category. These were the Cock Lane Ghost, whom Samuel Johnson investigated; the Tedworth Drummer, who annoyed the natives of a small village with his racket; and the ghost who harassed the family of Samuel Wesley.

The largest difference between popular belief and fiction, however, lies in the reason for a haunting. The ghost in the fiction of Mrs. Riddell and her contemporaries usually has a reason for appearing. It wants something. It must reveal information, confess to a crime, tell where the will or the love letters are hidden, undo some hurt it has done, or reveal the murderer of its body. To show how didactic some of the revelatory ghosts can be, let me quote from the anonymous story "Haunted" from *A Stable for Nightmares*, a Christmas annual published in 1867:

> The Colonel fired . . . .
> "Colonel Demarion," spake the deep, solemn voice of the perforated stranger, "In vain you shoot me—I am dead already."
> The soldier, with all his bravery, gasped, spell-bound. The firelight gleamed through the hole in the body.
> "Fear nothing," spake the mournful presence. "I seek but to divulge my wrongs. Until my death shall be avenged, my unquiet spirit lingers here. Listen."
> . . . . .
> In the same terse, solemn manner, the ghostly visitor gave the real and assumed names of his murderer, described his person and dress at the present time, described a curious ring he was then wearing, together with other distinguishing characteristics; all being carefully noted down by Colonel Demarion, who, by degrees, recovered his self-possession, and pledged himself to use every endeavour to bring the murderer to justice.

The idea that a ghost brings justice is not common in the factual ghost stories of this period. Almost all ghosts who appeared at this time (not retellings of older experiences) are ghosts without motivation.

In earlier years, however, the older link between ghosts and justice still held. The expression "murder will out" had a supernatural connotation in the seventeenth and eighteenth centuries, as, indeed, it still had in William Gilmore Simms's American story "Grayling, or Murder Will Out." It implied that the universe was so constructed that a crime would be revealed by the will of God. One early writer, John Reynolds of the seventeenth century, compiled a large book entitled *Triumphs of God's Revenge against Murther*. A large collection of stories (largely from French sources) which often involved super-natural revealment of crime, it went through many editions up into the nineteenth century. But presumably the worldly, materialistic Victorians could no longer swallow the notion of Providence, except in fiction.

Mrs. Riddell strayed only occasionally beyond these boundaries in her fiction: the haunted house, the death warning, the prophetic or clairvoyant dream, or the unquiet ghost. The Höllenfahrt and hypostatized guilt in "Sandy the Tinker" are somewhat unusual, as is the Presence in "The Last of Squire Ennismore." Despite her Irish background Irish folklore does not enter into her stories (either natural or supernatural) very much, and the occasional banshee (which may also be a conscience symbol) is probably used more to intrigue the English than for its own sake.

We do not know how Mrs. Riddell felt about the supernatural, but since there is no evidence to the contrary, it seems most reasonable to guess that ghosts and other supernaturalisms were for her simply literary devices. She was a strong-minded, hard-headed woman. More appealing to her, in all probability, was the morality latent in the fictional ghost situations.

IV

TODAY, if anyone wants to read a ghost story, he can buy a collection of ghost stories, like this one, very easily, or with a little effort he can find a magazine on the newsstands. Forty years or so ago, during the Golden Age of American weird fiction, the rewards were even richer, for the newsstands carried several magazines with new, creative fiction.

Back in Mrs. Riddell's day, however, the supernatural story had a very odd cultural characteristic: it was seasonal. It was strongly linked to Christmas, a linkage which did not weaken until the 1880's. While an occasional ghost story might be found in the fiction periodicals or might appear in a short story collection, much the most frequent locus was, as was mentioned in the report by the Society for Psychical Research, the Christmas annual.

The Christmas annual was a book of entertainments published specially for the Christmas season. Book publishers issued such books annually; to name a few of the better-known series, *Routledge's Christmas Annual, Warne's Christmas Annual, Beeton's Christmas*

Annual. The magazines also published Christmas annuals or Christmas issues, which would appear fairly early in December, out of numerical sequence, to be sold separately.

The mood of such journals, in general, was one of "letting down hair," even in the stuffier journals. They stressed stories of physical adventure and perils, often set in strange places, with emphasis on thrills. The annuals might also contain rebuses, charades, cartoon strips, full Christmas masques, pantomime texts, carols and songs, special illustrations and poetry for Christmas, puzzles and magical stunts, jokes, and similar amusements. And, of course, ghost stories. Occasionally, as was the case with Mrs. Riddell's supernatural novels, the entire volume consisted of a single, long ghost story.

Just why the ghost story was so closely associated with Christmas in Victorian England is not quite clear. The image of old people sitting before the fire, in earlier days, telling ghost stories is almost a cliché, yet there does not seem to be much evidence for it. Thomas J. Hervey's *Book of Christmas, Descriptive of the Customs, Ceremonies, Traditions, Superstitions, Fun, Feeling and Festivities of the Christmas Season* (1845), a fine, full survey of the traditional Christmas, does not even mention the ghost story as an oral matter. Dickens's *Christmas Carol* (1843), in all probability, had much to do with linking Christmas with ghosts, but it is not clear whether it reinflated an older, weak tradition or created a new configuration.

Before 1860 a Christmas book was a small, daintily bound, pretentious collection of sugary verse and mushy engravings, a gift for a maiden aunt or a platonic sweetheart. It had little or nothing to do with Christmas, except that it was in itself a gift. From the 1860's on—I do not know the volume that broke new paths—the Christmas book became not a gift, but laic Christmas itself, in compressed form.

It offered things to do. It entertained the adults, both individually and in groups. It gave ways to keep under control the children, who were home for the holidays—games, charades, playlets, songs, thrillers. Such was the heart of the Victorian Christmas situation: the great family was to gather, as a social sacrament, once a year, and everyone was to be Merry or be damned to them.

Only an occasional voice was to be heard against this social interpretation of Christmas as a sacrament to the great family. Ebenezer Scrooge, of course, was one. Another, surprisingly enough, was

Mrs. J. H. Riddell—"surprisingly" since she had so much of her precarious living from Christmas. In her essay "The Miseries of Christmas," published in *On the Cards, Routledge's Christmas Annual* for 1867, she contrasts the "official" myth with the verities: commercialism, extravagances, hypocrisy, inconvenience. People were not Merry on Christmas, she claimed, and Christmas in real life was not always so pleasant as in fiction:

> Owing to the absurd customs of our country, we can rarely get our kind on Christmas-day, though we almost always can our kin, "whom it is your duty to ask"—say the proper ones again. . . . These annual reunions become penances instead of pleasures, and a day which might be passed in a really agreeable manner is made dull, heavy, wearisome, monotonous. . . .
>
> And then, again, why call Christmas, with such a nightmare entertainment hanging over British establishments, "merry." "Merry"—good heavens! where is there anything merry about it? Is it the height of jollity to give away Christmas-boxes, . . . Is it very merry to feel that whatever the state of the domestic finances may be, Jack, Tom, and Harry must be suitably remembered? Is there not a ghastly sort of pleasantry in bidding a man be "merry" when the yearly bills are coming in, when quarter day is just passed, . . . when, in fact, in the dull, dead, heavy Christmas weather every disagreeable [thing] which the close of a year can furnish is heaped together to make a cairn over the grave of merriment?

Mrs. Riddell's overall position was that Christmas was a humbug, and that Charles Dickens was to blame for much of this situation, since his *Christmas Carol* had so overwhelmed England. Dickens had set up the equation that humanity, good will and the internal spirit must be balanced against sentimental externals, and it is due to Dickens's theatricality (she does not use the word) that the Christmas of the day took the form it did.

"The Miseries of Christmas" was an astonishing essay to appear in a Christmas annual, and I wish we knew how it was received by its readers. Some must have been annoyed, since Victorian journalism, on the whole, did not debunk institutional sacred cows; others may have recognized much truth in it.

Despite her feelings, journalistic or personal, about the celebration of Christmas, Mrs. Riddell continued to contribute to the annuals as a lead writer, and came, in a sense, to be almost synonymous with one aspect of Christmas in mid-Victorian Great Britain, the well-written domestic ghost story.

V

Mrs. Riddell's supernatural fiction was outstanding in several respects. She had a fine knack of evoking the supernatural out of very convincing domestic or social backgrounds; very few have been her equal at verisimilitude. Related to this was her formal strength. The supernatural novel is a very difficult form to fulfill, and it is to her credit that she brought the feat off well four times.

She was also able to enshroud the ghost story in verities that her more perceptive readers might have seen. She was not concerned with writing a thriller primarily, but used a highly conventionalized, rigid form to suggest the evanescence of life, the tragic nature of man, and the inevitability of ultimate morality.

Apart from J. S. LeFanu, no other writer of the Victorian period could handle better the emergence of the supernormal. This is the reason for this collection of her short ghost stories.

E. F. BLEILER

Photograph of Mrs. Riddell around 1890.

Letter from Mrs. J. H. Riddell.

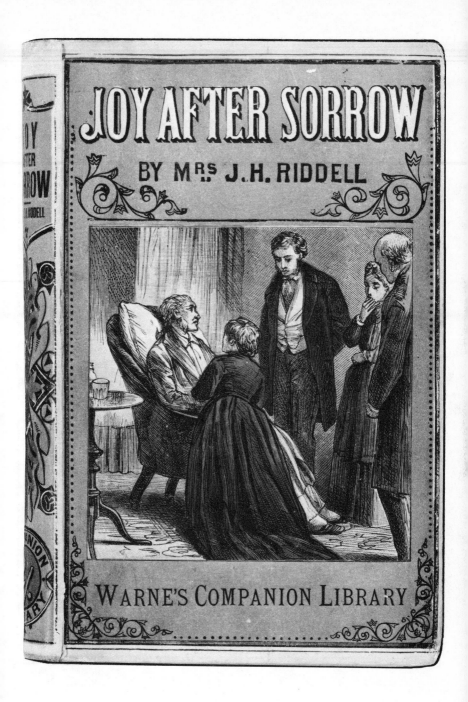

Yellowback publication of *Joy after Sorrow*.

Yellowback publication of *The Ruling Passion*.

Yellowback publication of *The World in the Church*.

THE COLLECTED
GHOST STORIES OF
MRS. J. H. RIDDELL

NUT BUSH FARM

Chapter One

WHEN I entered upon the tenancy of Nut Bush Farm almost the first piece of news which met me, in the shape of a whispered rumour, was that "something" had been seen in the "long field."

Pressed closely as to what he meant, my informant reluctantly stated that the "something" took the "form of a man," and that the wood and the path leading thereto from Whittleby were supposed to be haunted.

Now, all this annoyed me exceedingly. I do not know when I was more put out than by this intelligence. It is unnecessary to say I did not believe in ghosts or anything of that kind, but my wife being a very nervous, impressionable woman, and our only child a delicate weakling, in the habit of crying himself into fits if left alone at night without a candle, I really felt at my wits' end to imagine what I should do if a story of this sort reached their ears.

And reach them I knew it must if they came to Nut Bush Farm, so the first thing I did when I heard people did not care to venture down the Beech Walk or through the copse, or across the long field after dark, or indeed by day, was to write to say I thought they had both better remain on at my father-in-law's till I could get the house thoroughly to rights.

After that I lit my pipe and went out for a stroll; when I knocked the ashes out of my pipe and re-entered the sitting-room I had made up my mind. I could not afford to be frightened away from my tenancy. For weal or for woe I must stick to Nut Bush Farm.

It was quite by chance I happened to know anything of the place at first. When I met with that accident in my employers' service, which they rated far too highly and recompensed with a liberality I never can feel sufficiently grateful for, the doctors told me plainly if I could not give up office work and leave London altogether, they would not give a year's purchase for my life.

Life seemed very sweet to me then—it always has done—but just at

1

that period I felt the pleasant hopes of convalescence, and with that thousand pounds safely banked, I *could* not let it slip away from me.

"Take a farm," advised my father-in-law. "Though people say a farmer's is a bad trade, I know many a man who is making money out of it. Take a farm, and if you want a helping hand to enable you to stand the racket for a year or two, why, you know I am always ready."

I had been bred and born on a farm. My father held something like fifteen hundred acres under the principal landowner in his county, and though it so happened I could not content myself at home, but must needs come up to London to see the lions and seek my fortune, still I had never forgotten the meadows and the cornfields, and the cattle, and the orchards, and the woods and the streams, amongst which my happy boyhood had been spent. Yes, I thought I should like a farm—one not too far from London; and "not too big," advised my wife's father.

"The error people make nowadays," he went on, "is spreading their butter over too large a surface. It is the same in business as in land—they stretch their arms out too far—they will try to wade in deep waters—and the consequence is they know a day's peace, and end mostly in the bankruptcy court."

He spoke as one having authority, and I knew what he said was quite right. He had made his money by a very different course of procedure, and I felt I could not follow a better example.

I knew something about farming, though not very much. Still, agriculture is like arithmetic: when once one knows the multiplication table the rest is not so difficult. I had learned unconsciously the alphabet of soils and crops and stock when I was an idle young dog, and liked nothing better than talking to the labourers, and accompanying the woodman when he went out felling trees; and so I did not feel much afraid of what the result would be, more especially as I had a good business head on my shoulders, and enough money to "stand the racket," as my father-in-law put it, till the land began to bring in her increase.

When I got strong and well again after my long illness—I mean strong and well enough to go about—I went down to look at a farm which was advertised as to let in Kent.

According to the statement in the newspaper, there was no charm that farm lacked; when I saw it I discovered the place did not possess one virtue, unless, indeed, an old Tudor house fast falling to ruins, which would have proved invaluable to an artist, could be so considered. Far from a railway, having no advantages of water carriage, remote from a market, apparently destitute of society. Nor could these drawbacks be accounted the worst against it. The land, poor originally, seemed to have been totally exhausted. There were fields on which I do not think a goose could have found subsistence—nothing grew luxuriantly save weeds; it would have taken all my capital to get the ground clean. Then I saw the fences were dilapidated, the hedges in a deplorable condition, and the farm buildings in such a state of decay I would not have stabled a donkey in one of them.

Clearly, the King's Manor, which was the modest name of the place, would not do at any price, and yet I felt sorry, for the country around was beautiful, and already the sweet, pure air seemed to have braced up my nerves and given me fresh energy. Talking to mine host at the "Bunch of Hops," in Whittleby, he advised me to look over the local paper before returning to London.

"There be a many farms vacant," he said, "mayhap you'll light on one to suit."

To cut a long story short, I did look in the local paper and found many farms to let, but not one to suit. There was a drawback to each— a drawback at least so far as I was concerned. I felt determined I would not take a large farm. My conviction was then what my conviction still remains, that it is better to cultivate fifty acres thoroughly than to crop, stock, clean, and manure a hundred insufficiently. Besides, I did not want to spend my strength on wages, or take a place so large I could not oversee the workmen on foot. For all these reasons and many more I came reluctantly to the conclusion that there was nothing in that part of the country to suit a poor unspeculative plodder like myself.

It was a lovely afternoon in May when I turned my face towards Whittleby, as I thought, for the last time. In the morning I had taken train for a farm some ten miles distant and worked my way back on foot to a "small cottage with land" a local agent thought might suit me. But neither the big place not the little answered my requirements much to the disgust of the auctioneer, who had himself accompanied us to the cottage under the impression I would immediately purchase it and so secure his commission.

Somewhat sulkily he told me a short cut back to Whittleby, and added, as a sort of rider to all previous statements, the remark:

"You had best look out for what you want in Middlesex. You'll find nothing of that sort hereabouts."

As to the last part of the foregoing sentence I was quite of his opinion, but I felt so oppressed with the result of all my wanderings that I thought upon the whole I had better abandon my search altogether, or else pursue it in some county very far away indeed—perhaps in the land of dreams for that matter!

As has been said, it was a lovely afternoon in May—the hedges were snowy with hawthorn blossom, the chestnuts were bursting into flower, the birds were singing fit to split their little throats, the lambs were dotting the hillsides, and I—ah, well, I was a boy again, able to relish all the rich banquet God spreads out day by day for the delight and nourishment of His too often thankless children.

When I came to a point half way up some rising ground where four lanes met and then wound off each on some picturesque diverse way, I paused to look around regretfully.

As I did so—some distance below me—along what appeared to be a never-before-traversed lane, I saw the gleam of white letters on a black board.

"Come," I thought, "I'll see what this is at all events," and bent my steps towards the place, which might, for all I knew about it, have been a ducal mansion or a cockney's country villa.

The board appeared modestly conspicuous in the foreground of a young fir plantation, and simply bore this legend:

To be let, House and Land,
Apply at the "White Dragon."

"It is a mansion," I thought, and I walked on slowly, disappointed.

All of a sudden the road turned a sharp corner and I came in an instant upon the prettiest place I had ever seen or ever desire to see.

I looked at it over a low laurel hedge growing inside an open paling about four feet high. Beyond the hedge there was a strip of turf, green as emeralds, smooth as a bowling green—then came a sunk fence, the most picturesque sort of protection the ingenuity of man ever devised; beyond that, a close-cut lawn which sloped down to the sunk fence from a house with projecting gables in the front, the recessed portion of the building having three windows on the first floor. Both gables were covered with creepers, the lawn was girt in by a semi-circular sweep of forest trees, the afternoon sun streamed over the grass and tinted the swaying foliage with a thousand tender lights. Hawthorn bushes, pink and white, mingled with their taller and grander brothers. The chestnuts here were in flower, the copper beech made a delightful contrast of colour, and a birch rose delicate and graceful close beside.

It was like a fairy scene. I passed my hand across my eyes to assure myself it was all real. Then I thought "if this place be even nearly within my means I will settle here. My wife will grow stronger in this paradise—my boy get more like other lads. Such things as nerves must be unknown where there is not a sight or sound to excite them. Nothing but health, purity, and peace."

Thus thinking, I tore myself away in search of the "White Dragon," the landlord of which small public-house sent a lad to show me over the farm.

"As for the rent," he said, "you will have to speak to Miss Gostock herself—she lives at Chalmont, on the road between here and Whittleby."

In every respect the place suited me; it was large enough, but not too large; had been well farmed, and was amply supplied with water—a stream indeed flowing through it; a station was shortly to be opened, at about half-a-mile's distance; and most of the produce could be disposed of to dealers and tradesmen at Crayshill, a town to which the communication by rail was direct.

I felt so anxious about the matter, it was quite a disappointment to find Miss Gostock from home. Judging from the look of her house, I did not suppose she could afford to stick out for a long rent, or to let a farm lie idle for any considerable period. The servant who appeared in answer to my summons was a singularly red armed and rough handed Phyllis. There was only a strip of carpeting laid down in the hall, the windows were bare of draperies, and the avenue gate, set a little back from the main road, was such as I should have felt ashamed to put in a farmyard.

Next morning I betook myself to Chalmont, anxiously wondering as I walked along what the result of my interview would prove.

When I neared the gate, to which uncomplimentary reference has already been made, I saw standing on the other side a figure wearing a man's broad-brimmed straw hat, a man's coat, and a woman's skirt.

I raised my hat in deference to the supposed sex of this stranger. She put up one finger to the brim of hers, and said, "Servant, sir."

Not knowing exactly what to do, I laid my hand upon the latch of the gate and raised it, but she did not alter her position in the least.

She only asked, "What do you want?"

"I want to see Miss Gostock," was my answer.

"I am Miss Gostock," she said; "what is your business with me?"

I replied meekly that I had come to ask the rent of Nut Bush Farm.

"Have you viewed it?" she inquired.

"Yes." I told her I had been over the place on the previous afternoon.

"And have you a mind to take it?" she persisted. "For I am not going to trouble myself answering a lot of idle inquiries."

So far from my being an idle inquirer, I assured the lady that if we could come to terms about the rent, I should be very glad indeed to take the farm. I said I had been searching the neighbourhood within a circuit of ten miles for some time unsuccessfully, and added, somewhat unguardedly, I suppose, Nut Bush Farm was the only place I had met with which at all met my views.

Standing in an easy attitude, with one arm resting on the top bar of the gate and one foot crossed over the other, Miss Gostock surveyed me, who had unconsciously taken up a similar position, with an amused smile.

"You must think me a very honest person, young man," she remarked.

I answered that I hoped she was, but I had not thought at all about the matter.

"Or else," proceeded this extraordinary lady, "you fancy I am a much greater flat than I am."

"On the contrary," was my reply. "If there be one impression stronger than another which our short interview has made upon me it is that you are a wonderfully direct and capable woman of business."

She looked at me steadily, and then closed one eye, which performance, done under the canopy of that broad-brimmed straw hat, had the most ludicrous effect imaginable.

"You won't catch me napping," she observed, "but, however, as you seem to mean dealing, come in; I can tell you my terms in two minutes," and opening the gate—a trouble she would not allow me to take off her hands—she gave me admission.

The Miss Gostock took off her hat, and swinging it to and fro began slowly walking up the ascent leading to Chalmont, I beside her.

"I have quite made up my mind," she said, "not to let the farm again without a premium; my last tenant treated me abominably——"

I intimated I was sorry to hear that, and waited for further information.

"He had the place at a low rent—a very low rent. He should not have got it so cheap but for his covenanting to put so much money in the soil; and well—I'm bound to say he acted fair so far as that—he fulfilled that part of his contract. Nearly two years ago we had a bit of a quarrel about—well, it's no matter what we fell out over—only the upshot of the affair was he gave me due notice to leave at last winter quarter. At that time he owed about a year-and-a-half's rent—for he was a man who never could bear parting with money—and like a fool I did not push him for it. What trick do you suppose he served me for my pains?"

It was simply impossible for me to guess, so I did not try.

"On the twentieth of December," went on Miss Gostock, turning her broad face and curly grey hair—she wore her hair short like a man —towards me, "he went over to Whittleby, drew five thousand pounds out of the bank, was afterwards met going towards home by a gentleman named Waite, a friend of his. Since then he has never been seen nor heard of."

"Bless my soul!" I exclaimed involuntarily.

"You may be very sure I did not bless his soul," she snarled out angrily. "The man bolted with the five thousand pounds, having previously sold off all his stock and the bulk of his produce, and when I distrained for my rent, which I did pretty smart, I can tell you, there was scarce enough on the premises to pay the levy."

"But what in the world made him bolt?" I asked, quite unconsciously adopting Miss Gostock's expressive phrase; "as he had so much money, why did he not pay you your rent?"

"Ah! Why, indeed?" mocked Miss Gostock. "Young sir, I am afraid you are a bit of a humbug, or you would have suggested at once there was a pretty girl at the bottom of the affair. He left his wife and children, and me—all in the lurch—and went off with a slip of a girl, whom I once took, thinking to train up as a better sort of servant, but was forced to discharge. Oh, the little hussy !"

Somehow I did not fancy I wanted to hear anything more about her late tenant and the pretty girl, and consequently ventured to inquire how that gentleman's defalcations bore upon the question of the rent I should have to pay.

"I tell you directly," she said, and as we had by this time arrived at the house, she invited me to enter, and led the way into an old-fashioned parlour that must have been furnished about the time chairs and tables were first invented and which did not contain a single feminine belonging—not even a thimble.

"Sit down," she commanded, and I sat. "I have quite made up my mind," she began, "not to let the farm again, unless I get a premium sufficient to insure me against the chances of possible loss. I mean to ask a very low rent and—a premium."

"And what amount of premium do you expect ?" I inquired, doubtfully.

"I want—— " and here Miss Gostock named a sum which fairly took my breath away.

"In that case," I said as soon as I got it again, "it is useless to prolong this interview; I can only express my regret for having intruded, and wish you good morning." And arising, I was bowing myself out when she stopped me.

"Don't be so fast," she cried, "I only said what I wanted. Now what are you prepared to give ?"

"I can't be buyer and seller too," I answered, repeating a phrase the precise meaning of which, it may here be confessed, I have never been able exactly to understand.

"Nonsense," exclaimed Miss Gostock—I am really afraid the lady used a stronger term—"if you are anything of a man of business, fit at all to commence farming, you must have an idea on the subject. You shall have the land at a pound an acre, and you will give me for premium—come, how much ?"

By what mental process I instantly jumped to an amount it would be impossible to say, but I did mention one which elicited from Miss Gostock the remark :

"That won't do at any price."

"Very well, then," I said, "we need not talk any more about the matter."

"But what *will* you give ?" asked the lady.

"I have told you," was my answer, "and I am not given either to haggling or beating down."

"You won't make a good farmer," she observed.

"If a farmer's time were of any value, which it generally seems as if it were not," I answered, "he would not waste it in splitting a sixpence."

She laughed, and her laugh was not musical.

"Come now," she said, "make another bid."

"No," I replied, "I have made one and that is enough. I won't offer another penny."

"Done then," cried Miss Gostock, "I accept your offer—we'll just sign a little memorandum of agreement, and the formal deeds can be prepared afterwards. You'll pay a deposit, I suppose ?"

I was so totally taken aback by her acceptance of my offer I could only stammer out I was willing to do anything that might be usual.

"It does not matter much whether it is usual or not," she said; "either pay it or I won't keep the place for you. I am not going to have my land lying idle and my time taken up for your pleasure."

"I have no objection to paying you a deposit," I answered.

"That's right," she exclaimed; "now if you will just hand me over the writing-desk we can settle the matter, so far as those thieves of lawyers will let us, in five minutes."

Like one in a dream I sat and watched Miss Gostock while she wrote. Nothing about the transaction seemed to me real. The farm itself resembled nothing I had ever before seen with my waking eyes, and Miss Gostock appeared to me but as some monstrous figure in a story of giants and hobgoblins. The man's coat, the woman's skirt, the hobnailed shoes, the grisly hair, the old straw hat, the bare, unfurnished room, the bright sunshine outside, all struck me as mere accessories in a play—as nothing which had any hold on the outside, everyday world.

It was drawn—we signed our names. I handed Miss Gostock over a cheque. She locked one document in an iron box let into the wall, and handed me the other, adding, as a rider, a word of caution about "keeping it safe and taking care it was not lost."

Then she went to a corner cupboard, and producing a square decanter half full of spirits, set that and two tumblers on the table.

"You don't like much water, I suppose," she said, pouring out a measure which frightened me.

"I could not touch it, thank you, Miss Gostock," I exclaimed; "I dare not do so; I should never get back to Whittleby."

For answer she only looked at me contemptuously and said, "D—d nonsense."

"No nonsense, indeed," I persisted; "I am not accustomed to anything of that sort."

Miss Gostock laughed again, then crossing to the sideboard she returned with a jug of water, a very small portion of the contents of which she mixed with the stronger liquor, and raised the glass to her lips.

"To your good health and prosperity," she said, and in one instant the fiery potion was swallowed.

"You'll mend of all that," she remarked, as she laid down her glass, and wiped her lips in the simplest manner by passing the back of her hand over them.

"I hope not, Miss Gostock," I ventured to observe.

"Why, you look quite shocked," she said; "did you never see a lady take a mouthful of brandy before?"

I ventured to hint that I had not, more particularly so early in the morning.

"Pooh!" she said. "Early in the morning or late at night, where's the difference? However, there was a time when I—but that was before I had come through so much trouble. Good-bye for the present, and I hope we shall get on well together."

I answered I trusted we should, and was half-way to the hall-door, when she called me back.

"I forgot to ask you if you were married," she said.

"Yes, I have been married some years," I answered.

"That's a pity," she remarked, and dismissed me with a wave of her hand.

"What on earth would have happened had I not been married?" I considered as I hurried down the drive. "Surely she never contemplated proposing to me herself ? But nothing she could do would surprise me."

Chapter Two

THERE were some repairs I had mentioned it would be necessary to have executed before I came to live at Nut Bush Farm, but when I found Miss Gostock intended to do them herself—nay, was doing them all herself—I felt thunderstruck.

On one memorable occasion I came upon her with a red handkerchief tied round her head, standing at a carpenter's bench in a stable yard, planing away, under a sun which would have killed anybody but a negro or my landlady.

She painted the gates, and put sash lines in some of the windows; she took off the locks, oiled, and replaced them; she mowed the lawn, and offered to teach me how to mow; and lastly, she showed me a book where she charged herself and paid herself for every hour's work done.

"I've made at least twenty pounds out of your place," she said triumphantly. "Higgs at Whittleby would not have charged me a half-penny less for the repairs. The tradesmen here won't give me a contract—they say it is just time thrown away, but I know that would have been about his figure. Well, the place is ready for you now, and if you take my advice, you'll get your grass up as soon as possible. It's a splendid crop, and if you hire hands enough, not a drop of rain need spoil it. If this weather stands you might cut one day and carry the next."

I took her advice, and stacked my hay in magnificent condition. Miss Gostock was good enough to come over and superintend the building of the stack, and threatened to split one man's head open with the pitchfork, and proposed burying another—she called him a "lazy blackguard"—under a pile of hay.

"I will say this much for Hascot," she remarked, as we stood together beside the stream; "he was a good farmer; where will you see better or cleaner land ? A pattern I call it—and to lose his whole future for the sake of a girl like Sally Powner; leaving his wife and children on the parish, too !"

"You don't mean that ?" I said.

"Indeed I do. They are all at Crayshill. The authorities did talk of shifting them, but I know nothing about what they have done."

I stood appalled. I thought of my own poor wife and the little lad, and wondered if any Sally on the face of the earth could make me desert them.

"It has given the place a bad sort of name," remarked Miss Gostock, looking at me sideways: "but, of course, that does not signify anything to you."

"Oh, of course not," I agreed.

"And don't you be minding any stories; there are always a lot of stories going about places."

I said I did not mind stories. I had lived too long in London to pay much attention to them.

"That's right," remarked Miss Gostock, and negativing my offer to see her home she started off to Chalmont.

It was not half an hour after her departure when I happened to be walking slowly round the meadows, from which the newly mown hay had been carted, that I heard the rumour which vexed me—"Nut Bush Farm haunted." I thought, "I said the whole thing was too good to last."

"What, Jack, lost in reverie ? " cried my sister, who had come up from Devonshire to keep me company, and help to get the furniture a little to rights, entering at the moment, carrying lights; "supper will be ready in a minute, and you can dream as much as you like after you have had something to eat."

I did not say anything to her about my trouble, which was then indeed no bigger than a man's hand, but which grew and grew till it attained terrible proportions.

What was I to do with my wife and child ? I never could bring them to a place reputed to be haunted. All in vain I sauntered up and down the Beech Walk night after night; walked through the wood—as a rule selected that route when I went to Whittleby. It did not produce the slightest effect. Not a farm servant but eschewed that path townward; not a girl but preferred spending her Sunday at home rather than venture under the interlacing branches of the beech trees, or through the dark recesses of the wood.

It was becoming serious—I did not know what to do.

One wet afternoon Lolly came in draggled but beaming.

"I've made a new acquaintance, Jack," she said; "a Mrs. Waite—such a nice creature, but in dreadfully bad health. It came on to rain when I was coming home, and so I took refuge under a great tree at the gate of a most picturesque old house. I had not stood there long before a servant with an umbrella appeared at the porch to ask if I would not please to walk in until the storm abated. I waited there ever so long, and we had such a pleasant talk. She is a most delightful woman, with a melancholy, pathetic sort of expression that has been haunting me ever since. She apologised for not having called—said she was not strong and could not walk so far. They keep no conveyance she can drive. Mr. Waite, who is not at home at present, rides into Whittleby when anything is wanted.

"I hoped she would not think of standing on ceremony with me. I was only a farmer's daughter, and accustomed to plain, homely ways, and I asked her if I might walk round and bid her good-bye before I went home."

"You must not go home yet, Lolly," I cried, alarmed; "what in the world should I do without you?"

"Well, you would be a lonely boy," she answered, complacently, "with no one to sew on a button or darn your socks, or make you eat or go to bed, or do anything you ought to do."

I had not spoken a word to her about the report which was troubling me, and I knew there must be times when she wondered why I did not go up to London and fetch my wife and child to enjoy the bright summer-time; but Lolly was as good as gold, and never asked me a question, or even indirectly inquired if Lucy and I had quarrelled, as many another sister might.

She was as pleasant and fresh to look upon as a spring morning, with her pretty brown hair smoothly braided, her cotton or muslin dresses never soiled or crumpled, but as nice as though the laundress had that moment sent them home—a rose in her belt and her hands never idle—for ever busy with curtain or blind, or something her housewifely eyes thought had need of making or mending.

About ten days after that showery afternoon when she found shelter under Mr. Waite's hospitable roof, I felt surprised when, entering the parlour a few minutes before our early dinner, I found Lolly standing beside one of the windows apparently hopelessly lost in the depths of a brown study.

"Why, Lolly," I exclaimed, finding she took no notice of me, "where have you gone to now? A penny for your thoughts, young lady."

"They are not worth a penny," she said, and turning from the window took some work and sat down at a little distance from the spot where I was standing.

I was so accustomed to women, even the best and gayest of them, having occasional fits of temper or depression—times when silence on my part seemed the truest wisdom—that, taking no notice of my sister's manner, I occupied myself with the newspaper till dinner was announced.

During the progress of that meal she talked little and ate still less, but when I was leaving the room, in order to go out to a field of barley where the reapers were at work, she asked me to stop a moment.

"I want to speak to you, Jack," she said.

"Speak, then," I answered, with that lack of ceremony which obtains amongst brothers and sisters.

She hesitated for a moment, but did not speak.

"What on earth is the matter with you, Lolly?" I exclaimed. "Are you sick, or cross, or sorry, or what?"

"If it must be one of the four," she answered, with a dash of her usual manner, "it is 'or what,' Jack," and she came close up to where I stood and took me sorrowfully by the button-hole.

"Well?" I said, amused, for this had always been a favourite habit of Lolly's when she wanted anything from one of the males of her family.

"Jack, you won't laugh at me?"

"I feel much more inclined to be cross with you," I answered. "What are you beating about the bush for, Lolly?"

She lifted her fair face a moment and I saw she was crying.

"Lolly, Lolly!" I cried, clasping her to my heart, "what is it, dear? Have you bad news from home, or have you heard anything about Lucy or the boy? Don't keep me in suspense, there's a darling. No matter what has happened, let me know the worst."

She smiled through her tears, and Lolly has the rarest smile! It quieted my anxious heart in a moment, even before she said:

"No, Jack—it is nothing about home, or Lucy, or Teddy, but—but —but——" and then she relinquished her hold on the button-hole, and fingered each button on the front of my coat carefully and lingeringly. "Did you ever hear—Jack—anybody say anything about this place ?"

I knew in a moment what she meant; I knew the cursed tattle had reached her ears, but I only asked:

"What sort of thing, Lolly ?"

She did not answer me; instead, she put another question.

"Is that the reason you have not brought Lucy down ?"

I felt vexed—but I had so much confidence in her good sense, I could not avoid answering without a moment's delay.

"Well, yes; I do not want her to come till this foolish report has completely died away."

"Are you quite sure it is a foolish report ?" she inquired.

"Why, of course; it could not be anything else."

She did not speak immediately, then all at once:

"Jack," she said, "I must tell you something. Lock the door that we may not be interrupted."

"No," I answered; "come into the barley field. Don't you remember Mr. Fenimore Cooper advised, if you want to talk secrets, choose the middle of a plain ?"

I tried to put a good face on the matter, but the sight of Lolly's tears, the sound of Lolly's doleful voice, darkened my very heart. What had she to tell me which required locked doors or the greater privacy of a half-reaped barley field. I could trust my sister—she was no fool—and I felt perfectly satisfied that no old woman's story had wrought the effect produced on her.

"Now, Lolly," I said, as we paced side by side along the top of the barley field in a solitude all the more complete because life and plenty of it was close at hand.

"You know what they say about the place, Jack ?"

This was interrogative, and so I answered. "Well, no, Lolly, I can't say that I do, for the very good reason that I have always refused to listen to the gossip. What do they say ?"

"That a man haunts the Beech Walk, the long meadow, and the wood."

"Yes, I have heard that," I replied.

"And they say further, the man is Mr. Hascot, the late tenant."

"But he is not dead," I exclaimed; "how, then, can they see his ghost ?"

"I cannot tell. I know nothing but what I saw this morning. After breakfast I went to Whittleby, and as I came back I observed a man before me on the road. Following him, I noticed a curious thing, that none of the people he met made way for him or he for them. He walked straight on, without any regard to the persons on the side path, and yet no one seemed to come into collision with him. When I reached the field path I saw him going on still at the same pace. He did not look to right or left, and did not seem to walk—the motion was gliding——"

"Yes, dear."

"He went on, and so did I, till we reached the hollow where the nut-bushes grow, then he disappeared from sight. I looked down among the trees, thinking I should be able to catch a glimpse of his figure through the underwood, but no, I could see no signs of him, neither could I hear any. Everything was as still as death; it seemed to me that my ear had a spell of silence laid upon it."

"And then ?" I asked hoarsely, as she paused.

"Why, Jack, I walked on and crossed the little footbridge and was just turning into the Beech Walk when the same man bustled suddenly across my path, so close to me if I had put out my hands I could have touched him. I drew back, frightened for a minute, then, as he had not seemed to see me, I turned and looked at him as he sped along down the little winding path to the wood. I thought he must be some silly creature, some harmless sort of idiot, to be running here and there without any apparent object. All at once, as he neared the wood, he stopped, and, half wheeling round, beckoned to me to follow him."

"You did not, Lolly ?"

"No, I was afraid. I walked a few steps quietly till I got among the beech trees and so screened from sight, and then I began to run. I could not run fast, for my knees trembled under me; but still I did run as far nearly as that seat round the 'Priest's Tree.' I had not got quite up to the seat when I saw a man rise from it and stand upright as if waiting for me. *It was the same person, Jack !* I recognised him instantly, though I had not seen his face clearly before. He stood quiet for a moment, and then, with the same gliding motion, silently disappeared."

"Someone must be playing a very nice game about Nut Bush Farm," I exclaimed.

"Perhaps so, dear," she said doubtfully.

"Why, Lolly, you don't believe it was a ghost you met in the broad daylight ?" I cried incredulously.

"I don't think it was a living man, Jack," she answered.

"Living or dead, he dare not bring himself into close quarters with me," was my somewhat braggart remark. "Why, Lolly, I have walked the ground day after day and night after night in the hope of seeing your friend, and not a sign of an intruder, in the flesh or out of it, could I find. Put the matter away, child, and don't ramble in that direction again. If I can ascertain the name of the person who is trying to frighten the household and disgust me with Nut Bush Farm he shall go to jail if the magistrates are of my way of thinking. Now, as you have told me this terrible story, and we have reduced your great mountain to a molehill, I will walk back with you to the house."

She did not make any reply : we talked over indifferent matters as we paced along. I went with her into the pleasant sunshiny drawing-room and looked her out a book and made her promise to read something amusing; then I was going, when she put up her lips for me to kiss her, and said—

"Jack, you won't run any risks ?"

"Risks—pooh, you silly little woman ! " I answered ; and so left my sister and repaired to the barley field once more.

When it was time for the men to leave off work I noticed that one after another began to take a path leading immediately to the main road, which was a very circuitous route to the hamlet, where most of them had either cottages or lodgings.

I noticed this for some time, and then asked a brawny young fellow.

"Why don't you go home through the Beech Walk ? It is not above half the distance."

He smiled and made some almost unintelligible answer.

"Why are you all afraid of taking the shortest way," I remarked, "seeing there are enough of you to put half a dozen ghosts to the rout ?"

"Likely, sir," was the answer ; "but the old master was a hard man living, and there is not many would care to meet him dead."

"What old master ?" I inquired.

"Mr. Hascot : it's him as walks. I saw him as plain as I see you now, sir, one moonlight night, just this side of the wood, and so did

Nat Tyler and James Monsey, and James Monsey's father—wise Ben."

"But Mr. Hascot is not dead; how can he 'walk,' as you call it?" was my natural exclamation.

"If he is living, then, sir, where is he?" asked the man. "There is nobody can tell that, and there is a many, especially just lately, think he must have been made away with. He had a cruel lot of money about him—where is all that money gone to?"

The fellow had waxed quite earnest in his interrogations, and really for the first time the singularity of Mr. Hascot's disappearance seemed to strike me.

I said, after an instant's pause, "The money is wherever he is. He went off with some girl, did he not?"

"It suited the old people to say so," he answered; "but there is many a one thinks they know more about the matter than is good for them. I can't help hearing, and one of the neighbours did say Mrs. Ockfield was seen in church last Sunday with a new dress on and a shawl any lady might have worn."

"And who is Mrs. Ockfield?" I inquired.

"Why, Sally Powner's grandmother. The old people treated the girl shameful while she was with them, and now they want to make her out no better than she should be."

And with a wrathful look the young man, who I subsequently discovered had long been fond of Sally, took up his coat and his tin bottle and his sickle, and with a brief "I think I'll be going, sir; good night," departed.

It was easy to return to the house, but I found it impossible to shake the effect produced by this dialogue off my mind.

For the first time I began seriously to consider the manner of Mr. Hascot's disappearance, and more seriously still commenced trying to piece together the various hints I had received as to his character.

A hard man—a hard master, all I ever heard speak considered him, but just, and in the main not unkind. He had sent coals to one widow, and kept a poor old labourer off the parish, and then in a minute, for the sake of a girl's face, left his own wife and children to the mercy of the nearest Union.

As I paced along it seemed to me monstrous, and yet how did it happen that till a few minutes previously I had never heard even a suspicion of foul play?

Was it not more natural to conclude the man must have been made away with, than that, in one brief day, he should have changed his nature and the whole current of his former life?

Upon the other hand, people must have had some strong reason for imagining he was gone off with Miss Powner. The notion of a man disappearing in this way—vanishing as if the earth had opened to receive him and closed again—for the sake of any girl, however attractive, was too unnatural an idea for anyone to have evolved out of his internal consciousness. There must have been some substratum of fact, and then, upon the other hand, there seemed to me more than a substratum of possibility in the theory started of his having been murdered.

Supposing he had been murdered, I went on to argue, what then? Did I imagine he "walked"? Did I believe he could not rest wherever he was laid?

Pooh—nonsense! It might be that the murderer haunted the place of his crime—that he hovered about to see if his guilt were still undetected, but as to anything in the shape of a ghost tenanting the Beech Walk, long meadow, and wood, I did not believe it—I could not, and I added, "if I saw it with my own eyes, I would not."

Having arrived at which decided and sensible conclusion, I went in to supper.

Usually a sound sleeper, I found it impossible that night when I lay down to close my eyes. I tossed and turned, threw off the bedclothes under the impression I was too hot and drew them tight up round me the next instant, feeling cold. I tried to think of my crops, of my land, of my wife, of my boy, of my future—all in vain. A dark shadow, a wall-like night stood between me and all the ordinary interests of my life—I could not get the notion of Mr. Hascot's strange disappearance out of my mind. I wondered if there was anything about the place which made it in the slightest degree probable I should ever learn to forget the wife who loved, the boy who was dependent on me. Should I ever begin to think I might have done better as regards my choice of a wife, that it would be nicer to have healthy merry children than my affectionate delicate lad?

When I got to this point, I could stand it no longer. I felt as though some mocking spirit were taking possession of me, which eventually would destroy all my peace of mind, if I did not cast it out promptly and effectually.

I would not lie there supine to let any demon torment me; and, accordingly, springing to the floor, I dressed in hot haste, and flinging wide the window, looked out over a landscape bathed in the clear light of a most lovely moon.

"How beautiful !" I thought. "I have never yet seen the farm by night, I'll just go and take a stroll round it and then turn in again—after a short walk I shall likely be able to sleep."

So saying, I slipped downstairs, closed the hall door softly after me, and went out into the moonlight.

Chapter Three

As I stood upon the lawn, looking around with a keen and subtle pleasure, I felt, almost for the first time in my life, the full charm and beauty of night. Every object was as clearly revealed as though the time had been noon instead of an hour past midnight, but there lay a mystic spell on tree and field and stream the garish day could never equal. It was a fairy light and a fairy scene, and it would scarcely have astonished me to see fantastic elves issue from the foxglove's flowers or dart from the shelter of concealing leaves and dance a measure on the emerald sward.

For a minute I felt—as I fancy many and many a commonplace man must have done when first wedded to some miracle of grace and beauty—a sense of amazement and unreality.

All this loveliness was mine—the moonlit lawn—the stream murmuring through the fir plantation, singing soft melodies as it pursued its glittering way—the trees with a silvery gleam tinting their foliage—the roses giving out their sweetest, tenderest perfumes—the wonderful silence around—the fresh, pure air—the soft night wind—the prosperity with which God had blessed me. My heart grew full, as I turned and gazed first on this side and then on that, and I felt vexed and angry to remember I had ever suffered myself to listen to idle stories and to be made uncomfortable by reason of village gossip.

On such a night it really seemed a shame to go to bed, and, acccord-ingly, though the restlessness which first induced me to rise had vanished, and in doing so left the most soothing calm behind, I wan-dered on away from the house, now beside the stream, and again across a meadow, where faint odours from the lately carried hay still lin-gered.

Still the same unreal light over field and copse—still the same witching glamour—still the same secret feeling. I was seeing some-thing and experiencing some sensation I might never again recall on this side of the grave !

A most lovely night—one most certainly not for drawn curtains and closed eyelids—one rather for lovers' tête-à-tête or a dreamy reverie—for two young hearts to reveal their secrets to each other or one soul to commune alone with God.

Still rambling, I found myself at last beside a stile, opening upon a path, which, winding upwards, led past the hollow where the nut trees grew, and then joined the footway leading through the long field to Whittleby. The long field was the last in that direction belonging to Nut Bush Farm. It joined upon a portion of the land surrounding Chalmont, and the field path continued consequently to pass through Miss Gostock's property till the main road was reached. It cut off a long distance, and had been used generally by the inhabitants of the villages and hamlets dotted about my place until the rumour being circulated that something might be "seen" or "met" deterred people from venturing by a route concerning which such evil things were whispered. I had walked it constantly, both on account of the time it saved and also in order to set a good example to my labourers and my neighbours, but I might as well have saved my pains.

I was regarded merely as foolhardy, and I knew people generally supposed I should one day have cause to repent my temerity.

As I cleared the stile and began winding my upward way to the higher ground beyond, the thought did strike me what a likely place for a murder Nut Bush Hollow looked. It was a deep excavation, out of which, as no one supposed it to be natural, hundreds and thousands of loads of earth must at some time or other have been carted. From top to bottom it was clothed with nut trees—they grew on every side, and in thick, almost impenetrable masses. For years and years they seemed to have had no care bestowed on them, the Hollow forming in this respect a remarkable contrast to the rest of Mr. Hascot's careful farming, and, as a fir plantation ran along the base of the Hollow, while the moon's light fell clear and full on some of the bushes, the others lay in densest shadow.

The road that once led down into the pit was now completely overgrown with nut bushes which grew luxuriantly to the very edge of the Beech Walk, and threatened ere long to push their way between the trunks of the great trees, which were the beauty and the pride of my lovely farm.

At one time, so far as I could understand, the nut bushes had the whole place almost to themselves, and old inhabitants told me that formerly, in the days when their parents were boys and girls, the nuts used to pay the whole of the rent. As years passed, however, whether from want of care or some natural cause, they gradually ceased to bear, and had to be cut down and cleared off the ground—those in the dell, however, being suffered to remain, the hollow being useless for husbandry, and the bushes which flourished there producing a crop of nuts sufficient for the farmer's family.

All this recurred to my mind as I stood for a moment and looked down into the depths of rustling green below me. I thought of the boys who must have gone nutting there, of all the nests birds had built in the branches so closely interlaced, of the summers' suns which had shone full and strong upon that mass of foliage, of the winters' snows which had lain heavy on twig and stem and happed the strong roots in a warm covering of purest white.

And then the former idea again asserted itself—what a splendid place for a tragedy; a sudden blow—a swift stab—even a treacherous push—and the deed could be done—a man might be alive and well one minute, and dead the next !

False friend, or secret enemy; rival or thief, it was competent for either in such a place at any lonely hour to send a man upon his last long journey. Had Mr. Hascot been so served ? Down, far down, was he lying in a quiet, dreamless sleep ? At that very moment was there anyone starting from fitful slumber to grapple with his remorse for crime committed, or shrink with horror from the dread of detection ?

"Where was my fancy leading me ?" I suddenly asked myself. This was worse than in my own chamber preventing the night watches. Since I had been standing there my heart felt heavier than when tossing from side to side in bed, and wooing unsuccessfully the slumber which refused to come for my asking.

What folly ! what nonsense ! and into what an insane course of speculation had I not embarked. I would leave the eerie place and get once again into the full light of the moon's bright beams.

Hush ! hark ! what was that ? deep down amongst the underwood —a rustle, a rush, and a scurry—then silence—then a stealthy movement amongst the bushes—then whilst I was peering down into the abyss lined with waving green below, SOMETHING passed by me swiftly, something which brought with it a cold chill as though the hand of one dead had been laid suddenly on my heart.

Instantly I turned and looked around. There was not a living thing in sight—neither on the path, nor on the sward, nor on the hillside, nor skirting the horizon as I turned my eyes upward.

For a moment I stood still in order to steady my nerves, then re-assuring myself with the thought it must have been an animal of some kind, I completed the remainder of the ascent without further delay.

"The ghost, I suspect," I said to myself as I reached the long field and the path leading back to the farm, "will resolve itself into a hare or pheasant—is not the whirr of a cock pheasant rising, for instance, enough, when coming unexpectedly, to frighten any nervous person out of his wits ? And might not a hare, or a cat, or, better still, a stoat— yes, a stoat, with its gliding, almost noiseless, movements—mimic the footfall of a suppositious ghost ?"

By this time I had gained the summit of the incline, and slightly out of breath with breasting the ascent, stood for a moment contemplating the exquisite panorama stretched out beneath me. I linger on that moment because it was the last time I ever saw beauty in the moonlight. Now I cannot endure the silvery gleam of the queen of night— weird, mournful, fantastic if you like, but to be desired—no.

Whenever possible I draw the blinds and close the shutters, yet withal on moonlight nights I cannot sleep, the horror of darkness is to my mind nothing in comparison to the terror of a full moon. But I drivel ; let me hasten on.

From the crest of the hill I could see lying below a valley of dream-like beauty—woods in the foreground—a champagne country spreading away into the indefinite distance—a stream winding in and out, dancing and glittering under the moon's beams—a line of hills dimly seen against the horizon, and already a streak of light appearing above them the first faint harbinger of dawn.

"It is morning, then, already," I said, and with the words turned my face homewards. As I did so I saw before me on the path—*clearly*—the figure of a man.

He was walking rapidly and I hurried my pace in order to overtake him. Now to this part of the story I desire to draw particular attention. *Let me hurry as I might I never seemed able to get a foot nearer to him.*

At intervals he paused, as if on purpose to assist my desire, but the moment I seemed gaining upon him the distance between us suddenly increased. I could not tell how he did it, the fact only remained—it was like pursuing some phantom in a dream.

All at once when he reached the bridge he stood quite still. He did not move hand or limb as I drew near—the way was so narrow I knew I should have to touch him in passing; nevertheless, I pressed forward. My foot was on the bridge—I was close to him—I felt my breath coming thick and fast—I clasped a stick I had picked up in the plantation firmly in my hand—I stopped, intending to speak—I opened my mouth, intending to do so—and then—then—without any movement on his part—I was alone !

Yes, as totally alone as though he had never stood on the bridge—never preceded me along the field-path—never loitered upon my footsteps—never paused for my coming.

I was appalled.

"Lord, what is this ?" I thought. "Am I going mad ?" I felt as if I were. On my honour, I know I was as nearly insane at that moment as a man ever can be who is still in the possession of his senses.

Beyond lay the farm of which in my folly I had felt so proud to be the owner, where I once meant to be so happy and win health for my wife and strength for my boy. I saw the Beech Walk I had gloried in—the ricks of hay it seemed so good to get thatched geometrically as only one man in the neighbourhood was said to be able to lay the straw.

What was farm, or riches, or beech trees, or anything, to me now ? Over the place there seemed a curse—better the meanest cottage than a palace with such accessories.

If I had been incredulous before, I was not so now—I could not distrust the evidence of my own eyes—and yet as I walked along, I tried after a minute or two to persuade myself imagination had been playing some juggler's trick with me. The moon, I argued, always lent herself readily to a game of hide-and-seek. She is always open to join in fantastic gambols with shadows—with thorn bushes—with a waving branch—aye, even with a clump of gorse. I must have been mistaken—I had been thinking weird thoughts as I stood by that dismal dell—I had seen no man walking—beheld no figure disappear !

Just as I arrived at this conclusion I beheld someone coming towards me down the Beech Walk. It was a man walking leisurely with a firm, free step. The sight did me good. Here was something tangible—something to question. I stood still, in the middle of the path—the Beech Walk being rather a grassy glade with a narrow footway dividing it, than anything usually understood by the term walk—so that I might speak to the intruder when he drew near, and ask him what he meant by trespassing on my property, more especially at such an hour. There were no public rights on my land except as regarded the path across the long field and through the wood. No one had any right or business to be in the Beech Walk, by day or night, save those employed about the farm, and this person was a gentleman; even in the distance I could distinguish that. As he came closer I saw he was dressed in a loose Palmerston suit, that he wore a low-crowned hat, and that he carried a light cane. The moonbeams dancing down amongst the branches and between the leaves fell full upon his face, and catching sight of a ring he had on his right hand, made it glitter with as many different colours as a prism.

A middle-aged man, so far as I could judge, with a set, determined expression of countenance, dark hair, no beard or whiskers, only a small moustache. A total stranger to me. I had never seen him nor any one like him in the neighbourhood. Who could he be, and what in the wide world was he doing on my premises at that unearthly hour of the morning ?

He came straight on, never moving to right or left—taking no more notice of me than if he had been blind. His easy indifference, his contemptuous coolness, angered me, and planting myself a little more in his way, I began :

"Are you aware, sir——"

I got no further. Without swerving in the slightest degree from the path, he passed me ! I felt something like a cold mist touch me for an instant, and the next, I saw him pursuing his steady walk down the centre of the glade. I was sick with fear, but for all that I ran after him faster than I had ever done since boyhood.

All to no purpose ! I might as well have tried to catch the wind. Just where three ways joined I stood still and looked around. I was quite alone ! Neither sign nor token of the intruder could I discover. On my left lay the dell where the nut trees grew, and above it the field path to Whittleby showing white and clear in the moonlight; close at hand was the bridge; straight in front the wood looked dark and solemn. Between me and it lay a little hollow, down which a narrow path wound tortuously. As I gazed I saw that, where a moment before no one had been, a man was walking now. But I could not follow. My limbs refused their office. He turned his head, and lifting his hand on which the ring glittered, beckoned me to come. He might as well have asked one seized with paralysis. On the confines of the wood he stood motionless as if awaiting my approach; then, when I made no sign of movement, he wrung his hands with a despairing gesture, and disappeared.

At the same moment, moon, dell, bridge, and stream faded from my sight—and I fainted.

Chapter Four

IT was not much past eight o'clock when I knocked at Miss Gostock's hall door, and asked if I could see that lady.

After that terrible night vision I had made up my mind. Behind Mr. Hascot's disappearance I felt sure there lurked some terrible tragedy— living, no man should have implored my help with such passionate earnestness without avail, and if indeed one had appeared to me from the dead I would right him if I could.

But never for a moment did I then think of giving up the farm. The resolve I had come to seemed to have braced up my courage—let what might come or go, let crops remain unreaped and men neglect their labour, let monetary loss and weary, anxious days be in store if they would, I meant to go on to the end.

The first step on my road clearly led in the direction of Miss Gostock's house. She alone could give me all the information I required— to her alone could I speak freely and fully about what I had seen.

I was instantly admitted, and found the lady, as I had expected, at breakfast. It was her habit, I knew, to partake of that meal while the labourers she employed were similarly engaged. She was attired in an easy *négligé* of a white skirt and a linen coat which had formerly belonged to her brother. She was not taking tea or coffee like any other woman—but was engaged upon about a pound of smoking steak which she ate covered with mustard and washed down with copious draughts of home-brewed beer.

She received me cordially and invited me to join in the banquet—a request I ungallantly declined, eliciting in return the remark I should never be good for much till I ceased living on "slops" and took to "good old English" fare.

After these preliminaries I drew my chair near the table and said:

"I want you to give me some information, Miss Gostock, about my predecessor."

"What sort of information?" she asked, with a species of frost at once coming over her manner.

"Can you tell me anything of his personal appearance?"

"Why do you ask?"

I did not immediately answer, and seeing my hesitation she went on:

"Because if you mean to tell me you or anyone else have seen him about your place I would not believe it if you swore it—there!"

"I do not ask you to believe it, Miss Gostock," I said.

"And I give you fair warning, it is of no use coming here and asking me to relieve you of your bargain, because I won't do it. I like you well enough—better than I ever liked a tenant; but I don't intend to be a shilling out of pocket by you."

"I hope you never may be," I answered meekly.

"I'll take very good care I never am," she retorted; "and so don't come here talking about Mr. Hascot. He served me a dirty turn, and I would not put it one bit past him to try and get the place a bad name."

"Will you tell me what sort of looking man he was?" I asked determinedly.

"No, I won't," she snapped, and while she spoke she rose, drained the last drop out of a pewter measure, and after tossing on the straw hat with a defiant gesture, thumped its crown well down on her head. I took the hint, and rising, said I must endeavour to ascertain the particulars I wanted elsewhere.

"You won't ascertain them from me," retorted Miss Gostock, and so we parted as we had never done before—on bad terms.

Considerably perplexed, I walked out of the house. A rebuff of this sort was certainly the last thing I could have expected, and as I paced along I puzzled myself by trying to account for Miss Gostock's extraordinary conduct, and anxiously considering what I was to do under present circumstances. All at once the recollection of mine host of the "Bunch of Hops" flashed across my mind. He must have seen Mr. Hascot often, and I could address a few casual questions to him without exciting his curiosity.

No sooner thought than done. Turning my face towards Whittleby, I stepped briskly on.

"Did I ever see Mr. Hascot?" repeated the landlord—when after some general conversation about politics, the weather, the crops, and many other subjects, I adroitly turned it upon the late tenant of Nut Bush Farm. "Often, sir. I never had much communication with him, for he was one of your stand-aloof, keep-your-distance, sort of gentlemen—fair dealing and honourable—but neither free nor generous. He has often sat where you are sitting now, sir, and not so much as said—'it is a fine day,' or, 'I am afraid we shall have rain.'

"You had but to see him walking down the street to know what he was. As erect as a grenadier, with a firm easy sort of marching step, he looked every inch a gentleman—just in his everyday clothes, a *Palmerston suit* and a *round hat*, he was, as many a one said, fit to go to court. His hands were not a bit like a farmer's, but white and delicate as any lady's, and the *diamond ring* he wore flashed like a star when he stroked the *slight bit of a moustache* that was *all the hair he had upon his face*. No—not a handsome gentleman, but fine looking, with a presence—bless and save us all to think of his giving up everything for the sake of that slip of a girl."

"She was very pretty, wasn't she?" I inquired.

"Beautiful—we all said she was too pretty to come to any good. The old grandmother, you see, had serious cause for keeping so tight a hold over her, but it was in her, and 'what's bred in bone,' you know, sir."

"And you really think they did go off together?"

"Oh, yes, sir; nobody had ever any doubt about that."

On this subject his tone was so decided I felt it was useless to continue the conversation, and having paid him for the modest refreshment of which I had partaken I sauntered down the High Street and turned into the Bank, where I thought of opening an account.

When I had settled all preliminaries with the manager he saved me the trouble of beating about the bush by breaking cover himself and asking if anything had been heard of Mr. Hascot.

"Not that I know of," I answered.

"Curious affair, wasn't it?" he said.

"It appears so, but I have not heard the whole story."

"Well, the whole story is brief," returned the manager. "He comes over here one day and without assigning any reason withdraws the whole of his balance, which was very heavy—is met on the road homeward but never returns home—the same day the girl Powner is also missing—what do you think of all that?"

"It is singular," I said, "very."

"Yes, and to leave his wife and family totally unprovided for."

"I cannot understand that at all."

"Nor I—it was always known he had an extreme partiality for the young person—he and Miss Gostock quarrelled desperately on the subject—but no one could have imagined an attachment of that sort would have led a man so far astray—Hascot more especially. If I had been asked to name the last person in the world likely to make a fool of himself for the sake of a pretty face I should have named the late tenant of Nut Bush Farm."

"There never was a suspicion of foul play," I suggested.

"Oh, dear, no! It was broad daylight when he was last seen on the Whittleby road. The same morning it is known he and the girl were talking earnestly together beside the little wood on your property, and two persons answering to their description were traced to London, that is to say, a gentleman came forward to say he believed he had travelled up with them as far as New Cross on the afternoon in question."

"He was an affectionate father I have heard," I said.

"A *most* affectionate parent—a most devoted husband. Dear, dear! It is dreadfully sad to think how a bad woman may drag the best of men down to destruction. It is terrible to think of his wife and family being inmates of the Union."

"Yes, and it is terrible to consider not a soul has tried to get them out of it," I answered, a little tartly.

"H—m, perhaps so; but we all know we are contributing to their support," he returned with an effort at jocularity, which, in my then frame of mind, seemed singularly *mal-apropos*.

"There is something in that," I replied with an effort, and leaving the Bank next turned my attention to the Poorhouse at Crayshill.

At that time many persons thought what I did quixotic. It is so much the way of the world to let the innocent suffer for the guilty, that I believe Mr. Hascot's wife might have ended her days in Crayshill Union but for the action I took in the matter.

Another night I felt I could not rest till I had arranged for a humble lodging she and her family could occupy till I was able to form some plan for their permanent relief. I found her a quiet, ladylike woman, totally unable to give me the slightest clue as to where her husband might be found. "He was just at the stile on the Chalmont fields," she said, "when Mr. Waite met him; no one saw him afterwards, unless it might be the Ockfields, but, of course, there is no information to be got from them. The guardians have tried every possible means to discover his whereabouts without success. My own impression is he and Sally Powner have gone to America, and that some day we may hear from him. He cannot harden his heart for ever and forget——" Here Mrs. Hascot's sentence trailed off into passionate weeping.

"It is too monstrous!" I considered; "the man never did such a thing as desert his wife and children. Someone knows all about the matter," and then in a moment I paused in the course of my meditations.

Was that person Miss Gostock?

It was an ugly idea, and yet it haunted me. When I remembered the woman's masculine strength, when I recalled her furious impetuosity when I asked her a not very exasperating question, as I recalled the way she tossed off that brandy, when I considered her love of money, her eagerness to speak ill of her late tenant, her semi-references to some great trouble prior to which she was more like other women, or, perhaps, to speak more correctly, less unlike them—doubts came crowding upon my mind.

It was when entering her ground Mr. Hascot was last seen. He had a large sum of money in his possession. She was notoriously fond of rambling about Nut Bush Farm, and what my labouring men called "spying around," which had been the cause of more than one pitched battle between herself and Mr. Hascot.

"The old master could not a-bear her," said one young fellow.

I hated myself for the suspicion; and yet, do what I would, I could not shake it off. Not for a moment did I imagine Miss Gostock had killed her former tenant in cold blood; but it certainly occurred to me that the dell was deep, and the verge treacherous, that it would be easy to push a man over, either by accident or design, that the nut-bushes grew thick, that a body might lie amongst them till it rotted, ere even the boys who went nutting there, season after season, happened to find 'it.

Should I let the matter drop ? No, I decided. With that mute appeal haunting my memory, I should know no rest or peace till I had solved the mystery of Mr. Hascot's disappearance, and cleared his memory from the shameful stain circumstances had cast upon it.

What should I do next ? I thought the matter over for a few days, and then decided to call on Mr. Waite, who never yet had called on me. As usual, he was not at home; but I saw his wife, whom I found just the sort of woman Lolly described—a fair, delicate creature who seemed fading into the grave.

She had not much to tell me. It was her husband who saw Mr. Hascot at the Chalmont stile; it was he also who had seen Mr. Hascot and the girl Powner talking together on the morning of their disappearance. It so happened he had often chanced to notice them together before. "She was a very, very pretty girl," Mrs. Waite added, "and I always thought a modest. She had a very sweet way of speaking—quite above her station—inherited, no doubt, for her father was a gentleman. Poor little Sally !"

The words were not much, but the manner touched me sensibly. I felt drawn to Mrs. Waite from that moment, and told her more of what I had beheld and what I suspected than I had mentioned to anyone else.

As to my doubts concerning Miss Gostock, I was, of course, silent but I said quite plainly I did not believe Mr. Hascot had gone off with any girl or woman either, that I thought he had come to an unfair end, and that I was of opinion the stories circulated, concerning a portion of Nut Bush Farm being haunted, had some foundation in fact.

"Do you believe in ghosts then ?" she asked, with a curious smile.

"I believe in the evidence of my senses," I answered, "and I declare to you, Mrs. Waite, that one night, not long since, I saw as plainly as I see you what I can only conclude to have been the semblance of Mr. Hascot."

She did not make any reply, she only turned very pale, and blaming myself for having alarmed one in her feeble state of health, I hastened to apologise and take my leave.

As we shook hands, she retained mine for a moment, and said, "When you hear anything more, if you should, that is, you will tell us, will you not? Naturally we feel interested in the matter, he was such a near neighbour, and—we knew him."

I assured her I would not fail to do so, and left the room.

Before I reached the front door I found I had forgotten one of my gloves, and immediately retraced my steps.

The drawing-room door was ajar, and somewhat unceremoniously, perhaps, I pushed it open and entered.

To my horror and surprise, Mrs. Waite, whom I had left apparently in her ordinary state of languid health, lay full length on the sofa, sobbing as if her heart would break. What I said so indiscreetly had brought on an attack of violent hysterics—a malady with the signs and tokens of which I was not altogether unacquainted.

Silently I stole out of the room without my glove, and left the house, closing the front door noiselessly behind me.

A couple of days elapsed, and then I decided to pay a visit to Mrs. Ockfield. If she liked to throw any light on the matter, I felt satisfied she could. It was, to say the least of it, most improbable her granddaughter, whether she had been murdered or gone away with Mr. Hascot, should disappear and not leave a clue by which her relatives could trace her.

The Ockfields were not liked, I found, and I flattered myself if they had any hand in Mr. Hascot's sudden disappearance I should soon hit on some weak spot in their story.

I found the old woman, who was sixty-seven, and who looked two hundred, standing over her washing tub.

"Can I tell you where my grand-daughter is," she repeated, drawing her hands out of the suds and wiping them on her apron. "Surely, sir, and very glad I am to be able to tell everybody, gentle and simple, where to find our Sally. She is in a good service down in Cheshire. Mr. Hascot got her the place, but we knew nothing about it till yesterday; she left us in a bit of a pet, and said she wouldn't have written me only something seemed to tell her she must. Ah ! she'll have a sore heart when she gets my letter and hears how it has been said that the master and she went off together. She thought a deal of the master, did Sally; he was always kind and stood between her and her grand-father."

"Then do you mean to say," I asked, "that she knows nothing of Mr. Hascot's disappearance ?"

"Nothing, sir, thank God for all His mercies; the whole of the time since the day she left here she has been in service with a friend of his. You can read her letter if you like."

Though I confess old Mrs. Ockfield neither charmed nor inspired me with confidence, I answered that I should like to see the letter very much indeed.

When I took it in my hand I am bound to say I thought it had been written with a purpose, and intended less for a private than for the public eye, but as I read I fancied there was a ring of truth about the epistle, more especially as the writer made passing reference to a very bitter quarrel which had preceded her departure from the grand-paternal roof.

"It is very strange," I said, as I returned the letter, "it is a most singular coincidence that your grand-daughter and Mr. Hascot should have left Whittleby on the same day, and yet that she should know nothing of his whereabouts, as judging from her letter seems to be the case."

"Are you quite sure Mr. Hascot ever did leave Whittleby, sir ?" asked the old woman with a vindictive look in her still bright old eyes. "There are those as think he never went very far from home, and that the whole truth will come out some day."

"What do you mean ?" I exclaimed, surprised.

"Least said soonest mended," she answered shortly; "only I hopes if ever we do know the rights of it, people as do hold their heads high enough, and have had plenty to say about our girl, and us too for that matter, will find things not so pleasant as they find them at present. The master had a heap of money about him, and we know that often those as has are those as wants more !"

"I cannot imagine what you are driving at," I said, for I feared every moment she would mention Miss Gostock, and bring her name into the discussion. "If you think Mr. Hascot met with any foul play you ought to go to the police about the matter."

"Maybe I will some time," she answered, "but just now I have my washing to do."

"This will buy you some tea to have afterwards," I said, laying down half-a-crown, and feeling angry with myself for this momentary irritation. After all, the woman had as much right to her suspicions as I to mine.

Thinking over Miss Powner's letter, I came to the conclusion it might be well to see the young lady for myself. If I went to the address she wrote from I could ascertain at all events whether her statement regarding her employment was correct. Yes, I would take train and travel into Cheshire; I had commenced the investigation and I would follow it to the end.

I travelled so much faster than Mrs. Ockfield's letter—which, indeed, that worthy woman had not then posted—that when I arrived at my journey's end I found the fair Sally in total ignorance of Mr. Hascot's disappearance and the surmises to which her own absence had given rise.

Appearances might be against the girl's truth and honesty, yet I felt she was dealing fairly with me.

"A better gentleman, sir," she said, "than Mr. Hascot never drew breath. And so they set it about he had gone off with me—they little know—they little know ! Why, sir, he thought of me and was careful for me as he might for a daughter. The first time I ever saw him grandfather was beating me, and he interfered to save me. He knew they treated me badly, and it was after a dreadful quarrel I had at home he advised me to go away. He gave me a letter to the lady I am now with, and a ten-pound note to pay my travelling expenses and keep something in my pocket. 'You'll be better away from the farm, little girl,' he said the morning I left; 'people are beginning to talk, and we can't shut their mouths if you come running to me every time your grandmother speaks sharply to you.'"

"But why did you not write sooner to your relatives ?" I asked.

"Because I was angry with my grandmother, sir, and I thought I would give her a fright. I did not bring any clothes or anything and I hoped—it was a wicked thing I know, sir—but I hoped she would believe I had made away with myself. Just lately, however, I began to consider that if she and grandfather had not treated we well, I was treating them worse, so I made up a parcel of some things my mistress gave me and sent it to them with a letter. I am glad it reached them safely."

"What time was it when you saw Mr. Hascot last ?" I inquired.

"About two o'clock, sir, I know that, because he was in a hurry. He had got some news about the Bank at Whittleby not being quite safe, and he said he had too much money there to run any risk of loss. 'Be a good girl,' were the last words he said, and he walked off sharp and quick by the field path to Whittleby. I stood near the bridge crying for a while. Oh, sir ! do you think anything ill can have happened to him ?"

For answer, I only said the whole thing seemed most mysterious.

"He'd never have left his wife and children, sir," she went on; "never. He must have been made away with."

"Had he any enemies, do you think ?" I asked.

"No, sir; not to say enemies. He was called hard because he would have a day's work for a day's wage, but no one that ever I heard of had a grudge against him. Except Miss Gostock and Mr. Waite, he agreed well with all the people about. He did not like Miss Gostock, and Mr. Waite was always borrowing money from him. Now Mr. Hascot did not mind giving, but he could not bear lending."

I returned to Nut Bush Farm perfectly satisfied that Mr. Hascot had been, as the girl expressed the matter, "made away with." On the threshold of my house I was met with a catalogue of disasters. The female servants had gone in a body; the male professed a dislike to be in the stable-yard in the twilight. Rumour had decided that Nut Bush Farm was an unlucky place even to pass. The cattle were out of condition because the men would not go down the Beech Walk, or turn a single sheep into the long field. Reapers wanted higher wages. The labourers were looking out for other service.

"Poor fellow ! This is a nice state of things for you to come home to," said Lolly compassionately. "Even the poachers won't venture into the wood, and the boys don't go nutting."

"I will clear away the nut trees and cut down the wood," I declared savagely.

"I don't know who you are going to get to cut them," answered Lolly, "unless you bring men down from London."

As for Miss Gostock, she only laughed at my dilemma, and said, "You're a pretty fellow to be frightened by a ghost. If he was seen at Chalmont I'd ghost him."

While I was in a state of the most cruel perplexity, I bethought me of my promise to Mrs. Waite, and walked over one day to tell her the result of my inquiries.

I found her at home, and Mr. Waite, for a wonder, int he drawing-room. He was not a bad-looking fellow, and welcomed my visit with a heartiness which ill accorded with the discourtesy he had shown in never calling upon me.

Very succinctly I told what I had done, and where I had been. I mentioned the terms in which Sally Powner spoke of her benefactor. We discussed the whole matter fully—the *pros* and *cons* of anyone knowing Mr. Hascot had such a sum of money on his person, and the possibility of his having been murdered. I mentioned what I had done about Mrs. Hascot, and begged Mr. Waite to afford me his help and co-operation in raising such a sum of money as might start the poor lady in some business.

"I'll do all that lies in my power," he said heartily, shaking hands at the same time, for I had risen to go.

"And for my part," I remarked, "it seems to me there are only two things more I can do to elucidate the mystery, and those are—root every nut-tree out of the dell and set the axe to work in the wood."

There was a second's silence. Then Mrs. Waite dropped to the floor as if she had been shot.

As he stooped over her he and I exchanged glances, and then *I knew*. Mr. Hascot *had* been murdered, and Mr. Waite was the murderer !

*   *   *   *   *

That night I was smoking and Lolly at needlework. The parlour windows were wide open, for it was warm, and not a breath of air seemed stirring.

There was a stillness on everything which betokened a coming thunderstorm; and we both were silent, for my mind was busy and Lolly's heart anxious. She did not see, as she said, how I was to get on at all, and for my part I could not tell what I ought to do.

All at once something whizzed through the window furthest from where we sat, and fell noisily to the floor.

"What is that?" Lolly cried, springing to her feet. "Oh, Jack ! What is it?"

Surprised and shaken myself, I closed the windows and drew down the blinds before I examined the cause of our alarm. It proved to be an oblong package weighted with a stone. Unfastening it cautiously, for I did not know whether it might not contain some explosive, I came at length to a pocket book. Opening the pocket book, I found it stuffed full of bank notes.

"What are they? Where can they have come from?" exclaimed Lolly.

"They are the notes Mr. Hascot drew from Whittleby bank the day he disappeared," I answered with a sort of inspiration, but I took no notice of Lolly's last question.

For good or for evil that was a secret which lay between myself and the Waites, and which I have never revealed till now.

If the vessel in which they sailed for New Zealand had not gone to the bottom I should have kept the secret still.

When they were out of the country and the autumn well advanced, I had the wood thoroughly examined, and there in a gully, covered with a mass of leaves and twigs and dead branches, we found Mr. Hascot's body. His watch was in his waistcoat pocket—his ring on his finger; save for these possessions no one could have identified him.

His wife married again about a year afterwards and my brother took Nut Bush Farm off my hands. He says the place never was haunted— that I never saw Mr. Hascot except in my own imagination—that the whole thing originated in a poor state of health and a too credulous disposition !

I leave the reader to judge between us.

THE OPEN DOOR

SOME people do not believe in ghosts. For that matter, some people do not believe in anything. There are persons who even affect incredulity concerning that open door at Ladlow Hall. They say it did not stand wide open—that they could have shut it; that the whole affair was a delusion; that they are sure it must have been a conspiracy; that they are doubtful whether there is such a place as Ladlow on the face of the earth; that the first time they are in Meadowshire they will look it up.

That is the manner in which this story, hitherto unpublished, has been greeted by my acquaintances. How it will be received by strangers is quite another matter. I am going to tell what happened to me exactly as it happened, and readers can credit or scoff at the tale as it pleases them. It is not necessary for me to find faith and comprehension in addition to a ghost story, for the world at large. If such were the case, I should lay down my pen.

Perhaps, before going further, I ought to premise there was a time when I did not believe in ghosts either. If you had asked me one summer's morning years ago when you met me on London Bridge if I held such appearances to be probable or possible, you would have received an emphatic "No" for answer.

But, at this rate, the story of the Open Door will never be told; so we will, with your permission, plunge into it immediately.

"Sandy !"

"What do you want ?"

"Should you like to earn a sovereign ?"

"Of course I should."

A somewhat curt dialogue, but we were given to curtness in the office of Messrs. Frimpton, Frampton and Fryer, auctioneers and estate agents, St. Benet's Hill, City.

(My name is not Sandy or anything like it, but the other clerks so styled me because of a real or fancied likeness to some character, an ill-looking Scotchman, they had seen at the theatre. From this it may be inferred I was not handsome. Far from it. The only ugly specimen in my family, I knew I was very plain; and it chanced to be no secret to me either that I felt grievously discontented with my lot.

I did not like the occupation of clerk in an auctioneer's office, and I did not like my employers.

We are all of us inconsistent, I suppose, for it was a shock to me to find they entertained a most cordial antipathy to me.)

"Because," went on Parton, a fellow, my senior by many years—a fellow who delighted in chaffing me, "I can tell you how to lay hands on one."

"How ?" I asked, sulkily enough, for I felt he was having what he called his fun.

"You know that place we let to Carrison, the tea-dealer ? "

Carrison was a merchant in the China trade, possessed of fleets of vessels and towns of warehouses; but I did not correct Parton's expression, I simply nodded.

"He took it on a long lease, and he can't live in it; and our governor said this morning he wouldn't mind giving anybody who could find out what the deuce is the matter, a couple of sovereigns and his travelling expenses."

"Where is the place ?" I asked, without turning my head; for the convenience of listening I had put my elbows on the desk and propped up my face with both hands.

"Away down in Meadowshire, in the heart of the grazing country."

"And what *is* the matter ?" I further inquired.

"A door that won't keep shut."

"What ?"

"A door that will keep open, if you prefer that way of putting it," said Parton.

"You are jesting."

"If I am, Carrison is not, or Fryer either. Carrison came here in a nice passion, and Fryer was in a fine rage; I could see he was, though he kept his temper outwardly. They have had an active correspondence it appears, and Carrison went away to talk to his lawyer. Won't make much by that move, I fancy."

"But tell me," I intreated, "why the door won't keep shut ?"

"They say the place is haunted."

"What nonsense !" I exclaimed.

"Then you are just the person to take the ghost in hand. I thought so while old Fryer was speaking."

"If the door won't keep shut," I remarked, pursuing my own train of thought, "why can't they let it stay open?"

"I have not the slightest idea. I only know there are two sovereigns to be made, and that I give you a present of the information."

And having thus spoken, Parton took down his hat and went out, either upon his own business or that of his employers.

There was one thing I can truly say about our office, we were never serious in it. I fancy that is the case in most offices nowadays; at all events, it was the case in ours. We were always chaffing each other, playing practical jokes, telling stupid stories, scamping our work, looking at the clock, counting the weeks to next St. Lubbock's Day, counting the hours to Saturday.

For all that we were all very earnest in our desire to have our salaries raised, and unanimous in the opinion no fellows ever before received such wretched pay. I had twenty pounds a year, which I was aware did not half provide for what I ate at home. My mother and sisters left me in no doubt on the point, and when new clothes were wanted I always hated to mention the fact to my poor worried father.

We had been better off once, I believe, though I never remember the time. My father owned a small property in the country, but owing to the failure of some bank, I never could understand what bank, it had to be mortgaged; then the interest was not paid, and the mortgagees foreclosed, and we had nothing left save the half-pay of a major, and about a hundred a year which my mother brought to the common fund.

We might have managed on our income, I think, if we had not been so painfully genteel; but we were always trying to do something quite beyond our means, and consequently debts accumulated, and creditors ruled us with rods of iron.

Before the final smash came, one of my sisters married the younger son of a distinguished family, and even if they had been disposed to live comfortably and sensibly she would have kept her sisters up to the mark. My only brother, too, was an officer, and of course the family thought it necessary he should see we preserved appearances.

It was all a great trial to my father, I think, who had to bear the brunt of the dunning and harass, and eternal shortness of money; and it would have driven me crazy if I had not found a happy refuge when matters were going wrong at home at my aunt's. She was my father's sister, and had married so "dreadfully below her" that my mother refused to acknowledge the relationship at all.

For these reasons and others, Parton's careless words about the two sovereigns stayed in my memory.

I wanted money badly—I may say I never had sixpence in the world of my own—and I thought if I could earn two sovereigns I might buy some trifles I needed for myself, and present my father with a new umbrella. Fancy is a dangerous little jade to flirt with, as I soon discovered.

She led me on and on. First I thought of the two sovereigns; then I recalled the amount of the rent Mr. Carrison agreed to pay for Ladlow Hall; then I decided he would gladly give more than two sovereigns if he could only have the ghost turned out of possession. I fancied I might get ten pounds—twenty pounds. I considered the matter all day, and I dreamed of it all night, and when I dressed myself next morning I was determined to speak to Mr. Fryer on the subject.

I did so—I told that gentleman Parton had mentioned the matter to me, and that if Mr. Fryer had no objection, I should like to try whether I could not solve the mystery. I told him I had been accustomed to lonely houses, and that I should not feel at all nervous; that I did not believe in ghosts, and as for burglars, I was not afraid of them.

"I don't mind your trying," he said at last. "Of course you understand it is no cure, no pay. Stay in the house for a week; if at the end of that time you can keep the door shut, locked, bolted, or nailed up, telegraph for me, and I will go down—if not, come back. If you like to take a companion there is no objection."

I thanked him, but said I would rather not have a companion.

"There is only one thing, sir, I should like," I ventured.

"And that—— ?" he interrupted.

"Is a little more money. If I lay the ghost, or find out the ghost, I think I ought to have more than two sovereigns."

"How much more do you think you ought to have ?" he asked.

His tone quite threw me off my guard, it was so civil and conciliatory, and I answered boldly:

"Well, if Mr. Carrison cannot now live in the place perhaps he wouldn't mind giving me a ten-pound note."

Mr. Fryer turned, and opened one of the books lying on his desk. He did not look at or refer to it in any way—I saw that.

"You have been with us how long, Edlyd ?" he said.

"Eleven months to-morrow," I replied.

"And our arrangement was, I think, quarterly payments, and one month's notice on either side ?"

"Yes, sir." I heard my voice tremble, though I could not have said what frightened me.

"Then you will please to take your notice now. Come in before you leave this evening, and I'll pay you three months' salary, and then we shall be quits."

"I don't think.I quite understand," I was beginning, when he broke in :

"But I understand, and that's enough. I have had enough of you and your airs, and your indifference, and your insolence here. I never had a clerk I disliked as I do you. Coming and dictating terms, forsooth ! No, you shan't go to Ladlow. Many a poor chap"—(he said "devil")—"would have been glad to earn half a guinea, let alone two sovereigns ; and perhaps you may be before you are much older."

"Do you mean that you won't keep me here any longer, sir ?" I asked in despair. "I had no intention of offending you. I——"

"Now you need not say another word," he interrupted, "for I won't bandy words with you. Since you have been in this place you have never known your position, and you don't seem able to realise it. When I was foolish enough to take you, I did it on the strength of your connexions, but your connexions have done nothing for me. I have never had a penny out of any one of your friends—if you have any. You'll not do any good in business for yourself or anybody else, and the sooner you go to Australia"—(here he was very emphatic)—"and get off these premises, the better I shall be pleased."

I did not answer him—I could not. He had worked himself to a white heat by this time, and evidently intended I should leave his premises then and there. He counted five pounds out of his cash-box, and, writing a receipt, pushed it and the money across the table, and bade me sign and be off at once.

My hand trembled so I could scarcely hold the pen, but I had presence of mind enough left to return one pound ten in gold, and three shillings and fourpence I had, quite by the merest good fortune, in my waistcoat pocket.

"I can't take wages for work I haven't done," I said, as well as sorrow and passion would let me. "Good-morning," and I left his office and passed out among the clerks.

I took from my desk the few articles belonging to me, left the papers it contained in order, and then, locking it, asked Parton if he would be so good as to give the key to Mr. Fryer.

"What's up?" he asked. "Are you going?"

I said, "Yes, I am going."

"Got the sack?"

"That is exactly what has happened."

"Well, I'm——!" exclaimed Mr. Parton.

I did not stop to hear any further commentary on the matter, but bidding my fellow-clerks good-bye, shook the dust of Frimpton's Estate and Agency Office from off my feet.

I did not like to go home and say I was discharged, so I walked about aimlessly, and at length found myself in Regent Street. There I met my father, looking more worried than usual.

"Do you think, Phil," he said (my name is Theophilus), "you could get two or three pounds from your employers?"

Maintaining a discreet silence regarding what had passed, I answered:

"No doubt I could."

"I shall be glad if you will then, my boy," he went on, "for we are badly in want of it."

I did not ask him what was the special trouble. Where would have been the use? There was always something—gas, or water, or poor-rates, or the butcher, or the baker, or the bootmaker. Well, it did not much matter, for we were well accustomed to the life; but, I thought, "if ever I marry, we will keep within our means." And then there rose up before me a vision of Patty, my cousin—the blithest, prettiest, most useful, most sensible girl that ever made sunshine in a poor man's house.

My father and I had parted by this time, and I was still walking aimlessly on, when all at once an idea occurred to me. Mr. Fryer had not treated me well or fairly. I would hoist him on his own petard. I would go to headquarters, and try to make terms with Mr. Carrison direct.

No sooner thought than done. I hailed a passing omnibus, and was ere long in the heart of the city. Like other great men, Mr. Carrison was difficult of access—indeed, so difficult of access, that the clerk to whom I applied for an audience told me plainly I could not see him at all. I might send in my message if I liked, he was good enough to add, and no doubt it would be attended to. I said I should not send in a message, and was then asked what I would do. My answer was simple. I meant to wait till I did see him. I was told they could not have people waiting about the office in this way.

I said I supposed I might stay in the street. "Carrison didn't own that," I suggested.

The clerk advised me not to try that game, or I might get locked up.

I said I would take my chance of it.

After that we went on arguing the question at some length, and we were in the middle of a heated argument, in which several of Carrison's "young gentlemen," as they called themselves, were good enough to join, when we were all suddenly silenced by a grave-looking individual, who authoritatively inquired:

"What is all this noise about?"

Before anyone could answer I spoke up:

"I want to see Mr. Carrison, and they won't let me."

"What do you want with Mr. Carrison?"

"I will tell that to himself only."

"Very well, say on—I am Mr. Carrison."

For a moment I felt abashed and almost ashamed of my persistency; next instant, however, what Mr. Fryer would have called my "native audacity" came to the rescue, and I said, drawing a step or two nearer to him, and taking off my hat:

"I wanted to speak to you about Ladlow Hall, if you please, sir."

In an instant the fashion of his face changed, a look of irritation succeeded to that of immobility; an angry contraction of the eyebrows disfigured the expression of his countenance.

"Ladlow Hall!" he repeated; "and what have you got to say about Ladlow Hall?"

"That is what I wanted to tell you, sir," I answered, and a dead hush seemed to fall on the office as I spoke.

The silence seemed to attract his attention, for he looked sternly at the clerks, who were not using a pen or moving a finger.

"Come this way, then," he said abruptly; and next minute I was in his private office.

"Now, what is it?" he asked, flinging himself into a chair, and addressing me, who stood hat in hand beside the great table in the middle of the room.

I began—I will say he was a patient listener—at the very beginning, and told my story straight through. I concealed nothing. I enlarged on nothing. A discharged clerk I stood before him, and in the capacity of a discharged clerk I said what I had to say. He heard me to the end, then he sat silent, thinking.

At last he spoke.

"You have heard a great deal of conversation about Ladlow, I suppose?" he remarked.

"No sir; I have heard nothing except what I have told you."

"And why do you desire to strive to solve such a mystery?"

"If there is any money to be made, I should like to make it, sir."

"How old are you?"

"Two-and-twenty last January."

"And how much salary had you at Frimpton's?"

"Twenty pounds a year."

"Humph! More than you are worth, I should say."

"Mr. Fryer seemed to imagine so, sir, at any rate," I agreed, sorrowfully.

"But what do you think?" he asked, smiling in spite of himself.

"I think I did quite as much work as the other clerks," I answered.

"That is not saying much, perhaps," he observed. I was of his opinion, but I held my peace.

"You will never make much of a clerk, I am afraid," Mr. Carrison proceeded, fitting his disparaging remarks upon me as he might on a lay figure. "You don't like desk work?"

"Not much, sir."

"I should judge the best thing you could do would be to emigrate," he went on, eyeing me critically.

"Mr. Fryer said I had better go to Australia or——" I stopped, remembering the alternative that gentleman had presented.

"Or where?" asked Mr. Carrison.

"The——, sir," I explained, softly and apologetically.

He laughed—he lay back in his chair and laughed—and I laughed myself, though ruefully.

After all, twenty pounds was twenty pounds, though I had not thought much of the salary till I lost it.

We went on talking for a long time after that; he asked me all about my father and my early life, and how we lived, and where we lived, and the people we knew; and, in fact, put more questions than I can well remember.

"It seems a crazy thing to do," he said at last; "and yet I feel disposed to trust you. The house is standing perfectly empty. I can't live in it, and I can't get rid of it; all my own furniture I have removed, and there is nothing in the place except a few old-fashioned articles belonging to Lord Ladlow. The place is a loss to me. It is of no use trying to let it, and thus, in fact, matters are at a deadlock. You won't be able to find out anything, I know, because, of course, others have tried to solve the mystery ere now; still, if you like to try you may. I will make this bargain with you. If you like to go down, I will pay your reasonable expenses for a fortnight; and if you do any good for me, I will give you a ten-pound note for yourself. Of course I must be satisfied that what you have told me is true and that you are what you represent. Do you know anybody in the city who would speak for you?"

I could think of no one but my uncle. I hinted to Mr. Carrison he was not grand enough or rich enough, perhaps, but I knew nobody else to whom I could refer him.

"What!" he said, "Robert Dorland, of Cullum Street. He does business with us. If he will go bail for your good behaviour I shan't want any further guarantee. Come along." And to my intense amazement, he rose, put on his hat, walked me across the outer office and along the pavements till we came to Cullum Street.

"Do you know this youth, Mr. Dorland?" he said, standing in front of my uncle's desk, and laying a hand on my shoulder.

"Of course I do, Mr. Carrison," answered my uncle, a little apprehensively; for, as he told me afterwards, he could not imagine what mischief I had been up to. "He is my nephew."

"And what is your opinion of him—do you think he is a young fellow I may safely trust?"

My uncle smiled, and answered, "That depends on what you wish to trust him with."

"A long column of addition, for instance."

"It would be safer to give that task to somebody else."

"Oh, uncle !" I remonstrated; for I had really striven to conquer my natural antipathy to figures—worked hard, and every bit of it against the collar.

My uncle got off his stool, and said, standing with his back to the empty fire-grate:

"Tell me what you wish the boy to do, Mr. Carrison, and I will tell you whether he will suit your purpose or not. I know him, I believe, better than he knows himself."

In an easy, affable way, for so rich a man, Mr. Carrison took possession of the vacant stool, and nursing his right leg over his left knee, answered:

"He wants to go and shut the open door at Ladlow for me. Do you think he can do that ?"

My uncle looked steadily back at the speaker, and said, "I thought, Mr. Carrison, it was quite settled no one could shut it ?"

Mr. Carrison shifted a little uneasily on his seat, and replied: "*I* did not set your nephew the task he fancies he would like to undertake."

"Have nothing to do with it, Phil," advised my uncle, shortly.

"You don't believe in ghosts, do you, Mr. Dorland ?" asked Mr. Carrison, with a slight sneer.

"Don't you, Mr. Carrison ?" retorted my uncle.

There was a pause—an uncomfortable pause—during the course of which I felt the ten pounds, which, in imagination, I had really spent, trembling in the scale. I was not afraid. For ten pounds, or half the money, I would have faced all the inhabitants of spirit land. I longed to tell them so; but something in the way those two men looked at each other stayed my tongue.

"If you ask me the question here in the heart of the city, Mr. Dorland," said Mr. Carrison, at length, slowly and carefully, "I answer 'No'; but if you were to put it to me on a dark night at Ladlow, I should beg time to consider. I do not believe in supernatural phenomena myself, and yet—the door at Ladlow is as much beyond my comprehension as the ebbing and flowing of the sea."

"And you can't live at Ladlow ?" remarked my uncle.

"I can't live at Ladlow, and what is more, I can't get anyone else to live at Ladlow."

"And you want to get rid of your lease?"

"I want so much to get rid of my lease that I told Fryer I would give him a handsome sum if he could induce anyone to solve the mystery. Is there any other information you desire, Mr. Dorland? Because if there is, you have only to ask and have. I feel I am not here in a prosaic office in the city of London, but in the Palace of Truth."

My uncle took no notice of the implied compliment. When wine is good it needs no bush. If a man is habitually honest in his speech and in his thoughts, he desires no recognition of the fact.

"I don't think so," he answered; "it is for the boy to say what he will do. If he be advised by me he will stick to his ordinary work in his employers' office, and leave ghost-hunting and spirit-laying alone."

Mr. Carrison shot a rapid glance in my direction, a glance which, implying a secret understanding, might have influenced my uncle could I have stooped to deceive my uncle.

"I can't stick to my work there any longer," I said. "I got my marching orders to-day."

"What *had* you been doing, Phil?" asked my uncle.

"I wanted ten pounds to go and lay the ghost!" I answered, so dejectedly, that both Mr. Carrison and my uncle broke out laughing.

"Ten pounds!" cried my uncle, almost between laughing and crying. "Why, Phil boy, I had rather, poor man though I am, have given thee ten pounds than that thou should'st go ghost-hunting or ghost-laying."

When he was very much in earnest my uncle went back to thee and thou of his native dialect. I liked the vulgarism, as my mother called it, and I knew my aunt loved to hear him use the caressing words to her. He had risen, not quite from the ranks it is true, but if ever a gentleman came ready born into the world it was Robert Dorland, upon whom at our home everyone seemed to look down.

"What will you do, Edlyd?" asked Mr. Carrison; "you hear what your uncle says, 'Give up the enterprise,' and what I say; I do not want either to bribe or force your inclinations."

"I will go, sir," I answered quite steadily. "I am not afraid, and I should like to show you——" I stopped. I had been going to say, "I should like to show you I am not such a fool as you all take me for," but I felt such an address would be too familiar, and refrained.

Mr. Carrison looked at me curiously. I think he supplied the end of the sentence for himself, but he only answered:

"I should like you to show me that door fast shut; at any rate, if you can stay in the place alone for a fortnight, you shall have your money."

"I don't like it, Phil," said my uncle: "I don't like this freak at all."

"I am sorry for that, uncle," I answered, "for I mean to go."

"When?" asked Mr. Carrison.

"To-morrow morning," I replied.

"Give him five pounds, Dorland, please, and I will send you my cheque. You will account to me for that sum, you understand," added Mr. Carrison, turning to where I stood.

"A sovereign will be quite enough," I said.

"You will take five pounds, and account to me for it," repeated Mr. Carrison, firmly; "also, you will write to me every day, to my private address, and if at any moment you feel the thing too much for you, throw it up. Good-afternoon," and without more formal leave-taking he departed.

"It is of no use talking to you, Phil, I suppose?" said my uncle.

"I don't think it is," I replied; "you won't say anything to them at home, will you?"

"I am not very likely to meet any of them, am I?" he answered, without a shade of bitterness—merely stating a fact.

"I suppose I shall not see you again before I start," I said, "so I will bid you good-bye now."

"Good-bye, my lad; I wish I could see you a bit wiser and steadier."

I did not answer him; my heart was very full, and my eyes too. I had tried, but office-work was not in me, and I felt it was just as vain to ask me to sit on a stool and pore over writing and figures as to think a person born destitute of musical ability could compose an opera.

Of course I went straight to Patty; though we were not then married, though sometimes it seemed to me as if we never should be married, she was my better half then as she is my better half now.

She did not throw cold water on the project; she did not discourage me. What she said, with her dear face aglow with excitement, was, "I only wish, Phil, I was going with you." Heaven knows, so did I.

Next morning I was up before the milkman. I had told my people over-night I should be going out of town on business. Patty and I settled the whole plan in detail. I was to breakfast and dress there, for I meant to go down to Ladlow in my volunteer garments. That was a subject upon which my poor father and I never could agree; he called volunteering child's play, and other things equally hard to bear; whilst my brother, a very carpet warrior to my mind, was never weary of ridiculing the force, and chaffing me for imagining I was "a soldier."

Patty and I had talked matters over, and settled, as I have said, that I should dress at her father's.

A young fellow I knew had won a revolver at a raffle, and willingly lent it to me. With that and my rifle I felt I could conquer an army.

It was a lovely afternoon when I found myself walking through leafy lanes in the heart of Meadowshire. With every vein of my heart I loved the country, and the country was looking its best just then: grass ripe for the mower, grain forming in the ear, rippling streams, dreamy rivers, old orchards, quaint cottages.

"Oh that I had never to go back to London," I thought, for I am one of the few people left on earth who love the country and hate cities. I walked on, I walked a long way, and being uncertain as to my road, asked a gentleman who was slowly riding a powerful roan horse under arching trees—a gentleman accompanied by a young lady mounted on a stiff white pony—my way to Ladlow Hall.

"That is Ladlow Hall," he answered, pointing with his whip over the fence to my left hand. I thanked him and was going on, when he said:

"No one is living there now."

"I am aware of that," I answered.

He did not say anything more, only courteously bade me good-day, and rode off. The young lady inclined her head in acknowledgment of my uplifted cap, and smiled kindly. Altogether I felt pleased, little things always did please me. It was a good beginning—half-way to a good ending !

When I got to the Lodge I showed Mr. Carrison's letter to the woman, and received the key.

"You are not going to stop up at the Hall alone, are you, sir?" she asked.

"Yes, I am," I answered, uncompromisingly, so uncompromisingly that she said no more.

The avenue led straight to the house; it was uphill all the way, and bordered by rows of the most magnificent limes I ever beheld. A light iron fence divided the avenue from the park, and between the trunks of the trees I could see the deer browsing and cattle grazing. Ever and anon there came likewise to my ear the sound of a sheep-bell.

It was a long avenue, but at length I stood in front of the Hall—a square, solid-looking, old-fashioned house, three stories high, with no basement; a flight of steps up to the principal entrance; four windows to the right of the door, four windows to the left; the whole building flanked and backed with trees; all the blinds pulled down, a dead silence brooding over the place: the sun westering behind the great trees studding the park. I took all this in as I approached, and afterwards as I stood for a moment under the ample porch; then, re-membering the business which had brought me so far, I fitted the great key in the lock, turned the handle, and entered Ladlow Hall.

For a minute—stepping out of the bright sunlight—the place looked to me so dark that I could scarcely distinguish the objects by which I was surrounded; but my eyes soon grew accustomed to the comparative darkness, and I found I was in an immense hall, lighted from the roof; a magnificent old oak staircase conducted to the upper rooms.

The floor was of black and white marble. There were two fireplaces, fitted with dogs for burning wood; around the walls hung pictures, antlers, and horns, and in odd niches and corners stood groups of statues, and the figures of men in complete suits of armour.

To look at the place outside, no one would have expected to find such a hall. I stood lost in amazement and admiration, and then I began to glance more particularly around.

Mr. Carrison had not given me any instructions by which to identify the ghostly chamber—which I concluded would most probably be found on the first floor.

I knew nothing of the story connected with it—if there were a story. On that point I had left London as badly provided with mental as with actual luggage—worse provided, indeed, for a hamper, packed by Patty, and a small bag were coming over from the station; but regard-ing the mystery I was perfectly unencumbered. I had not the faintest idea in which apartment it resided. Well, I should discover that, no doubt, for myself ere long.

I looked around me—doors—doors—doors. I had never before

seen so many doors together all at once. Two of them stood open—
one wide, the other slightly ajar.

"I'll just shut them as a beginning," I thought, "before I go upstairs."

The doors were of oak, heavy, well-fitting, furnished with good
locks and sound handles. After I had closed I tried them. Yes, they
were quite secure. I ascended the great staircase feeling curiously like
an intruder, paced the corridors, entered the many bed-chambers—
some quite bare of furniture, others containing articles of an ancient
fashion, and no doubt of considerable value—chairs, antique dressing-
tables, curious wardrobes, and such like. For the most part the doors
were closed, and I shut those that stood open before making my way
into the attics.

I was greatly delighted with the attics. The windows lighting them
did not, as a rule, overlook the front of the Hall, but commanded wide
views over wood, and valley, and meadow. Leaning out of one, I
could see, that to the right of the Hall the ground, thickly planted,
shelved down to a stream, which came out into the daylight a little
distance beyond the plantation, and meandered through the deer park.
At the back of the Hall the windows looked out on nothing save a
dense wood and a portion of the stable-yard, whilst on the side nearest
the point from whence I had come there were spreading gardens surrounded by thick yew hedges, and kitchen-gardens protected by high
walls; and further on a farmyard, where I could perceive cows and
oxen, and, further still, luxuriant meadows, and fields glad with
waving corn.

"What a beautiful place !" I said. "Carrison must have been a duffer
to leave it." And then I thought what a great ramshackle house it was
for anyone to be in all alone.

Getting heated with my long walk, I suppose, made me feel chilly,
for I shivered as I drew my head in from the last dormer window, and
prepared to go downstairs again.

In the attics, as in the other parts of the house I had as yet explored,
I closed the doors, when there were keys locking them; when there
were not, trying them, and in all cases, leaving them securely fastened.

When I reached the ground floor the evening was drawing on apace,
and I felt that if I wanted to explore the whole house before dusk I
must hurry my proceedings.

"I'll take the kitchens next," I decided, and so made my way to a wilderness of domestic offices lying to the rear of the great hall. Stone passages, great kitchens, an immense servants'-hall, larders, pantries, coal-cellars, beer-cellars, laundries, brewhouses, housekeeper's room —it was not of any use lingering over these details. The mystery that troubled Mr. Carrison could scarcely lodge amongst cinders and empty bottles, and there did not seem much else left in this part of the building.

I would go through the living-rooms, and then decide as to the apartments I should occupy myself.

The evening shadows were drawing on apace, so I hurried back into the hall, feeling it was a weird position to be there all alone with those ghostly hollow figures of men in armour, and the statues on which the moon's beams must fall so coldly. I would just look through the lower apartments and then kindle a fire. I had seen quantities of wood in a cupboard close at hand, and felt that beside a blazing hearth, and after a good cup of tea, I should not feel the solitary sensation which was oppressing me.

The sun had sunk below the horizon by this time, for to reach Ladlow I had been obliged to travel by cross lines of railway, and wait besides for such trains as condescended to carry third-class passengers; but there was still light enough in the hall to see all objects distinctly. With my own eyes I saw that one of the doors I had shut with my own hands was standing wide !

I turned to the door on the other side of the hall. It was as I had left it—closed. *This, then, was the room—this with the open door.* For a second I stood appalled; I think I was fairly frightened.

That did not last long, however. There lay the work I had desired to undertake, the foe I had offered to fight; so without more ado I shut the door and tried it.

"Now I will walk to the end of the hall and see what happens," I considered. I did so. I walked to the foot of the grand staircase and back again, and looked.

The door stood wide open.

I went into the room, after just a spasm of irresolution—went in and pulled up the blinds: a good-sized room, twenty by twenty (I knew, because I paced it afterwards), lighted by two long windows.

The floor, of polished oak, was partially covered with a Turkey carpet. There were two recesses beside the fireplace, one fitted up as a bookcase, the other with an old and elaborately carved cabinet. I was astonished also to find a bedstead in an apartment so little retired from the traffic of the house; and there were also some chairs of an obsolete make, covered, so far as I could make out, with faded tapestry. Beside the bedstead, which stood against the wall opposite to the door, I perceived another door. It was fast locked, the only locked door I had as yet met with in the interior of the house. It was a dreary, gloomy room: the dark panelled walls; the black, shining floor; the windows high from the ground; the antique furniture; the dull four-poster bedstead, with dingy velvet curtains; the gaping chimney; the silk counterpane that looked like a pall.

"Any crime might have been committed in such a room," I thought pettishly; and then I looked at the door critically.

Someone had been at the trouble of fitting bolts upon it, for when I passed out I not merely shut the door securely, but bolted it as well.

"I will go and get some wood, and then look at it again," I soliloquised. When I came back it stood wide open once more.

"Stay open, then !" I cried in a fury. "I won't trouble myself any more with you to-night !"

Almost as I spoke the words, there came a ring at the front door. Echoing through the desolate house, the peal in the then state of my nerves startled me beyond expression.

It was only the man who had agreed to bring over my traps. I bade him lay them down in the hall, and, while looking out some small silver, asked where the nearest post-office was to be found. Not far from the park gates, he said; if I wanted any letter sent, he would drop it in the box for me; the mail-cart picked up the bag at ten o'clock.

I had nothing ready to post then, and told him so. Perhaps the money I gave was more than he expected, or perhaps the dreariness of my position impressed him as it had impressed me, for he paused with his hand on the lock, and asked:

"Are you going to stop here all alone, master ?"

"All alone," I answered, with such cheerfulness as was possible under the circumstances.

"That's the room, you know," he said, nodding in the direction of the open door, and dropping his voice to a whisper.

"Yes, I know," I replied.

"What, you've been trying to shut it already, have you ? Well, you are a game one !" And with this complimentary if not very respectful comment he hastened out of the house. Evidently he had no intention of proffering his services towards the solution of the mystery.

I cast one glance at the door—it stood wide open. Through the windows I had left bare to the night, moonlight was beginning to stream cold and silvery. Before I did aught else I felt I must write to Mr. Carrison and Patty, so straightway I hurried to one of the great tables in the hall, and lighting a candle my thoughtful little girl had provided, with many other things, sat down and dashed off the two epistles.

Then down the long avenue, with its mysterious lights and shades, with the moonbeams glinting here and there, playing at hide-and-seek round the boles of the trees and through the tracery of quivering leaf and stem, I walked as fast as if I were doing a match against time.

It was delicious, the scent of the summer odours, the smell of the earth; if it had not been for the door I should have felt too happy As it was——

"Look here, Phil," I said, all of a sudden; "life's not child's play, as uncle truly remarks. That door is just the trouble you have now to face, and you must face it ! But for that door you would never have been here. I hope you are not going to turn coward the very first night. Courage !—that is your enemy—conquer it."

"I will try," my other self answered back. "I can but try. I can but fail."

The post-office was at Ladlow Hollow, a little hamlet through which the stream I had remarked dawdling on its way across the park flowed swiftly, spanned by an ancient bridge.

As I stood by the door of the little shop, asking some questions of the postmistress, the same gentleman I had met in the afternoon mounted on his roan horse, passed on foot. He wished me good-night as he went by, and nodded familiarly to my companion, who curtseyed her acknowledgments.

"His lordship ages fast," she remarked, following the retreating figure with her eyes.

"His lordship," I repeated. "Of whom are you speaking ?"

"Of Lord Ladlow," she said.

"Oh ! I have never seen him," I answered, puzzled.

"Why, *that* was Lord Ladlow !" she exclaimed.

You may be sure I had something to think about as I walked back to the Hall—something beside the moonlight and the sweet night-scents, and the rustle of beast and bird and leaf, that make silence seem more eloquent than noise away down in the heart of the country.

Lord Ladlow ! my word, I thought he was hundreds, thousands of miles away; and here I find him—he walking in the opposite direction from his own home—I an inmate of his desolate abode. Hi !—what was that ? I heard a noise in a shrubbery close at hand, and in an instant I was in the thick of the underwood. Something shot out and darted into the cover of the further plantation. I followed, but I could catch never a glimpse of it. I did not know the lie of the ground sufficiently to course with success, and I had at length to give up the hunt—heated, baffled, and annoyed.

When I got into the house the moon's beams were streaming down upon the hall; I could see every statue, every square of marble, every piece of armour. For all the world it seemed to me like something in a dream; but I was tired and sleepy, and decided I would not trouble about fire or food, or the open door, till the next morning : I would go to sleep.

With this intention I picked up some of my traps and carried them to a room on the first floor I had selected as small and habitable. I went down for the rest, and this time chanced to lay my hand on my rifle.

It was wet. I touched the floor—it was wet likewise.

I never felt anything like the thrill of delight which shot through me. I had to deal with flesh and blood, and I would deal with it, heaven helping me.

The next morning broke clear and bright. I was up with the lark—had washed, dressed, breakfasted, explored the house before the postman came with my letters.

One from Mr. Carrison, one from Patty, and one from my uncle : I gave the man half a crown, I was so delighted, and said I was afraid my being at the Hall would cause him some additional trouble.

"No, sir," he answered, profuse in his expressions of gratitude; "I pass here every morning on my way to her ladyship's."

"Who is her ladyship ?" I asked.

"The Dowager Lady Ladlow," he answered—"the old lord's widow."

"And where is her place ?" I persisted.

"If you keep on through the shrubbery and across the waterfall, you come to the house about a quarter of a mile further up the stream."

He departed, after telling me there was only one post a day; and I hurried back to the room in which I had breakfasted, carrying my letters with me.

I opened Mr. Carrison's first. The gist of it was, "Spare no expense; if you run short of money telegraph for it."

I opened my uncle's next. He implored me to return; he had always thought me hair-brained, but he felt a deep interest in and affection for me, and thought he could get me a good berth if I would only try to settle down and promise to stick to my work. The last was from Patty. O Patty, God bless you ! Such women, I fancy, the men who fight best in battle, who stick last to a sinking ship, who are firm in life's struggles, who are brave to resist temptation, must have known and loved. I can't tell you more about the letter, except that it gave me strength to go on the end.

I spent the forenoon considering that door. I looked at it from within and from without. I eyed it critically. I tried whether there was any reason why it should fly open, and I found that so long as I remained on the threshold it remained closed; if I walked even so far away as the opposite side of the hall, it swung wide.

Do what I would, it burst from latch and bolt. I could not lock it because there was no key. Well, before two o'clock I confess I was baffled.

At two there came a visitor—none other than Lord Ladlow himself. Sorely I wanted to take his horse round to the stables, but he would not hear of it.

"Walk beside me across the park, if you will be so kind," he said; "I want to speak to you."

We went together across the park, and before we parted I felt I could have gone through fire and water for this simple-spoken nobleman.

"You must not stay here ignorant of the rumours which are afloat," he said. "Of course, when I let the place to Mr. Carrison I knew nothing of the open door."

"Did you not, sir ?—my lord, I mean," I stammered.

He smiled. "Do not trouble yourself about my title, which, indeed, carries a very empty state with it, but talk to me as you might to a friend. I had no idea there was any ghost story connected with the Hall, or I should have kept the place empty."

I did not exactly know what to answer, so I remained silent.

"How did you chance to be sent here ?" he asked, after a pause.

I told him. When the first shock was over, a lord did not seem very different from anybody else. If an emperor had taken a morning canter across the park, I might, supposing him equally affable, have spoken as familiarly to him as to Lord Ladlow. My mother always said I entirely lacked the bump of veneration !

Beginning at the beginning, I repeated the whole story, from Parton's remark about the sovereign to Mr. Carrison's conversation with my uncle. When I had left London behind in the narrative, however, and arrived at the Hall, I became somewhat more reticent. After all, it was *his* Hall people could not live in—*his* door that would not keep shut; and it seemed to me these were facts he might dislike being forced upon his attention.

But he would have it. What had *I* seen ? What did *I* think of the matter ? Very honestly I told him I did not know what to say. The door certainly would not remain shut, and there seemed no human agency to account for its persistent opening; but then, on the other hand, ghosts generally did not tamper with fire-arms, and my rifle, though not loaded, had been tampered with—I was sure of that.

My companion listened attentively. "You are not frightened, are you ?" he inquired at length.

"Not now," I answered. "The door did give me a start last evening, but I am not afraid of that since I find someone else is afraid of a bullet."

He did not answer for a minute; then he said:

"The theory people have set up about the open door is this: As in that room my uncle was murdered, they say the door will never remain shut till the murderer is discovered."

"Murdered !" I did not like the word at all; it made me feel chill and uncomfortable.

"Yes—he was murdered sitting in his chair, and the assassin has never been discovered. At first many persons inclined to the belief that I killed him; indeed, many are of that opinion still."

"But you did not, sir—there is not a word of truth in that story, is there ?"

He laid his hand on my shoulder as he said:

"No, my lad; not a word. I loved the old man tenderly. Even when he disinherited me for the sake of his young wife, I was sorry, but not angry; and when he sent for me and assured me he had resolved to repair that wrong, I tried to induce him to leave the lady a handsome sum in addition to her jointure. "If you do not, people may think she has not been the source of happiness you expected," I added.

"Thank you, Hal," he said. "You are a good fellow; we will talk further about this to-morrow." And then he bade me good-night.

"Before morning broke—it was in the summer two years ago—the household was aroused by a fearful scream. It was his death-cry. He had been stabbed from behind in the neck. He was seated in his chair writing—writing a letter to me. But for that I might have found it harder to clear myself than was in the case; for his solicitors came forward and said he had signed a will leaving all his personalty to me— he was very rich—unconditionally, only three days previously. That, of course, supplied the motive, as my lady's lawyer put it. She was very vindictive, spared no expense in trying to prove my guilt, and said openly she would never rest till she saw justice done, if it cost her the whole of her fortune. The letter lying before the dead man, over which blood had spurted, she declared must have been placed on his table by me; but the coroner saw there was an animus in this, for the few opening lines stated my uncle's desire to confide in me his reasons for changing his will—reasons, he said, that involved his honour, as they had destroyed his peace. 'In the statement you will find sealed up with my will in——' At that point he was dealt his death-blow. The papers were never found, and the will was never proved. My lady put in the former will, leaving her everything. Ill as I could afford to go to law, I was obliged to dispute the matter, and the lawyers are at it still, and very likely will continue at it for years. When I lost my good name, I lost my good health, and had to go abroad; and while I was away Mr. Carrison took the Hall. Till I returned, I never heard a word about the open door. My solicitors said Mr. Carrison was behaving badly; but I think now I must see them or him, and consider what can be done in the affair. As for yourself, it is of vital importance to me that this mystery should be cleared up, and if you are really not timid, stay on. I am too poor to make rash promises, but you won't find me ungrateful."

"Oh, my lord !" I cried—the address slipped quite easily and naturally off my tongue—"I don't want any more money or anything, if I can only show Patty's father I am good for something——"

"Who is Patty ?" he asked.

He read the answer in my face, for he said no more.

"Should you like to have a good dog for company ?" he inquired after a pause.

I hesitated; then I said:

"No, thank you. I would rather watch and hunt for myself."

And as I spoke, the remembrance of that "something" in the shrubbery recurred to me, and I told him I thought there had been someone about the place the previous evening.

"Poachers," he suggested; but I shook my head.

"A girl or a woman I imagine. However, I think a dog might hamper me."

He went away, and I returned to the house. I never left it all day. I did not go into the garden, or the stable-yard, or the shrubbery, or anywhere; I devoted myself solely and exclusively to that door.

If I shut it once, I shut it a hundred times, and always with the same result. Do what I would, it swung wide. Never, however, when I was looking at it. So long as I could endure to remain, it stayed shut—the instant I turned my back, it stood open.

About four o'clock I had another visitor; no other than Lord Ladlow's daughter—the Honourable Beatrice, riding her funny little white pony.

She was a beautiful girl of fifteen or thereabouts, and she had the sweetest smile you ever saw.

"Papa sent me with this," she said; "he would not trust any other messenger," and she put a piece of paper in my hand.

"*Keep your food under lock and key ; buy what you require yourself. Get your water from the pump in the stable-yard.* I am going from home; but if you want anything, go or send to my daughter."

"Any answer ?" she asked, patting her pony's neck.

"Tell his lordship, if you please, I will 'keep my powder dry '!" I replied.

"You have made papa look so happy," she said, still patting that fortunate pony.

"If it is in my power, I will make him look happier still, Miss——" and I hesitated, not knowing how to address her.

"Call me Beatrice," she said, with an enchanting grace; then added, slily, "Papa promises me I shall be introduced to Patty ere long," and before I could recover from my astonishment, she had tightened the bit and was turning across the park.

"One moment, please," I cried. "You can do something for me."

"What is it?" and she came back, trotting over the great sweep in front of the house.

"Lend me your pony for a minute."

She was off before I could even offer to help her alight—off, and gathering up her habit dexterously with one hand, led the docile old sheep forward with the other.

I took the bridle—when I was with horses I felt amongst my own kind—stroked the pony, pulled his ears, and let him thrust his nose into my hand.

Miss Beatrice is a countess now, and a happy wife and mother; but I sometimes see her, and the other night she took me carefully into a conservatory and asked:

"Do you remember Toddy, Mr. Edlyd?"

"Remember him!" I exclaimed; "I can never forget him!"

"He is dead!" she told me, and there were tears in her beautiful eyes as she spoke the words. "Mr. Edlyd, *I loved Toddy!*"

Well, I took Toddy up to the house, and under the third window to the right hand. He was a docile creature, and let me stand on the saddle while I looked into the only room in Ladlow Hall I had been unable to enter.

It was perfectly bare of furniture, there was not a thing in it—not a chair or table, not a picture on the walls, or ornament on the chimney-piece.

"That is where my grand-uncle's valet slept," said Miss Beatrice. "It was he who first ran in to help him the night he was murdered."

"Where is the valet?" I asked.

"Dead," she answered. "The shock killed him. He loved his master more than he loved himself."

I had seen all I wished, so I jumped off the saddle, which I had carefully dusted with a branch plucked from a lilac tree; between jest and earnest pressed the hem of Miss Beatrice's habit to my lips as I arranged its folds; saw her wave her hand as she went at a hand-gallop across the park; and then turned back once again into the lonely house, with the determination to solve the mystery attached to it or die in the attempt.

Why, I cannot explain, but before I went to bed that night I drove a gimlet I found in the stables hard into the floor, and said to the door:

"Now *I* am keeping you open."

When I went down in the morning the door was close shut, and the handle of the gimlet, broken off short, lying in the hall.

I put my hand to wipe my forehead; it was dripping with perspiration. I did not know what to make of the place at all! I went out into the open air for a few minutes; when I returned the door again stood wide.

If I were to pursue in detail the days and nights that followed, I should weary my readers. I can only say they changed my life. The solitude, the solemnity, the mystery, produced an effect I do not profess to understand, but that I cannot regret.

I have hesitated about writing of the end, but it must come, so let me hasten to it.

Though feeling convinced that no human agency did or could keep the door open, I was certain that some living person had means of access to the house which I could not discover. This was made apparent in trifles which might well have escaped unnoticed had several, or even two people occupied the mansion, but that in my solitary position it was impossible to overlook. A chair would be misplaced, for instance; a path would be visible over a dusty floor; my papers I found were moved; my clothes touched—letters I carried about with me, and kept under my pillow at night; still, the fact remained that when I went to the post-office, and while I was asleep, someone did wander over the house. On Lord Ladlow's return I meant to ask him for some further particulars of his uncle's death, and I was about to write to Mr. Carrison and beg permission to have the door where the valet had slept broken open, when one morning, very early indeed, I spied a hairpin lying close beside it.

What an idiot I had been! If I wanted to solve the mystery of the open door, of course I must keep watch in the room itself. The door would not stay wide unless there was a reason for it, and most certainly a hairpin could not have got into the house without assistance.

I made up my mind what I should do—that I would go to the post early, and take up my position about the hour I had hitherto started for Ladlow Hollow. I felt on the eve of a discovery, and longed for the day to pass, that the night might come.

It was a lovely morning; the weather had been exquisite during the whole week, and I flung the hall-door wide to let in the sunshine and the breeze. As I did so, I saw there was a basket on the top step—a basket filled with rare and beautiful fruit and flowers.

Mr. Carrison had let off the gardens attached to Ladlow Hall for the season—he thought he might as well save something out of the fire, he said, so my fare had not been varied with delicacies of that kind. I was very fond of fruit in those days, and seeing a card addressed to me, I instantly selected a tempting peach, and ate it a little greedily perhaps.

I might say I had barely swallowed the last morsel, when Lord Ladlow's caution recurred to me. The fruit had a curious flavour—there was a strange taste hanging about my palate. For a moment, sky. trees and park swam before my eyes; then I made up my mind what to do.

I smelt the fruit—it had all the same faint odour; then I put some in my pocket—took the basket and locked it away—walked round to the farmyard—asked for the loan of a horse that was generally driven in a light cart, and in less than half an hour was asking in Ladlow to be directed to a doctor.

Rather cross at being disturbed so early, he was at first inclined to pooh-pooh my idea; but I made him cut open a pear and satisfy himself the fruit had been tampered with.

"It is fortunate you stopped at the first peach," he remarked, after giving me a draught, and some medicine to take back, and advising me to keep in the open air as much as possible. "I should like to retain this fruit and see you again to-morrow."

We did not think then on how many morrows we should see each other!

Riding across to Ladlow, the postman had given me three letters, but I did not read them till I was seated under a great tree in the park, with a basin of milk and a piece of bread beside me.

Hitherto, there had been nothing exciting in my correspondence. Patty's epistles were always delightful, but they could not be regarded as sensational; and about Mr. Carrison's there was a monotony I had begun to find tedious. On this occasion, however, no fault could be found on that score. The contents of his letter greatly surprised me. He said Lord Ladlow had released him from his bargain—that I could, therefore, leave the Hall at once. He enclosed me ten pounds, and said he would consider how he could best advance my interests; and that I had better call upon him at his private house when I returned to London.

"I do not think I shall leave Ladlow yet awhile," I considered, as I replaced his letter in its envelope. "Before I go I should like to make it hot for whoever sent me that fruit; so unless Lord Ladlow turns me out I'll stay a little longer."

Lord Ladlow did not wish me to leave. The third letter was from him.

"I shall return home to-morrow night," he wrote, "and see you on Wednesday. I have arranged satisfactorily with Mr. Carrison, and as the Hall is my own again, I mean to try to solve the mystery it contains myself. If you choose to stop and help me to do so, you would confer a favour, and I will try to make it worth your while."

"I will keep watch to-night, and see if I cannot give you some news to-morrow," I thought. And then I opened Patty's letter—the best, dearest, sweetest letter any postman in all the world could have brought me.

If it had not been for what Lord Ladlow said about his sharing my undertaking, I should not have chosen that night for my vigil. I felt ill and languid—fancy, no doubt, to a great degree inducing these sensations. I had lost energy in a most unaccountable manner. The long, lonely days had told upon my spirits—the fidgety feeling which took me a hundred times in the twelve hours to look upon the open door, to close it, and to count how many steps I could take before it opened again, had tried my mental strength as a perpetual blister might have worn away my physical. In no sense was I fit for the task I had set myself, and yet I determined to go through with it. Why had I never before decided to watch in that mysterious chamber? Had I been at the bottom of my heart afraid? In the bravest of us there are depths of cowardice that lurk unsuspected till they engulf our courage.

The day wore on—the long, dreary day; evening approached—the night shadows closed over the Hall. The moon would not rise for a couple of hours more. Everything was still as death. The house had never before seemed to me so silent and so deserted.

I took a light, and went up to my accustomed room, moving about for a time as though preparing for bed; then I extinguished the candle, softly opened the door, turned the key, and put it in my pocket, slipped softly downstairs, across the hall, through the open door. Then I knew I had been afraid, for I felt a thrill of terror as in the dark I stepped over the threshold. I paused and listened—there was not a sound—the night was still and sultry, as though a storm were brewing. Not a leaf seemed moving—the very mice remained in their holes ! Noiselessly I made my way to the other side of the room. There was an old-fashioned easy-chair between the bookshelves and the bed; I sat down in it, shrouded by the heavy curtain.

The hours passed—were ever hours. so long ? The moon rose, came and looked in at the windows, and then sailed away to the west; but not a sound, no, not even the cry of a bird. I seemed to myself a mere collection of nerves. Every part of my body appeared twitching. It was agony to remain still; the desire to move became a form of torture. Ah ! a streak in the sky; morning at last, Heaven be praised ! Had ever anyone before so welcomed the dawn ? A thrush began to sing—was there ever heard such delightful music ? It was the morning twilight, soon the sun would rise; soon that awful vigil would be over, and yet I was no nearer the mystery than before. Hush ! what was that ? *It had come.* After the hours of watching and waiting; after the long night and the long suspense, it came in a moment.

The locked door opened—so suddenly, so silently, that I had barely time to draw back behind the curtain, before I saw a woman in the room. She went straight across to the other door and closed it, securing it as I saw with bolt and lock. Then just glancing around, she made her way to the cabinet, and with a key she produced shot back the wards. I did not stir, I scarcely breathed, and yet she seemed uneasy. Whatever she wanted to do she evidently was in haste to finish, for she took out the drawers one by one, and placed them on the floor; then, as the light grew better, I saw her first kneel on the floor, and peer into every aperture, and subsequently repeat the same process, standing on a chair she drew forward for the purpose. A slight, lithe woman, not a lady, clad all in black—not a bit of white about her. What on earth could she want ? In a moment if flashed upon me—THE WILL AND THE LETTER! SHE IS SEARCHING FOR THEM.

I sprang from my concealment—I had her in my grasp; but she tore herself out on my hands, fighting like a wild-cat: she bit, scratched, kicked, shifting her body as though she had not a bone in it, and at last slipped herself free, and ran wildly towards the door by which she had entered.

If she reached it, she would escape me. I rushed across the room and just caught her dress as she was on the threshold. My blood was up, and I dragged her back: she had the strength of twenty devils, I think, and struggled as surely no woman ever did before.

"I do not want to kill you," I managed to say in gasps, "but I will if you do not keep quiet."

"Bah !" she cried; and before I knew what she was doing she had the revolver out of my pocket and fired.

She missed: the ball just glanced off my sleeve. I fell upon her—I can use no other expression, for it had become a fight for life, and no man can tell the ferocity there is in him till he is placed as I was then—fell upon her, and seized the weapon. She would not let it go, but I held her so tight she could not use it. She bit my face; with her disengaged hand she tore my hair. She turned and twisted and slipped about like a snake, but I did not feel pain or anything except a deadly horror lest my strength should give out.

Could I hold out much longer ? She made one desperate plunge, I felt the grasp with which I held her slackening; she felt it too, and seizing her advantage tore herself free, and at the same instant fired again blindly, and again missed.

Suddenly there came a look of horror into her eyes—a frozen expression of fear.

"See!" she cried; and flinging the revolver at me, fled.

I saw, as in a momentary flash, that the door I had beheld locked stood wide—that there stood beside the table an awful figure, with uplifted hand—and then I saw no more. I was struck at last; as she threw the revolver at me she must have pulled the trigger, for I felt something like red-hot iron enter my shoulder, and I could but rush from the room before I fell senseless on the marble pavement of the hall.

When the postman came that morning, finding no one stirring, he looked through one of the long windows that flanked the door; then he ran to the farmyard and called for help.

"There is something wrong inside," he cried. "That young gentleman is lying on the floor in a pool of blood."

As they rushed round to the front of the house they saw Lord Ladlow riding up the avenue, and breathlessly told him what had happened.

"Smash in one of the windows," he said; "and go instantly for a doctor."

They laid me on the bed in that terrible room, and telegraphed for my father. For long I hovered between life and death, but at length I recovered sufficiently to be removed to the house Lord Ladlow owned on the other side of the Hollow.

Before that time I had told him all I knew, and begged him to make instant search for the will.

"Break up the cabinet if necessary," I entreated, "I am sure the papers are there."

And they were. His lordship got his own, and as to the scandal and the crime, one was hushed up and the other remained unpunished. The dowager and her maid went abroad the very morning I lay on the marble pavement at Ladlow Hall—they never returned.

My lord made that one condition of his silence.

Not in Meadowshire, but in a fairer county still, I have a farm which I manage, and make both ends meet comfortably.

Patty is the best wife any man ever possessed—and I—well, I am just as happy if a trifle more serious than of old; but there are times when a great horror of darkness seems to fall upon me, and at such periods I cannot endure to be left alone.

THE LAST OF SQUIRE ENNISMORE

"DID I see it myself? No, sir; I did not see it; and my father before me did not see it; nor his father before him, and he was Phil Regan, just the same as myself. But it is true, for all that; just as true as that you are looking at the very place where the whole thing happened. My great-grandfather (and he did not die till he was ninety-eight) used to tell, many and many's the time, how he met the stranger, night after night, walking lonesome-like about the sands where most of the wreckage came ashore."

"And the old house, then, stood behind that belt of Scotch firs?"

"Yes; and a fine house it was, too. Hearing so much talk about it when a boy, my father said, made him often feel as if he knew every room in the building, though it had all fallen to ruin before he was born. None of the family ever lived in it after the squire went away. Nobody else could be got to stop in the place. There used to be awful noises, as if something was being pitched from the top of the great staircase down in to the hall; and then there would be a sound as if a hundred people were clinking glasses and talking all together at once. And then it seemed as if barrels were rolling in the cellars; and there would be screeches, and howls, and laughing, fit to make your blood run cold. They say there is gold hid away in the cellars; but not one has ever ventured to find it. The very children won't come here to play; and when the men are plowing the field behind, nothing will make them stay in it, once the day begins to change. When the night is coming on, and the tide creeps in on the sand, more than one thinks he has seen mighty queer things on the shore."

"But what is it really they think they see? When I asked my landlord to tell me the story from beginning to end, he said he could not remember it; and, at any rate, the whole rigmarole was nonsense, put together to please strangers."

"And what is he but a stranger himself? And how should he know the doings of real quality like the Ennismores? For they were gentry, every one of them—good old stock; and as for wickedness, you might have searched Ireland through and not found their match. It is a sure thing, though, that if Riley can't tell you the story, I can; for, as I said, my own people were in it, of a manner of speaking. So, if your honour will rest yourself off your feet, on that bit of a bank, I'll set down my creel and give you the whole pedigree of how Squire Ennismore went away from Ardwinsagh."

It was a lovely day, in the early part of June; and, as the Englishman cast himself on a low ridge of sand, he looked over Ardwinsagh Bay with a feeling of ineffable content. To his left lay the Purple Headland; to his right, a long range of breakers, that went straight out into the Atlantic till they were lost from sight; in front lay the Bay of Ardwinsagh, with its bluish-green water sparkling in the summer sunlight, and here and there breaking over some sunken rock, against which the waves spent themselves in foam.

"You see how the current's set, Sir? That is what makes it dangerous for them as doesn't know the coast, to bathe here at any time, or walk when the tide is flowing. Look how the sea is creeping in now, like a race-horse at the finish. It leaves that tongue of sand bars to the last, and then, before you could look round, it has you up to the middle. That is why I made bold to speak to you; for it is not alone on the account of Squire Ennismore the bay has a bad name. But it is about him and the old house you want to hear. The last mortal being that tried to live in it, my great-grandfather said, was a creature, by name Molly Leary; and she had neither kith nor kin, and begged for her bite and sup, sheltering herself at night in a turf cabin she had built at the back of a ditch. You may be sure she thought herself a made woman when the agent said, 'Yes: she might try if she could stop in the house; there was peat and bog-wood,' he told her, 'and half-a-crown a week for the winter, and a golden guinea once Easter came,' when the house was to be put in order for the family; and his wife gave Molly some warm clothes and a blanket or two; and she was well set up.

"You may be sure she didn't choose the worst room to sleep in; and for a while all went quiet, till one night she was wakened by feeling the bedstead lifted by the four corners and shaken like a carpet. It was a heavy four-post bedstead, with a solid top: and her life seemed to go out of her with the fear. If it had been a ship in a storm off the Headland, it couldn't have pitched worse and then, all of a sudden, it was dropped with such a bang as nearly drove the heart into her mouth.

"But that, she said, was nothing to the screaming and laughing, and hustling and rushing that filled the house. If a hundred people had been running hard along the passages and tumbling downstairs, they could not have made greater noise.

"Molly never was able to tell how she got clear of the place; but a man coming late home from Ballycloyne Fair found the creature crouched under the old thorn there, with very little on her—saving your honour's presence. She had a bad fever, and talked about strange things, and never was the same woman after."

"But what was the beginning of all this? When did the house first get the name of being haunted?"

"After the old Squire went away: that was what I purposed telling you. He did not come here to live regularly till he had got well on in years. He was near seventy at the time I am talking about; but he held himself as upright as ever, and rode as hard as the youngest; and could have drunk a whole roomful under the table, and walked up to bed as unconcerned as you please at the dead of the night.

"He was a terrible man. You couldn't lay your tongue to a wickedness he had not been in the forefront of—drinking, duelling, gambling, —all manner of sins had been meat and drink to him since he was a boy almost. But at last he did something in London so bad, so beyond the beyonds, that he thought he had best come home and live among people who did not know so much about his goings on as the English. It was said that he wanted to try and stay in this world for ever; and that he had got some secret drops that kept him well and hearty. There was something wonderful queer about him, anyhow.

"He could hold foot with the youngest; and he was strong, and had a fine fresh colour in his face; and his eyes were like a hawk's; and there was not a break in his voice—and him near upon threescore and ten!

"At last and at long last it came to be the March before he was seventy—the worst March ever known in all these parts—such blowing, sleeting, snowing, had not been experienced in the memory of man; when one blusterous night some foreign vessel went to bits on the Purple Headland. They say it was an awful sound to hear the death-cry that went up high above the noise of the wind; and it was as bad a sight to see the shore there strewed with corpses of all sorts and sizes, from the little cabin-boy to the grizzled seaman.

"They never knew who they were or where they came from, but

some of the men had crosses, and beads, and such like, so the priest said they belonged to him, and they were all buried deeply and decently in the chapel graveyard.

"There was not much wreckage of value drifted on shore. Most of what is lost about the Head stays there; but one thing did come into the bay—a puncheon of brandy.

"The Squire claimed it; it was his right to have all that came on his land, and he owned this sea-shore from the Head to the breakers—every foot—so, in course, he had the brandy; and there was sore illwill because he gave his men nothing, not even a glass of whiskey.

"Well, to make a long story short, that was the most wonderful liquor anybody ever tasted. The gentry came from far and near to take share, and it was cards and dice, and drinking and story-telling night after night—week in, week out. Even on Sundays, God forgive them! The officers would drive over from Ballyclone, and sit emptying tumbler after tumbler till Monday morning came, for it made beautiful punch.

"But all at once people quit coming—a word went round that the liquor was not all it ought to be. Nobody could say what ailed it, but it got about that in some way men found it did not suit them.

"For one thing, they were losing money very fast.

"They could not make head against the Squire's luck, and a hint was dropped the puncheon ought to have been towed out to sea, and sunk in fifty fathoms of water.

"It was getting to the end of April, and fine, warm weather for the time of year, when first one and then another, and then another still, began to take notice of a stranger who walked the shore alone at night. He was a dark man, the same colour as the drowned crew lying in the chapel graveyard, and had rings in his ears, and wore a strange kind of hat, and cut wonderful antics as he walked, and had an ambling sort of gait, curious to look at. Many tried to talk to him, but he only shook his head; so, as nobody could make out where he came from or what he wanted, they made sure he was the spirit of some poor wretch who was tossing about the Head, longing for a snug corner in holy ground.

"The priest went and tried to get some sense out of him.

"'Is it Christian burial you're wanting?' asked his reverence; but the creature only shook his head.

"'Is it word sent to the wives and daughters you've left orphans and widows, you'd like?' But no; it wasn't that.

"'Is it for sin committed you're doomed to walk this way? Would masses comfort ye? There's a heathen,' said his reverence; 'Did you ever hear tell of a Christian that shook his head when masses were mentioned?'

"'Perhaps he doesn't understand English, Father,' says one of the officers who was there; 'Try him with Latin.'

"No sooner said than done. The priest started off with such a string of aves and paters that the stranger fairly took to his heels and ran.

"'He is an evil spirit,' explained the priest, when he stopped, tired out, 'and I have exorcised him.'

"But next night my gentleman was back again, as unconcerned as ever.

"'And he'll just have to stay,' said his reverence, 'For I've got lumbago in the small of my back, and pains in all my joints—never to speak of a hoarseness with standing there shouting; and I don't believe he understood a sentence I said.'

"Well, this went on for a while, and people got that frightened of the man, or appearance of a man, they would not go near the sand; till in the end, Squire Ennismore, who had always scoffed at the talk, took it into his head he would go down one night, and see into the rights of the matter. He, maybe, was feeling lonesome, because, as I told your honour before, people had left off coming to the house, and there was nobody for him to drink with.

"Out he goes, then, bold as brass; and there were a few followed him. The man came forward at sight of the Squire and took off his hat with a foreign flourish. Not to be behind in civility, the Squire lifted his.

"'I have come, sir,' he said, speaking very loud, to try to make him understand, 'to know if you are looking for anything, and whether I can assist you to find it.'

"The man looked at the Squire as if he had taken the greatest liking to him, and took off his hat again.

"'Is it the vessel that was wrecked you are distressed about?'

"There came no answer, only a mournful shake of the head.

"'Well, *I* haven't your ship, you know; it went all to bits months ago; and, as for the sailors, they are snug and sound enough in consecrated ground.'

"The man stood and looked at the Squire with a queer sort of smile on his face.

"' What *do* you want?' asked Mr. Ennismore in a bit of a passion. 'If anything belonging to you went down with the vessel, it's about the Head you ought to be looking for it, not here—unless, indeed, its after the brandy you're fretting!'

"Now, the Squire had tried him in English and French, and was now speaking a language you'd have thought nobody could understand; but, faith, it seemed natural as kissing to the stranger.

"'Oh! That's where you are from, is it?' said the Squire. 'Why couldn't you have told me so at once? I can't give you the brandy, because it mostly is drunk; but come along, and you shall have as stiff a glass of punch as ever crossed your lips.' And without more to-do off they went, as sociable as you please, jabbering together in some outlandish tongue that made moderate folks' jaws ache to hear it.

"That was the first night they conversed together, but it wasn't the last. The stranger must have been the height of good company, for the Squire never tired of him. Every evening, regularly, he came up to the house, always dressed the same, always smiling and polite, and then the Squire called for brandy and hot water, and they drank and played cards till cock-crow, talking and laughing into the small hours.

"This went on for weeks and weeks, nobody knowing where the man came from, or where he went; only two things the old house-keeper did know—that the puncheon was nearly empty, and that the Squire's flesh was wasting off him; and she felt so uneasy she went to the priest, but he could give her no manner of comfort.

"She got so concerned at last that she felt bound to listen at the dining-room door; but they always talked in that foreign gibberish, and whether it was blessing or cursing they were at she couldn't tell.

"Well, the upshot of it came one night in July—on the eve of the Squire's birthday—there wasn't a drop of spirit left in the puncheon—no, not as much as would drown a fly. They had drunk the whole lot clean up—and the old woman stood trembling, expecting every minute to hear the bell ring for more brandy, for where was she to get more if they wanted any?

"All at once the Squire and the stranger came out into the hall. It was a full moon, and light as day.

"'I'll go home with you to-night by way of a change,' says the Squire.

"'Will you so?' asked the other.

"'That I will,' answered the Squire.

"'It is your own choice, you know.'

"'Yes; it is my own choice; let us go.'

"So they went. And the housekeeper ran up to the window on the great staircase and watched the way they took. Her niece lived there as housemaid, and she came and watched, too; and, after a while, the butler as well. They all turned their faces this way, and looked after their master walking beside the strange man along these very sands. Well, they saw them walk on, and on, and on, and on, till the water took them to their knees, and then to their waists, and then to their arm-pits, and then to their throats and their heads; but long before that the women and the butler were running out on the shore as fast as they could, shouting for help."

"Well?" said the Englishman.

"Living or dead, Squire Ennismore never came back again. Next morning, when the tides ebbed again, one walking over the sand saw the print of a cloven foot—that he tracked to the water's edge. Then everybody knew where the Squire had gone, and with whom."

"And no more search was made?"

"Where would have been the use searching?"

"Not much, I suppose. It's a strange story, anyhow."

"But true, your honour—every word of it."

"Oh! I have no doubt of that," was the satisfactory reply.

A STRANGE CHRISTMAS GAME

WHEN, through the death of a distant relative, I, John Lester, succeeded to the Martingdale Estate, there could not have been found in the length and breadth of England a happier pair than myself and my only sister Clare.

We were not such utter hypocrites as to affect sorrow for the loss of our kinsman, Paul Lester, a man whom we had never seen, of whom we had heard but little, and that little unfavourable, at whose hands we had never received a single benefit—who was, in short, as great a stranger to us as the then Prime Minister, the Emperor of Russia, or any other human being utterly removed from our extremely humble sphere of life.

His loss was very certainly our gain. His death represented to us, not a dreary parting from one long loved and highly honoured, but the accession of lands, houses, consideration, wealth, to myself—John Lester, Esquire, Martingdale, Bedfordshire, whilom Jack Lester, artist and second floor lodger at 32, Great Smith Street, Bloomsbury.

Not that Martingdale was much of an estate as county properties go. The Lesters who had succeeded to that domain from time to time during the course of a few hundred years, could by no stretch of courtesy have been called prudent men. In regard of their posterity they were, indeed, scarcely honest, for they parted with manors and farms, with common rights and advowsons, in a manner at once so baronial and so unbusiness-like, that Martingdale at length in the hands of Jeremy Lester, the last resident owner, melted to a mere little dot in the map of Bedfordshire.

Concerning this Jeremy Lester there was a mystery. No man could say what had become of him. He was in the oak parlour at Martingdale one Christmas-eve, and before the next morning he had disappeared—to reappear in the flesh no more.

Over night, one Mr. Warley, a great friend and boon companion of Jeremy's, had sat playing cards with him until after twelve o'clock chimed, then he took leave of his host and rode home under the moonlight. After that, no person, as far as could be ascertained, ever saw Jeremy Lester alive.

His ways of life had not been either the most regular, or the most respectable, and it was not until a new year had come in without any tidings of his whereabouts reaching the house, that his servants became seriously alarmed concerning his absence.

Then inquiries were set on foot concerning him—inquiries which grew more urgent as weeks and months passed by without the slightest clue being obtained as to his whereabouts. Rewards were offered, advertisements inserted, but still Jeremy made no sign; and so in course of time the heir-at-law, Paul Lester, took possession of the house, and went down to spend the summer months at Martingdale with his rich wife, and her four children by a first husband. Paul Lester was a barrister—an over-worked barrister, who, every one supposed would be glad enough to leave the bar and settle at Martingdale, where his wife's money and the fortune he had accumulated could not have failed to give him a good standing even among the neighbouring county families; and perhaps it was with such intention that he went down into Bedfordshire.

If this were so, however, he speedily changed his mind, for with the January snows he returned to London, let off the land surrounding the house, shut up the Hall, put in a caretaker, and never troubled himself further about his ancestral seat.

Time went on, and people began to say the house was haunted, that Paul Lester had "seen something," and so forth—all which stories were duly repeated for our benefit, when, forty-one years after the disappearance of Jeremy Lester, Clare and I went down to inspect our inheritance.

I say "our," because Clare had stuck bravely to me in poverty—grinding poverty, and prosperity was not going to part us now. What was mine was hers, and that she knew, God bless her, without my needing to tell her so.

The transition from rigid economy to comparative wealth was in our case the more delightful also, because we had not in the least degree anticipated it. We never expected Paul Lester's shoes to come to us, and accordingly it was not upon our consciences that we had ever in our dreariest moods wished him dead.

Had he made a will, no doubt we never should have gone to

Martingdale, and I, consequently, never written this story; but, luckily for us, he died intestate, and the Bedfordshire property came to me.

As for the fortune, he had spent it in travelling, and in giving great entertainments at his grand house in Portman Square. Concerning his effects, Mrs. Lester and I came to a very amicable arrangement, and she did me the honour of inviting me to call upon her occasionally, and, as I heard, spoke of me as a very worthy and presentable young man "for my station," which, of course, coming from so good an authority, was gratifying. Moreover, she asked me if I intended residing at Martingdale, and on my replying in the affirmative, hoped I should like it.

It struck me at the time that there was a certain significance in her tone, and when I went down to Martingdale and heard the absurd stories which were afloat concerning the house being haunted, I felt confident that if Mrs. Lester had hoped much, she had feared more.

People said Mr. Jeremy "walked" at Martingdale. He had been seen, it was averred, by poachers, by gamekeepers, by children who had come to use the park as a near cut to school, by lovers who kept their tryst under the elms and beeches.

As for the caretaker and his wife, the third in residence since Jeremy Lester's disappearance, the man gravely shook his head when questioned, while the woman stated that wild horses, or even wealth untold, should not draw her into the red bedroom, nor into the oak parlour, after dark.

"I have heard my mother tell, sir—it was her as followed old Mrs. Reynolds, the first caretaker—how there were things went on in these self same rooms as might make any Christian's hair stand on end. Such stamping, and swearing, and knocking about on furniture; and then tramp, tramp, up the great staircase; and along the corridor and so into the red bedroom, and then bang, and tramp, tramp again. They do say, sir, Mr. Paul Lester met him once, and from that time the oak parlour has never been opened. I never was inside it myself."

Upon hearing which fact, the first thing I did was to proceed to the oak parlour, open the shutters, and let the August sun stream in upon the haunted chamber. It was an old-fashioned, plainly furnished apartment, with a large table in the centre, a smaller in a recess by the fire-place, chairs ranged against the walls, and a dusty moth-eaten carpet on the floor. There were dogs on the hearth, broken and rusty; there was a brass fender, tarnished and battered; a picture of some sea-fight over the mantel-piece, while another work of art about equal in merit hung between the windows. Altogether, an utterly prosaic and yet not uncheerful apartment, from out of which the ghosts flitted as soon as daylight was let into it, and which I proposed, as soon as I "felt my feet," to redecorate, refurnish, and convert into a pleasant morning-room. I was still under thirty, but I had learned prudence in that very good school, Necessity; and it was not my intention to spend much money until I had ascertained for certain what were the actual revenues derivable from the lands still belonging to the Martingdale estates, and the charges upon them. In fact, I wanted to know what I was worth before committing myself to any great extravagances, and the place had for so long been neglected, that I experienced some difficulty in arriving at the state of my real income.

But in the meanwhile, Clare and I found great enjoyment in exploring every nook and corner of our domain, in turning over the contents of old chests and cupboards, in examining the faces of our ancestors looking down on us, from the walls, in walking through the neglected gardens, full of weeds, overgrown with shrubs and birdweed, where the boxwood was eighteen feet high, and the shoots of the rosetrees yards long. I have put the place in order since then; there is no grass on the paths, there are no trailing brambles over the ground, the hedges have been cut and trimmed, and the trees pruned and the boxwood clipped. But I often say nowadays that in spite of all my improvements, or rather, in consequence of them, Martingdale does not look one half so pretty as it did in its pristine state of uncivilized picturesqueness.

Although I determined not to commence repairing and decorating the house till better informed concerning the rental of Martingdale, still the state of my finances was so far satisfactory that Clare and I decided on going abroad to take our long-talked-of holiday before the fine weather was past. We could not tell what a year might bring forth, as Clare sagely remarked; it was wise to take our pleasure while we could; and accordingly, before the end of August arrived we were wandering about the continent, loitering at Rouen, visiting the galleries at Paris, and talking of extending our one month of enjoyment into three. What decided me on this course was the circumstance of our becoming acquainted with an English family who intended wintering in Rome. We met accidentally, but discovering that we were near neighbours in England—in fact that Mr. Cronson's property lay close beside Martingdale—the slight acquaintance soon ripened into intimacy, and ere long we were travelling in company.

From the first, Clare did not much like this arrangement. There was "a little girl" in England she wanted me to marry, and Mr. Cronson had a daughter who certainly was both handsome and attractive. The little girl had not despised John Lester, artist, while Miss Cronson indisputably set her cap at John Lester of Martingdale, and would have turned away her pretty face from a poor man's admiring glance—all this I can see plainly enough now, but I was blind then and should have proposed for Maybel—that was her name—before the winter was over, had news not suddenly arrived of the illness of Mrs. Cronson, senior. In a moment the programme was changed; our pleasant days of foreign travel were at an end. The Cronsons packed up and departed, while Clare and I returned more slowly to England, a little out of humour, it must be confessed, with each other.

It was the middle of November when we arrived at Martingdale, and we found the place anything but romantic or pleasant. The walks were wet and sodden, the trees were leafless, there were no flowers save a few late pink roses blooming in the garden.

It had been a wet season, and the place looked miserable. Clare would not ask Alice down to keep her company in the winter months, as she had intended; and for myself, the Cronsons were still absent in Norfolk, where they meant to spend Christmas with old Mrs. Cronson, now recovered.

Altogether, Martingdale seemed dreary enough, and the ghost stories we had laughed at while sunshine flooded the rooms became less unreal when we had nothing but blazing fires and wax candles to dispel the gloom. They became more real also when servant after servant left us to seek situations elsewhere; when "noises" grew frequent in the house; when we ourselves, Clare and I, with our own ears heard the tramp, tramp, the banging and the clattering which had been described to us.

My dear reader, you are doubtless free from superstitious fancies. You pooh-pooh the existence of ghosts, and only "wish you could find a haunted house in which to spend a night," which is all very brave and praiseworthy, but wait till you are left in a dreary, desolate old country mansion, filled with the most unaccountable sounds, without a servant, with no one save an old caretaker and his wife, who, living at the extremest end of the building, heard nothing of the tramp, tramp, bang, bang, going on at all hours of the night.

At first I imagined the noises were produced by some evil-disposed persons, who wished, for purposes of their own, to keep the house uninhabited; but by degrees Clare and I came to the conclusion the visitation must be supernatural, and Martingdale by consequence untenantable. Still being practical people, and unlike our predecessors, not having money to live where and how we liked, we decided to watch and see whether we could trace any human influence in the matter. If not, it was agreed we were to pull down the right wing of the house and the principal staircase.

For nights and nights we sat up till two or three o'clock in the morning, Clare engaged in needlework, I reading, with a revolver lying on the table beside me; but nothing, neither sound nor appearance, rewarded our vigil.

This confirmed my first idea that the sounds were not supernatural; but just to test the matter, I determined on Christmas-eve, the anniversary of Mr. Jeremy Lester's disappearance, to keep watch by myself in the red bed-chamber. Even to Clare I never mentioned my intention.

About ten, tired out with our previous vigils, we each retired to rest. Somewhat ostentatiously, perhaps, I noisily shut the door of my room, and when I opened it half an hour afterwards, no mouse could have pursued its way along the corridor with greater silence and caution than myself.

Quite in the dark I sat in the red room. For over an hour I might as well have been in my grave for any thing I could see in the apartment; but at the end of that time the moon rose and cast strange lights across the floor and upon the wall of the haunted chamber.

Hitherto I had kept my watch opposite the window; now I changed my place to a corner near the door, where I was shaded from observation by the heavy hangings of the bed, and an antique wardrobe.

Still I sat on, but still no sound broke the silence. I was weary with many nights' watching; and tired of my solitary vigil, I dropped at last into a slumber from which I was awakened by hearing the door softly opened.

"John," said my sister, almost in a whisper; "John, are you here?"

"Yes, Clare," I answered; "but what are you doing up at this hour?"

"Come downstairs," she replied; "*they* are in the oak parlour."

I did not need any explanation as to whom she meant, but crept downstairs, after her, warned by an uplifted hand of the necessity for silence and caution.

By the door—by the open door of the oak parlour, she paused, and we both looked in.

There was the room we left in darkness overnight, with a bright wood fire blazing on the hearth, candles on the chimney-piece, the small table pulled out from its accustomed corner, and two men seated beside it, playing at cribbage.

We could see the face of the younger player; it was that of a man of about five-and-twenty, of a man who had lived hard and wickedly; who had wasted his substance and his health; who had been while in the flesh, Jeremy Lester. It would be difficult for me to say how I knew this, how in a moment I identified the features of the player with those of the man who had been missing for forty-one years—forty-one years that very night. He was dressed in the costume of a bygone period; his hair was powdered, and round his wrists there were ruffles of lace.

He looked like one who, having come from some great party, had sat down after his return home to play at cards with an intimate friend. On his little finger there sparkled a ring, in the front of his shirt there gleamed a valuable diamond. There were diamond buckles in his shoes, and, according to the fashion of his time, he wore knee-breeches and silk stockings, which showed off advantageously the shape of a remarkably good leg and ankle.

He sat opposite to the door, but never once lifted his eyes to it. His attention seemed concentrated on the cards.

For a time there was utter silence in the room, broken only by the monotonous* counting of the game.

In the doorway we stood, holding our breath, terrified, and yet fascinated by the scene which was being acted before us.

The ashes dropped on the hearth softly and like the snow; we could hear the rustle of the cards as they were dealt out and fell upon the

* In the text , "momentous."

table: we listened to the count—fifteen-one, fifteen-two, and so forth—but there was no other word spoken till at length the player, whose face we could not see, exclaimed, "I win; the game is mine."

Then his opponent took up the cards, sorted them over negligently in his hand, put them close together, and flung the whole pack in his guest's face, exclaiming, "Cheat! Liar! Take that!"

There was a bustle and a confusion—a flinging over of chairs, and fierce gesticulation, and such a noise of passionate voices mingling, that we could not hear a sentence which was uttered.

All at once, however, Jeremy Lester strode out of the room in so great a hurry that he almost touched us where we stood; out of the room, and tramp, tramp up the staircase, to the red room, whence he descended in a few minutes with a couple of rapiers under his arm.

When he reentered the room he gave, as it seemed to us, the other man his choice of the weapons, and then he flung open the window, and after ceremoniously giving place to his opponent to pass out first, he walked forth into the night-air, Clare and I following.

We went through the garden and down a narrow winding walk to a smooth piece of turf sheltered from the north by a plantation of young fir-trees. It was a bright moonlit* night by this time, and we could distinctly see Jeremy Lester measuring off the ground.

"When you say 'three,'" he said to the man whose back was still toward us. They had drawn lots for the ground, and the lot had fallen against Mr. Lester. He stood thus with the moonbeams falling full upon him, and a handsomer fellow I would never desire to behold.

"One," began the other; "two," and before our kinsman had the slightest suspicion of his design, he was upon him, and his rapier through Jeremy Lester's breast. At the sight of that cowardly treachery, Clare screamed aloud. In a moment the combatants had disappeared, the moon was obscured behind a cloud, and we were standing in the shadow of the fir-plantation, shivering with cold and terror.

But we knew at last what had become of the late owner of Martingdale: that he had fallen, not in fair fight, but foully murdered by a false friend.

When, late on Christmas morning, I awoke, it was to see a white world, to behold the ground, and trees, and shrubs all laden and

* In the text, "moonlight."

covered with snow. There was snow everywhere, such snow as no person could remember having fallen for forty-one years.

"It was on just such a Christmas as this that Mr. Jeremy disappeared," remarked the old sexton to my sister who had insisted on dragging me through the snow to church, whereupon Clare fainted away and was carried into the vestry, where I made a full confession to the Vicar of all we had beheld the previous night.

At first that worthy individual rather inclined to treat the matter lightly, but when a fortnight after, the snow melted away and the fir-plantation came to be examined, he confessed there might be more things in heaven and earth than his limited philosophy had dreamed of.

In a little clear space just within the plantation, Jeremy Lester's body was found. We knew it by the ring and the diamond buckles, and the sparkling breast-pin; and Mr. Cronson, who in his capacity as magistrate came over to inspect these relics, was visibly perturbed at my narrative.

"Pray, Mr. Lester, did you in your dream see the face of—of the gentleman—your kinsman's opponent?"

"No," I answered, "he sat and stood with his back to us all the time."

"There is nothing more, of course, to be done in the matter," observed Mr. Cronson.

"Nothing," I replied; and there the affair would doubtless have terminated, but that a few days afterwards when we were dining at Cronson Park, Clare all of a sudden dropped the glass of water she was carrying to her lips, and exclaiming, "Look, John, there he is!" rose from her seat, and with a face as white as the table cloth, pointed to a portrait hanging on the wall.

"I saw him for an instant when he turned his head towards the door as Jeremy Lester left it," she exclaimed; "that is he."

Of what followed after this identification I have only the vaguest recollection. Servants rushed hither and thither; Mrs. Cronson dropped off her chair into hysterics; the young ladies gathered round their mamma; Mr. Cronson, trembling like one in an ague fit, attempted some kind of explanation, while Clare kept praying to be taken away—only to be taken away.

I took her away, not merely from Cronson Park, but from Martingdale. Before we left the latter place, however, I had an interview with

Mr. Cronson, who said the portrait Clare had identified was that of his wife's father, the last person who saw Jeremy Lester alive.

"He is an old man now," finished Mr. Cronson, "a man of over eighty, who has confessed everything to me. You won't bring further sorrow and disgrace upon us by making this matter public?"

I promised him I would keep silence, but the story gradually oozed out, and the Cronsons left the country.

My sister never returned to Martingdale; she married and is living in London. Though I assure here there are no strange noises now in my house, she will not visit Bedfordshire, where the "little girl" she wanted me so long ago to "think seriously of," is now my wife and the mother of my children.

THE OLD HOUSE IN VAUXHALL WALK

Chapter One

"HOUSELESS—homeless—hopeless !"

Many a one who had before him trodden that same street must have uttered the same words—the weary, the desolate, the hungry, the forsaken, the waifs and strays of struggling humanity that are always coming and going, cold, starving and miserable, over the pavements of Lambeth Parish; but it is open to question whether they were ever previously spoken with a more thorough conviction of their truth, or with a feeling of keener self-pity, than by the young man who hurried along Vauxhall Walk one rainy winter's night, with no overcoat on his shoulders and no hat on his head.

A strange sentence for one-and-twenty to give expression to—and it was stranger still to come from the lips of a person who looked like and who was a gentleman. He did not appear either to have sunk very far down in the good graces of Fortune. There was no sign or token which would have induced a passer-by to imagine he had been worsted after a long fight with calamity. His boots were not worn down at the heels or broken at the toes, as many, many boots were which dragged and shuffled and scraped along the pavement. His clothes were good and fashionably cut, and innocent of the rents and patches and tatters that slunk wretchedly by, crouched in doorways, and held out a hand mutely appealing for charity. His face was not pinched with famine or lined with wicked wrinkles, or brutalised by drink and debauchery, and yet he said and thought he was hopeless, and almost in his young despair spoke the words aloud.

It was a bad night to be about with such a feeling in one's heart. The rain was cold, pitiless and increasing. A damp, keen wind blew down the cross streets leading from the river. The fumes of the gas works seemed to fall with the rain. The roadway was muddy; the pavement greasy; the lamps burned dimly; and that dreary district of London looked its very gloomiest and worst.

Certainly not an evening to be abroad without a home to go to, or a sixpence in one's pocket, yet this was the position of the young gentleman who, without a hat, strode along Vauxhall Walk, the rain beating on his unprotected head.

Upon the houses, so large and good—once inhabited by well-to-do citizens, now let out for the most part in floors to weekly tenants—he looked enviously. He would have given much to have had a room, or even part of one. He had been walking for a long time, ever since dark in fact, and dark falls soon in December. He was tired and cold and hungry, and he saw no prospect save of pacing the streets all night.

As he passed one of the lamps, the light falling on his face revealed handsome young features, a mobile, sensitive mouth, and that particular formation of the eyebrows—not a frown exactly, but a certain draw of the brows—often considered to bespeak genius, but which more surely accompanies an impulsive organisation easily pleased, easily depressed, capable of suffering very keenly or of enjoying fully. In his short life he had not enjoyed much, and he had suffered a good deal. That night, when he walked bareheaded through the rain, affairs had come to a crisis. So far as he in his despair felt able to see or reason, the best thing he could do was to die. The world did not want him; he would be better out of it.

The door of one of the houses stood open, and he could see in the dimly lighted hall some few articles of furniture waiting to be removed. A van stood beside the curb, and two men were lifting a table into it as he, for a second, paused.

"Ah," he thought, "even those poor people have some place to go to, some shelter provided, while I have not a roof to cover my head, or a shilling to get a night's lodging." And he went on fast, as if memory were spurring him, so fast that a man running after had some trouble to overtake him.

"Master Graham ! Master Graham !" this man exclaimed, breathlessly ; and, thus addressed, the young fellow stopped as if he had been shot.

"Who are you that know me ?" he asked, facing round.

"I'm William; don't you remember William, Master Graham ? And, Lord's sake, sir, what are you doing out a night like this without your hat ?"

"I forgot it," was the answer; "and I did not care to go back and fetch it."

"Then why don't you buy another, sir ? You'll catch your death of cold; and besides, you'll excuse me, sir, but it does look odd."

"I know that," said Master Graham grimly; "but I haven't a halfpenny in the world."

"Have you and the master, then———" began the man, but there he hesitated and stopped.

"Had a quarrel ? Yes, and one that will last us our lives," finished the other, with a bitter laugh.

"And where are you going now ? "

"Going ! Nowhere, except to seek out the softest paving stone, or the shelter of an arch."

"You are joking, sir."

"I don't feel much in a mood for jesting either."

"Will you come back with me, Master Graham ? We are just at the last of our moving, but there is a spark of fire still in the grate, and it would be better talking out of this rain. Will you come, sir ? "

"Come ! Of course I will come," said the young fellow, and, turning, they retraced their steps to the house he had looked into as he passed along.

An old, old house, with long, wide hall, stairs low, easy of ascent, with deep cornices to the ceilings, and oak floorings, and mahogany doors, which still spoke mutely of the wealth and stability of the original owner, who lived before the Tradescants and Ashmoles were thought of, and had been sleeping far longer than they, in St. Mary's churchyard, hard by the archbishop's palace.

"Step upstairs, sir," entreated the departing tenant; "it's cold down here, with the door standing wide."

"Had you the whole house, then, William ?" asked Graham Coulton, in some surprise.

"The whole of it, and right sorry I, for one, am to leave it; but nothing else would serve my wife. This room, sir," and with a little conscious pride, William, doing the honours of his late residence, asked his guest into a spacious apartment occupying the full width of the house on the first floor.

Tired though he was, the young man could not repress an exclamation of astonishment.

"Why, we have nothing so large as this at home, William," he said.

"It's a fine house," answered William, raking the embers together as he spoke and throwing some wood upon them; "but, like many a good family, it has come down in the world."

There were four windows in the room, shuttered close; they had deep, low seats, suggestive of pleasant days gone by; when, well-curtained and well-cushioned, they formed snug retreats for the children, and sometimes for adults also; there was no furniture left, unless an oaken settle beside the hearth, and a large mirror let into the panelling at the opposite end of the apartment, with a black marble console table beneath it, could be so considered; but the very absence of chairs and tables enabled the magnificent proportions of the chamber to be seen to full advantage, and there was nothing to distract the attention from the ornamented ceiling, the panelled walls the old-world chimney-piece so quaintly carved, and the fire-place lined with tiles, each one of which contained a picture of some scriptural or allegorical subject.

"Had you been staying on here, William," said Coulton, flinging himself wearily on the settle, "I'd have asked you to let me stop where I am for the night."

"If you can make shift, sir, there is nothing as I am aware of to prevent you stopping," answered the man, fanning the wood into a flame. "I shan't take the key back to the landlord till to-morrow, and this would be better for you than the cold streets at any rate."

"Do you really mean what you say?" asked the other eagerly. "I should be thankful to lie here; I feel dead beat."

"Then stay, Master Graham, and welcome. I'll fetch a basket of coals I was going to put in the van, and make up a good fire, so that you can warm yourself; then I must run round to the other house for a minute or two, but it's not far, and I'll be back as soon as ever I can."

"Thank you, William; you were always good to me," said the young man gratefully. "This is delightful," and he stretched his numbed hands over the blazing wood, and looked round the room with a satisfied smile.

"I did not expect to get into such quarters," he remarked, as his friend in need reappeared, carrying a half-bushel basket full of coals, with which he proceeded to make up a roaring fire. "I am sure the last thing I could have imagined was meeting with anyone I knew in Vauxhall Walk."

"Where were you coming from, Master Graham ?" asked William curiously.

"From old Melfield's. I was at his school once, you know, and he has now retired, and is living upon the proceeds of years of robbery in Kennington Oval. I thought, perhaps he would lend me a pound, or offer me a night's lodging, or even a glass of wine; but, oh dear, no. He took the moral tone, and observed he could have nothing to say to a son who defied his father's authority. He gave me plenty of advice, but nothing else, and showed me out into the rain with a bland courtesy, for which I could have struck him."

William muttered something under his breath which was not a blessing, and added aloud :

"You are better here, sir, I think, at any rate. I'll be back in less than half an hour."

Left to himself, young Coulton took off his coat, and shifting the settle a little, hung it over the end to dry. With his handkerchief he rubbed some of the wet out of his hair; then, perfectly exhausted, he lay down before the fire and, pillowing his head on his arm, fell fast asleep.

He was awakened nearly an hour afterwards by the sound of some-one gently stirring the fire and moving quietly about the room. Starting into a sitting posture, he looked around him, bewildered for a moment, and then, recognising his humble friend, said laughingly :

"I had lost myself; I could not imagine where I was."

"I am sorry to see you here, sir," was the reply; "but still this is better than being out of doors. It has come on a nasty night. I brought a rug round with me that, perhaps, you would wrap yourself in."

"I wish, at the same time, you had brought me something to eat," said the young man, laughing.

"Are you hungry, then, sir ?" asked William, in a tone of concern.

"Yes; I have had nothing to eat since breakfast. The governor and I commenced rowing the minute we sat down to luncheon, and I rose and left the table. But hunger does not signify; I am dry and warm, and can forget the other matter in sleep."

"And it's too late now to buy anything," soliloquised the man;

"the shops are all shut long ago. Do you think, sir," he added, brightening, "you could manage some bread and cheese ?"

"Do I think—I should call it a perfect feast," answered Graham Coulton. "But never mind about food to-night, William; you have had trouble enough, and to spare, already."

William's only answer was to dart to the door and run downstairs. Presently he reappeared, carrying in one hand bread and cheese wrapped up in paper, and in the other a pewter measure full of beer.

"It's the best I could do, sir," he said apologetically. "I had to beg this from the landlady."

"Here's to her good health !" exclaimed the young fellow gaily, taking a long pull at the tankard. "That tastes better than champagne in my father's house."

"Won't he be uneasy about you ?" ventured William, who, having by this time emptied the coals, was now seated on the inverted basket, looking wistfully at the relish with which the son of the former master was eating his bread and cheese.

"No," was the decided answer. "When he hears it pouring cats and dogs he will only hope I am out in the deluge, and say a good drenching will cool my pride."

"I do not think you are right there," remarked the man.

"But I am sure I am. My father always hated me, as he hated my mother."

"Begging your pardon, sir; he was over fond of your mother."

"If you had heard what he said about her to-day, you might find reason to alter your opinion. He told me I resembled her in mind as well as body; that I was a coward, a simpleton, and a hypocrite."

"He did not mean it, sir."

"He did, every word. He does think I am a coward, because I— I——" And the young fellow broke into a passion of hysterical tears.

"I don't half like leaving you here alone," said William, glancing round the room with a quick trouble in his eyes; "but I have no place fit to ask you to stop, and I am forced to go myself, because I am night watchman, and must be on at twelve o'clock."

"I shall be right enough," was the answer. "Only I mustn't talk any more of my father. Tell me about yourself, William. How did you manage to get such a big house, and why are you leaving it ?"

"The landlord put me in charge, sir; and it was my wife's fancy not to like it."

"Why did she not like it ?"

"She felt desolate alone with the children at night," answered William, turning away his head; then added, next minute: "Now, sir, if you think I can do no more for you, I had best be off. Time's getting on. I'll look round to-morrow morning."

"Good night," said the young fellow, stretching out his hand, which the other took as freely and frankly as it was offered. "What should I have done this evening if I had not chanced to meet you ?"

"I don't think there is much chance in the world, Master Graham," was the quiet answer. "I do hope you will rest well, and not be the worse for your wetting."

"No fear of that," was the rejoinder, and the next minute the young man found himself all alone in the Old House in Vauxhall Walk.

Chapter Two

LYING on the settle, with the fire burnt out, and the room in total darkness, Graham Coulton dreamed a curious dream. He thought he awoke from deep slumber to find a log smouldering away upon the hearth, and the mirror at the end of the apartment reflecting fitful gleams of light. He could not understand how it came to pass that, far away as he was from the glass, he was able to see everything in it; but he resigned himself to the difficulty without astonishment, as people generally do in dreams.

Neither did he feel surprised when he beheld the outline of a female figure seated beside the fire, engaged in picking something out of her lap and dropping it with a despairing gesture.

He heard the mellow sound of gold, and knew she was lifting and dropping sovereigns. He turned a little so as to see the person engaged in such a singular and meaningless manner, and found that, where there had been no chair on the previous night, there was a chair now, on which was seated an old, wrinkled hag, her clothes poor and ragged, a mob cap barely covering her scant white hair, her cheeks sunken, her nose hooked, her fingers more like talons than aught else as they dived down into the heap of gold, portions of which they lifted but to scatter mournfully.

"Oh ! my lost life," she moaned, in a voice of the bitterest anguish. "Oh ! my lost life—for one day, for one hour of it again !"

Out of the darkness—out of the corner of the room where the shadows lay deepest—out from the gloom abiding near the door—out from the dreary night, with their sodden feet and the wet dripping from their heads, came the old men and the young children, the worn women and the weary hearts, whose misery that gold might have relieved, but those wretchedness it mocked.

Round that miser, who once sat gloating as she now sat lamenting, they crowded—all those pale, sad shapes—the aged of days, the infant of hours, the sobbing outcast, honest poverty, repentant vice; but one low cry proceeded from those pale lips—a cry for help she might have given, but which she withheld.

They closed about her, all together, as they had done singly in life; they prayed, they sobbed, they entreated; with haggard eyes the figure regarded the poor she had repulsed, the children against whose cry she had closed her ears, the old people she had suffered to starve and die for want of what would have been the merest trifle to her; then, with a terrible scream, she raised her lean arms above her head, and sank down—down—the gold scattering as it fell out of her lap, and rolling along the floor, till its gleam was lost in the outer darkness beyond.

Then Graham Coulton awoke in good earnest, with the perspiration oozing from every pore, with a fear and an agony upon him such as he had never before felt in all his existence, and with the sound of the heart-rending cry—"Oh ! my lost life"—still ringing in his ears.

Mingled with all, too, there seemed to have been some lesson for him which he had forgotten, that, try as he would, eluded his memory, and which, in the very act of waking, glided away.

He lay for a little thinking about all this, and then, still heavy with sleep, retraced his way into dreamland once more.

It was natural, perhaps, that, mingling with the strange fantasies which follow in the train of night and darkness, the former vision should recur, and the young man ere long found himself toiling through scene after scene wherein the figure of the woman he had seen seated beside a dying fire held principal place.

He saw her walking slowly across the floor munching a dry crust—

she who could have purchased all the luxuries wealth can command; on the hearth, contemplating her, stood a man of commanding presence, dressed in the fashion of long ago. In his eyes there was a dark look of anger, on his lips a curling smile of disgust, and somehow, even in his sleep, the dreamer understood it was the ancestor to the descendant he beheld—that the house put to mean uses in which he lay had never so far descended from its high estate, as the woman possessed of so pitiful a soul, contaminated with the most despicable and insidious vice poor humanity knows, for all other vices seem to have connection with the flesh, but the greed of the miser eats into the very soul.

Filthy of person, repulsive to look at, hard of heart as she was, he yet beheld another phantom, which, coming into the room, met her almost on the threshold, taking her by the hand, and pleading, as it seemed, for assistance. He could not hear all that passed, but a word now and then fell upon his ear. Some talk of former days; some mention of a fair young mother—an appeal, as it seemed, to a time when they were tiny brother and sister, and the accursed greed for gold had not divided them. All in vain; the hag only answered him as she had answered the children, and the young girls, and the old people in his former vision. Her heart was as invulnerable to natural affection as it had proved to human sympathy. He begged, as it appeared, for aid to avert some bitter misfortune or terrible disgrace, and adamant might have been found more yielding to his prayer. Then the figure standing on the hearth changed to an angel, which folded its wings mournfully over its face, and the man, with bowed head, slowly left the room.

Even as he did so the scene changed again; it was night once more, and the miser wended her way upstairs. From below, Graham Coulton fancied he watched her toiling wearily from step to step. She had aged strangely since the previous scenes. She moved with difficulty; it seemed the greatest exertion for her to creep from step to step, her skinny hand traversing the balusters with slow and painful deliberateness. Fascinated, the young man's eyes followed the progress of that feeble, decrepid woman. She was solitary in a desolate house, with a deeper blackness than the darkness of night waiting to engulf her.

It seemed to Graham Coulton that after that he lay for a time in a still, dreamless sleep, upon awaking from which he found himself entering a chamber as sordid and unclean in its appointments as the woman of his previous vision had been in her person. The poorest labourer's wife would have gathered more comforts around her than that room contained. A four-poster bedstead without hangings of any kind—a blind drawn up awry—an old carpet covered with dust, and dirt on the floor—a rickety washstand with all the paint worn off it—an ancient mahogany dressing table, and a cracked glass spotted all over—were all the objects he could at first discern, looking at the room through that dim light which oftentimes obtains in dreams.

By degrees, however, he perceived the outline of someone lying huddled on the bed. Drawing nearer, he found it was that of the person whose dreadful presence seemed to pervade the house. What a terrible sight she looked, with her thin white locks scattered over the pillow, with what were mere remnants of blankets gathered about her shoulders, with her claw-like fingers clutching the clothes, as though even in sleep she was guarding her gold !

An awful and a repulsive spectacle, but not with half the terror in it of that which followed. Even as the young man looked he heard stealthy footsteps on the stairs. Then he saw first one man and then his fellow steal cautiously into the room. Another second, and the pair stood beside the bed, murder in their eyes.

Graham Coulton tried to shout—tried to move, but the deterrent power which exists in dreams only tied his tongue and paralysed his limbs. He could but hear and look, and what he heard and saw was this : aroused suddenly from sleep, the woman started, only to receive a blow from one of the ruffians, whose fellow followed his lead by plunging a knife into her breast.

Then, with a gurgling scream, she fell back on the bed, and at the same moment, with a cry, Graham Coulton again awoke, to thank heaven it was but an illusion.

Chapter Three

" I hope you slept well, sir." It was William, who, coming into the hall with the sunlight of a fine bright morning streaming after him, asked this question: "Had you a good night's rest ?"

Graham Coulton laughed, and answered:

"Why, faith, I was somewhat in the case of Paddy, 'who could not slape for dhraming.' I slept well enough, I suppose, but whether it was in consequence of the row with my dad, or the hard bed, or the cheese —most likely the bread and cheese so late at night—I dreamt all the night long, the most extraordinary dreams. Some old woman kept cropping up, and I saw her murdered."

"You don't say that, sir?" said William nervously.

"I do, indeed," was the reply. "However, that is all gone and past. I have been down in the kitchen and had a good wash, and I am as fresh as a daisy, and as hungry as a hunter; and, oh, William, can you get me any breakfast?"

"Certainly, Master Graham. I have brought round a kettle, and I will make the water boil immediately. I suppose, sir"—this tentatively —"you'll be going home to-day?"

"Home!" repeated the young man. "Decidedly not. I'll never go home again till I return with some medal hung to my coat, or a leg or arm cut off. I've thought it all out, William. I'll go and enlist. There's a talk of war; and, living or dead, my father shall have reason to retract his opinion about my being a coward."

"I am sure the admiral never thought you anything of the sort, sir," said William. "Why, you have the pluck of ten!"

"Not before him," answered the young fellow sadly.

"You'll do nothing rash, Master Graham; you won't go 'listing, or aught of that sort, in your anger?"

"If I do not, what is to become of me?" asked the other. "I cannot dig—to beg I am ashamed. Why, but for you, I should not have had a roof over my head last night."

"Not much of a roof, I am afraid, sir."

"Not much of a roof!" repeated the young man. "Why, who could desire a better? What a capital room this is," he went on, looking around the apartment, where William was now kindling a fire; "one might dine twenty people here easily!"

"If you think so well of the place, Master Graham, you might stay here for a while, till you have made up your mind what you are going to do. The landlord won't make any objection, I am very sure."

"Oh! nonsense; he would want a long rent for a house like this."

"I daresay; *if he could get it*," was William's significant answer.

"What do you mean? Won't the place let?"

"No, sir. I did not tell you last night, but there was a murder done here, and people are shy of the house ever since."

"A murder! What sort of a murder? Who was murdered?"

"A woman, Master Graham—the landlord's sister; she lived here all alone, and was supposed to have money. Whether she had or not, she was found dead from a stab in her breast, and if there ever was any money, it must have been taken at the same time, for none ever was found in the house from that day to this."

"Was that the reason your wife would not stop here?" asked the young man, leaning against the mantelshelf, and looking thoughtfully down on William.

"Yes, sir. She could not stand it any longer; she got that thin and nervous no one would have believed it possible; she never saw anything, but she said she heard footsteps and voices, and then when she walked through the hall, or up the staircase, someone always seemed to be following her. We put the children to sleep in that big room you had last night, and they declared they often saw an old woman sitting by the hearth. Nothing ever came my way," finished William, with a laugh; "I was always ready to go to sleep the minute my head touched the pillow."

"Were not the murderers discovered?" asked Graham Coulton.

"No, sir; the landlord, Miss Tynan's brother, had always lain under the suspicion of it—quite wrongfully, I am very sure—but he will never clear himself now. It was known he came and asked her for help a day or two before the murder, and it was also known he was able within a week or two to weather whatever trouble had been harassing him. Then, you see, the money was never found; and, altogether, people scarce knew what to think."

"Humph!" ejaculated Graham Coulton, and he took a few turns up and down the apartment. "Could I go and see this landlord?"

"Surely, sir, if you had a hat," answered William, with such a serious decorum that the young man burst out laughing.

"That is an obstacle, certainly," he remarked, "and I must make a note do instead. I have a pencil in my pocket, so here goes."

Within half an hour from the dispatch of that note William was back again with a sovereign; the landlord's compliments, and he would be much obliged if Mr. Coulton could "step round."

"You'll do nothing rash, sir," entreated William.

"Why, man," answered the young fellow, "one may as well be picked off by a ghost as a bullet. What is there to be afraid of?"

William only shook his head. He did not think his young master was made of the stuff likely to remain alone in a haunted house and solve the mystery it assuredly contained by dint of his own unassisted endeavours. And yet when Graham Coulton came out of the landlord's house he looked more bright and gay than usual, and walked up the Lambeth road to the place where William awaited his return, humming an air as he paced along.

"We have settled the matter," he said. "And now if the dad wants his son for Christmas, it will trouble him to find him."

"Don't say that, Master Graham, don't," entreated the man, with a shiver; "maybe after all it would have been better if you had never happened to chance upon Vauxhall Walk."

"Don't croak, William," answered the young man; "if it was not the best day's work I ever did for myself I'm a Dutchman."

During the whole of that forenoon and afternoon, Graham Coulton searched diligently for the missing treasure Mr. Tynan assured him had never been discovered. Youth is confident and self-opinionated, and this fresh explorer felt satisfied that, though others had failed, he would be successful. On the second floor he found one door locked, but he did not pay much attention to that at the moment, as he believed if there was anything concealed it was more likely to be found in the lower than the upper part of the house. Late into the evening he pursued his researches in the kitchen and cellars and old-fashioned cupboards, of which the basement had an abundance.

It was nearly eleven, when, engaged in poking about amongst the empty bins of a wine cellar as large as a family vault, he suddenly felt a rush of cold air at his back. Moving, his candle was instantly extinguished, and in the very moment of being left in darkness he saw, standing in the doorway, a woman, resembling her who had haunted his dreams overnight.

He rushed with outstretched hands to seize her, but clutched only air. He relit his candle, and closely examined the basement, shutting off communication with the ground floor ere doing so. All in vain. Not a trace could he find of living creature—not a window was open—not a door unbolted.

"It is very odd," he thought, as, after securely fastening the door at the top of the staircase, he searched the whole upper portion of the house, with the exception of the one room mentioned.

"I must get the key of that to-morrow," he decided, standing gloomily with his back to the fire and his eyes wandering about the drawing-room, where he had once again taken up his abode.

Even as the thought passed through his mind, he saw standing in the open doorway a woman with white dishevelled hair, clad in mean garments, ragged and dirty. She lifted her hand and shook it at him with a menacing gesture, and then, just as he was darting towards her, a wonderful thing occurred.

From behind the great mirror there glided a second female figure, at the sight of which the first turned and fled, uttering piercing shrieks as the other followed her from story to story.

Sick almost with terror, Graham Coulton watched the dreadful pair as they fled upstairs past the locked room to the top of the house.

It was a few minutes before he recovered his self-possession. When he did so, and searched the upper apartments, he found them totally empty.

That night, ere lying down before the fire, he carefully locked and bolted the drawing-room door; before he did more he drew the heavy settle in front of it, so that if the lock were forced no entrance could be effected without considerable noise.

For some time he lay awake, then dropped into a deep sleep, from which he was awakened suddenly by a noise as if of something scuffling stealthily behind the wainscot. He raised himself on his elbow and listened, and, to his consternation, beheld seated at the opposite side of the hearth the same woman he had seen before in his dreams, lamenting over her gold.

The fire was not quite out, and at that moment shot up a last tongue of flame. By the light, transient as it was, he saw that the figure pressed a ghostly finger to its lips, and by the turn of its head and the attitude of its body seemed to be listening.

He listened also—indeed, he was too much frightened to do aught else; more and more distinct grew the sounds which had aroused him, a stealthy rustling coming nearer and nearer—up and up it seemed, behind the wainscot.

"It is rats," thought the young man, though, indeed, his teeth were almost chattering in his head with fear. But then in a moment he saw what disabused him of that idea—*the gleam of a candle or lamp through a crack in the panelling.* He tried to rise, he strove to shout—all in vain; and, sinking down, remembered nothing more till he awoke to find the grey light of an early morning stealing through one of the shutters he had left partially unclosed.

For hours after his breakfast, which he scarcely touched, long after William had left him at mid-day, Graham Coulton, having in the morning made a long and close survey of the house, sat thinking before the fire, then, apparently having made up his mind, he put on the hat he had bought, and went out.

When he returned the evening shadows were darkening down, but the pavements were full of people going marketing, for it was Christmas Eve, and all who had money to spent seemed bent on shopping.

It was terribly dreary inside the old house that night. Through the deserted rooms Graham could feel that ghostly semblance was wandering mournfully. When he turned his back he knew she was flitting from the mirror to the fire, from the fire to the mirror; but he was not afraid of her now—he was far more afraid of another matter he had taken in hand that day.

The horror of the silent house grew and grew upon him. He could hear the beating of his own heart in the dead quietude which reigned from garret to cellar.

At last William came; but the young man said nothing to him of what was in his mind. He talked to him cheerfully and hopefully enough—wondered where his father would think he had got to, and hoped Mr. Tynan might send him some Christmas pudding. Then the man said it was time for him to go, and, when Mr. Coulton went downstairs to the hall-door, remarked the key was not in it.

"No," was the answer, "I took it out to-day, to oil it."

"It wanted oiling," agreed William, "for it worked terribly stiff." Having uttered which truism he departed.

Very slowly the young man retraced his way to the drawing-room, where he only paused to lock the door on the outside; then taking off his boots he went up to the top of the house, where, entering the front attic, he waited patiently in darkness and in silence.

It was a long time, or at least it seemed long to him, before he heard the same sound which had aroused him on the previous night—a stealthy rustling—then a rush of cold air—then cautious footsteps— then the quiet opening of a door below.

It did not take as long in action as it has required to tell. In a moment the young man was out on the landing and had closed a portion of the panelling on the wall which stood open; noiselessly he crept back to the attic window, unlatched it, and sprung a rattle, the sound of which echoed far and near through the deserted streets, then rushing down the stairs, he encountered a man who, darting past him, made for the landing above; but perceiving that way of escape closed, fled down again, to find Graham struggling desperately with his fellow.

"Give him the knife—come along," he said savagely; and next instant Graham felt something like a hot iron through his shoulder, and then heard a thud, as one of the men, tripping in his rapid flight, fell from the top of the stairs to the bottom.

At the same moment there came a crash, as if the house was falling, and faint, sick, and bleeding, young Coulton lay insensible on the threshold of the room where Miss Tynan had been murdered.

When he recovered he was in the dining-room, and a doctor was examining his wound.

Near the door a policeman stiffly kept guard. The hall was full of people; all the misery and vagabondism the streets contain at that hour was crowding in to see what had happened.

Through the midst two men were being conveyed to the station-house; one, with his head dreadfully injured, on a stretcher, the other handcuffed, uttering frightful imprecations as he went.

After a time the house was cleared of the rabble, the police took possession of it, and Mr. Tynan was sent for.

"What was that dreadful noise?" asked Graham feebly, now seated on the floor, with his back resting against the wall.

"I do not know. Was there a noise?" said Mr. Tynan, humouring his fancy, as he thought.

"Yes, in the drawing-room, I think; the key is in my pocket."

Still humouring the wounded lad, Mr. Tynan took the key and ran upstairs.

When he unlocked the door, what a sight met his eyes ! The mirror had fallen—it was lying all over the floor shivered into a thousand pieces; the console table had been borne down by its weight, and the marble slab was shattered as well. But this was not what chained his attention. Hundreds, thousands of gold pieces were scattered about, and an aperture behind the glass contained boxes filled with securities and deeds and bonds, the possession of which had cost his sister her life.

*   *   *   *   *

"Well, Graham, and what do you want?" asked Admiral Coulton that evening as his eldest born appeared before him, looking somewhat pale but otherwise unchanged.

"I want nothing," was the answer, "but to ask your forgiveness. William has told me all the story I never knew before; and, if you let me, I will try to make it up to you for the trouble you have had. I am provided for," went on the young fellow, with a nervous laugh; "I have made my fortune since I left you, and another man's fortune as well."

"I think you are out of your senses," said the Admiral shortly.

"No, sir, I have found them," was the answer; "and I mean to strive and make a better thing of my life than I should ever have done had I not gone to the Old House in Vauxhall Walk."

"Vauxhall Walk! What is the lad talking about?"

"I will tell you, sir, if I may sit down," was Graham Coulton's answer, and then he told this story.

SANDY THE TINKER

" BEFORE commencing my story, I wish to state it is perfectly true in every particular."

"We quite understand that," said the sceptic of our party, who was wont, in the security of friendly intercourse, to characterise all such prefaces as mere introductions to some tremendous 'blank,' 'blank,' 'blank,' which trio the reader can fill up at his own pleasure and leisure.

On the occasion in question, however, we had donned our best behaviour, a garment which did not sit ungracefully on some of us; and our host, who was about to draw out from the stores of memory one narrative for our entertainment, was scarcely the person before whom even Jack Hill would have cared to express his cynical and unbelieving views.

We were seated, an incongruous company of ten persons, in the best room of an old manse among the Scottish hills. Accident had thrown us together, and accident had driven us under the minister's hospitable roof. Cold, wet, and hungry, drenched with rain, sorely beaten by the wind, we had crowded through the door opened by a friendly hand, and now, wet no longer, the pangs of hunger assuaged with smoking rashers of ham, poached eggs, and steaming potatoes, we sat around a blazing fire, drinking toddy out of tumblers, whilst the two ladies who graced the assemblage partook of a modicum of the same beverage from wine glasses.

Everything was eminently comfortable, but conducted upon the most correct principles. Jack could no more have taken it upon him to shock the minister's ear with some of the opinions he aired in Fleet Street than he could have asked for more whisky with his water.

"Yes, it is perfectly true," continued the minister, looking thoughtfully at the fire. "I can't explain it, I cannot even try to explain it. I will tell you the story as it occurred, however, and leave you to draw your own deductions from it."

None of us answered. We fell into listening attitudes instantly, and eighteen eyes fixed themselves by one accord upon our host.

He was an old man, but hale. The weight of eighty winters had whitened his head, but not bowed it. He seemed young as any of us— younger than Jack Hill, who was a reviewer and a newspaper hack, and whose way through life had not been altogether on easy lines.

"Thirty years ago, upon a certain Friday morning in August," began the minister, "I was sitting at breakfast in the room on the other side of the passage, where you ate your supper, when the servant girl came in with a letter she said a laddie, all out of breath, had brought over from Dendeldy Manse. 'He was bidden rin a' the way,' she went on, 'and he's fairly beaten.'

"I told her to make the messenger sit down, and put food before him; and then, when she went to do my bidding, proceeded, I must confess with some curiosity, to break the seal of a missive forwarded in such hot haste.

"It was from the minister at Dendeldy, who had been newly chosen to occupy the pulpit his deceased father occupied for a quarter of a century and more.

"The call from the congregation originated rather out of respect to the father's memory than any extraordinary liking for the son. He had been reared for the most part in England, and was somewhat distant and formal in his manners; and, though full of Greek and Latin and Hebrew, wanted the true Scotch accent, that goes straight to the heart of those accustomed to the broad, honest, tender Scottish tongue.

"His people were proud of him, but they did not just like all his ways. They could remember him a lad running about the whole countryside, and they could not understand, and did not approve of, his holding them at arm's length, and shutting himself up among his books and refusing their hospitality, and sending out word he was busy when maybe some very decent man wanted speech of him. I had taken upon myself to point out that I thought he was wrong, and that he would alienate his flock from him. Perhaps it was for this very reason, because I was blunt and plain, he took to me kindly, and never got on his high horse, no matter what I said to him.

"Well, to return to the letter. It was written in the wildest haste, and entreated me not to lose a moment in coming to him, as he was in the very *greatest distress* and *anxiety*. 'Let *nothing* delay you,' he proceeded. 'If I cannot speak to you soon I believe I shall go out of my senses.'

" 'What could be the matter ?' I thought. 'What in all the wide earth could have happened ?'

"I had seen him but a few days before, and he was in good health and spirits, getting on better with his people, feeling hopeful of so altering his style of preaching as to touch their hearts more sensibly.

" 'I must lay aside Southern ideas as well as accent, if I can,' he went on, smiling. 'Men who live such lives of hardship and privation, who cast their seed into the ground under such rigorous skies, and cut their corn in fear and trembling at the end of late, uncertain summers, who take the sheep out of the snowdrifts and carry the lambs into shelter beside their own humble hearths, must want a different sort of sermon from those who sleep softly and walk delicately.'

"I had implied something of all this myself, and it amused me to find my own thoughts come back clothed in different fashion and presented to me quite as strangers. Still, all I wanted was his good, and I felt glad he showed such aptitude to learn.

"What could have happened, however, puzzled me sorely. As I made my hurried preparations for setting out I fairly perplexed myself with speculation. I went into the kitchen, where his messenger was eating some breakfast, and asked him if Mr. Cawley was ill.

" 'I dinna ken,' he answered. 'He mad' no complaint, but he luiked awfu' bad, just awfu'.'

" 'In what way ?' I enquired.

" 'As if he had seen a ghaist,' was the reply.

"This made me very uneasy, and I jumped to the conclusion the trouble was connected with money matters. Young men will be young men." And here the minister looked significantly at the callow bird of our company, a youth who had never owed a sixpence in his life or given away a cent; while Jack Hill—no chicken, by the way—was over head and ears in debt, and could not keep a sovereign in his pocket, though spending or bestowing it involved going dinnerless the next day.

"Young men will be young men," repeated the minister, in his best pulpit manner ("Just as though anyone expected them to be young women !" grumbled Jack to me afterwards), "and I feared that now he was settled and comfortably off, some old creditor he had been paying as best he could might have become pressing. I knew nothing of his liabilities, or, beyond the amount of the stipend paid him, the state of his pecuniary affairs; but, having once in my own life made myself responsible for a debt, I was aware of all the trouble putting your arm out further than you can draw it back involves, and I considered that most probably money, which is the root of all evil" ("and all good," Jack's eyes suggested to me), "was the cause of my young friend's agony of mind. Blessed with a large family—every one of whom is now alive and doing well, I thank God, out in the world—you may imagine I had not much opportunity for laying by; still, I had put aside a little for a rainy day, and that little I placed in my pocket-book, hoping even a small sum might prove of use in case of emergency."

"Come, you *are* a trump," I saw written plainly on Jack Hill's face; and he settled himself to listen to the remainder of the minister's story in a manner which could not be considered other than complimentary.

Duly and truly I knew quite well he had already devoted the first five-guinea cheque he received to the poor of that minister's parish.

"By the road," proceeded out host, "Dendeldy is distant from here ten long miles, but by a short cut across the hills it can be reached in something under six. For me it was nothing of a walk, and accordingly I arrived at the manse ere noon."

He paused, and, though thirty years had elapsed, drew a handkerchief across his forehead ere he continued his narrative.

"I had to climb a steep brae to reach the front door, but ere I could breast it my friend met me.

"'Thank God you are come,' he said, pressing my hand in his. 'Oh, I am grateful.'

"He was trembling with excitement. His face was of a ghastly pallor. His voice was that of a person suffering from some terrible shock, labouring under some awful fear.

"'What *has* happened, Edward?' I asked. I had known him when he was a little boy. 'I am distressed to see you in such a state. Rouse yourself; be a man; whatever may have gone wrong can possibly be righted. I have come over to do all that lies in my power for you. If it is a matter of money——'

"'No, no; it is not money,' he interrupted; 'would that it were!' and he began to tremble again so violently that really he communicated some part of his nervousness to me, and put me into a state of perfect terror.

"'Whatever it is, Cawley, out with it,' I said; 'have you murdered anybody?'

"'No, it is worse than that,' he answered.

"'But that's just nonsense,' I declared. 'Are you in your right mind, do you think?'

"'I wish I were not,' he returned. 'I'd like to know I was stark staring mad; it would be happier for me—far, far happier.'

"'If you don't tell me this minute what is the matter, I shall turn on my heel and tramp my way home again,' I said, half in a passion, for what I thought his folly angered me.

"'Come into the house,' he entreated, 'and try to have patience with me; for indeed, Mr. Morison, I am sorely troubled. I have been through my deep waters, and they have gone clean over my head.'

"We went into his little study and sat down. For a while he remained silent, his head resting upon his hand, struggling with some strong emotion; but after about five minutes he asked, in a low, subdued voice:

"'Do you believe in dreams?'

"'What has my belief to do with the matter in hand?' I inquired.

"'It is a dream, an awful dream, that is troubling me.'

"I rose from my chair.

"'Do you mean to say,' I asked, 'you have brought me from my business and my parish to tell me you have had a bad dream?'

"'That is just what I do mean to say,' he answered. 'At least, it was not a dream—it was a vision; no, I don't mean a vision—I can't tell you what it was; but nothing I ever went through in actual life was half so real, and I have bound myself to go through it all again. There is no hope for me, Mr. Morison. I sit before you a lost creature, the most miserable man on the face of the whole earth.'

"'What did you dream?' I inquired.

"A dreadful fit of trembling again seized him; but at last he managed to say:

"'I have been like this ever since, and I shall be like this for evermore, till—till—the end comes.'

"'When did you have your bad dream?' I asked.

"'Last night, or rather this morning,' he answered. 'I'll tell you all about it in a minute.' And he covered his face with his hands again.

"'I was as well when I went to bed about eleven o'clock as ever I was in my life,' he began, putting a great restraint upon himself, as I could see by the nervous way he kept knotting and unknotting his fingers. 'I had been considering my sermon, and felt satisfied I should be able to deliver a good one next Sunday morning. I had taken nothing after my tea, and I lay down in my bed feeling at peace with all mankind, satisfied with my lot, thankful for the many blessings vouchsafed to me. How long I slept, or what I dreamt about at first, if I dreamt at all, I don't know; but after a time the mists seemed to clear from before my eyes, to roll away like clouds from a mountain summit, and I found myself walking on a beautiful summer's evening beside the river Deldy.'

"He paused for a moment, and an irrepressible shudder shook his frame.

"'Go on,' I said, for I felt afraid of his breaking down again.

"He looked at me pitifully, with a hungry entreaty in his weary eyes, and continued,

"'It was a lovely evening. I had never thought the earth so beautiful before: a gentle breeze just touched my cheek; the water flowed on clear and bright; the mountains in the distance looked bright and glowing, covered with purple heather. I walked on and on, till I came to that point where, as you may perhaps remember, the path, growing very narrow, winds round the base of a great crag, and leads the wayfarer suddenly into a little green amphitheatre, bounded on one side by the river and on the other by rocks that rise in places sheer to a height of a hundred feet and more.'

"'I remember it,' I said; 'a little further on three streams meet and fall with a tremendous roar into the Witches' Caldron. A fine sight in the winter-time, only that there is scarce any reaching it from below, as the path you mention and the little green oasis are mostly covered with water.'

"'I had not been there before since I was a child,' he went on mournfully, 'but I recollected it as one of the most solitary spots possible; and my astonishment was great, to see a man standing in the pathway, with a drawn sword in his hand. He did not stir as I drew near, so I stepped aside on the grass. Instantly he barred my way.

"'"You can't pass here," he said.

"'"Why not?" I asked.

"'"Because I say so," he answered.

""" And who are you that say so ?" I inquired, looking full at him.

"' He was like a god. Majesty and power were written on every feature, were expressed in every gesture; but oh, the awful scorn on his smile, the contempt with which he regarded me ! The beams of the setting sun fell full upon him, and seemed to bring out, as in letters of fire, the wickedness and hate and sin that underlay the glorious and terrible beauty of his face.

"' I felt afraid; but I managed to say:

""" Stand out of my way; the river-brink is as free to me as to you."

"""Not this part of it," he answered; " this place belongs to me."

""" Very well,"I agreed, for I did not want to stand there bandying words with him, and a sudden darkness seemed to be falling around. "It is getting late, and so I'll e'en turn back."

"' He gave a laugh, the like of which never fell on human ear before, and made reply :

""" You can't turn back; of your own free will you have come on my ground, and from it there is no return."

"'I did not speak; I just turned round, and made as fast as I could for the path at the foot of the crag. He did not pass me, yet before I could reach the point I desired he stood barring my progress, with the scornful smile still on his lips, and his gigantic form assuming tremendous proportions in the narrow way.

""" Let me pass," I entreated, " and I will never come here again, never trespass more on your ground."

""" No, you shall not pass."

""" Who are you that takes such power on yourself ?" I asked.

""" Come closer, and I will tell you," he said.

"'I drew a step nearer, and he spoke one word. I had never heard it before, but, by some extraordinary intuition, I knew what it meant. He was the Evil One; the name seemed to be taken up by the echoes, and repeated from rock to rock and crag to crag; the whole air seemed full of that one word; and then a great horror of darkness came about us, only the place where we stood remained light. We occupied a small circle walled round with the thick blackness of night.

""" You must come with me," he said.

"'I refused; and then he threatened me. I implored and entreated and wept; but at last I agreed to do what he wanted if he would promise to let me return. Again he laughed, and said, yes, I should return; and the rocks and trees and mountains, ay, and the very rivers, seemed to take up the answer, and bear it in sobbing whispers away into the darkness.'

"He stopped, and lay back in his chair, shivering like one in an ague fit.

"'Go on,' I repeated again; 'twas but a dream, you know.'

"'Was it?' he murmured mournfully. 'Ah, you have not heard the end of it yet.'

"'Let me hear it, then,' I said. 'What happened afterwards?'

"'The darkness seemed in part to clear away, and we walked side by side across the sward in the tender twilight straight up to the bare black wall of rock. With the hilt of his sword he struck a heavy blow, and the solid rock opened as though it were a door. We passed through, and it closed behind us with a tremendous clang; yes, it closed behind us.' And at that point he fairly broke down, crying and sobbing as I had never seen a man even in the most frightful grief cry and sob before."

The minister paused in his narrative. At that moment there came a most tremendous blast of wind, which shook the windows of the manse, and burst open the hall-door, and caused the candles to flicker and the fire to go roaring up the chimney. It is not too much to say that, what with the uncanny story, and what with the howling storm, we every one felt that creeping sort of uneasiness which so often seems like the touch of something from another world—a hand stretched across the boundary-line of time and eternity, the coldness and mystery of which make the stoutest heart tremble.

"I am telling you this tale," said Mr. Morison, resuming his seat after a brief absence to see that the fastenings of the house were properly attended to, "exactly as I heard it. I am not adding a word or comment of my own, nor, so far as I know, am I omitting any incident, however trivial. You must draw your own deductions from the facts I put before you. I have no explanation to give or theory to propound. Part of that great and terrible region in which he found himself, my friend went on to tell me, he penetrated, compelled by a power he could not resist to see the most awful sights, the most frightful sufferings. There was no form of vice that had not there its representative. As they moved along his companion told him the special sin for which such horrible punishment was being inflicted. Shuddering, and in mortal agony, he was yet unable to withdraw his eyes from the dreadful spectacle; the atmosphere grew more unendurable the sights more and more terrible; the cries, groans, blasphemies, more awful and heart-rending.

"'I can bear no more,' he gasped at last; 'let me go !'

"With a mocking laugh, the Presence beside him answered this appeal; a laugh which was taken up, even by the lost and anguished spirits around.

"'There is no return,' said the pitiless voice.

"'But you promised,' he cried; 'you promised me faithfully.'

"'What are promises here ?' And the words were as the sound of doom.

"Still he prayed and entreated; he fell on his knees, and in his agony spoke words that seemed to cause the purpose of the Evil One to falter.

"'You shall go,' he said, 'on one condition: that you agree to return to me on Wednesday next, or send a substitute.'

"'I could not do that,' said my friend. 'I could not send any fellow-creature here. Better stop myself than do that.'

"'Then stop,' said Satan, with the bitterest contempt; and he was turning away, when the poor distracted soul asked for a minute more ere he made his choice.

"He was in an awful strait: on the one hand, how could he remain himself ? On the other, how doom another to such fearful torments ? Who could he send ? Who would come ? And then suddenly there flashed through his mind the thought of an old man to whom it could not signify much whether he took up his abode in this place a few days sooner or a few days later. He was travelling to it as fast as he knew how; he was the reprobate of the parish; the sinner without hope successive ministers had striven in vain to reclaim from the error of his ways; a man marked and doomed—Sandy the Tinker; Sandy, who was mostly drunk, and always godless; Sandy, who, it was said, believed in nothing, and gloried in his infidelity; Sandy, whose soul really did not signify much. He would send him. Lifting his eyes, he saw those of his tormentor surveying him scornfully.

"'Well, have you made your choice ?' he asked.

"'Yes; I think I can send a substitute,' was the hesitating answer.

"'See you do, then,' was the reply; 'for if you do not, and fail to return yourself, *I shall come for you*. Wednesday, remember, before midnight.' And with these words ringing in his ears he was flung violently through the rock, and found himself in the middle of his bedroom floor, as if he had just been kicked there."

"That is not the end of the story, is it?" asked one of the party, as the minister came to a full stop, and looked earnestly at the fire.

"No," he answered, "it is not the end; but before proceeding I must ask you to bear carefully in mind the circumstances already recounted. Specially remember the date mentioned—*Wednesday next, before midnight.*

"Whatever I thought, and you may think, about my friend's dream, it made the most remarkable impression upon *his* mind. He could not shake off its influence; he passed from one state of nervousness to another. It was in vain I entreated him to exert his common sense, and call all his strength of mind to his assistance. I might as well have spoken to the wind. He implored me not to leave him, and I agreed to remain; indeed, to leave him in his then frame of mind would have been an act of the greatest cruelty. He wanted me also to preach in his place on the Sunday ensuing; but this I flatly refused.

"'If you do not make an effort now,' I said, 'you will never make it. Rouse yourself, get on with your sermon, and if you buckle to work you will soon forget all about that foolish dream.'

"Well, to cut a long story short, the sermon was somehow composed and Sunday came, and my friend, a little better and getting over his fret, walked up into the pulpit to preach. He looked dreadfully ill; but I thought the worst was now over, and that he would go on mending.

"Vain hope! He gave out the text and then looked over the congregation: the first person on whom his eyes lighted was Sandy the Tinker—Sandy, who had never before been known to enter a place of worship of any sort; Sandy, whom he had mentally chosen as his substitute, and who was *due on the following Wednesday*—sitting just below him, quite sober, and comparatively clean, waiting with a great show of attention for the opening words of the sermon.

"With a terrible cry, my friend caught the front of the pulpit, then swayed back and fell down in a fainting fit. He was carried home and a doctor sent for. I said a few words, addressed apparently to the congregation, but really to Sandy, for my heart, somehow, came into my mouth at the sight of him; and then, after I had dismissed the people, I paced slowly back to the manse, almost afraid of what might meet me there.

"Mr. Cawley was not dead; but he was in the most dreadful state of physical exhaustion and mental agitation. It was dreadful to hear him. How could he go himself? How could he send Sandy—poor old Sandy, whose soul, in the sight of God, was just as precious as his own?

"His whole cry was for us to deliver him from the Evil One; to save him from committing a sin which would render him a wretched man for life. He counted the hours and the minutes before he must return to that horrible place.

"'I can't send Sandy,' he would moan. 'I cannot, oh, I cannot save myself at such a price!'

"And then he would cover his face with the bedclothes, only to start up and wildly entreat me not to leave him; to stand between the enemy and himself, to save him, or, if that were impossible, to give him courage to do what was right.

"'If this continues,' said the doctor, 'Wednesday will find him either dead or a raving lunatic.'

"We talked the matter over, the doctor and I, in the gloaming, as we walked to and fro in the meadow behind the manse; and we decided, having to make our choice of two evils, to risk giving him such an opiate as should carry him over the dreaded interval. We knew it was a perilous thing to do with one in his condition, but, as I said before, we could only take the lesser of two evils.

"What we dreaded most was his awaking before the time expired; so I kept watch beside him. He lay like one dead through the whole of Tuesday night and Wednesday, and Wednesday evening. Eight, nine, ten, eleven o'clock came and passed; twelve. 'God be thanked!' I said, as I stooped over him and heard he was breathing quietly.

"'He will do now, I hope,' said the doctor, who had come in just before midnight; 'you will stay with him till he wakes?'

"I promised that I would, and in the beautiful dawn of a summer's morning he opened his eyes and smiled. He had no recollection then of what had occurred; he was as weak as an infant, and when I bade him try to go to sleep again, turned on his pillow and sank to rest once more.

"Worn out with watching, I stepped softly from the room and

passed into the fresh, sweet air. I strolled down to the garden gate, and stood looking at the great mountains and the fair country, and the Deldy wandering like a silver thread through the green fields below.

"All at once my attention was attracted by a group of people coming slowly along the road leading from the hills. I could not at first see that in their midst something was being borne on men's shoulders; but when at last I made this out, I hurried to meet them and learn what was the matter.

"'Has there been an accident ?' I asked, as I drew near.

"They stopped, and one man came towards me.

"'Ay,' he said, 'the warst accident that could befa' him, puir fella'. He's deid.'

"'Who is it ?' I asked, pressing forward; and lifting the cloth they had flung over his face, I saw *Sandy the Tinker*!

"'He had been fou' coming home, I tak' it,' remarked one who stood by; 'puir Sandy, and gaed over the cliff afore he could save himsel'. We found him just on this side of the Witches' Caldron, where there's a bonny strip of green turf, and his cuddy was feeding on the hilltop with the bit cart behind her.'"

There was silence for a minute; then one of the ladies said softly, "Poor Sandy !"

"And what became of Mr. Cawley ?" asked the other.

"He gave up his parish and went abroad as a missionary. He is still living."

"What a most extraordinary story !" I remarked.

"Yes *I* think so," said the minister. "If you like to go round to Dendeldy to-morrow, my son, who now occupies the manse, would show you the scene of the occurrence."

The next day we all stood looking at the "bonny strip of green," at the frowning cliffs, and at the Deldy, swollen by recent rains, rushing on its way.

The youngest of the party went up to the rock, and knocked upon it loudly with his cane.

"Oh, don't do that, pray !" cried both the ladies nervously; the spirit of the weird story still brooded over us.

"What do you think of the coincidence, Jack ?" I inquired of my friend, as we talked apart from the others.

"Ask me when we get back to Fleet Street," he answered.

FOREWARNED, FOREARMED

THE story I am about to tell is not a chapter out of my own life. The incidents which go to furnish it were enacted years before I was born; the performers in it died forty years ago, and have left nor son nor heir to inherit the memory.

I question whether the man live (the woman may, seeing women are more enduring than men) who could identify the names of the persons concerning whom I shall have hereafter to speak, but the facts happened, nevertheless.

Many a time I have heard them rehearsed, many a night I have sat on the hearthrug fascinated, listening to how Mr. Dwarris dreamt a dream, and many a night I have passed through the folding-doors that led from the outer to the lesser hall, and walked to bed along the corridors thinking tremblingly of the face which continually reappeared—of the journey in the coach and the post-chaise—all the particulars of which I purpose in due time to recount. Further, it is in my memory, that I was wont to place a pillow against my back in the night season, lest some vague enemy should enter my room and strike me under the fifth rib; and I went through much anguish when the Storm King was abroad, fancying I heard stealthy footsteps in the long gallery, and the sound of another persons' breathing in the room beside my own.

But in spite of this, Mr. Dwarris' dream was one of the awful delights of my childhood; and when strangers gathered around the social hearth, and the conversation turned upon supernatural appearances, as it often did in those remote days in lonely country houses, it was always with a thrill of pleasure that I greeted the opening passages of this, the only inexplicable yet true story we possessed.

It was the fact of this possession, perhaps, which made the tale dear to me—other stories belonged to other people; it was their friends or their relatives who had seen ghosts, and been honoured with warnings, but Mr. Dwarris' dream was our property.

We owned it as we owned the old ash tree that grew on the lawn. Though Mr. Dwarris was dead and gone, though at the age of three-score years and ten he had departed from a world which had used him

very kindly, and which he had enjoyed thoroughly, to another world
that he only knew anything of by hearsay, that in fact he only believed
in after the vague gentlemanly sceptical fashion which was considered
the correct thing about the beginning of this century, still he had been
a friend of our quiet and non-illustrious family.

In our primitive society he had been considered a man of fashion, a
person whose opinions might safely be repeated, whose decisions
were not to be lightly contradicted. He was kind enough in the days
when postage was very high (would those days could come back
again) to write long letters to his good friends who lived far away
from Court, and craved for political and fashionable gossip—long
letters filled with scraps of news and morsels of scandal, which furnished topics of conversation for many days and weeks, and made
pleasant little breaks in the monotony of that country existence.

By my parents, and by the chosen friends who were invited to dinner
when he honoured our poor house with his presence, he was looked up
to as a learned and travelled man of the world.

He had read everything at a time when people did not read much as
is the case at present. He had not merely made the grand tour, but he
had wintered frequently abroad, and the names of princesses, duchesses
and counts flowed as glibly off his tongue as those of the vicar and
family doctor from the lips of less fortunate mortals.

The best china was produced, and the children kept well out of the
way while he remained in the house.

The accessories of his toilette table were a fearful mystery to our
servants, and the plan he had of leaving his vails under his bolster or
the soap dish, a more inscrutable mystery still.

He did not smoke, and though that was a time when the reputation
of hard drinking carried with it no stigma—quite the reverse indeed—
he was temperate to a degree. While not utterly insensible to the charms
of female beauty, he regarded the sex rather as a critical than a devoted
admirer, and he was wont to consider any unusually handsome women
as practically thrown away on our society.

He used to talk much of the "West End," and, to sum up the matter,
he spoke as one having authority.

Looking back at his pretensions from a point of observation which
has not been attained without a considerable amount of acquaintance,
pleasant and otherwise, with men of the same rank in life and standing

in society, I am inclined to think that Mr. Dwarris was, to a certain extent, a humbug; that he was not such a great man as our neighbours imagined, and that the style in which he lived at home was much less luxurious than that in which my parents considered it necessary to indulge when he honoured us with a visit.

Further, I believe the time he spent with us, instead of proving irksome and uncongenial to his superior mind, were periods of the most thorough enjoyment. Looking over his letters—which still remain duly labeled and tied up—I can see the natural man breaking through the conventional. I can perceive how happy a change it was for him to leave a life passed amongst people, richer, better born, cleverer, more fashionable than himself, in order to stay with friends who looked up to him, and believed in their simplicity it was an honour to receive so great a man.

I understand that he had no genius, that he had little talent, that he loved the world and the high places thereof, that he had no passion for anything whether in nature or art, but that he had acquired a superficial knowledge of most subjects, and that he affected a fondness for painting, music, sculpture, literature, because he considered such fondness the mark of a refined mind, and because the men and the women with whom he associated were content to think so too.

But when he recalls with words of pleasure the journey he and my father made through the wilds of Connemara, when he speaks with tenderest affection of his old friend Woodville—(my maternal grand-father's name was Woodville)—when he sends a word of kindly remembrance to each of the servants, who have been always happy to see, and wait upon him, I feel that the gloss and the pretension of learning were but superficial, that the man had really a heart, which, under auspices, would have rendered him a more useful and beloved member of society, instead of an individual in whose acquaintance we merely felt a pride, who was, as I have before said, one of our cherished possessions.

He was never married; he had no near relatives so far as we ever knew, and he lived all alone in a large house in a large English town, which, for sufficient reasons, I shall call Callersfield.

In his early youth he had been engaged in business, but the death of a distant relative leaving him independent of his own exertions, he severed all connection with trade, and went abroad to study whatever may be, in foreign parts, analogous to "Shakespeare and the musical glasses" in England.

To the end of his life—long after travelling became a much easier and safer matter than it was towards the close of the last century—he retained his fondness for continental wanderings, and my mother's cabinets and my father's hot-houses bore ample testimony to the length of his journeys and the strength of his friendship. Seeds of rare plants, and bulbs from almost every country in Europe, found their way to our remote home, whilst curiosities of all kinds were sent with the best wishes of "an old friend," to swell that useless olio of oddities that were at once the wonder and admiration of my juvenile imagination.

But at length all these good gifts came to an end. No more lava snuff-boxes and Pompeian vases; no more corals, or fans, or cameos, or inlaid boxes; no more gorgeous lilies or rare exotics; for news arrived one morning that the donor had started on his last journey, and gone to the land whence no presents can be delivered by coach, railway, or parcels company, to assuage the grief of bereaved relatives. He was dead, and in due time there arrived at our house two of the most singular articles (as the matter appears to me now), that were ever forwarded without accessories of any kind to set them off, to people who had really been on terms of closest intimacy with the deceased.

One was a plaster bust of Mr. Dwarris, the other a lithograph likeness of the same gentleman.

The intrinsic value of the two might in those days have been five shillings, but then, as his heirs delicately put it, they knew my parents would value these mementoes of their lamented friend far beyond any actual worth which they might possess.

Where, when the old home was broken up, and the household goods scattered, that bust vanished I can form no idea, but the lithograph is still in my possession; and as I look at it I feel my mother's statement to have been utterly true, namely, that Mr. Dwarris was not a man either to be deluded by his imagination, or to tell a falsehood wittingly.

Perhaps in the next world some explanation may have been vouchsafed to him about his dream, but on this side the grave he always professed himself unable to give the slightest solution of it.

"I am not a man," he was wont to declare, "inclined to believe in the supernatural;" and indeed he was not, whether in nature or religion.

To be sure he was secretly disposed to credit that great superstition which many persons now openly profess—of a universe without a Creator, of a future without a Redeemer—but still this form of credulity proceeds rather from an imperfect development of the reason than from a disordered state of the imagination.

In the ordinary acceptation of the word he was not superstitious. He was hard headed and he was cold-blooded—essentially a man to be trusted implicitly when he said such and such a thing had happened within his own experience.

"I never could account for it in any way," he declared—"and if it had chanced to another person, I should have believed he had made some mistake in the matter. For this reason, I have always felt shy of repeating my dream—but I do not mind telling it to you to-night."

And then he proceeded to relate the story which thenceforth became our property—the most enduring gift he ever gave us.

This is the tale he told while the wind was howling outside, and the snow falling upon the earth, and the woodfire crackling and leaping as a fit accompaniment.

I did not hear him recite his adventures—but I have often sat and listened while the story was rehearsed to fresh auditors—almost in his own words.

"The first time that I went abroad," he began, "I made acquaintance with Sir Harry Hareleigh. How our acquaintance commenced is of no consequence—but it soon ripened into a close friendship, which was only broken by his death. His father and my father had been early friends also—but worldly reverses had long separated our family from that of the Hareleighs, and it was only by the merest chance I resumed my connection with it. Sir Harry was the youngest son—but his brothers having all died before their father, he came into his title early—though he did not at the same time succeed to any very great amount of property.

"A large but unentailed estate, owned by a bachelor Ralph Hareleigh, would, people imagined, ultimately come into his hands—but Sir Harry himself considered this doubtful—for there was a cousin of his own who longed for the broad acres, and spent much of his time at Dulling Court, which was the name of Mr. Ralph Hareleigh's seat.

"'No one,' Sir Harry declared, 'should ever be able to say he sat watching for dead men's shoes;' and so he spent all his time abroad—

visiting picture galleries and studios, and mixing much among artists and patrons and lovers of art.

"It seemed to me in those days that he was wasting his existence, and that a man of his rank and abilities ought to have remained more in his own country, and associated more with those of his own standing in society—but whenever I ventured to hint this to him, he only answered that—

"'England had been a cruel stepdame to him, and that of his own free-will he would never spend a day in his native country again.'

"He had a villa near Florence, where he resided when he was not wandering over the earth; and there I spent many happy weeks in his society—before returning, as it was needful and expedient for me to do, to Callersfield.

"We had been separated for some years—during the whole of the time we corresponded regularly, when one night I dreamt a dream which is as vivid to me now as it was a quarter of a century ago.

"I know I was well in health at the time—that I was undisturbed in my mind—that especially my thoughts had not been straying after Sir Harry Hareleigh. I had heard from him about a month previously, and he said in his letter that he purposed wintering in Vienna, where it would be a great pleasure if I could join him. I had replied that I could not join him at Vienna, but that it was not impossible we might meet the following spring if he felt disposed to spend a couple of months with me in Spain, a country which I then desired to visit.

"I was, therefore, not expecting to see him for half a year, at all events—and had certainly no thought of his arrival in England, and yet when I went to bed on the night in question, this was what happened to me.

"I dreamt that towards the close of an autumn day I was sitting reading by the window of my library—you remember how my house is situated at the corner of two streets, and that there is a slight hill from the town up to it—you may recollect, also, perhaps, that the windows of my library face on this ascent, while the hall door opens into King Charles Street. Well, I was sitting reading as I have said, with the light growing dimmer and dimmer, and the printed characters getting more and more indistinct, when all at once my attention was aroused by the appearance of a hackney coach driven furiously up Martyr Hill.

"The man was flogging his horses unmercifully, and they cantered up the ascent at a wonderful pace. I rose and watched the vehicle turn the corner of King Charles Street, when of course it disappeared from my observation. I remained, however, standing at the window looking out on the gathering twilight, and but little curious concerning a loud double knock which resounded through the house. Next moment, however, the library door opened, and in walked Sir Harry Hareleigh.

"'I want you to do me a favour, Dwarris,' were almost his first words. 'Can you—will you—come with me on a journey? Your man will just have time to pack a few clothes up for you, and then we shall be able to catch the coach that leaves "The Maypole" at seven. I have this moment arrived from Italy, and will explain everything as we go along. Can you give me a crust of bread and a glass of wine?'

"I rang the bell and ordered in refreshments. While he was hastily swallowing his food, Sir Harry told me that Ralph Hareleigh was dead and had left him every acre of land he owned and every guinea of money he possessed. 'He heard, it appears,' added Sir Harry, 'that my cousin George had raised large sums of money on the strength of certainly being his heir, so he cut him out and left the whole to me, saddled with only one condition, namely, that I should marry within six months from the date of his death.'

"'And when do the six months expire?' I inquired.

"'There's the pull!' he answered. 'By some accident my lawyer's first letter never reached me; and if by good fortune it had not occurred to him to send one of his clerks with a second epistle, I should have been done out of my inheritance. There is only a bare month left for me to make all my arrangements.'

"'And where are you going now?' I asked.

"'To Dulling Court,' he returned, 'and we have not a moment to lose if we are to catch the mail.'

"Those were the days in which gentlemen travelled with their pistols ready for use, and you may be sure I did not forget mine. My *valise* was carried out to the hackney carriage; Sir Harry and I stepped into the vehicle, and before I had time to wonder at my friend's sudden appearance, we were at the 'Maypole,' and taking our places as inside passengers to Warweald, from whence our route lay across country to Dulling.

"When we had settled ourselves comfortably, put on our travelling-caps, and buttoned our great coats up to our throats, I looked out to see whether any other passengers were coming.

"As I did so, my eyes fell on a man who stood back a little from the crowd that always surrounds a coach at starting time, and there was something about him which riveted my attention, though I could not have told why.

"He was an evil-looking man, dressed in decent but very common clothes, and he stood leaning up against the wall of the 'Maypole,' and, as it chanced, directly under the light of an oil-lamp.

"It was this circumstance which enabled me to get so good a view of his face, of his black hair and reddish whiskers, of his restless brown eyes, and dark complexion.

"The contrast between his complexion and his whiskers I remember struck me forcibly, as did also a certain discrepancy between his dress and his appearance.

"He did not stand exactly as a man of his apparent class would stand, and I noticed that he bit his nails nervously, a luxury I never observed an ordinary working man indulge in.

"Further, he stared not at what was going on, but persistently at the coach window until he discovered my scrutiny, when he turned on his heel and walked away down the street.

"Somehow I seemed to breathe more freely when once he was gone; but as the coach soon started, I forgot all about him, until two or three stages after, happening to get out of the coach for a glass of brandy, I beheld the same man standing at a little distance and watching the coach as before.

"My first impulse was to go up and speak to him, but a moment's reflection showed me that I should only place myself in a ridiculous position by doing so. No doubt the man was merely a passenger like ourselves, and if he chose to lean up against the wall of the inn while the horses were being changed, it was clearly no business of mine.

"At the next stage, however, when I looked out for him he was nowhere to be seen, and I thought no more of the matter till on arriving at Warweald I chanced to put my head out of the window furthest from the inn, when by the light of one of the coach lamps I saw my gentleman drop down from the roof and walk away into the darkness.

We went into the inn parlour whilst post horses were put to, and then I told Sir Harry what I had witnessed.

"'Very likely a Bow Street runner,' he said, 'keeping some poor wretch well in sight. I should not wonder if the old gentleman who snored so persistently for the last twenty miles be a hardened criminal on whom your friend will clap handcuffs, the moment he gets the warrant to arrest him.'

"The explanation seemed so reasonable that I marvelled it had not occurred to me before, and then I suppose I went off into deeper sleep, for I have a vague recollection of dreaming afterwards, how we travelled miles and miles in a post chaise, how we ploughed through heavy country lanes, how we passed through dark plantations, and how we stopped at last in front of an old-fashioned way-side house.

"It was a fine night when we arrived there, but the wind was high and drifted black clouds over the moon's face. We alighted at this point and I remember how the place was engraved on my memory.

"It was an old inn, with a large deep door-way, two high gables, and small latticed windows. There were tall trees in front of it, and from one of these the sign 'A Bleeding Heart,' depended, rocking moanfully to and fro in the breeze. There were only a few leaves left on the branches, but the wind caught up those which lay scattered on the ground, and whirled them through the air. Not a soul appeared as our chaise drove up to the door. The postilion, however, applied the butt end of his whip with such vigour to the door that a head was soon thrust from one of the windows, and a gruff voice demanded, 'what the devil we wanted.'

"Just as he was about to answer, moved by some sudden impulse, I turned suddenly round and beheld stealing away in the shadow, my friend with the dark complexion and the red whiskers.

"At this juncture I awoke—always at this juncture I awoke, for I dreamt the same dream over and over again, till I really grew afraid of going to bed at night.

"I used to wake up bathed in perspiration with a horror on me such as I have never felt in my waking moments. I could not get the man's face out of my mind—waking I was constantly thinking of it, sleeping I reproduced it in my dreams—and at length I became so nervous that I had determined to seek relief either in medical advice or change of scene—when one evening in the late autumn as I sat reading in my library—the identical coach I had beheld in my dream drove up Martyr Hill, and next moment Sir Harry and I grasped hands.

"Though I had the dream in my mind all the while, something withheld me from mentioning it to him. We had always laughed at warnings and such things as old woman's tales, and so I let him talk on just as he had talked to me in my dream, and he ate and drank, and we went down together to the 'Maypole' and took our seats in the coach.

"You may be sure I looked well up the street, and down the street, to see if there were any sign of my friend with the whiskers, but not a trace of him could I discern. Somewhat relieved by this I leaned back in my corner, and really in the interest of seeing and talking to my old companion again, I forgot all about my dream, until the arrival of another passenger caused me to shift my position a little, when I glanced out again, and there standing under the lamp—with his restless brown eyes, his dark complexion and his red whiskers—stood the person whom I had never before seen in the flesh, biting his nails industriously.

"'Just look out for a moment, Hareleigh,' I said drawing back from the window 'there is a man standing under the lamp I want you to notice.'

"'I see no man,' answered Sir Harry, and when I looked out again neither did I.

"As in my dream, however, I had beheld the stranger at different stages of our journey, so I beheld him at different stages with my waking eyes.

"Standing at the hotel at Warweald, I spoke seriously to my companion concerning the mysterious passenger, when to my amazement he repeated the same words I had heard in my dream.

"'Now, Hareleigh,' I said, 'this is getting past a joke. You know I am not superstitious, or given to take fancies, and yet I tell you I have had a warning about that man and I feel confident he means mischief,' and then I told Sir Harry my dream, and described to him the inn upon our arrival at which I had invariably awakened.

"'There is no such inn anywhere on the road between here and Dulling,' he answered after a moment's silence, and then he turned towards the fire again and knit his brow, and there ensued a disagreeable pause.

"'If I have offended you,' I remarked at last.

"'My dear friend,' he replied in an earnest voice, 'I am not offended, I am only alarmed. When I left the continent I hoped that I had put the sea between myself and my enemy; but what you say makes me fear that I am being dogged to my death. I have narrowly escaped assassination twice within the last three months, and I know every movement of mine has been watched, that there have been spies upon me. Even on board the vessel by which I returned to England I was nearly pitched overboard; at the time I regarded it as an accident, but if your dream be true, that was, as this is, the result of a premeditated plan.'

"'Then let us remain here for the night,' I urged.

"'Impossible,' he answered. 'I must reach Dulling before to-morrow morning, or otherwise the only woman I ever wanted to marry or ever shall marry will have dropped out of my life a second time.'

"'And she,' I suggested.

"'Is the widow of Lord Warweald, and she leaves for India to-morrow with her brother the Honourable John Moffat.'

"'Then,' said I, 'you can have no difficulty in fulfilling the conditions of Mr. Ralph Hareleigh's will.'

"'Not if she agree to marry me,' he answered.

"At that moment the chaise was announced, and we took our places in it.

"Over the country roads, along lonely lanes, we drove almost in silence.

"Somehow Sir Harry's statement and the memory of my own dream made me feel anxious and nervous. Who could this unknown enemy be? had my friend played fast and loose with some lovely Italian, and was this her nearest of kin dogging him to his death?

"Most certainly the man who stood under the lamp at Callersfield had no foreign blood in his veins; spite of his complexion, he was English, in figure, habit and appearance.

"Could there be any dark secret in Sir Harry's life? I then asked myself. His reluctance to visit England, his reserve about the earlier part of his existence, almost inclined me to belief; and I was just about settling in my own mind what this secret might probably be, when the postilion suddenly pulled up, and after an examination of his horses' feet informed us that one of them had cast a shoe, and that it was impossible the creature could travel the nine miles which still intervened between us and the next stage.

"'There is an inn, however,' added the boy, 'about a mile from here on the road to Rindon; and if you could make shift to stop there for the night, I will undertake to have you at Dulling Court by nine o'clock in the morning.'

"Hearing this, I looked in the moonlight at my friend, and Sir Harry looked hard at me.

"'It is to happen so,' he said, and flinging himself back in the chaise, fell into a fit of moody musing.

"Meanwhile, as the horses proceeded slowly along, I looked out of the window, and once I could have sworn I saw the shadow of a man flung across the road.

"When I opened the door, however, and jumped out, I could see nothing except the dark trees almost meeting overhead, and the denser undergrowth lying to right and left.

"It was a fine night when we arrived at our destination, just such a night as I had dreamed was to come—moonlight, but with heavy black clouds drifting across the sky.

"There was the inn, there swung the sign, the dead leaves swirled about us as we stood waiting while the post-boy hammered for admittance.

"It all came about as I had dreamt, save that I did *not* see waking as I had done in my sleep a stealing figure creeping away in the shadow of the house.

"I saw the figure afterwards, but not then.

"We ate in the house, but we did not drink—we made a feint of doing so; but we really poured away the liquor upon the hot ashes that lay underneath the hastily replenished fire, though I believe this caution to have been unnecessary.

"We selected our bed chambers, Sir Harry choosing one which looked out on what our host called the Wilderness, and I selecting another that commanded a view of the garden.

"There were no locks or bolts to the doors, but we determined to pull up such furniture as the rooms afforded, and erect barricades for our protection.

"I wanted to remain in the same apartment with my friend, but he would not hear of such an arrangement.

"'We shall only delay the end,' he said stubbornly, in the answer to my entreaties, 'and I have an ounce of lead ready for any one who tries to meddle with me.' So we bade each other good night, and separated.

"I had not the slightest intention of going to bed, so I sat and read my favourite poet till, overpowered by fatigue, I dropped asleep in my chair.

"When I awoke it was with a start; the candle had burnt out, and the moonlight was streaming through the white blind into the room.

"Was it fancy, or did I hear some one actually try my door? I held my breath, and then I knew it was no fancy, for the latch snicked in the lock, then stealthy footsteps crept along the passage and down the stairs.

"In a moment my resolution was taken. Opening my window, I crept on to the sill, and closing the casement after me, dropped into the garden.

"Keeping close against the wall, I crept to the corner of the house, where I concealed myself behind an *arbor vitæ*.

"A minute afterwards the man I was watching for came round the opposite corner, and stood for a second looking at the window of Sir Harry's room. There was a pear tree trained against the wall on this side of the house, and up it he climbed with more agility than I should have expected from his appearance.

"I had my pistol in my hand, and felt inclined to wing him while he was fighting with the crazy fastening, and trying to open the window without noise, but I refrained. I wanted to see the play out; I desired to see his game, and so the moment he was in the room I climbed the pear tree also, and raising my eyes just above the sill, and lifting the blind about an inch, looked in.

"Like myself, Hareleigh had not undressed, but he lay stretched on the bed with his right hand under his head, and his left flung across his body.

"He was fast asleep, his pistols lay on a chair beside him, and I could see he had so far followed my advice as to have dragged an ancient secretaire across the door.

"By the moonlight I got a good view now of the individual who had for so long a time troubled my dreams. As he stealthily moved the pistols, he turned his profile a little towards the window, and then I knew what I already suspected, viz., that the man who had travelled with us from Callersfield was identical with the man who now stood beside Sir Harry meaning to murder him.

"It was the dream in that hour which seemed the reality, and the reality the dream.

"For an instant he stooped over my friend, and then I saw him raise his hand to strike, but the same moment I took deliberate aim, and before the blow could fall, fired and shot him in the right shoulder.

"There was a shriek and an imprecation, a rush to the window, where we met, he trying to get out, I striving to get in.

"I grappled with him, but having no secure foothold the impetus of his body was too much for me, and we both fell to the ground together. The force of the fall stunned me, I suppose, for I remember nothing of what followed till I found myself lying on a sofa in the inn, with Hareleigh sitting beside me.

"Don't talk! for God's sake don't talk!' he entreated. 'We shall be out of this in five minute's time if you think you can bear the shaking. I have made the landlord lend us another horse, and we shall be at Dulling in two hours' time. There you shall tell me all about it.'

"But there I never told him all about it. Before we reached our next stage, I was far too ill to travel further, and for weeks I lay between life and death at the Green Man and Still, Aldney.

"When I was strong enough to sit up with him, Harry and Lady Hareleigh came over from Dulling to see me, but it was months before I could bear to speak of the events of that night, and though I never dreamed my dream again, it left its traces on me for life.

"Till the day of his death, however, Sir Harry always regarded me as his preserver, and the warmest welcome to Dulling Court was given by his wife to one whom she honoured by calling her dearest friend.

"When Sir Harry died, he left me joint guardian with Lady Hareleigh of his children. So carefully worded a will, I never read—in the event of the death of his children without issue, he bequeathed Dulling Court to various charitable institutions.

"'A most singular disposition of his property,' I remarked to his lawyer.

"'Depend upon it, my dear sir, he had his reasons,' that individual replied.

"'And those——' I suggested.

"'I must regard as strictly private and confidential.'

"The most singular part of my narrative has yet to come," Mr. Dwarris continued after a pause.

"Many years after Sir Harry's death, it chanced I arrived at a friend's house on the evening before the nomination day of an election, which it was expected would be hotly contested.

"'Mr. Blair's wealth of course gives him a great advantage,' sighed my hostess, 'and we all do dislike him so cordially—I would give anything to see him lose.'

"Accustomed to such thoroughly feminine and logical sentiments, I attached little importance to the lady's remarks, and with only a very slight feeling of interest in the matter, next morning accompanied my friend to the county town where the nomination was to take place.

"We were rather late in starting, and before our arrival Mr. Blair had commenced his harangue to the crowd.

"He was talking loudly and gesticulating violently with his *left* hand when I first caught sight of him. He was telling the free and independent electors that they knew who he was, what he was, and why he supported such and such a political party.

"At intervals he was interrupted by 'cheers and hisses,' but at the end of one of his most brilliant perorations, I who had been elbowing my way through the crowd, shouted out at the top of my voice—

"'How about the man you tried to murder at "The Bleeding Heart"?'"

"For a moment there was a dead silence, then the mob took up my cry—

"'How about the man you tried to murder at "The Bleeding Heart"?'"

"I saw him look round as if a ghost had spoken, then he fell suddenly back, and his friends carried him off the platform.

"My hostess had her wish, for his opponent walked over the course, and a few weeks afterwards I read in the papers—

"'Died—At Hollingford Hall, in his forty-sixth year, George Hareleigh Blair, Esq., nephew of the late Ralph Hareleigh, Esq., of Dulling Court.'

"'He married a Miss Blair, I presume,' I said to my host.

"'Yes, for her money,' was the reply, 'she had two hundred thousand pounds.'

"So the mystery of 'The Bleeding Heart' was cleared up at last; but on this side the grave I do not expect to understand how I chanced to dream of a man I had never seen—of places I had never visited—of events of which I was not then cognizant—of conversations which had then still to take place."

HERTFORD O'DONNELL'S
WARNING

MANY a year ago, before chloroform was thought of, there lived in an old rambling house in Gerrard Street, Soho, a young Irishman called Hertford O'Donnell.

After Hertford O'Donnell he was entitled to write M.R.C.S., for he had studied hard to gain this distinction, and the elder surgeons at Guy's (his hospital) considered him, in their secret hearts, one of the most rising operators of the day.

Having said chloroform was unknown at the time this story opens, it will strike my readers that, if Hertford O'Donnell were a rising and successful operator in those days, of necessity he combined within himself a larger number of striking qualities than are by any means necessary to form a successful operator in these.

There was more than mere hand skill, more than even thorough knowledge of his profession, needful for the man who, dealing with conscious subjects, essayed to rid them of some of the diseases to which flesh is heir. There was greater courage required in the manipulator of old than is altogether essential now. Then, as now, a thorough mastery of his instruments—a steady hand—a keen eye—a quick dexterity, were indispensable to a good operator; but, added to all these things, there were formerly required a pulse which knew no quickening—a mental strength which never faltered—a ready power of adaptation in unexpected circumstances—fertility of resource in difficult cases, and a brave front under all emergencies.

If I refrain from adding that a hard as well as a courageous heart was an important item in the programme, it is only out of deference to general opinion, which, amongst other delusions, clings to the belief that courage and hardness are antagonistic qualities.

Hertford O'Donnell, however, was hard as steel. He understood his work, and he did it thoroughly; but he cared no more for quivering nerves and contracting muscles, for screams of agony, for faces white with pain, and teeth clenched in the extremity of anguish, than he did for the stony countenance of the dead, which sometimes in the dissecting room appalled younger and less experienced men.

He had no sentiment, and he had no sympathy. The human body was to him an ingenious piece of mechanism, which it was at once a pleasure and a profit to understand. Precisely as Brunel loved the Thames Tunnel, or any other singular engineering feat, so O'Donnell loved a patient on whom he operated successfully, more especially if the ailment possessed by the patient were of a rare and difficult character.

And for this reason he was much liked by all who came under his hands, for patients are apt to mistake a surgeon's interest in their cases for interest in themselves; and it was gratifying to John Dicks, plasterer, and Timothy Regan, labourer, to be the happy possessors of remarkable diseases, which produced a cordial understanding between them and the handsome Irishman.

If he were hard and cool at the moment of hewing them to pieces, that was all forgotten, or remembered only as a virtue, when, after being discharged from hospital like soldiers who have served in a severe campaign, they met Mr. O'Donnell in the street, and were accosted by that rising individual, just as though he considered himself nobody.

He had a royal memory, this stranger in a strange land, both for faces and cases; and, like the rest of his countrymen, he never felt it beneath his dignity to talk cordially to corduroy and fustian.

In London, as at Calgillan, he never held back his tongue from speaking a cheery or a kindly word. His manners were pliable enough, if his heart were not; and the porters, and the patients, and the nurses, and the students at Guy's all were pleased to see Hertford O'Donnell.

Rain, hail, sunshine, it was all the same; there was a life, and a brightness about the man which communicated itself to those with whom he came in contact. Let the mud out in Smithfield be a foot deep, or the London fog thick as pea-soup, Mr. O'Donnell never lost his temper, never uttered a surly reply to the gatekeeper's salutation, but spoke out blithely and cheerfully to his pupils and his patients, to the sick and to the well, to those below and to those above him.

And yet, spite of all these good qualities—spite of his handsome face, his fine figure, his easy address and his unquestionable skill as an operator, the dons, who acknowledged his talent, shook their heads gravely when two or three of them, in private and solemn conclave, talked confidentially of their younger brother.

If there were many things in his favour, there were more in his disfavour. He was Irish—not merely by the accident of birth, which might have been forgiven, since a man cannot be held accountable for such caprices of Nature, but by every other accident and design which is objectionable to the orthodox and respectable and representative English mind.

In speech, appearance, manner, habits, modes of expression, habits of life, Hertford O'Donnell was Irish. To the core of his heart he loved the island which he, nevertheless, declared he never meant to revisit; and amongst the English he moved, to all intents and purposes, a foreigner who was resolved, so said the great prophets at Guy's, to go to destruction as fast as he could and let no man hinder him.

"He means to go the whole length of his tether," observed one of the ancient wiseacres to another; which speech implied a conviction that Hertford O'Donnell, having sold himself to the Evil One, had determined to dive the full length of his rope into wickedness before being pulled to the shore where even wickedness is negative—where there are no mad carouses, no wild, sinful excitement, nothing but impotent wailing and gnashing of teeth.

A reckless, graceless, clever, wicked devil—going to his natural home as fast as in London a man can possibly progress thither: this was the opinion his superiors held of the man who lived all alone with a housekeeper and her husband (who acted as butler) in his big house near Soho.

Gerrard Street was not then an utterly shady and forgotten locality: carriage patients found their way to the rising young surgeon—some great personages thought it not beneath them to fee an individual whose consulting rooms were situated on what was even then the wrong side of Regent Street. He was making money; and he was spending it; he was over head and ears in debt—useless, vulgar debt—senselessly contracted, never bravely faced. He had lived at an awful pace ever since he came to London, at a pace which only a man who hopes and expects to die young can ever travel.

Life! what good was it? Death! was he a child, or a woman, or a coward, to be afraid of that hereafter? God knew all about the trifle which had upset his coach better than the dons at Guy's; and he did not dread facing his Maker, and giving an account to Him, even of the disreputable existence he had led since he came to London.

Hertford O'Donnell knew the world pretty well, and the ways thereof were to him as roads often traversed; therefore, when he said that at the day of judgment he felt certain he should come off better than many of those who censured him, it may be assumed that, although his views of post-mortem punishment were vague, unsatisfactory, and infidel, still his information as to the peccadilloes of his neighbours was such as consoled himself.

And yet, living all alone in the old house near Soho Square, grave thoughts would intrude frequently into the surgeon's mind—thoughts which were, so to say, italicized by peremptory letters, and still more peremptory visits, from people who wanted money.

Although he had many acquaintances, he had no single friend, and accordingly these thoughts were received and brooded over in solitude, in those hours when, after returning from dinner or supper, or congenial carouse, he sat in his dreary room smoking his pipe and considering means and ways, chances and certainties.

In good truth he had started in London with some vague idea that as his life in it would not be of long continuance, the pace at which he elected to travel could be of little consequence; but the years since his first entry into the metropolis were now piled one on the top of another, his youth was behind him, his chances of longevity, spite of the way he had striven to injure his constitution, quite as good as ever. He had come to that time in existence, to that narrow strip of table land whence the ascent of youth and the descent of age are equally discernible— when, simply because he has lived for so many years, it strikes a man as possible he may have to live for just as many more, with the ability for hard work gone, with the boon companions scattered abroad, with the capacity for enjoying convivial meetings a mere memory, with small means, perhaps, with no bright hopes, with the pomp and the equipage, and the fairy carriages, and the glamour which youth flings over earthly objects, faded away like the pageant of yesterday, while the dreary ceremony of living has to be gone through to-day and to-morrow and the morrow after, as though the gay cavalcade and the martial music, and the glittering helmets and the prancing steeds were still accompanying the wayfarer to his journey's end.

Ah! my friends, there comes a moment when we must all leave the coach with its four bright bays, its pleasant outside freight, its cheery company, its guard who blows the horn so merrily through villages and along lonely country roads.

Long before we reach that final stage, where the black business claims us for its own especial property, we have to bid good-bye to all easy thoughtless journeying, and betake ourselves, with what zest we will, to traversing the common of Reality. There is no royal road across it that ever I heard of. From the king on his throne to the labourer who vaguely imagines what manner of being a king is, we have all to tramp across that desert at one period of our lives, at all events, and that period usually is when, as I have said, a man starts to find the hopes and the strength and the buoyancy of youth left behind, while years and years of life lie stretching out before him.

Even supposing a man's spring-time to have been a cold and un-genial one, with bitter easterly winds and nipping frosts, biting the buds and retarding the blossom, still it was spring for all that—spring, with the young green leaves sprouting forth, with the flowers unfolding tenderly, with the songs of birds and the rush of waters, with the summer before and the autumn afar off, and winter remote as death and eternity; but when once the trees have donned their summer foliage, when the pure white blossoms have disappeared, and a gorgeous red and orange, and purple blaze of many-coloured flowers fills the gardens; then, if there comes a wet, dreary day, the idea of autumn and winter is not so difficult to realise. When once twelve o'clock is reached, the evening and night become facts, not possibilities; and it was of the afternoon and the evening and the night, Hertford O'Donnell sat thinking on the Christmas Eve when I crave permission to introduce him to my readers.

A good-looking man, ladies considered him. A tall, dark-complex-ioned, black-haired, straight-limbed, deeply, divinely blue-eyed fellow, with a soft voice, with a pleasant brogue, who had ridden like a Centaur over the loose stone walls in Connemara, who had danced all night at the Dublin balls, who had walked over the Bennebeola mountains, gun in hand, day after day without weariness: who had led a mad, wild life while "studying for a doctor"—as the Irish phrase goes—in Dublin, and who, after the death of his eldest brother left him free to return to Calgillan and pursue the usual utterly useless, utterly purposeless, utterly pleasant life of an Irish gentleman possessed of health, birth, and expectations, suddenly kicked over the paternal traces, bade adieu to Calgillan Castle and the blandishments of a certain beautiful Miss Clifden, beloved of his mother, and laid out to be his wife, walked down the avenue without even so much company as a gossoon to carry his carpet-bag, shook the dust from his feet at the lodge-gates, and took his seat on the coach, never once looking back at Calgillan, where his favourite mare was standing in the stable, his greyhounds chasing one another round the home paddock, his gun at half-cock in his dressing-room, and his fishing-tackle all in order and ready for use.

He had not kissed his mother nor asked for his father's blessing; he left Miss Clifden arrayed in her bran-new-riding-habit, without a word of affection or regret; he had spoken no syllable of farewell to any servant about the place; only when the old woman at the lodge bade him good morning and God-blessed his handsome face, he recommended her bitterly to look well at it, for she would never see it more.

Twelve years and a half had passed since then without either Nancy Blake or any other one of the Calgillan people having set eyes on Master Hertford's handsome face. He had kept his vow to himself— he had not written home; he had not been indebted to mother or father for even a tenpenny-piece during the whole of that time; he had lived without God—so far as God ever lets a man live without him— and his own private conviction was that he could get on very well without either. One thing only he felt to be needful—money; money to keep him when the evil days of sickness, or age, or loss of practice came upon him. Though a spendthrift, he was not a simpleton. Around him he saw men, who, having started with fairer prospects than his own, were nevertheless reduced to indigence; and he knew that what had happened to others might happen to himself.

An unlucky cut, slipping on a bit of orange-peel in the street, the merest accident imaginable, is sufficient to change opulence to beggary in the life's programme of an individual whose income depends on eye, on nerve, on hand; and besides the consciousness of this fact, Hertford O'Donnell knew that beyond a certain point in his profession progress was not easy.

It did not depend quite on the strength of his own bow or shield whether he counted his earnings by hundreds or thousands. Work may achieve competence; but mere work cannot, in a profession at all events, compass wealth.

He looked around him, and he perceived that the majority of great men—great and wealthy—had been indebted for their elevation more to the accidents of birth, patronage, connection, or marriage than to personal ability.

Personal ability, no doubt, they possessed; but then, little Jones, who lived in Frith Street, and who could barely keep himself and his wife and family, had ability, too, only he lacked the concomitants of success.

He wanted something or some one to puff him into notoriety—a brother at court—a lord's leg to mend—a rich wife to give him prestige in society; and, lacking this something or some one, he had grown grey-haired and faint-hearted in the service of that world which utterly despises its most obsequious servants.

"Clatter along the streets with a pair of hired horses, snub the middle classes, and drive over the commonalty—that is the way to compass wealth and popularity in England," said Hertford O'Donnell bitterly; and, as the man desired wealth and popularity, he sat before his fire, with a foot on each hob, and a short pipe in his mouth, considering how he might best obtain the means to clatter along the streets in his carriage, and splash plebeians with mud from his wheels like the best.

In Dublin he could, by means of his name and connection, have done well; but then he was not in Dublin, neither did he want to be. The bitterest memories of his life were inseparable from the name of the Green Island, and he had no desire to return to it.

Besides, in Dublin, heiresses are not quite so plentiful as in London; and an heiress, Hertford O'Donnell had decided, would do more for him than years of steady work.

A rich wife could clear him of debt, introduce him to fashionable practice, afford him that measure of social respectability which a medical bachelor invariably lacks; deliver him from the loneliness of Gerrard Street, and the domination of Mr. and Mrs. Coles.

To most men, deliberately bartering away their dependence for money seems so prosaic a business that they strive to gloss it over even to themselves, and to assign every reason for their choice, save that which is really the influencing one.

Not so, however, with Hertford O'Donnell. He sat beside the fire scoffing over his proposed bargain—thinking of the lady's age—her

money-bags—her desirable house in town—her seat in the country—
her snobbishness—her folly.

"It would be a fitting ending," he sneered; "and why I did not
settle the matter to-night passes my comprehension. I am not a fool,
to be frightened with old women's tales; and yet I must have turned
white. I felt I did, and she asked me whether I was ill. And then to
think of my being such an idiot as to ask her if she had heard anything
like a cry, as though she would be likely to hear *that*—she, with her
poor *parvenu* blood, which, I often imagine, must have been mixed
with some of her father's strong pickling vinegar. What the deuce
could I have been dreaming about? I wonder what it really was?" and
Hertford O'Donnell pushed his hair back from his forehead and took
another draught from the too familiar tumbler, which was placed
conveniently on the chimney piece.

"After expressly making up my mind to propose, too!" he mentally
continued. "Could it have been conscience—that myth, which
somebody, who knew nothing of the matter, said 'makes cowards of
us all?' I don't believe in conscience; and even if there be such a thing
capable of being developed by sentiment and cultivation, why should it
trouble me? I have no intention of wronging Miss Janet Price Ingot—
not the least. Honestly and fairly I shall marry her; honestly and fairly
I shall act by her. An old wife is not exactly an ornamental article of
furniture in a man's house; and I do not know that the fact of her being
well gilded makes her look any more ornamental. But she shall have no
cause for complaint; and I will go and dine with her to-morrow and
settle the matter."

Having arrived at which resolution, Mr. O'Donnell arose, kicked
down the fire—burning hollow—with the heel of his boot, knocked
the ashes out of his pipe, emptied his tumbler, and bethought him it
was time to go to bed. He was not in the habit of taking rest so early
as a quarter to twelve o'clock; but he felt unusually weary—tired
mentally and bodily—and lonely beyond all power of expression.

"The fair Janet would be better than this," he said, half aloud; and
then, with a start and a shiver and a blanched face, he turned sharply
round, whilst a low, sobbing, wailing cry echoed mournfully through
the room. No form of words could give an idea of the sound. The
plaintiveness of the Eolian harp—that plaintiveness which so soon
affects and lowers the highest spirits—would have seemed wildly gay

in comparison to the sadness of the cry which seemed floating in the air. As the summer wind comes and goes amongst the trees, so that mournful wail came and went—came and went. It came in a rush of sound, like a gradual crescendo managed by a skilful musician, and it died away like a lingering note, so that the listener could scarcely tell the exact moment when it faded away into silence

I say faded away, for it disappeared as the coast line disappears in the twilight, and there was utter stillness in the apartment.

Then for the first time, Hertford O'Donnell looked at his dog, and, beholding the creature crouched into a corner beside the fireplace, called upon him to come out.

His voice sounded strange, even to himself, and apparently the dog thought so too, for he made no effort to obey the summons.

"Come out, sir," his master repeated, and then the animal came crawling reluctantly forward, with his hair on end, his eyes almost starting from his head, trembling violently, as the surgeon, who caressed him, felt.

"So you heard it, Brian?" he said to the dog. "And so your ears are sharper than hers, old fellow? It's a mighty queer thing to think of, being favoured with a visit from a banshee in Gerrard Street; and as the lady has travelled so far, I only wish I knew whether there is any sort of refreshment she would like to take after her long journey."

He spoke loudly and with a certain mocking defiance, seeming to think the phantom he addressed would reply; but when he stopped at the end of his sentence, no sound came through the stillness. There was utter silence in the room—silence broken only by the falling of the cinders on the hearth, and the breathing of the dog.

"If my visitor would tell me," he proceeded, "for whom this lamentation is being made, whether for myself, or for some member of my illustrious family, I should feel immensely obliged. It seems too much honour for a poor surgeon to have such attention paid him. Good heavens! What is that?" he exclaimed, as a ring, loud and peremptory, woke all the echoes in the house, and brought his housekeeper, in a state of distressing dishabille, "out of her warm bed," as she subsequently stated, to the head of the staircase.

Across the hall Hertford O'Donnell strode, relieved at the prospect of speaking to any living being. He took no precaution of putting up the chain, but flung the door wide. A dozen burglars would have proved welcome in comparison to that ghostly intruder; and, as I have said, he threw the door open, admitting a rush of wet, cold air, which made poor Mrs. Coles's few remaining teeth chatter in her head.

"Who is there?—what do you want?" asked the surgeon, seeing no person, and hearing no voice. "Who is there?—why the devil can't you speak?"

But when even this polite exhortation failed to elicit an answer, he passed out into the night, and looked up the street, and down the street, to see nothing but the drizzling rain and the blinking lights.

"If this goes on much longer, I shall soon think I must be either mad or drunk," he muttered, as he re-entered the house and locked and bolted the door once more.

"Lord's sake! what is the matter, sir?" asked Mrs. Coles, from the upper flight, careful only to reveal the borders of her nightcap to Mr. O'Donnell's admiring gaze "Is anybody killed?—have you to go out, sir?"

"It was only a runaway ring," he answered, trying to reassure himself with an explanation he did not in his heart believe.

"Runaway!—I'd runaway them," murmured Mrs. Coles, as she retired to the conjugal couch, where Coles was, to quote her own expression, "snoring like a pig through it all." Almost immediately afterwards she heard her master ascend the stairs and close his bedroom door.

"Madam will surely be too much of a gentlewoman to intrude here," thought the surgeon, scoffing even at his own fears; but when he lay down he did not put out his light, and he made Brian leap up and crouch on the coverlet beside him.

The man was fairly frightened, and would have thought it no discredit to his manhood to acknowledge as much. He was not afraid of death, he was not afraid of trouble, he was not afraid of danger; but he was afraid of the banshee; and as he lay with his hand on the dog's head, he thought over all the stories he had ever heard about this family retainer in the days of his youth. He had not thought about her for years and years. Never before had he heard her voice himself. When his brother died, she had not thought it necessary to travel up to Dublin and give him notice of the impending catastrophe. "If she had, I would have gone down to Calgillan, and perhaps saved his life," considered the surgeon. "I wonder who this is for! If for me, that will settle my debts and my marriage. If I could be quite certain it was either of the old people, I would start for Ireland to-morrow." And then vaguely his mind wandered on to think of every banshee story he had ever heard in his life. About the beautiful lady with the wreath of flowers, who sat on the rocks below Red Castle, in the County Antrim, crying till one of the sons died for love of her; about the Round Chamber at Dunluce, which was swept clean by the banshee every night; about the bed in a certain great house in Ireland, which was slept in constantly, although no human being passed ever in or out after dark; about that general officer who, the night before Waterloo, said to a friend, "I have heard the banshee, and shall not come off the field alive to-morrow; break the news gently to poor Carry;" and who, nevertheless, coming safe off the field, had subsequently news about poor Carry broken tenderly and pitifully to him; about the lad who, aloft in the rigging, hearing through the night a sobbing and wailing coming over the waters, went down to the captain and told him he was afraid they were somehow out of their reckoning, just in time to save the ship, which when morning broke, they found, but for his warning, would have been on the rocks. It was blowing great guns, and the sea was all fret and turmoil, and they could sometimes see in the trough of the waves, as down a valley, the cruel black reefs they had escaped.

On deck the captain stood speaking to the boy who had saved them, and asking how he knew of their danger; and when the lad told him, the captain laughed, and said her ladyship had been outwitted that time.

But the boy answered, with a grave shake of his head, that the warning was either for him or his, and that if he got safe to port there would be bad tidings waiting for him from home; whereupon the captain bade him go below, and get some brandy and lie down.

He got the brandy, and he laid down, but he never rose again; and when the storm abated—when a great calm succeeded to the previous tempest—there was a very solemn funeral at sea; and on their arrival at Liverpool the captain took a journey to Ireland to tell a widowed mother how her only son died, and to bear his few effects to the poor, desolate soul.

And Hertford O'Donnell thought again about his own father, riding full-chase across country, and hearing, as he galloped by a clump of plantation, something like a sobbing and wailing. The hounds were in full cry; but he still felt, as he afterwards expressed it, that there was something among those trees he could not pass; and so he jumped off his horse, and hung the reins over the branch of a fir and beat the cover well, but not a thing could he find in it.

Then, for the first time in his life, Miles O'Donnell turned his horse's head *from* the hunt, and, within a mile of Calgillan, met a man running to tell him Mr. Martin's gun had burst and hurt him badly.

And he remembered the story, also, of how Mary O'Donnell, his great-aunt, being married to a young Englishman, heard the banshee as she sat one evening waiting for his return; and of how she, thinking the bridge by which he often came home unsafe for horse and man, went out in a great panic, to meet and entreat him go round by the main road for her sake. Sir Everard was riding alone in the moonlight, making straight for the bridge, when he beheld a figure dressed all in white upon it. Then there was a crash, and the figure disappeared.

The lady was rescued and brought back to the hall; but next morning there were two dead bodies within its walls—those of Lady Eyreton and her still-born son.

Quicker than I write them, these memories chased one another through Hertford O'Donnell's brain; and there was one more terrible memory than any, which would recur to him, concerning an Irish nobleman who, seated alone in his great town-house in London, heard the banshee, and rushed out to get rid of the phantom, which wailed in his ear, nevertheless, as he strode down Piccadilly. And then the surgeon remembered how he went with a friend to the opera, feeling sure that there no banshee, unless she had a box, could find admittance, until suddenly he heard her singing up amongst the highest part of the scenery, with a terrible mournfulness, with a pathos which made the prima donna's tenderest notes seem harsh by comparison.

As he came out, some quarrel arose between him and a famous fire-eater, against whom he stumbled; and the result was that the next afternoon there was a new Lord——, *vice* Lord ——, killed in a duel with Captain Bravo.

Memories like these are not the most enlivening possible; they are apt to make a man fanciful, and nervous, and wakeful; but as time ran on, Hertford O'Donnell fell asleep, with his candle still burning and Brian's cold nose pressed against his hand.

He dreamt of his mother's family—the Hertfords, of Artingbury, Yorkshire, far-off relatives of Lord Hertford—so far off that even Mrs. O'Donnell held no clue to the genealogical maze.

He thought he was at Artingbury, fishing; that it was a misty summer's morning and the fish rising beautifully. In his dream he hooked one after another, and the boy who was with him threw them into the basket.

At last there was one more difficult to land than the others; and the boy, in his eagerness to watch the sport, drew nearer and nearer to the brink, while the fisher, intent on his prey, failed to notice his companion's danger.

Suddenly there was a cry, a splash, and the boy disappeared from sight.

Next instant he rose again, however, and then, for the first time, Hertford O'Donnel saw his face.

It was one he knew well.

In a moment he plunged into the water, and struck out for the lad. He had him by the hair, he was turning to bring him back to land, when the stream suddenly changed into a wide, wild, shoreless sea, where the billows were chasing one another with a mad, demoniac mirth.

For a while O'Donnell kept the lad and himself afloat. They were swept under the waves, and came forth again, only to see larger waves rushing towards them; but through all the surgeon never loosened his hold until a tremendous billow engulfing them both, tore the boy from him.

With the horror of that he awoke, to hear a voice saying quite distinctly: "Go to the hospital!—go at once!"

The surgeon started up in bed, rubbed his eyes and looked about him. The candle was flickering faintly in its socket. Brian, with his ears pricked forward, had raised his head at his master's sudden jump.

Everything was quiet, but still those words were ringing in his ear— "Go to the hospital!—go at once!"

The tremendous peal of the bell overnight, and this sentence, seemed to be simultaneous.

That he was wanted at Guy's—wanted imperatively—came to O'Donnell like an inspiration.

Neither sense nor reason had anything to do with the conviction that roused him out of bed, and made him dress as speedily as possible and grope his way down the staircase, Brian following.

He opened the front door and passed out into the darkness. The rain was over, and the stars were shining as he pursued his way down Newport Market, and thence, winding in and out in a south-east direction, through Lincoln's Inn Fields and Old Square to Chancery Lane, whence he proceeded to St. Paul's.

Along the deserted streets he resolutely continued his walk. He did not know what he was going to Guy's for. Some instinct was urging him on, and he neither strove to combat nor control it. Only once had the thought of turning back occurred, and that was at the archway leading into Old Square. There he had paused for a moment, asking himself whether he were not gone stark, staring mad; but Guy's seemed preferable to the haunted house in Gerrard Street, and he walked resolutely on, determining to say, if any surprise were expressed at his appearance, that he had been sent for.

On, thinking of many things: of his wild life in London; of the terrible cry he had heard overnight—that terrible wail which he could not drive away from his memory, even as he entered Guy's, and confronted the porter, who said:

"You have just been sent for, sir; did you meet the messenger?"

Like one in a dream, Hertford O'Donnell heard him; like one in a dream, also, he asked what was the matter.

"Bad accident, sir: fire; fall of a balcony—unsafe—old building. Mother and child—a son; child with compound fracture of thigh." This, the joint information of porter and house-surgeon, mingled together, and made a roar in Mr. O'Donnell's ears like the sound of the sea breaking on a shingly shore.

Only one sentence he understood perfectly—"Immediate amputation necessary." At this point he grew cool; he was the careful, cautious, successful surgeon in a moment.

"The child, you say?" he answered; "let me see him."

In the days of which I am writing, the two surgeons had to pass a staircase leading to the upper stories. On the lower step of this staircase, partially in shadow, Hertford O'Donnell beheld as he came forward, an old woman seated.

An old woman with streaming grey hair, with attenuated arms, with head bowed forward, with scanty clothing, with bare feet; who never looked up at their approach, but sat unnoticing, shaking her head and wringing her hands in an extremity of grief.

"Who is that?" asked Mr. O'Donnell, almost involuntarily.

"Who is what?" demanded his companion.

"That—that woman," was the reply.

"What woman?"

"There—are you blind?—seated on the bottom step of the staircase. What is she doing?" persisted Mr. O'Donnell.

"There is no woman near us," his companion answered, looking at the rising surgeon very much as though he suspected him of seeing double.

"No woman!" scoffed Hertford. "Do you expect me to disbelieve the evidence of my own eyes?" and he walked up to the figure, meaning to touch it.

But as he essayed to do so, the woman seemed to rise in the air and float away, with her arms stretched high up over her head, uttering such a wail of pain, and agony, and distress, as caused the Irishman's blood to curdle.

"My God! did you hear that?" he said to his companion.

"What?" was the reply.

Then, although he knew the sound had fallen on deaf ears, he answered—

"The wail of the banshee! Some of my people are doomed!"

"I trust not," answered the house-surgeon.

With nerves utterly shaken, Mr. O'Donnell walked forward to the accident ward. There, with his face shaded from the light, lay his patient—a young boy, with a compound fracture of the thigh.

In that ward, in the face of actual pain or danger capable of relief, the surgeon had never known faltering nor fear; and now he carefully examined the injury, felt the pulse, inquired as to the treatment pursued, and ordered the sufferer to be carried to the operating room.

While he was laying out his instruments he heard the boy lying on the table murmur faintly—

"Tell her not to cry so—tell her not to cry."

"What is he talking about?" Hertford O'Donnell inquired.

"The nurse says he has been speaking about some woman crying ever since he came in—his mother, most likely," answered one of the attendants.

"He is delirious, then?" observed the surgeon.

"No, sir," pleaded the boy excitedly. "No; it is that woman—that woman with the grey hair. I saw her looking from the upper window before the balcony gave way. She has never left me since, and she won't be quiet, wringing her hands and crying."

"Can you see her now?" Hertford O'Donnell inquired, stepping to the side of the table. "Point out where she stands."

Then the lad stretched forth a feeble finger in the direction of the door, where clearly, as he had seen her seated on the stairs, the surgeon saw a woman standing—a woman with grey hair and scanty clothing, and upstretched arms and bare feet.

"A word with you, sir," O'Donnell said to the house surgeon, drawing him back from the table. "I cannot perform this operation: send for some other person. I am ill; I am incapable."

"But," pleaded the other, "there is no time to get anyone else. We sent for Mr. —— before we troubled you, but he was out of town, and all the rest of the surgeons live so far away. Mortification may set in at any moment, and——" then Hertford O'Donnell fell fainting on the floor.

How long he lay in that dead-like swoon I cannot say: but when he returned to consciousness, the principal physician of Guy's was standing beside him in the cold grey light of the Christmas morning.

"The boy?" murmured O'Donnell faintly.

"Now, my dear fellow, keep yourself quiet," was the reply.

"The boy?" he repeated irritably. "Who operated?"

"No one," Dr. —— answered. "It would have been useless cruelty. Mortification had set in, and——"

Hertford O'Donnell turned his face to the wall, and his friend could not see it.

"Do not distress yourself," went on the physician kindly. "Allington says he could not have survived the operation in any case. He was quite delirious from the first, raving about a woman with grey hair, and——"

"Yes, I know," Hertford O'Donnell interrupted; "and the boy had a mother, they told me, or I dreamt it."

"Yes; bruised and shaken, but not seriously injured."

"Has she blue eyes and fair hair—fair hair rippling and wavy? Is she white as a lily, with just a faint flush of colour in her cheeks? Is she young, and trusting, and innocent? No; I am wandering. She must be nearly thirty now. Go, for God's sake, and tell me if you can find a woman that you could imagine having been as a girl such as I describe."

"Irish?" asked the doctor; and O'Donnell made a gesture of assent.

"It is she then," was the reply; "a woman with the face of an angel."

"A woman who should have been my wife," the surgeon answered; "whose child was my son."

"Lord help you!" ejaculated the doctor. Then Hertford O'Donnell raised himself from the sofa where they had laid him, and told his companion the story of his life—how there had been bitter feud between his people and her people—how they were divided by old animosities and by difference of religion—how they had met by stealth, and exchanged rings and vows, all for nought—how his family had insulted hers, so that her father, wishful for her to marry a kinsman of his own, bore her off to a far-away land, and made her write him a letter of eternal farewell—how his own parents had kept all knowledge of the quarrel from him till she was utterly beyond his reach—how they had vowed to discard him unless he agreed to marry according to their wishes—how he left home, and came to London, and pushed his fortune. All this Hertford O'Donnell repeated; and when he had finished, the bells were ringing for morning service—ringing loudly—ringing joyfully: "Peace on earth, good will towards men."

But there was little peace that morning for Hertford O'Donnell. He had to look on the face of his dead son, wherein he beheld, as though reflected, the face of the boy in his dream.

Stealthily he followed his friend, and beheld, with her eyes closed, her cheeks pale and pinched, her hair thinner, but still falling like a veil over her, the love of his youth, the only woman he had ever loved devotedly and unselfishly.

There is little space left here to tell of how the two met at last—of how the stone of the years seemed suddenly rolled away from the tomb of their past, and their youth arose and returned to them, amid their tears.

She had been true to him, through persecution, through contumely, through kindness, which was more trying; through shame, and grief, and poverty, she had been loyal to the lover of her youth; and before the new year dawned there came a letter from Calgillan, saying that the banshee had been heard there, and praying Hertford, if he was still alive, to let bygones be bygones, in consideration of the long years of estrangement—the anguish and remorse of his afflicted parents.

More than that, Hertford O'Donnell, if a reckless man, was an honourable one; and so, on the Christmas Day, when he was to have proposed for Miss Ingot, he went to that lady and told her how he had wooed and won in the years of his youth one who, after many days, was miraculously restored to him. And from the hour in which he took her into his confidence he never thought her either vulgar or foolish, but rather he paid homage to the woman who, when she had heard the whole tale repeated, said simply, "Ask her to come to me till you claim her—and God bless you both."

WALNUT-TREE HOUSE

Chapter One

THE NEW OWNER

Many years ago there stood at the corner of a street leading out of Upper Kennington Lane a great red brick house, covering a goodly area of ground, and surrounded by gardens magnificent in their proportions when considered in relation to the populous neighbourhood mentioned.

Originally a place of considerable pretention; a gentleman's seat in the country probably when Lambeth Marsh had not a shop in the whole of it; when Vauxhall Gardens were still *in nubibus*; when no South-Western Railway was planned or thought of; when London was comparatively a very small place, and its present suburbs were mere country villages—hamlets lying quite remote from the heart of the city.

Once, the house in question had been surrounded by a small park, and at that time there were fish-ponds in the grounds, and quite a stretch of meadow-land within the walls. Bit by bit, however, the park had been cut up into building ground and let off on building leases; the meadows were covered with bricks and mortar, shops were run up where cows once chewed the cud, and the roar and rumble of London traffic sounded about the old house and the deserted garden, formerly quiet and silent as though situated in some remote part of the country.

Many a time in the course of the generations that had come and gone, been born and buried, since the old house was built, the freehold it covered changed hands. On most estates of this kind round London there generally is a residence, which passes like a horse from buyer to buyer. When it has served one man's need it is put up for sale and bid for by another. When rows and rows of houses, and line after line of streets, have obliterated all the familiar marks, it is impossible to cultivate a sentiment as regards property; and it is unlikely that the descendants of the first possessors of Walnut-Tree House who had grown to be country folk and lived in great state, oblivious of business people, and entertaining a great contempt for trade, knew that in a very undesirable part of London there still stood the residence where the first successful man of their family went home each day from his counting-house over against St. Mildred's Church, in The Poultry.

One very wet evening, in an autumn the leaves of which have been dead and gone this many a year, Walnut-Tree House, standing grim and lonely in the mournful twilight, looked more than ordinarily desolate and deserted.

There was not a sign of life about it; the shutters were closed—the rusty iron gates were fast locked—the approach was choked up with grass and weeds—through no chink did the light of a single candle flicker. For seven years it had been given over to rats and mice and blackbeetles; for seven years no one had been found to live in it; for seven years it had remained empty, while its owner wore out existence in fits of moody dejection or of wild frenzy in the madhouse close at hand; and now that owner was dead and buried and forgotten, and the new owner was returning to take possession. This new owner had written to his lawyers, or rather he had written to the lawyers of his late relative, begging them to request the person in charge of the house to have rooms prepared for his arrival; and, when the train drew into the station at Waterloo, he was met by one of the clerks in Messrs. Timpson and Co.'s office, who, picking out Mr. Stainton, delivered to that gentleman a letter from the firm, and said he would wait and hear if there were any message in reply.

Mr. Stainton read the letter—looked at the blank flyleaf—and then, turning back to the first words, read what his solicitors had to say all through once again, this time aloud.

"The house has stood empty for more than seven years," he said, half addressing the clerk and half speaking to himself. "Must be damp and uninhabitable; there is no one living on the premises. Under these circumstances we have been unable to comply with your directions, and can only recommend you to go to an hotel till we are able personally to discuss future arrangements."

"Humph," said the new owner, after he had finished. "I'll go and take a look at the place, anyhow. Is it far from here, do you know?" he asked, turning to the young man from Timpsons'.

"No, sir; not very far."

"Can you spare time to come over there with me ?" continued Mr. Stainton.

The young man believed that he could, adding, "If you want to go into the house we had better call for the key. It is at an estate agent's in the Westminster Bridge Road."

"I cannot say I have any great passion for hotels," remarked the new owner, as he took his seat in the cab.

"Indeed, sir ? "

"No; either they don't suit me, or I don't suit them. I have led a wild sort of life: not much civilisation in the bush, or at the goldfields, I can tell you. Rooms full of furniture, houses where a fellow must keep to the one little corner he has hired, seem to choke me. Then I have not been well, and I can't stand noise and the trampling of feet. I had enough of that on board ship; and I used to lie awake at nights and think how pleasant it would be to have a big house all to myself, to do as I liked in."

"Yes, sir," agreed the clerk.

"You see, I have been used to roughing it, and I can get along very well for a night without servants."

"No doubt, sir."

"I suppose the house is in substantial repair—roof tight, and all that sort of thing ? "

"I can't say, I am sure, sir."

"Well, if there is a dry corner where I can spread a rug, I shall sleep there to-night."

The clerk coughed. He looked out of the window, and then he looked at Messrs. Timpsons' client.

"I do not think——" he began, apologetically, and then stopped.

"You don't think what ?" asked the other.

"You'll excuse me, sir, but I don't think—I really do not think, if I were you, I'd go to that house to-night."

"Why not ?"

"Well, it has not been slept in for nearly seven years, and it must be blue mouldy with damp; and if you have been ill, that is all the more reason you should not run such a risk. And, besides——"

"Besides ? " suggested Mr. Stainton. "Out with it ! Like a post-script, no doubt, that 'besides' holds the marrow of the argument."

"The house has stood empty for years, sir, because—there is no use in making any secret of it—the place has a bad name."

"What sort of a bad name—unhealthy?"

"Oh, no!"

"Haunted?"

The clerk inclined his head. "You have hit it, sir," he said.

"And that is the reason no one has lived there?"

"We have been quite unable to let the house on that account."

"The sooner it gets unhaunted, then, the better," retorted Mr. Stainton. "I shall certainly stop there to-night. You are not disposed to stay and keep me company, I suppose?"

With a little gesture of dismay the clerk drew back. Certainly, this was one of the most unconventional of clients. The young man from Timpsons' did not at all know what to make of him.

"A rough sort of fellow," he said afterwards, when describing the new owner; "boorish; never mixed with good society, that sort of thing."

He did not in the least understand this rich man, who treated him as an equal, who objected to hotels, who didn't mind taking up his abode in a house where not even a drunken charwoman could be induced to stop, and who calmly asked a stranger on whom he had never set eyes before—a clerk in the respectable office of Timpson and Co., a young fellow anxious to rise in the world, careful as to his associates, particular about the whiteness of his shirts and the sit of his collar and the cut of his coats—to "rough" things with him in that dreadful old dungeon, where, perhaps, he might even be expected to light a fire.

Still, he did not wish to offend the new owner. Messrs. Timpson expected him to be a profitable client; and to that impartial firm the money of a boor would, he knew, seem as good as the money of a count.

"I am very sorry," he stammered; "should only have felt too much honoured; but the fact is—previous engagement——"

Mr. Stainton laughed.

"I understand," he said. "Adventures are quite as much out of your line as ghosts. And now tell me about this apparition. Does the 'old man' walk?"

"Not that I ever heard of," answered the other.

"Is it, then, the miserable beggar who tried to do for himself?"

"It is not the late Mr. Stainton, I believe," said the young man, in a tone which mildly suggested that reference to a client of Timpsons' as a "miserable beggar" might be considered bad taste.

"Then who on earth is it?" persisted Mr. Stainton.

"If you must know, sir, it is a child—a child who has driven every tenant in succession out of the house."

The new owner burst into a hearty laugh—a laugh which gave serious offence to Timpsons' clerk.

"That is too good a joke," said Mr. Stainton. "I do not know when I heard anything so delicious."

"It is a fact, whether it be delicious or not," retorted the young man, driven out of all his former propriety of voice and demeanour by the contemptuous ridicule this "digger" thought fit to cast on his story; "and I, for one, would not, after all I have heard about your house, pass a night in it—no, not if anybody offered me fifty pounds down."

"Make your mind easy, my friend," said the new owner, quietly. "I am not going to bid for your company. The child and I can manage, I'll be bound, to get on very comfortably by ourselves."

Chapter Two

THE CHILD

I⊤ was later on in the same evening; Mr. Stainton had an hour previously taken possession of Walnut-Tree House, dismissed his cab, bidden Timpsons' clerk good evening, and, having ordered in wood and coals from the nearest greengrocer, besides various other necessary articles from various other tradesmen, he now stood by the front gate waiting the coming of the goods purchased.

As he waited, he looked up at the house, which in the uncertain light of the street lamps appeared gloomier and darker than had been the case even in the gathering twilight.

The long rows of shuttered windows, the silent solemnity of the great trees, remnants of a once goodly avenue that had served to give its name to Walnut-Tree House; the appalling silence of everything within the place, when contrasted with the noise of passing cabs and whistling street boys, and men trudging home with unfurled umbrellas and women scudding along with draggled petticoats, might well have impressed even an unimpressionable man, and Edgar Stainton, spite of his hard life and rough exterior, was impressionable and imaginative.

"It has an 'uncanny' look, certainly," he considered; "but is not so cheerless for a lonely man as the 'bush'; and though I am not over-tired, I fancy I shall sleep more soundly in my new home than I did many a night at the goldfields. When once I can get a good fire up I shall be all right. Now, I wonder when those coals are coming!"

As he turned once again towards the road, he beheld on its way the sack of fuel with which the nearest greengrocer said he thought he could—indeed, said he would—"oblige" him. A ton—half a ton—quarter of a ton, the greengrocer affirmed would be impossible until the next day; but a sack—yes—he would promise that. Bill should bring it round; and Bill was told to put his burden on the truck, and twelve bundles of wood, "and we'll make up the rest to-morrow," added Bill's master, with the air of one who has conferred a favour.

In the distance Mr. Stainton descried a very grimy Bill, and a very small boy, coming along with the truck leisurely, as though the load had been Herculean.

Through the rain he watched the pair advancing and greeted Bill with a glad voice of welcome.

"So you've come at last; that's right. Better late than never. Bring them this way. I'll have this small lot shot in the kitchen for the night."

"Begging your pardon, sir," answered Bill, "I don't think you will—that is to say, not by me. As I told our governor, I'll take 'em to the house as you've sold 'em to the house, but I won't set a foot inside it."

"Do you mean to say you are going to leave them out on the pavement?" asked Mr. Stainton.

"Well, sir, I don't mind taking them to the front door if it'll be a convenience."

"That will do. You are a brave lot of people in these parts I must say."

"As for that," retorted Bill, with sack on back and head bent forward, "I dare say we're as brave about here as where you come from."

"It is not impossible,"retorted Mr. Stainton; "there are plenty of cowards over there too."

With a feint of being very much afraid, Bill, after he had shot his coals on the margin of the steps, retreated from the door, which stood partly open, and when the boy who brought up the wood was again out with the truck, said, putting his knuckles to his eyebrows:

"Beg pardon, sir, but I suppose you couldn't give us a drop of beer? Very wet night, sir."

"No, I could not," answered Mr. Stainton, very decidedly. "I shall have to shovel these coals into the house myself; and, as for the night, it is as wet for me as it is for you."

Nevertheless, as Bill shuffled along the short drive—shuffling wearily—like a man who, having nearly finished one day's hard work, was looking forward to beginning another hard day in the morning, the new owner relented.

"Here," he said, picking out a sixpence to give him, "it isn't your fault, I suppose, that you believe in old women's tales."

"Thank you kindly, sir," Bill answered; "I am sure I am extremely obliged; but if I was in your shoes I wouldn't stop in that house— you'll excuse me, sir, meaning no offence—but I wouldn't; indeed I wouldn't."

"It seems to have got a good name, at any rate," thought Mr. Stainton, while retracing his steps to the banned tenement. "Let us see what effect a fire will have in routing the shadows."

He entered the house, and, striking a match, lighted some candles he had brought in with him from a neighbouring oil-shop.

Years previously the gas company, weary of receiving no profit from the house, had taken away their meter and cut off their connections. The water supply was in the same case, as Mr. Stainton, going round the premises before it grew quite dark, had discovered.

Of almost all small articles of furniture easily broken by careless tenants, easily removed by charwomen, the place was perfectly bare; and as there were no portable candlesticks in which to place the lights the new tenant was forced to make his illumination by the help of some dingy mirrors provided with sconces, and to seek such articles as he needed by the help of a guttering mould candle stuck in the neck of a broken bottle. After an inspection of the ground-floor rooms he decided to take up his quarters for the night in one which had evidently served as a library.

In the centre of the apartment there was the table covered with leather. Around the walls were bookcases, still well filled with volumes, too uninviting to borrow, too valueless in the opinion of the ignorant to steal. In one corner stood a bureau, where the man, who for so many years had been dead even while living, kept his letters and papers.

The floor was bare. Once a Turkey carpet had been spread over the centre of the polished oak boards, but it lay in its wonted place no longer; between the windows hung a convex mirror, in which the face of any human being looked horrible and distorted; whilst over the mantle-shelf, indeed, forming a portion of it, was a long, narrow glass, bordered by a frame ornamented with a tracery of leaves and flowers. The ceiling was richly decorated, and, spite of the dust and dirt and neglect of years, all the appointments of the apartment he had selected gave Edgar Stainton the impression that it was a good thing to be the owner of such a mansion, even though it did chance to be situated as much out of the way of fashionable London as the diggings whence he had come.

"And there is not a creature but myself left to enjoy it all," he mused, as he sat looking into the blazing coals. "My poor mother, how she would have rejoiced to-night, had she lived to be the mistress of so large a place ! And my father, what a harbour this would have seemed after the storms that buffeted him ! Well, they are better off, I know; and yet I cannot help thinking how strange it all is—that I, who went away a mere beggar, should come home rich, to be made richer, and yet stand so utterly alone that in the length and breadth of England I have not a relative to welcome me or to say I wish you joy of your inheritance."

He had eaten his frugal supper, and now, pushing aside the table on which the remains of his repast were spread, he began walking slowly up and down the room, thinking over the past and forming plans for the future.

As he was buried in reflection, the fire began to die down without his noticing the fact; but a sudden feeling of chilliness at length causing him in-stinctively to look towards the hearth, he threw some wood into the grate, and, while the flames went blazing up the wide chimney, piled on coals as though he desired to set the house alight.

While he was so engaged there came a knock at the door of the room—a feeble, hesitating knock, which was repeated more than once before it attracted Mr. Stainton's attention.

When it did, being still busy with the fire, and forgetting he was alone in the house, he called out, "Come in."

Along the panels there stole a rustling sort of touch, as if someone were feeling uncertainly for the handle—a curious noise, as of a weak hand fumbling about the door in the dark; then, in a similar manner, the person seeking admittance tried to turn the lock.

"Come in, can't you?" repeated Mr. Stainton; but even as he spoke he remembered he was, or ought to be, the sole occupant of the mansion.

He was not alarmed ; he was too much accustomed to solitude and danger for that; but he rose from his stooping position and instinctively seized his revolver, which he had chanced, while unpacking some of his effects, to place on the top of the bureau.

"Come in, whoever you are," he cried; but seeing the door remained closed, though the intruder was evidently making futile efforts to open it, he strode half-way across the room, and then stopped, amazed.

For suddenly the door opened, and there entered, shyly and timidly, a little child—a child with the saddest face mortal ever beheld; a child with wistful eyes and long, ill-kept hair; a child poorly dressed, wasted and worn, and with the mournfullest expression on its countenance that face of a child ever wore.

"What a hungry little beggar," thought Mr. Stainton. "Well, young one, and what do you want here?" he added, aloud.

The boy never answered, never took the slightest notice of his questioner, but simply walked slowly round the room, peering into all the corners, as if looking for something. Searching the embrasures of the windows, examining the recesses beside the fire-place, pausing on the hearth to glance under the library table, and finally, when the doorway was reached once more, turning to survey the contents of the apartment with an eager and yet hopeless scrutiny.

"What _is_ it you want, my boy?" asked Mr. Stainton, glancing as he spoke at the child's poor thin legs, and short, shabby frock, and shoes wellnigh worn out, and arms bare and lean and unbeautiful. "Is it anything I can get for you?"

Not a word—not a whisper; only for reply a glance of the wistful brown eyes.

"Where do you come from, and who do you belong to?" persisted Mr. Stainton

The child turned slowly away.

"Come, you shall not get off so easily as you seem to imagine," persisted the new owner, advancing towards his visitor. "You have no business to be here at all; and before you go you must tell me how you chance to be in this house, and what you expected to find in this room."

He was close to the doorway by this time, and the child stood on the threshold, with its back towards him.

Mr. Stainton could see every detail of the boy's attire—his little plaid frock, which he had outgrown, the hooks which fastened it; the pinafore, soiled and crumpled, tied behind with strings broken and knotted; in one place the skirt had given from the body, and a piece of thin, poor flannel showed that the child's under habiliments matched in shabbiness his exterior garments.

"Poor little chap," thought Mr. Stainton. "I wonder if he would like something to eat. Are you hungry, my lad?"

The child turned and looked at him earnestly, but answered never a word.

"I wonder if he is dumb," marvelled Mr. Stainton; and, seeing he was moving away, put out a hand to detain him. But the child eluded his touch, and flitted out into the hall and up the wide staircase with swift, noiseless feet.

Only waiting to snatch a candle from one of the sconces, Mr. Stainton pursued as fast as he could follow.

Up the easy steps he ran at the top of his speed; but, fast as he went, the child went faster. Higher and higher he beheld the tiny creature mounting, then, still keeping the same distance between them, it turned when it reached the top story and trotted along a narrow corridor with rooms opening off to right and left. At the extreme end of this passage a door stood ajar. Through this the child passed, Mr. Stainton still following.

"I have run you to earth at last," he said, entering and closing the door. "Why, where has the boy gone?" he added, holding the candle above his head and gazing round the dingy garret in which he found himself.

The room was quite empty. He examined it closely, but could find no possible outlet save the door, and a skylight which had evidently not been opened for years.

There was no furniture in the apartment, except a truckle bedstead, a rush-bottomed chair, and a rickety washstand. No wardrobe, or box or press where even a kitten might have lain concealed.

"It is very strange," muttered Mr. Stainton, as he turned away baffled. "Very strange !" he repeated, while he walked along the corridor. "I don't understand it at all," he decided, proceeding slowly down the topmost flight of stairs; but then all at once he stopped.

"It is the child !" he exclaimed aloud, and the sound of his own voice woke strange echoes through the silence of that desolate house. "It is the child !" And he descended the principal staircase very slowly, with bowed head, and his grave, thoughtful face graver and more thoughtful than ever.

Chapter Three

SEEKING FOR INFORMATION

It was enough to make any man look grave; and as time went on the new owner of Walnut-Tree House found himself pondering continually as to what the mystery could be which attached to the child he had found in possession of his property, and who had already driven tenant after tenant out of the premises. Inclined at first to regard the clerk's story as a joke, and his own experience on the night of his arrival a delusion, it was impossible for him to continue incredulous when he found, even in broad daylight, that terrible child stealing down the staircase and entering the rooms, looking—looking, for something it never found.

Never after the first horror was over did Mr. Stainton think of leaving the house in consequence of that haunting presence which had kept the house tenantless. It would have been worse than useless, he felt. With the ocean stretching between, his spirit would still be in the old mansion at Lambeth—his mental vision would always be watching the child engaged in the weary search to which there seemed no end— that never appeared to produce any result.

At bed and at board he had company, or the expectation of it. No apartment in the building was secure from intrusion. It did not matter where he lay; it did not matter where he ate; between sleeping and waking, between breakfast and dinner, whenever the notion seized it, the child came gliding in, looking, looking, looking, and never finding; not lingering longer than was necessary to be certain the object of its search was absent, but wandering hither and thither, from garret to kitchen, from parlour to bed-chamber, in that quest which still seemed fresh as when first begun.

Mr. Stainton went to his solicitors as the most likely persons from whom to obtain information on the subject, and plunged at once into the matter.

"Who is the child supposed to be, Mr. Timpson?" he asked, making no secret that he had seen it.

"Well, that is really very difficult to say," answered Mr. Timpson.

"There *was* a child once, I suppose—a real child—flesh and blood?"

Mr. Timpson took off his spectacles and wiped them.

"There were two ; yes, certainly, in the time of Mr. Felix Stainton —a boy and a girl."

"In that house?"

"In that house. They survived him."

"And what became of them?"

"The girl was adopted by a relation of her father's, and the—boy —died."

"Oh ! the boy died, did he ? Do you happen to know what he died of ?"

"No; I really do not. There was nothing wrong about the affair, however, if that is what you are thinking of. There never was a hint of that sort."

Mr. Stainton sat silent for a minute; then he said :

"Mr. Timpson, I can't shake off the idea that somehow there has been foul play with regard to those children. Who were they ?"

"Felix Stainton's grandchildren. His daughter made a low marriage, and he cast her adrift. After her death the two children were received at Walnut-Tree House on sufferance—fed and clothed, I believe, that was all; and when the old man died the heir-at-law permitted them to remain."

"Alfred Stainton ? "

"Yes; the unhappy man who became insane. His uncle died in-testate, and he consequently succeeded to everything but the per-sonalty, which was very small, and of which these children had a share."

"There was never any suspicion, you say, of foul play on the part of the late owner ? "

"Dear, dear ! No; quite the contrary."

"Then can you throw the least light on the mystery ? "

"Not the least; I wish I could."

For all that, Mr. Stainton carried away an impression Mr. Timpson knew more of the matter than he cared to tell; and was confirmed in this opinion by a chance remark from Mr. Timpson's partner, whom he met in the street almost immediately after.

"Why can't you let the matter rest, Mr. Stainton ? " asked the Co. with some irritation of manner when he heard the object of their client's visit. "What is the use of troubling your head about a child who has been lying in Lambeth Churchyard these dozen years ? Take my advise, have the house pulled down and let or sell the ground for building. You ought to get a pot of money for it in that neighbour-hood. If there were a wrong done it is too late to set it right now."

"What wrong do you refer to ? " asked Mr. Stainton eagerly, think-ing he had caught Timpson's partner napping. But that gentleman was too sharp for him.

"I remarked *if* there were a wrong done—not that there had been one," he answered; and then, without a pause, added, "We shall hope to hear from you that you have decided to follow our advice."

But Mr. Stainton shook his head.

"I will not pull down the old house just yet," he said, and walked slowly away.

"There is a mystery behind it all," he considered. "I must learn more about these children. Perhaps some of the local tradespeople may recollect them."

But the local tradespeople for the most part were newcomers—or else had not supplied "the house."

"So far as ever I could understand," said one "family butcher," irascibly sharpening his knife as he spoke, "there was not much to supply. *That* custom was not worth speaking of. I hadn't it, so what I am saying is not said on my own account. A scrag end of neck of mutton—a bit of gravy beef—two pennyworth of sheep's liver—that was the sort of thing. Misers, sir, misers; the old gentleman bad, and the nephew worse. A bad business, first and last. But what else could be expected ? When people as can afford to live on the fat of the land never have a sirloin inside their doors, why, worse must come of it. No, sir, I never set eyes on the children to my knowledge; I only knew there were children by hearing one of them was dead, and that it was the poorest funeral ever crossed a decent threshold."

"Poor little chap," thought Mr. Stainton, looking straight out into the street for a moment; then added, "lest the family misfortunes should descend to me, you had better send round a joint to Walnut-Tree House."

"Lor', sir, are you the gentleman as is living there ? I beg your pardon, I am sure, but I have been so bothered with questions in regard of that house and those children that I forget my manners when I talk about them. A joint, sir—what would you please to have ?"

The new owner told him; and while he counted out the money to pay for it Mr. Parker remarked :

"There is only one person I can think of, sir, likely to be able to give any information about the matter."

"And that is ?"

"Mr. Hennings, at the "Pedlar's Dog." He had some aquaintance with the old lady as was housekeeper both to Mr. Felix Stainton and the gentleman that went out of his mind."

Following the advice, the new owner repaired to the "Pedlar's Dog," where (having on his first arrival at Walnut-Tree House ordered some creature comforts from that well-known public) he experienced a better reception than had been accorded to him by Mr. Parker.

"Do I know Walnut-Tree House, sir ?" said Mr. Hennings, repeating his visitor's question. "Well, yes, rather. Why, you might as well ask me, do I know the "Pedlar's Dog." As boy and man I can remember the old house for close on five-and-fifty years. I remember Mr. George Stainton; he used to wear a skull-cap and knee-breeches. There was an orchard then where Stainton Street is now, and his whole time was taken up in keeping the boys out of it. Many a time I have run from him."

"Did you ever see anything of the boy and girl who were there, after Mr. Alfred succeeded to the property—Felix Stainton's grand-children, I mean ?" asked the new owner, when a pause in Mr. Henning's reminiscences enabled him to take his part in the conversation.

"Well, sir, I may have seen the girl, but I can't bring it to my recollection ; the boy I do remember, however. He came over here two or three times with Mrs. Toplis, who kept house for both Mr. Staintons, and I took notice of him, both because he looked so peaky ana old-fashioned, and also an account of the talk about him."

"There was talk about him, then ?"

"Bless you, yes, sir; as much talk while he was living as since he died. Everybody thought he ought to have been the heir."

"Why ?" enquired the new owner.

"Because there was a will made leaving the place to him."

Here was information. Mr. Stainton's heart seemed to stand still for a second and then leap on with excitement.

"Who made the will ?"

"The grandfather, Felix Stainton, to be sure; who else should make it ?"

"I did not mean that. Was it not drawn out by a solicitor ?"

"Oh ! Yes—now I understand you, sir. The will was drawn right enough by Mr. Quinance, in the Lambeth Road, a very clever lawyer."

"Not by Timpson, then ? How was that ?"

"The old man took the notion of making it late one night, and so Mrs. Toplis sent to the nearest lawyer she knew of."

"Yes; and then ? "

"Well, the will was made and signed and witnessed, and everything regular; and from that day to this no one knows what has become of it."

"How very strange."

"Yes, sir, it is more than strange—unaccountable. At first Mr. Quinance was suspected of having given it up to Mr. Alfred; but Mrs. Toplis and Quinance's clerk—he has succeeded to the business now—say that old Felix insisted upon keeping it himself. So, whether he destroyed it or the nephew got hold of it, Heaven only knows; for no man living does, I think."

"And the child—the boy, I mean ?"

"If you want to hear all about him, sir, Mrs. Toplis is the one to tell you. If you have a mind to give a shilling to a poor old lady who always did try to keep herself respectable, and who, I will say, paid her way honourable as long as she had a sixpence to pay it honourable with, you cannot do better than go and see Mrs. Toplis, who will talk to you for hours about the time she lived at Walnut-Tree House."

And with this delicate hint that his minutes were more valuable than the hours of Mrs. Toplis, Mr. Hennings would have closed the interview, but that his visitor asked where he should be able to find the housekeeper.

"A thousand pardons !" he answered, with an air; "forgetting the very cream and marrow of it, wasn't I ? Mrs. Toplis, sir, is to be found in Lambeth Workhouse—and a pity, too."

Edgar Stainton turned away, heart-sick. Was this all wealth had done for his people and those connected with them ?

No man seemed to care to waste a moment in speaking about their affairs; no one had a good word for or kindly memory of them. The poorest creature he met in the streets might have been of more use in the world then they. The house they had lived in mentioned as if a curse rested on the place; themselves only recollected as leaving everything undone which it befitted their station to do. An old servant allowed to end her days in the workhouse !

"Heaven helping me," he thought, "I will not so misuse the wealth which has been given me."

The slight put upon his family tortured and made him wince, and the face of the dead boy who ought to have been the heir seemed, as he hurried along the streets, to pursue and look on him with a wistful reproach.

"If I cannot lay that child I shall go mad," he said, almost audibly, "as mad, perhaps, as Alfred Stainton." And then a terrible fear took possession of him. The horror of that which is worse than any death made for the moment this brave, bold man more timid than a woman.

"God preserve my senses," he prayed, and then, determinedly putting that phantom behind him, he went on to the Workhouse.

Chapter Four

BROTHER AND SISTER

MR. STAINTON had expected to find Mrs. Toplis a decrepit crone, bowed with age and racked with rheumatism, and it was therefore like a gleam of sunshine streaming across his path to behold a woman, elderly, certainly, but carrying her years with ease, ruddy cheeked, clear eyed, upright as a dart, who welcomed him with respectful enthusiasm.

"And so you are Mr. Edgar, the son of the dear old Captain," she said, after the first greetings and explanations were over, after she had wiped her eyes and uttered many ejaculations of astonishment and expressions of delight. "Eh ! I remember him coming to the house just after he was married, and telling me about the sweet lady his wife. I never heard a gentleman so proud; he never seemed tired of saying the words, 'My wife'."

"She was a sweet lady," answered the new owner.

"And so the house has come to you, sir ? Well, I wish you joy. I hope you may have peace, and health, and happiness, and prosperity in it. And I don't see why you should not—no, indeed, sir."

Edgar Stainton sat silent for a minute, thinking how he should best approach his subject.

"Mrs. Toplis," he began at last, plunging into the very middle of the difficulty, "I want you to tell me about it. I have come here on purpose to ask you what it all means."

The old woman covered her face with her hands, and he could see that she trembled violently.

"You need not be afraid to speak openly to me," he went on. "I am quite satisfied there was some great wrong done in the house, and I want to put it right, if it lies in my power to do so. I am a rich man. I was rich when the news of this inheritance reached me, and I would gladly give up the property to-morrow if I could only undo whatever may have been done amiss."

Mrs. Toplis shook her head.

"Ah, sir; you can't do that," she said. "Money can't bring back the dead to life; and, if it could, I doubt if even you could prove as good a friend to the poor child sleeping in the churchyard yonder as his Maker did when He took him out of this troublesome world. It was just soul rending to see the boy the last few months of his life. I can't bear to think of it, sir! Often at night I wake in a fright, fancying I still hear the patter, patter of his poor little feet upon the stair."

"Do you know, it is a curious thing, but he doesn't frighten me," said Mr. Stainton; "that is when I am in the house; although when I am away from it the recollection seems to dog every step I take."

"What?" cried Mrs. Toplis. "*Have you, then, seen him too?* There! what am I talking about? I hope, sir, you will forgive my foolishness."

"I see him constantly," was the calm reply.

"I wonder what it means!—I wonder what it can mean!" exclaimed the housekeeper, wringing her hands in dire perplexity and dismay.

"I do not know," answered the new owner, philosophically; "but I want you to help me to find out. I suppose you remember the children coming there at first?"

"Well, sir—well, they were poor Miss Mary's son and daughter. She ran away, you know, with a Mr. Fenton—made a very poor match; but I believe he was kind to her. When they were brought to us, a shivering little pair, my master was for sending them here. Ay, and he would have done it, too, if somebody had not said he could be made to pay for their keep. You never saw brother and sister so fond of one another—never. They were twins. But, Lor'! the boy was more like a father to the little girl than aught else. He'd have kept an apple a month rather than eat it unless she had half; and the same with everything. I think it was seeing that—watching the love they had, he for her and she for him, coming upon them unsuspected, with their little arms round one another's necks, made the old gentleman alter his mind about leaving the place to Mr. Alfred; for he said to me, one day, thoughtful like, pointing to them, 'Wonderful fond, Toplis!' and I answered, 'Yes, sir; for all the world like the Babes in the Wood;' not thinking of how lonely that meant——

"Shortly afterwards he took to his bed; and while he was lying there, no doubt, better thoughts came to him, for he used to talk about his wife and Miss Mary, and the Captain, your father, sir, and ask if the children were gone to bed, and such like—things he never used to mention before.

"So when he made the will Mr. Quinance drew out I was not surprised—no, not a bit. Though before that time he always spoke of Mr. Alfred as his heir, and treated him as such."

"That will never was found," suggested Mr. Stainton, anxious to get at another portion of the narrative.

"Never, sir; we hunted for it high and low. Perhaps I wronged him, but I always thought Mr. Alfred knew what became of it. After the old gentleman's death the children were treated shameful—shameful. I don't mean beaten, or that like; but half-starved and neglected. He would not buy them proper clothes, and he would not suffer them to wear decent things if anybody else bought them. It was just the same with their food. I durs'n't give them even a bit of bread and butter unless it was on the sly; and, indeed, there was not much to give in that house. He turned regular miser. Hoarding came into the family with Mrs. Lancelot Stainton, Mr. Alfred's great grandmother, and they went on from bad to worse, each one closer and nearer than the last, begging your pardon for saying so, sir; but it is the truth."

"I fear so, Mrs. Toplis," agreed the man, who certainly was neither close nor near.

"Well, sir, at last, when the little girl was about six years old, she fell sick, and we didn't think she would get over the illness. While she was about at her worst, Mrs. May, her father's sister, chanced to be stopping up in London, and, as Mr. Alfred refused to let a doctor inside his doors, she made no more ado but wrapped the child up in blankets, sent for a cab, and carried her off to her own lodgings. Mr. Alfred made no objection to that. All he said as she went through the hall was :

" 'If you take her now, remember, you must keep her.'

" 'Very well,' she replied, 'I will keep her.' "

"And the boy ? the boy ?" cried Mr. Stainton, in an agony of impatience.

"I am coming to him, sir, if you please. He just dwindled away after his sister and he were parted, and died in December, as she was taken away in the July."

"What did he die of ?"

"A broken heart, sir. It seems a queer thing to say about a child; but if ever a heart was broken his was. At first he was always wandering about the house looking for her, but towards the end he used to go up to his room and stay there all by himself. At last I wrote to Mrs. May, but she was ill when the letter got to her, and when she did come up he was dead. My word, she talked to Mr. Alfred ! I never heard any one person say so much to another. She declared he had first cheated the boy of his inheritance, and then starved him to death; but that was not true, the child broke his heart fretting after his sister."

"Yes; and when he was dead———"

"Sir, I don't like to speak of it, but as true as I am sitting here, the night he was put in his coffin he came pattering down just as usual, looking, looking for his sister. I went straight upstairs, and if I had not seen the little wasted body lying there still and quiet, I must have thought he had come back to life. We were never without him afterwards, never; that, and nothing else, drove Mr. Alfred mad. He used to think he was fighting the child and killing it. When the worst fits were on him he tried to trample it under foot or crush it up in a corner, and then he would sob and cry, and pray for *it* to be taken away. I have heard he recovered a little before he died, and said his uncle told him there was a will leaving all to the boy, but he never saw such a paper. Perhaps it was all talk, though, or that he was still raving."

"You are quite positive there was no foul play as regards the child ?" asked Mr. Stainton, sticking to that question pertinaciously.

"Certain, sir; I don't say but Mr. Alfred wished him dead. That is not murder, though."

"I am not clear about that," answered Mr. Stainton.

Chapter Five

THE NEXT AFTERNOON

MR. STAINTON was trying to work off some portion of his perplexities by pruning the grimy evergreens in front of Walnut-Tree House, and chopping away at the undergrowth of weeds and couch grass which had in the course of years matted together beneath the shrubs, when his attention was attracted to two ladies who stood outside the great iron gate looking up at the house.

"It seems to be occupied now," remarked the elder, turning to her companion. "I suppose the new owner is going to live here. It looks just as dingy as ever; but you do not remember it, Mary."

"I think I do," was the answer. "As I look the place grows familiar to me. I do recollect some of the rooms, I am sure just like a dream, as I remember Georgie. What I would give to have a peep inside."

At this juncture the new owner emerged from amongst the bushes, and, opening the gate, asked if the ladies would like to look over the place.

The elder hesitated; whilst the younger whispered, "Oh, aunt, pray do !"

"Thank you," said Mrs. May to the stranger, whom she believed to be a gardener; "but perhaps Mr. Stainton might object."

"No; he wouldn't, I know," declared the new owner. "You can go through the house if you wish. There is no one in it. Nobody lives there except myself."

"Taking charge, I suppose ?" suggested Mrs. May blandly.

"Something of that sort," he answered.

"I do not think he is a caretaker," said the girl, as she and her relative passed into the old house together.

"What do you suppose he is, then ?" asked her aunt.

"Mr. Stainton himself."

"Nonsense, child !" exclaimed Mrs. May, turning, nevertheless, to one of the windows, and casting a curious glance towards the new owner, who was now, his hands thrust deep in his pockets, walking idly up and down the drive.

After they had been all over the place, from hall to garret, with a peep into this room and a glance into that, Mrs. May found the man who puzzled her leaning against one of the pillars of the porch, waiting, apparently, for their reappearance.

"I am sure we are very much obliged to you," she began, with a certain hesitation in her manner.

"Pray do not mention it," he said.

"This young lady has sad associations connected with the house," Mrs. May proceeded, still doubtfully feeling her way.

He turned his eyes towards the girl for a moment, and, though her veil was down, saw she had been weeping.

"I surmised as much," he replied. "She is Miss Fenton, is she not ?"

"Yes, certainly," was the answer; "and you are——"

"Edgar Stainton," said the new owner, holding out his hand.

"I am all alone here," he went on, after the first explanations were over. "But I can manage to give you a cup of tea. Pray do come in, and let me feel I am not entirely alone in England."

Only too well pleased, Mrs. May complied, and ten minutes later the three were sitting round a fire, the blaze of which leapt and flickered upon the walls and over the ceiling, casting bright lights on the dingy mirrors and the dark oak shelves.

"It is all coming back to me now," said the girl softly, addressing her aunt. "Many an hour Georgie and I have sat on that hearth seeing pictures in the fire."

But she did not see something which was even then standing close beside her, and which the new owner had witnessed approach with a feeling of terror that precluded speech.

It was the child! The child searching about no longer for something it failed to find, but standing at the girl's side still and motionless, with its eyes fixed upon her face, and its poor, wasted figure nestling amongst the folds of her dress.

"Thank Heaven she does not see it!" he thought, and drew his breath, relieved.

No; she did not see it—though its wan cheek touched her shoulder, though its thin hand rested on her arm, though through the long conversation which followed it never moved from her side, nor turned its wistful eyes from her face.

When she went away—when she took her fresh young beauty out of the house it seemed to gladden and light up—the child followed her to the threshold; and then in an instant it vanished, and Mr. Stainton watched for its flitting up the staircase all in vain.

But later on in the evening, when he was sitting alone beside the fire, with his eyes bent on the glowing coals, and perhaps seeing pictures there, as Mary said she and her brother had done in their lonely childhood, he felt conscious, even without looking round, that the boy was there once again.

And when he fell to thinking of the long, long years during which the dead child had kept faithful and weary watch for his sister, searching through the empty rooms for one who never came, and then bethought him of the sister to whom her dead brother had become but the vaguest of memories, of the summers and winters during the course of which she had probably forgotten him altogether, he sighed deeply; and heard his sigh echoed behind him in the merest faintest whisper.

More, when he, thinking deeply about his newly found relative and trying to recall each feature in her face, each tone of her voice, found it impossible to dissociate the girl grown to womanhood from the child he had pictured to himself as wandering about the old house in company with her twin brother, their arms twined together, their thoughts one, their sorrows one, their poor pleasures one—he felt a touch on his hand, and knew the boy was beside him, looking with wistful eyes into the firelight, too.

But when he turned he saw that sadness clouded those eyes no longer. She was found; the lost had come again to meet a living friend on the once desolate hearth, and up and down the wide, desolate staircase those weary little feet pattered no longer.

The quest was over, the search ended; into the darksome corners of that dreary house the child's glance peered no longer.

She was come ! Through years he had kept faithful watch for her, but the waiting was ended now.

That night Edgar Stainton slept soundly; and yet when morning dawned he knew that once in the darkness he wakened suddenly and was conscious of a small, childish hand smoothing his pillow and touching his brow.

Sweet were the dreams which visited his rest subsequently; sweet as ought to be the dreams of a man who had said to his own soul—and meant to hold fast by words he had spoken :

"As I deal by that orphan girl, so may God deal with me !"

Chapter Six

THE MISSING WILL

ERE long there were changes in the old house. Once again Mrs. Toplis reigned there, but this time with servants under her—with maids she could scold and lads she could harass.

The larder was well plenished, the cellars sufficiently stocked; windows formerly closely shuttered now stood open to admit the air; and on the drive grass grew no longer—too many footsteps passed that way for weeds to flourish.

It was Christmas-time. The joints in the butchers' shops were gay with ribbons; the grocers' windows were tricked out to delight the eyes of the children, young and old, who passed along. In Mr. May's house up the Clapham Road all was excitement, for the whole of the family—father, mother, grown-up sons and daughters—girls still in short frocks and boys in round jackets—were going to spend Christmas Eve with their newly-found cousin, whom they had adopted as a relation with a unanimity as rare as charming.

Cousin Mary also was going—Cousin Mary had got a new dress for the occasion, and was having her hair done up in a specially effective manner by Cissie May, when the toilette proceedings were interrupted by half a dozen young voices announcing:

"A gentleman in the parlour wants to see you, Mary. Pa says you are to make haste and come down immediately."

Obediently Mary made haste as bidden and descended to the parlour, to find there the clerk from Timpsons' who met Mr. Stainton on his arrival in London.

His business was simple, but important. Once again he was the bearer of a letter from Timpson and Co., this time announcing to Miss Fenton that the will of Mr. Felix Stainton had been found, and that under it she was entitled to the interest of ten thousand pounds, secured upon the houses in Stainton Street.

"Oh! aunt, Oh! uncle, how rich we shall be," cried the girl, running off to tell her cousins; but the uncle and aunt looked grave. They were wondering how this will might effect Edgar Stainton.

While they were still talking it over—after Timpsons' young man had taken his departure, Mr. Edgar Stainton himself arrived.

"Oh, it's all right!" he said, in answer to their questions. "I found the will in the room where Felix Stainton died. Walnut-Tree House and all the freeholds were left to the poor little chap who died, chargeable with Mary's ten thousand pounds, five hundred to Mrs. Toplis, and a few other legacies. Failing George, the property was to come to me. I have been to Quinance's successor, and found out the old man and Alfred had a grievous quarrel, and that in consequence he determined to cut him out altogether. Where is Mary? I want to wish her joy."

Mary was in the little conservatory, searching for a rose to put in her pretty brown hair.

He went straight up to her, and said:

"Mary, dear, you have had one Christmas gift to-night, and I want you to take another with it."

"What is it, Cousin Edgar?" she asked; but when she looked in his face she must have guessed his meaning, for she drooped her head, and began pulling her sweet rose to pieces.

He took the flower, and with it her fingers.

"Will you have me, dear?" he asked. "I am but a rough fellow, I know; but I am true, and I love you dearly."

Somehow, she answered him as he wished, and all spent a very happy evening in the old house.

Once, when he was standing close beside her in the familiar room, hand clasped in hand, Edgar Stainton saw the child looking at them.

There was no sorrow or yearning in his eyes as he gazed—only a great peace, a calm which seemed to fill and light them with an exquisite beauty.

OLD MRS. JONES

Chapter One

THERE could not have been found in his parish, which was a large one, a prouder or happier man than Richard Tippens, on the day when he took possession of the house which had been tenanted by Doctor Jones.

Never a better fellow drew breath than Mr. Richard Tippens. A good son, a loving husband, a fond father, his worst enemy could only say of him he had two faults—one, a tendency to be extra generous; the other, a perhaps undue fondness for an extra glass. But, earning money by the pocketful, as Dick did in those days, when there were fewer cabs and buses than at present, no tramcars, no Metropolitan or daylight route railway, to be free-handed seemed a virtue rather than a sin; whilst a man who had to be out in all weathers, and the period of whose meals was as uncertain as the climate, could scarcely be blamed for yielding to the solicitations of sporting or commercial-gent fares, and his own inclination, in the matter of little "gos" of rum and half-quarterns of gin, and whisky cold without, or with "just a drop of hot water and one lump of sugar, my dear, as my fingers is stiff with cold."

Mr. Tippens was a cheery fellow, with a jolly, honest, laughing face, merciful to the cattle he drove, proud of his newly-painted cab, of his silver-plated harness, of a fresh horse he had just bought, and—oh, far, far prouder of all—of having got the old house which Doctor Jones lived in, for so many a long and wicked year, for a mere song in the way of rent. It was precisely the sort of place he had been looking out for, he could scarcely remember how long; an old-fashioned house —not a grand old-fashioned house altogether above their position, but a rambling, ramshackle building, with a wide staircase, and lots of cupboards, and plenty of rooms they could let off to great advantage, and large cellars, and a paved yard at the back, where were also stables, and coach-house, and lofts, and wash-house, and brew-house, and ever so many other odd little places, telling unconsciously of the time when people, and things, and ways were different from what they are now; when wood enough for the whole winter had to be laid in at once, and bread was baked at home, and flitches of bacon were laid in the racks, and such modern innovations as tradesmen calling every day for orders, ladies only spending about thirty minutes a week in their kitchens, and no mistress's store-room, were matters still undreamt of.

"It is a splendid house," Mr. Richard Tippens joyfully exclaimed, when, opening the door with his own key, he walked into the premises with the old creature who was to do the repairs for him.

"Fit for any gentleman," capped the person in question, the accuracy of whose ideas on any social subject of that sort was indeed open to doubt, for he had only one definite notion on earth, and that was beer. His point of view was the nearest tap, and any road which led to the desired haven seemed to him filled with better company than the Row in the season.

He had been in a yard where Dick Tippens, then owning no horses of his own, was fain to work under a cab proprietor.

"I have known poor old Mickey," Dick was wont to say, "for a matter of thirty years, on and off, you know, and ever since I was as high as that," and the great burly fellow would indicate a height a child of five might have scoffed at. But Dick did not add how many a sixpence, and shilling, and half-crown, and good warm dinner had found their way to old Mickey since he met with the accident (when he was drunk) which made him for ever after a dependent on the charity of the ratepayers and the liberality of those who could remember him when he was earning from "thirty-three to forty bob a week, besides gettings." That Mickey, while in receipt of this princely income, might have put aside a trifle to help him over that rainy day, induced by "the cussedest brute that ever lashed out without a sign of warning," was an idea which never seemed to occur either to the various relieving officers he was under or to the many friends who "stood treat."

Neither was any weight attached to the horse's view of the question. How Michael himself would have liked his own toilet performed with the aid of a pitchfork, which was the implement he had taken up, apparently under the impression it was a curry-comb, nobody inquired. All that his own public considered was that Mickey, once the weekly recipient of "thirty-three to forty bob and gettings," which latter item probably amounted to as much more, had to go on the parish and feel thankful for half-crowns from the Board, and such odd jobs as Heaven, more merciful than the abhorred Board, put in his way.

For the rest he was a drunken, dissolute, lying, discontented, carneying old vagabond, who thrived on the kindness and folly of men like Dick Tippens, who likewise was not laying by a farthing but spending such of his superfluous cash as did not go in the best of good eating and drinking and smoking in the purchase of useless articles of various kinds, in fine household linen and damask, in a large stock of clothes for himself, which he could not possibly wear out before they grew old-fashioned, in shawls and dresses for his wife, each and all destined eventually to find their way to the pawnbroker as surely and infallibly as the sparks fly upwards.

For apparently a mere trifle, "just a bite of food, or a half-pint of beer, or an old pair of cast-off boots, or a coat you don't care to be seen about in any longer yourself, even in the worst of weather," thus, "poor old Mickey"; "or just whatever you are pleased to give me; or nothing at all, Mr. Tippens. I'll make the place clean and sweet for you. There is little here I can't do, except maybe the roof and a bit of bricklaying, that needs standing on a high ladder, or the pipes mending, or the gutter seeing to; but leave that all to me, plenty will be glad to earn a shilling or two, and I know where to go to look for them; don't you trouble yourself at all. Which had we best make a start with, the house, d'ye think, or the yard?"

Mr. Tippens thought the house. Once he was on the premises he could see to a bit of the loft and stables himself, and give Mike a helping hand; and his wife was all agog to get in, and put the place to rights while the fine weather lasted; and he had some fresh lodgers now, only waiting till he could take them in; and the children, poor things, were wild at the thought of the yard and the out-buildings.

"And fine children they are too," answered the worthy Michael; "but there, what would hinder them? You're not an ill-favoured man yourself, Mr. Tippens, and I mind the time when all the girls were setting their caps at you, and the like of your wife for beauty never stepped. The very sight of her seems to do my old eyes good, like the sunshine on a bright May morning. She always minds me somehow of primroses and violets and bluebells, and the scent of the wallflowers that used to grow along on the low wall of my father's garden down in

Surrey," and as he uttered these poetical similes, Michael's watery eyes wistfully followed the movements of Mr. Tippens' right hand while it fumbled in his pocket for a shilling, to bestow on the "poor old fellow, who had neither chick nor child, nor one belonging to him."

The expenditure of whitewash in that house was something awful; Westminster Abbey or the Tower of London could scarcely have required a larger outlay in whiting.

"You have no idea," said Mike, "of the quantity of wash them ceilings needs"—which, indeed, Mr. Tippens had not—floors, walls, and Mickey himself also received coat after coat; and the dust, according to the ex-helper's account, was so awful he was forced to keep a pot of beer constantly beside him, in one of the cupboards, to take a sip of at frequent intervals to prevent his choking.

At last, however, even Mike felt it would be dangerous any longer to defer announcing the completion of the repairs. He was brought to this state of mind by a visit from Mrs. Tippens, who, after declaring in tones not much like the birds in spring that she could have done the work herself in a quarter of the time, said, "Done or undone, she meant to have the "cleaning" begun on the following Monday," when she requested the favour of Mike's room instead of his company.

She saw clearly enough that individual was in a fuddled state, and whether the intoxication was produced by beer, or gin, or whitewash, or the lead in the paint, did not signify to her; even the praise of her children only elicited the answer that they were "well enough," and a more elaborate tribute to her own charms failed to soften the asperity with which she told him to "hold his tongue."

"I expect that Mickey has taken you in nicely, Dick," she said to her husband that night.

"Oh, it hasn't cost me so much," answered Mr. Tippens easily; "there was a whole lot of things to do."

As indeed he found when the rainy months and the snow came, and the water poured from the spouts, all of which leaked, and the wet soaked through the broken tiles that had never been replaced; and it was found necessary to open all the drains.

Long before winter arrived, however, Mrs. Tippens discovered that not a lock or bolt in the house worked properly; that the paint had only been smeared on the woodwork; that the whole of the repairs, in fact, had consisted in further dilapidation of the coats of Mr. Mike's stomach; and that almost all the money paid by her husband for "labour," "material," "extra help," "hire of ladders," "use of pulley," and so forth, had been spent over the counter of the "Guy Faux" tavern, situated round a near and convenient corner.

Meeting Mike one day, her just indignation found utterance, and, with feminine frankness, she reproached him for having deceived a man who had been so kind to him as her husband. Mrs. Tippens was in no sense of the word a shrew, but she could upon occasion speak out her mind, and on this occasion she did speak it very plainly.

Mike never attempted to deny the charge, he only tried to turn it into a victory by a strategic movement likely to divert her attention.

"What was the use," asked the hoary sinner, "of spending good money fitting a house up like a palace I knew you would never be able to live in ? "

"What would hinder us living in it ? " retorted Mrs. Tippens, more in the way of comment than inquiry.

"What would hinder you?—Why old Mrs. Jones, to be sure; she'll never let anybody live in the house till her bones are dug up out of the hole where her husband buried her."

"Oh, don't talk to me of your Mrs. Joneses !" exclaimed Mrs. Tippens, to whom the names was evidently not new. "At any rate, I never did any harm to the woman—never saw her, to my knowledge, so it's not likely she would come troubling me."

"She troubles everybody that tries to live in the house you're so set up with. Why, the last people did not stop a fortnight. It's well known she walks the place over, from the second floor down; and, if you take my advice, you won't go into the back-cellar alone after night."

Chapter Two

IT was Sunday evening. Mr. Tippens sat on one side of the fire and his wife on the other. They had partaken of tea, and it was not yet quite time for supper; the children were abed, three of them in a little room at the end of the passage Doctor Jones had used as a surgery, while the baby was, for a wonder, fast asleep in its cradle, which stood in a dark corner behind Mrs. Tippens' chair. The horses had long been fed and littered down. Mr. Tippens always took a look at them last thing, but last thing would not be yet for an hour or more. The house was as quiet as the grave, and through the smoke caused by his pipe Richard Tippens, with a delightful sense of well-being, and doing, and feeling, dreamily regarded his wife, who was certainly an extremely pretty woman, possessing further the reputation of being an extraordinarily good manager; neat in her own person, she always kept her children clean and tidy and well dressed; her rooms were regularly swept and scrubbed, and hearthstoned and blackleaded; she mended her husband's clothes, and sewed on his buttons, and with the help of a woman who came in to "chair," as it is generally called, did the family washing and the family ironing; she was a very fair cook, not in the least lazy—quite the contrary, indeed—and yet, if I may venture to say so, in the teeth of public opinion, which always favours women of her type, I do not think she was a good manager, for she spent up to the hilt of her income, whatever that might be. She was always considering how to increase her "gettings," but she never gave a thought as to how she might save them.

Her husband gave her a liberal allowance, and brought home from outlying regions, where he saw such articles marked up cheap, fowls, fish, necks of mutton, vegetables, and other welcome helps to housekeeping. She had a house full of regularly paying lodgers, who found their own latch-keys, and required no attendance. She took in needlework, at which, as she got it by favour, she was able to make a considerable amount of money—and yet, if she had told the truth to her own heart, she would have said, "We are not one bit better off than we were when Dick only gave me a pound certain every week, and paid the rent."

It is a pity someone, thoroughly up in financial questions, does not inform us why uncertain incomes lead almost invariably to extravagant living.

Your true economist, your excellent manager, your incomparable financier, is a labourer at a given weekly wage, a clerk on starvation salary, the lady left with the poorest of limited incomes. The moment "gettings," in any shape, enter into the question economy retires, worsted, from the contest. "You have got so much to-day, you may get so much more to-morrow," that is the reasoning. Now, why cannot the "gettings" be put aside? Why cannot they be left like an egg in the nest for more to be laid? We know, of course, they never are; but why is it?

Among my own somewhat varied acquaintances, I number, at this moment of writing, two persons—one, a lady whose income, all told, does not reach a hundred a year; on this amount she pays the rent of her rooms, she lives, she dresses; she is not young, and her health requires some few luxuries; yet she is never in debt, and she has always a trifle to spare for those who may be sick or sorry. The other is a youth who I do not think has yet counted eighteen summers; his health is perfect, his rank does not necessitate other than the most moderate expenditure for a bed; his hat covers his family; when he visits, his toilet is easily and perfectly made with a clean collar and a fancy tie; his weekly income has been from thirty to five-and-thirty shillings a week and "gettings"; and yet, lately, when he had been four days out of work, with the certainty of getting into work again on the next day but one, he had to pawn his watch!

Most certainly political economists of the age now coming towards us will find few more difficult questions to deal with than this of "gettings." Were an angel to descend from Heaven to-night and tell Mrs. Tippens what I know, that "gettings" had been the curse of herself, her husband, and her children, she would not believe him; so it would be worse than folly for me to speak—even if not cruel impertinence—now the inevitable end has come: the parish; the philanthropic society, the ever-decreasing bounty for which she is able to make interest; such casual help as she can get, and such work as she is able to obtain.

But no one that evening, looking at her and her husband, as they sat beside the fire, at the comfortable, well-furnished room, the bright blaze, the clean-swept hearth, could possibly have thought evil days were looming in the distance for both husband and wife. He, the picture of health and strength; she, a slight and still apparently quite young woman, with a refined style of beauty, and a cast of features altogether unusual in her rank. When her voice was not upraised and her temper tried, both of which had been the case during her encounter with that arch-hypocrite Mike, her mode of speaking accorded with the pure and delicate lines of her countenance. In truth, she had been well brought up, and from her youth knew how, with propriety, to address ladies—*real* ladies, as she was sometimes almost too careful to add; and since her marriage she had kept herself to herself; and in her own home, her children, her relations, and her husband found all the interest and society she required.

"Dick," she said, after they had sat in silence for some little time.

"I'm here, Luce," he answered; "what is it, my girl ?"

"You never told me this house was haunted."

"I told you people said it was haunted," he answered, "and you laughed at the idea; because, as you wisely remarked, 'when once people are buried they've done with this world, surely.' "

"But that's just what we don't know—whether old Mrs. Jones was ever buried or not."

"We don't know whether she is dead or not, for that matter."

"Then if she's not dead, where can she be ?"

"And if Doctor Jones isn't dead, where can he be ?" retorted Mr. Tippens.

"There's dreadful things said about this house, Dick."

"Well, you just turn a deaf ear to them, and they won't break your night's rest. What's Doctor or Mrs. Jones to us ? He was a bad man, we know; and she, if all accounts may be trusted, was a bit of a shrew, and held a tight grip on the money, which he married her for. He did not take her for her good looks, I'm sure; for a plainer, more ordinary woman you couldn't have met in a day's walk in London. She was more like a witch than anything else—a little bit of a woman, with eyes like black beads, and a face the colour of mahogany; but there—I've described her before, Luce, and I think we might find something pleasanter to talk about now."

"But they say, Dick—they do, indeed—she walks the house, and —— "

"Pack of rubbish," interrupted Mr. Tippens warmly; "who says it—at least, who says it to you ?"

"Why, mostly everybody—the baker, and the bootmaker down the street, and Mike——"

"She didn't hinder *him* staying in the house, at any rate," commented Dick.

"Well, Mr. Mowder lived here, you know."

"And he was turned out because he wouldn't pay a farthing of rent."

"He says," persisted Mrs. Tippens resolutely; "there was always like a cold air in the passage."

"You can't expect the hall to feel exactly sultry with those great underground kitchens and cellars. I've a mind to put a few spikes in the door, and so shut the whole of those caverns off the rest of the house."

"But then, Dick, dear, what should we and our lodgers do about coals ?"

"Aye, there you go," observed Dick. "Every woman's alike; the moment a man makes a suggestion, she's sure to raise some difficulty. Then I won't nail up the door; will that meet your views, Mrs. Tippens ?"

"Now, Dick, don't let us quarrel," entreated his better half; "there was enough of quarreling here, if all accounts be true, in the Joneses time, without our beginning the same game, and——"

He did not let her finish the sentence, he took his pipe out of his mouth, and drew his chair nearer to where she sat, and put his arm round her waist, and drew her head down on his shoulder, and stroked her hair tenderly, and said, "No fear of that, old girl—ghosts or no ghosts; Mrs. Jones or Mrs. Anybodyelse, we'll not take to quarrelling. Only, you see, I don't want you to be listening to foolish stories and the envious talk of people who, maybe, think we're getting on a bit too fast in the world. The house suits me and my business well, and I can't afford to have you set against it, and, likely as not, wanting to leave, and me bound for the rent for three years. Mind that, my lass," and he gave her a kiss so loud and hearty, neither of them heard the opening of the front door till the sound of several voices caused Mr. Tippens to exclaim :

"What noise is that, Luce ?"

"The Pendells coming in," she answered; "they've her brother and sister with them up from the country."

"It's about getting on for supper time, then, isn't it, Luce ?" asked Mr. Tippens tentatively. He was always ready for his meals on a Sunday, perhaps because he did not take out his cab and had nothing to do.

"Yes, I'll bring it is now," answered his wife; and as she spoke she passed into a lean-to, opening off the sitting-room, which she had metamorphosed into a tiny kitchen, perhaps to avoid the dark loneliness of those underground regions Mr. Tippens well described as caverns.

She had provided a nice little meal, and she looked pretty and grace-

ful as she flitted backwards and forwards, fetching one dish and then
another.

"Why, girl, this is a supper fit for the Lord Mayor," said Mr.
Tippens, looking approvingly at the contents of the table; "I don't
think the Queen herself——"

What he was going to say concerning Victoria by the Grace of God
will never now be known, for when he arrived at this point in his sentence there echoed through the silent house a shriek, which brought
both husband and wife to their feet, followed by a thud, as of something heavy falling to the ground.

"Lord bless and save us !" exclaimed Mr. Tippens, and seizing a
light he rushed out into the passage, followed by his wife.

It was a strangely built house; there were only six steps to the first
landing, where was a cupboard in the wall which Mrs. Pendell used as
a sort of pantry; half-way down this landing there were three steps
more, and then the flight that led direct to the rooms where the
Pendells lived.

As Dick Tippens and his wife ran up the half-dozen steps leading
from the hall, a posse of people came hurrying pell-mell from the upper
part of the house. "What is it ? What has happened ? Is it thieves ? Is
the house on fire ?" No, the house was not on fire, neither had thieves
set themselves at the unprofitable task of effecting an entry; it was only
that on the landing Mrs. Pendell lay in the deadest faint woman ever
fell into, a large dish she had evidently just taken out of the cupboard
smashed to atoms beside her, and the remnants of the joint the family
had operated upon in the middle of the day a few steps down, where it
had rolled when she dropped the dish.

Everything possible and impossible the house contained was
brought to revive Mrs. Pendell; everybody was talking at once, and
each individual had some pet theory to account for the phenomenon.

"I told her she was a-overdoing of it," said her husband, a slow,
florid, phlegmatic, pig-headed sort of man. "Didn't I, Bill ? Didn't I
say to her just on this side of Whitechapel Church, ' you've been a-
over-doing it, Mary, you'll have a turn of them spasms to-morrow'?"

Meantime, the subject of these remarks had been carried into the
inner chamber and laid on her bed, where every recognised experi-
mental and favourite personal expedient was tried in order to restore
her to consciousness; she was "poor deared," her dress was un-

fastened and her stays loosened, smelling salts of every degree of
strength were held to her nostrils, burnt feathers thrust almost up her
nose, her hands slapped, cold water dabbed on her forehead, an attempt
made to get some brandy down her throat, with various other ingenious efforts at torture, which almost drove Mrs. Tippens, who was
in the main a very sensible woman, distracted.

"If you'd only leave her to me and Susie," she said; "there's not a
breath of air in the room, with so many standing about the bed and the
doorway. She'll be right enough after a little, if you'll only not crowd
about her, and let me open the windows."

"She's right," observed Mr. Pendell, from the doorway. "Come
along, all of you, Mrs. Tippens knows what's what."

Mrs. Pendell, however, was so long in justifying this flattering
eulogy in Mrs. Tippens' favour, that Susie, the sister, who had come
up to see her, was just asking it it would not be better to send Bob for
the nearest doctor, when Mrs. Tippens, raising her hand to enforce
silence, said :

"Sh—sh—she's coming to now."

There was a pause, a pin might have been heard drop, so silent and
eager and expectant were the two watchers; then Mrs. Pendell,
recovering, opened her eyes a very little, and Mrs. Tippens, holding
her left hand, and softly rubbing it, said :

"Don't be frightened, dear, it's only me."

"What is it ? Where am I ?" murmured Mrs. Pendell, adding
suddenly, with a gesture of the extremest terror, "Oh ! I remember.
Keep her away from me, Mrs. Tippens ! Mrs. Tippens, won't you keep
her away—that dreadful woman, you know ?"

"She's a bit light-headed," said her sister; "I'm sure Bob had better
go for the doctor."

"I don't think there's any need," answered Mrs. Tippens, quietly
enough, though her very heart seemed to stand still at the words.
"There's nobody shall come near you, dear, but Susie and me. Don't
be looking about the room that way—indeed, there's no one here but
your sister and myself."

"She has long grey hair streaming over her shoulders. Oh, the
wickedest face I ever did see! I know her well, don't you, Mrs.
Tippens ?"

"Yes, yes, dear; but never mind her now; keep yourself quiet."

"She must be the smallest woman in the world," this after a moment's silence; "when I turned from the cupboard I felt like a rush of cold air, and then she stood on the top step but one."

"I think she *would* be the better for some sort of quieting draught," remarked Mrs. Tippens, *sotto voco* to Susan Hay—and it is no disparagement of a courageous woman's courage to say, after Susie left the room she looked fearfully around, while Mrs. Pendell rambled on about the dreadful sight which had struck her down like one dead.

"I have seen people in their coffins, who didn't look half so death-like," she whispered; "she was that dark, and her face and her eyes were so fierce, and her arms so shrivelled, and her hands so like claws going to make a clutch at me; and she had a red mark round her throat, as if she had been wearing a necklace too tight."

"Did she say anything to you?" Mrs. Tippens forced herself to ask.

"No; she was just going to speak when I screamed out with horror. Shall I ever forget her?—ever—ever!" and she buried her head despairingly in the pillow.

"Well, Polly, lass, how do you find yourself now?" said Mr. Pendell, coming into the room at this juncture, and causing a welcome diversion at least to Mrs. Tippens' fancy. "You're getting all right now, aren't you? Ah, I felt afraid what was coming; did I say to you, or did I not, on this side of Whitechapel Church, 'You've been a-over-doing of it, Mary; you'll have a turn of them spasms to-morrow'?"

For answer Mary only put her hand in her husband's and lay strangely still and quiet.

"Bob has gone for the doctor," proceeded Mr. Pendell, nodding across at Mrs. Tippens.

In replying, Mrs. Tippens looked at the patient and then nodded back at him.

Before morning broke Mrs. Pendell had brought a child prematurely into the world. That she lived and the baby lived the doctor assured Mr. Pendell was owing entirely to Mrs. Tippens' extraordinary devotion and excellent nursing; and Mr. Pendell declared solemnly to Mrs. Tippens he would never forget her goodness— "night or day, she had only to say what she wanted, and he would be quite at her service"—a promise he found it convenient to forget when evil days fell upon Dick and his wife.

While these events and exchanges of amenities were passing, there happened a curious experience to Mrs. Tippens one night while she was off duty.

Her husband was out on "a late job," and had told her not to sit up for him; and Mrs. Tippens having undressed and said her prayers, and placed a box of matches where she could instantly lay hand upon it, was about to blow out the candle and step into bed when from the little room at the end of the passage there came a chorus of "*Mother !* MOTHER ! MOTHER !" which caused her, without making any addition to her toilet beyond instinctively thrusting her bare feet into a pair of her husband's slippers, to snatch up the candle and rush to the place where her children slept.

"Now then, what is all this noise about?" she asked, seeing they were every one alive and each sitting bolt upright in bed. Theoretically Mrs. Tippens was nothing if not a disciplinarian, but the young ones twisted her round their little fingers for all that. "You'll bring all the lodgers down; I have a great mind to give each of you a good whipping."

"There was a woman in the room, mamma !" said Mrs. Tippens' second-born.

"And she came and touched me," added the youngest of the trio.

"Yes, that she did, I see her," exclaimed the eldest son; "a little woman with hair hanging about her like yours, only grey and not so long, and with eyes as black as Lucy's new doll's, the one Mr. Pendell gave her, and as dark as that man with the white turban we saw in the Strand and——"

"Hold your tongue this instant, and never let me hear your nonsense again," interrupted Mrs. Tippens angrily. "You had too much pudding for supper, that's what's the matter with you, and you got the nightmare and woke up thinking you saw all sorts of things."

"But we couldn't all have had nightmares," persisted Dick, who was a sturdy lad, and his father's pride and hope; "I saw her go up to Effie and lay her hand on her."

"It was cold, too," supplemented the child.

"And I saw her as well," capped Lucy, fearful of lagging behind the others in this little matter of renown and glory.

"You are very naughty children," answered Mrs. Tippens, in a superior sort of tone; then, descending to details, "it is so very likely, Dicky, you could see anyone in the dark."

"Oh, but she brought a light with her, a sort of a lamp."

At this point Mrs. Tippens collapsed. If old Mrs. Jones were able, not merely to go wandering about a house for which she paid no rent or taxes, but also to find her own light, what other feat might that lady not be expected to perform ? "Now, never let me hear any more of such folly," she said, however, valiantly, upon the principle that most noise is to be got out of an empty barrel; "I'll turn the key in the door, and then you'll know nobody can get in."

"No, leave the key inside, and I'll lock the door, and then, if she comes again, I'll holloa."

"You'd better not," retorted his mother, so sharply that Dick, discomfited, wrapped the bedclothes about his head, and twisting himself up like a hedgehog, lay repeating in a sort of rhyme the description of the woman who had broken in upon his rest.

That Mrs. Tippens did not sleep much during the course of the night—no, not even when her husband was snoring by her side, and the children had long sunk into slumber—will be readily imagined.

Chapter Three

FEW things had ever caused more excitement in a neighbourhood than the disappearance of Doctor and Mrs. Jones. Here to-day and gone to-morrow; gone, without beat of drum or sound of fife; gone, without the excitement of furniture moving, or cab laden with luggage, or funeral pomp and ceremony; even a one-horse hearse, without plumes or mutes, or decorous wands, or long black cloaks, or hatbands, or mourning coaches to follow, would have been better than this silent, mysterious flitting.

If the earth had suddenly opened and swallowed up husband and wife they could not have vanished more utterly. There was the house they had lived in, but where were they ?

What secret did that one night hold which all the intelligence of the whole parish failed to elucidate. Where was he ? What was more to the point, where was *she*? Upon this last question public opinion at length became unanimous. She was buried in the cellars. Her husband had murdered her—so it was finally decided—and after killing the "poor dear" had disposed of her remains in the manner indicated. That an industrious course of digging and grubbing brought no body or bones to light proved nothing but that "the doctor was a deep one," to quote the observations of local wiseacres.

"He used her cruel in her lifetime," said one.

"Ay, that he did," capped another. "And he wouldn't give her the chance of Christian burial. She's lying hidden away in some dark corner; no wonder the creature can't rest there. No; I wouldn't sleep a night in that house, not if you counted me down a hundred pounds in golden sovereigns."

"Neither would I, was it ever so."

"For there's not a doubt she walks."

"Of course she does. Didn't my own cousin, when she was coming along the passage one summer's night, feel like an icy wind at the nape of her neck, and as if a cold hand was laid flat on her shoulders? And she always says she knows if she had looked round she'd have seen the old woman with her grey hair——"

"That he used to d rag her about by——"

"Streaming down her back, and her eyes, filled with hunger and ill-treatment, staring through the darkness."

"The house ought to be pulled to the ground—that's what ought to be done with it——"

"And not one stone left on another——"

"And those cellars thoroughly examined."

"It's my belief there's some secret place in them that hasn't been found out yet."

"Very likely. You know it is reported there used to be a passage big enough for a man to creep along from there to the Thames."

"Bless and save us—maybe he has put her in the river."

"No, no; though he was wicked enough for that or anything else, she's in the house somewhere right enough, and if she could speak she would say so."

"I wonder where he is ?"

"Lord knows. Enjoying himself, most likely, beyond the seas."

"I suppose he was about the worst man you ever knew."

"I suppose he was about the worst man anybody ever knew."

"And the cleverest."

"Aye, he had brains to do anything, but they all turned to wickedness."

It often happens that a man obtains a reputation for talent in his own immediate circle on very slight and insufficient grounds; but in the case of Dr. Jones, popular rumour did not exaggerate the missing gentleman's abilities.

He was very clever indeed. He was so clever he might have risen to almost any height in his profession, had he not been at once lazy and self-indulgent. His father having lived and practised before, he succeeded to a prosperous business and a wide connection. When he first started on his own account, all the old houses in the street where he lived, and all the old houses in many other streets and squares and terraces and groves near at hand, were inhabited by well-to-do City people, by widows amply dowered, by men who had made their money in trade and were now living in affluent retirement.

It was a capital parish for a doctor to settle in; none of your new neighbourhoods, tenanted by mere birds of passage; once a medical man got a patient he had a chance of keeping him for many years. There were names on Dr. Jones' books of people and families who had been physicked by the Jones for more than half a century. Never a man began life under more auspicious circumstances.

He had the medical ball at his feet. Old ladies adored him, because he ordered them exactly what he knew they liked in the way of eating; old gentlemen were quite sure he understood their complaints, when he declared "a few glasses of sound wine could hurt no one." He met the best physicians and surgeons in consultation, and people agreed if any man could put a person on his legs again that man was Dr. Jones.

But as time went on, and Dr. Jones waxed more prosperous and less careful, it was found that, in spite of his many admirable virtues, he had grave faults. In no single respect did his moral character attain to that high standard which a doctor, above all other men, ought to try to reach. Things were whispered about him which mothers felt could not be spoken of before the younger members of the family; things indeed, which were, even among matrons, mentioned with chairs drawn close together, and bated breath and much uplifting of eyes and hands.

Fact is, the decency and restraint of respectable English society had become intolerable to the successful practitioner. For a long time he contented himself with sowing his bad wild oats at a distance from his dwelling—drinking, gambling, and leading the loosest of lives in the many disreputable haunts to be found on the north side of the Thames, instead of frequenting those in his own county of Surrey. But by degrees he began to fall into evil habits near home; then into the midst of that very sanctuary presided over by a maiden sister of uncertain age and rigid morality, he introduced all manner of wickedness.

The day came when Miss Jones could endure the drinking and the smoking and the card-playing and the boon-companions no longer. With a certain stately dignity she packed up her belongings and left the house where she had been born. Further, she employed a lawyer to disentangle her pecuniary affairs from those of her brother. Then all their little world knew dreadful things must be going on at Dr. Jones'. His character, or rather lack of character, was discussed both by church and chapel goers. His doings added a fresh zest to parish visiting, for, of course, the poor knew even more about the doctor's sins than their betters. His tastes led him to prefer bold, flaunting women to their more modest, if not less frail, sisters; and the brazen impudence of the "dreadful creatures" he successively selected for housekeepers furnished as constant a theme for comment and gossip as the shortcomings of Doctor Jones himself.

"He wants a wife to steady him," said one lady, whose daughter had been marriageable for nearly a third part of the time allotted by the Psalmist to man's sojourn on earth.

Alas ! poor soul, her wishes blinded her. All the wives of all the patriarchs could not have steadied Dr. Jones. He had started on a muck, and was running it blindly, like one possessed. Had he lived in the former days, one might have said that not one devil merely but a legion had taken for habitation the handsome fleshly temple of his body.

In the way of open sin, unblushing audacious wickedness, no medical man, perhaps, ever vied with Dr. Jones.

His house, after his sister's departure, became a scandal and a reproach, and yet so great was the doctor's skill he still had patients, and good paying patients too, but they were all of his own sex; the man did not live who could have sent for him to attend wife, or sister, or mother, or daughter.

So his family practice slipped into other and cleaner hands, and another and wiser general practitioner grew rich upon Doctor Jones' leavings.

All at once society was amazed by the rumour that the Doctor was going to be married to a lady possessed of great wealth; so report said, adding that ere long wonderful changes might be looked upon in the old house.

It was swept and garnished at any rate, the drawing-room smartened up, a brougham purchased, the latest and most utterly objectionable housekeeper dispatched about her business, whatever it might be, two respectable servants engaged, a man hired to look after the horse, answer the door, and prove a general credit to the street. Doctor Jones himself left off smoking pipes and took to cigars instead; he eschewed the local public houses, foreswore billiards, all packs of cards were cleared out of the dwelling; he washed, he shaved; he wore a coat instead of a dressing-gown, and he was to be found, by such patients as desired to see him, before twelve o'clock, till which time he had of late been in the habit of taking his rest in bed.

Things were looking up; the Mrs. Jones who was to be had, people felt, already achieved wonders; she was a credit to her sex; ladies admitted they could not possibly ever have the husband again as a medical man, but they might once more receive him as an acquaintance. Prodigals are always interesting, perhaps because no one ever really believes they will reform, and Doctor Jones was a specially delightful prodigal—so clever, so handsome, so reckless, so wicked, so extravagant.

He had studied at one time at a German University, and it had somehow been ascertained that no wilder spirit ever troubled the peace of the quaint old town that lay under the shadow of the frowning castle.

His world which, a short time previously, failed to find words strong enough to express its reprobation of his conduct, now began to make excuses for him. Perhaps his faults had been exaggerated, possibly there was only a modicum of truth in the reports which had been spread abroad concerning his doings: clever men always make enemies, the tattle of the lower orders could not be exactly depended upon; and in fine, to put the matter in a nutshell, it was at length unanimously decided to call on Mrs. Jones when she returned from the honeymoon.

There was something after these visits for gossips to talk about!

What countrywoman could she be ?—where had he met her ?—what was she ?—who was she ?—what had she been ?

Years seemed to stretch between her and the doctor—on the wrong side, of course.

She was little, she was old, she was plain, she was ignorant, and she was most furiously jealous. She could not endure her husband to look at or speak to any other woman. Even the elderly unmarried daughter of her mother, who was a widow, who would have liked Seraphina to undertake the doctor's case, even this innocent ewe lamb seemed unbearable to the bride.

No use now to think of pleasant little parties to which Mrs. Jones and her reformed husband might be bidden. No card-tables, no carpet-dances, no snug dinners, no safe and harmless social intercourse, which it had been hoped might prove to the repentant doctor as refreshing and non-intoxicating as a course of milk, lemonade, and cocoa to the once infuriated drunkard.

On the whole, perhaps, the matrons, in their hearts, thought Mrs. Jones' virtues worse than her husband's vices; tacitly it was agreed not to force acquaintanceship on her. Possibly she had her own set of friends, and it was felt it would be most undesirable to introduce foreigners of no respectable colour into the bosom of British families who had made their money in the City, as everybody knew; and who piqued themselves upon the strictness of their morals, the length of their purses, and the strength of their prejudices.

One gentleman, whose own face was as rosy as a peony, declared, with a mild asseveration, "Jones has married a blackamoor;" but Mrs. Jones was not black, only exceedingly brown, so brown that if she darkened much more, as time went on, she bade fair eventually to outvie the rich splendour of the old Spanish mahogany chairs, which had been recovered and repolished to do her honour.

Chapter Four

At the end of little more than three years from the date of his marriage, it might have been truly said of Doctor Jones that his last state was worse than his first. How many demons eventually took up their habitation within him it would be impossible to say; but the doings of the Jones' household, more particularly the doings of its master, became a terror and reproach to the neighbourhood.

How the case really stood no one ever exactly knew; all sorts of rumours and stories passed from mouth to mouth. She would not give him a shilling of her money, so gossip averred. He had stood over her with a cutting whip to compel her to sign papers, and then she would not; a mode of proceeding on the part of Doctor Jones to practise before witnesses, which was, to say the least of the matter, unlikely. Popular report asserted he starved her; but as she generally answered the street-door herself, was free to walk in and out if she pleased, and could have told any tradesmen to bring her anything she fancied, this was evidently a libel. At one time an idea got abroad that the whole tale of her fortune had been a myth; that the Doctor had been taken in, and that there were dreadful quarrels between them in consequence; but the boastings of various servants who declared they had seen her with "rolls on rolls" of banknotes and with such diamonds and rubies as the "Queen of Sheba or Solomon himself could have had nothing more splendid," negatived the truth of this statement.

Money or no money, however, the Jones, were a miserable couple. Mrs. Jones could not and would not endure a female servant about the house; as fast as they were engaged they went: a fortnight was a long time for any woman, young or old, to stop in the situation, and so ere long the house acquired that look of dirt and neglect some houses seem especially able to assume at the shortest notice. Little more than three years married and already the grass growing between the stones in the stableyard was nearly a foot high. The high-stepping horse had long been sold, and the brougham also; the new piano, never opened, followed suit; and about the same time Doctor Jones, giving up all idea of reformation and practice, and abandoning the rôle of a repentant prodigal, returned to his swine and his husks on the Middlesex side of the river; for he could not enjoy even such companionship and diet on his own side of the water, for fear Mrs. Jones might take it in her head to mar with her presence the delights of an evening in some low public house or lower music hall, or lower depth still; for, if all stories were to be believed, the Doctor went down very low indeed. Accordingly, when Christmas, for the fourth time after that inauspicious and, as some people went so far as to say, unchristian marriage, was approaching, people felt Doctor Jones had run about the length of his tether.

A change of some sort seemed imminent. He was in debt in the neighbourhood, a thing he had never been known to be in before. Even the few things sent into that evil house were not paid for, and hitherto the Doctor's credit had been so good that he owed in the neighbourhood more than might otherwise have been the case.

Mrs. Jones said she would not pay, and the Doctor said he could not. Nevertheless, after some parley, he promised to do what he could after Christmas—this was remembered afterwards—and the British tradesman, easily irritated, easily appeased, departed.

No joint, no turkey, no anything was ordered in for the 25th of that December. "Let him get his Christmas dinner where he gets his other dinners," said Mrs. Jones, in answer to a feeble remonstrance from the crone who came in daily to "put the place a bit to rights," a woman so old, so wrinkled, so ugly, so dirty, and so shabby that even Doctor Jones, his wife felt, was unlikely to chuck her under the chin, or exchange with her repartees more remarkable for wit than refinement. Apprised in due time of the fare he might expect at home, the once again unreformed prodigal announced his intention of accepting an invitation he said he had received to dine at a friend's house on Christmas Day.

Mrs. Jones tried hard to ascertain where this friend lived, but in vain, and still firm to her intention of providing no feast, even for herself, she told Mrs. Jubb, the charwoman, to bring in the tea tray and the kettle, and then to go.

About the events of that day and evening and the following morning Mrs. Jubb had afterwards much to tell, and she told it.

"As I come up from the kitchen," she was wont to observe, "and an awful kitchen that was too, full of black-beetles and slugs—just as I got on the top of the stairs, I saw the master, with his thick coat on, brushing his hat. He put it on and he took his umbrella, and he opened the door and slammed it after him, and that was the last I ever see of Doctor Jones. I took the tea-things into the drawing-room, and set the kettle on the hob, and I asked Mrs. Jones if she was sure I could not do anything else before I went.

"She said, 'Quite sure, Mrs. Jubb; good evening.'

"I had a sort of feeling on me, I did not like to leave her, though I knew John's children would be crying for me at home; and so I made believe to be putting the cup and saucer and plate nearer to her hand, and she looked round in her quick way, and asked sharp, as if I had angered her:

"'Didn't you hear me say "good evening," Mrs. Jubb? You can go.'

"So I went, and that was the last I ever saw of her. Goodness only knows where they both went to. It was not the next day, but the next day but one, the police got into the house through a window at the back that was left half an inch open (for I went down to the station, and told the inspector I was sure as sure murder had been done, for I could not make anybody hear, and the gas was burning, and the cat, poor thing, mewing in the area, and not another sign of life about the place); and there they found the tray just as I'd left it, and the fire out and the kettle on the hob, and high or low, in garret or cellar, not a trace of Doctor or Mrs. Jones."

There was nothing which gratified Mrs. Jubb's numerous friends and acquaintances more than to get her started on this theme.

The story was one which, properly managed, lasted for hours. Mrs. Jubb's feelings, Mrs. Jubb's doings, Mrs. Jubb's sayings, the remarks of the police, the fury and dismay of the tradespeople, and the many observations of the sprightly youth and beauty and strength of the neighbourhood, enabled the narrative to be spun out almost to the length of a three-volume novel.

"And after all, *where* did Doctor and Mrs. Jones go?" once asked an impatient and inquisitive auditor, who chanced to be listening for the first time to the oft-told tale.

"That'll never be known on this earth," answered Mrs. Jubb; "my own notion is, she started to follow him——"

"Then she can't be buried in the cellars," interposed another.

"You don't know what a man like that could do," said Mrs. Jubb; "why, even now, poor as I am, I wouldn't live in the house as them Tippenses are doing, no, not if you paved the hall with golden guineas."

"There's nobody going to tempt you, mother," remarked an incredulous youth; "I'd chance meeting all the ghosts out of the churchyard, let alone old Mrs. Jones, for a ten-pound note."

"You don't know what you are talking about, Jim," retorted Mrs. Jubb.

"Well, it was a queer start anyway," returned the undaunted Jim; "the Kilkenny cats left their tails behind them, but the Doctor and his wife took away every bit of their bodies——"

"And left clothes, and furniture, and bedding, and china, and plate, and linen, and all, just as if they had walked out of the house to spend a day at a friend's."

Which statement was, indeed, literally true; when the police entered the house they found no corpse, no confusion, no symptom of murder or premeditated departure. Nothing seemed to have been removed except the master and mistress, who had not taken with them even the typical "comb and toothbrush."

They were gone. Doctor Jones' creditors drew their own conclusions; the wealthy and respectable inhabitants did not know what to believe or think; the police felt disposed to consider the whole affair a make-up between the doctor and his wife; the general public, as usual, were not to be convinced by argument, or confounded by facts, they preferred to believe old Mrs. Jones had been murdered and her body what they called "put away" somewhere about the premises. Shortly after there followed a rumour of hidden treasure, then it was known for certain that the house was haunted, and, further, that no one who tried to live in it but was visited by some misfortune.

When the wind howled outside her dwelling, and shook the casements, and whistled through the keyholes, and the rain beat against the windows with a noise like slapping with an open hand, it was a dear delight to gossips to gather round Mrs. Jubb's fire, to which most who came contributed a billet and hear the whole story again, with additions of what had happened to those venturesome enough to try conclusions with old Mrs. Jones, out of the flesh.

"She was an awful woman to have much to say to when living," said Mrs. Jubb; "dead, she'll be a thousand times worse."

"I wonder what she wants wandering about the old house," said the irrepressible Jim; "if all accounts are true, she was none so happy in it."

"Ah, she knows that best herself, and she's not going to tell," returned Mrs. Jubb. "I wouldn't like to see her, that's all."

Chapter Five

To say that Mrs. Tippens wished to leave the house when her lodgers and children began to see visions is but to say she was a woman. She told her husband she "didn't know how she felt," which meant, as he was too well aware, that she desired to move. She likewise casually mentioned that "she seemed all nerves," and that "she was getting afraid of her own shadow."

To this Mr. Tippens replied he was very sorry, but he hoped she would try and pull herself together a bit, and not be frightened by a lot of lying stories. If they only held their tongues and stayed in the house for a while, people would soon quit talking about old Mrs. Jones, and then their lodgers would remain and not give notice because a door creaked.

He reminded her how he was answerable for the rent for three years, that he was not likely ever to get such cheap and convenient premises again, and he implored her, like a good girl, not to be foolish and be-lieve the house was haunted just because a parcel of old women, with Mrs. Jubb at their head, chose to give it a bad name.

"But, Dick," remonstrated Mrs. Tippens, "you know it is said that nobody thrives who stops here. There was old Mrs. Smith broke her leg in two places, and Mrs. Curtiss's child was run over in the street; and Mr. Perks, that was so respected, fell to robbing his employer, and is in jail now for taking more than a hundred pounds. And John Coombe turned teetotaller, and took to beating his wife—and——"

Mr. Tippens laughed outright. "Make your mind easy, Luce," he said; "I'm not likely either to turn teetotaller or take to beating you, lass; and as for the children, if you don't like them sleeping out of your sight, bring them in here till you get some of those notions blown off your mind; and when the days draw out a little, you and they shall have a week at the seaside, and you'll get so strong and well you'll laugh at ghosts, and make quite a joke of old Mrs. Jones."

Poor Mrs. Tippens! She only wished her lodgers could see the joke as well, for they were always going; except one old lady on the top floor who was blind and slightly deaf, not a soul stopped any time with her.

"I don't know how it is," she said to them, "for I have never seen anything in the house myself." Whereupon she was told "she was fortunate," or reminded "there were none so blind as those that would not see," or assured "her turn was certain to come," or advised, "clear out of the house before harm befell her and hers," "for it is just a-tempting of Providence to stop in it," said one person.

"Upon the other hand," as Mr. Tippens, determined to look on the bright side of things, remarked, "if lodgers were always going they were always coming; and you get such long prices for the rooms, Lucy, they can afford to stay empty part of a week now and then; and see how well the children are, having the yard to play in, which gives them plenty of air and keeps them out of the streets; and you are stronger and better yourself, and would be hearty if you would only stir about a bit more and not sit so constant at your needle." Further, business with Mr. Tippens was so good he had been forced to buy another horse, for which he paid seven pounds. "That very same horse," he often afterwards stated, "no more nor a month later I sold, as true as I am standing her, for twenty guineas. A fare took a fancy to him and bid me the money, and you may be sure I didn't say 'no.'"

It was, perhaps, on the strength of this transaction Mrs. Tippens and family travelled to Southend for the week previously mentioned to eat shrimps and repair dilapidations, returning to Doctor Jones's former residence, as Mr. Tippens declared, "in the best of health and spirits."

It was not long, however, after their return before Mrs. Tippens again began to feel her nerves troubling her. She did not say anything to her husband about the matter, but she mentioned to a few friends she had a "sort of weight on her," as if there was "something wrong, she did not know what," and "a fluttering round her heart," and "a weakness in her limbs," and "a creeping sensation at the back of her neck, when she came along the passage, as though, on the warmest day, a chill, clammy hand was laid there," after which lucid description of symptoms the whole question of old Mrs. Jones was again thoroughly gone into; the statements of all the lodgers repeated *in extenso*, and the gossip current in the neighbourhood retailed for the twentieth time.

Small marvel that when, after these conversations, almost exhaustive as they were of the Jones topic, Mrs. Tippens, returning to her house, felt a "waft of raw air" meet her the moment she opened the street door, and something "brush along the hall after her," as she passed into the sitting-room. She was braver than most women, and would, had she seen anything tangible, have tried to solve the enigma. But this pursuit by a shadow, this terror of the unseen, the feeling that there was a presence in the room with her which yet eluded her sight, began to prey on both her mind and body. She longed to cry out, "Take me away from this evil house or I shall die"; but when Dick entered, his honest face radiant with smiles, his tongue ready to tell of the gentlemen who had hired him to drive them to Chiswick, and given him about four times his proper fare, and some present in his hands for "Luce, old girl," the words died away on her lips, and she could only thank Dick for thinking so constantly about her, and hang round his neck with a fervour Mr. Tippens was not accustomed to from a somewhat undemonstrative wife.

"Who do you think I have had a letter from?" he asked one morning in the early summer, as he came in to breakfast, after a stroll down the street in search of a dried haddock or something savoury for Luce, who "seemed a bit peaked and off her feed"—Luce cannot speak of those days, and of her husband's constant thought for her, now without tears—"why, from my cousin, Anne Jane; I met the postman— and Luce, I couldn't get anything worth buying for you, only a nasty kipper, but I thought kippers were better than nothing, as you're tired of rashers; well, as I was saying, I met the postman, and he gave me a letter from Anne Jane. Her mistress and the whole family are going abroad, but they are keeping on Anne Jane, you see, though she doesn't go with them. While they are away she has a fancy for a change. She's tired of the sea and Brighton, and thinks she'd like to spend her holiday in London, so she writes to ask if we can take her in; she wants to pay for her board and lodging, but, of course, that's all nonsense; I shouldn't let my uncle's daughter pay a halfpenny for bread as long as I had a penny roll; what do you say, Luce? Shall I tell her to come; she's a good girl, as you know, and a quiet, and she'd be company for you while I am away. What d'ye say, girl?"

"I'd be only too glad for her to come, Dick; but where is she to sleep; we could only give her the room at the end of the passage, and——"

"If that's all, make your mind quite easy; she doesn't come of a family which trouble themselves about what you can't lay hold of. Then you're agreeable to have her, my girl; if you're not, just say the word——"

"I can't tell you how pleased I should be to have her, only——"

"I'll make that all right, old woman," and accordingly that very same day Dick went out and bought three sheets of notepaper for a penny, and three envelopes for the same price; and in the silent seclusion of the stable, while the horsekeeper was away for his dinner, indited an epistle to his cousin, in which he assured her of a warm welcome, of his determination not to take a farthing of her hard-earned wages, and of Lucy's delight at the prospect of showing her the London sights. "My wife's the best wife ever lived," he finished, "but she's a bit down at present, and I know you'll cheer her up.

"So no more at present, from your loving cousin,

"R. TIPPENS.

"P.S. I hope you're not afraid of ghosts, for folks will have it this house is haunted, though neither Luce or myself have ever seen anything worse nor ourselves."

All in good time Miss Anne Jane Tippens arrived at the house tenanted by her cousins from London Bridge Station in a four-wheeler, on the top of which appeared a trunk, encased in a neat holland cover, bound with red, the handiwork of Anne Jane, who paid the cabman his exact fare duly ascertained beforehand, and walked in the hall old Mrs. Jones was supposed to haunt, laden with all the impedimenta perishable creatures of the frailer sex are so fond of carrying whithersoever they go—a withered nosegay, a basket filled with seaweed and shells, a bandbox, another paper-box, oblong, and a few paper parcels were amongst the baggage; but at length everything was stowed away in the room Doctor Jones had used as a surgery, and Mrs. Tippens stood surveying the "very genteel figure" of her husband's cousin, as that young person, after refreshing laving of her dusty face, stood before the glass, "doing up" her hair.

Miss Tippens was the incarnation of the ideal sewing-maid in a good family.

Tall, but not too tall; thin, but not too thin; with pallid face, brown eyes, thick hair brushed back, and tightly plaited till it looked of no account, not pretty or ugly, quiet of movement, soft of voice; a good girl who—at last her toilet finished—turned to Mrs. Tippens and said:

"Now, dear, you'll let me help you all I can while I stay here."

Chapter Six

" I NEVER told her one single word about old Mrs. Jones; there seemed a spell on me," said Mrs. Tippens, using the approved formula of her class, when speaking, subsequently, concerning the events which rendered Miss Tippens' visit memorable. "That very first day as ever was she said, with that still sort of laugh of hers, Dick had warned her not to come if she felt anyways shy of ghosts. 'I have always had rather a wish to see a ghost,' she went on, making my very blood run cold with the light way she talked, and maybe old Mrs. Jones listening to her for aught I could tell. 'What sort of a ghost is it you keep here, Lucy?'

"'There has been a lot of chatter about the house,' I made answer, 'but I don't say anything on the subject indoors for fear of the children being frightened. People pretend there is something not right in the place, but nothing has come Dick's way or mine either'; and then I began talking of something else and Anne took the hint; she was a wonderfully wise, prudent sort of girl, as girls have to be who get into high families and want to keep their situations."

The day following Miss Tippens' arrival was devoted to showing her some of the London sights. She had been in London before, but only for a short time when "the family" came up to town, and she being kept hard at work under the eye of an exceedingly strict housekeeper was unable to see any of the wonders of the metropolis, except Kensal Green Cemetery, concerning which cheerful place she spoke with a good deal of enthusiasm. As a foretaste of the delights to come, Mrs. Tippens took her to the Abbey, showed her the exterior of the Houses of Parliament, the National Gallery, Northumberland House, the fountains in Trafalgar Square, Covent Garden, Somerset House, Temple Bar, St. Paul's, and the Monument. By the time they had arrived at Fish Street Hill, Anne Jane was tired out, and declining to climb Pope's "tall bully," asked Mrs. Tippens if they were very far from home, "because," she added, "I don't think I can walk much more."

"Dear me!" cried Mrs. Tippens, "I ought to have remembered you were not over strong; why, you look fit to drop. We'll go down to the pier and take the boat straight back, and you can rest all day to-morrow, for I shan't be able to stir out, as our first-floors are leaving, and I must see about getting the rooms fit for anyone to see."

"You'll sleep without rocking to-night, young woman," observed Mr. Tippens, as they all sat together over an early supper.

"I always sleep wonderfully sound," replied Miss Tippens, stating the fact as if some peculiar merit attached to it.

"And you'd better lie in in the morning, and I'll bring you a cup of tea," said Mrs. Tippens, kindly hospitable.

"Ay, make her stop a-bed," exclaimed Mr. Tippens. "I'll be bound she gets none too much sleep in service. I'd like well to see a bit of colour in your cheeks before you leave us."

Next morning Mrs. Tippens took a tray, on which was set out a nice little breakfast, into her visiter's bedchamber. Anne Jane did not look much the better for her night's rest and morning's sleep.

"I woke at five," she said, "and then went off again, and never roused till you came in, and yet I feel as tired as possible. I am not much accustomed to walking, and we did walk a long way yesterday."

"Yes, we went too far," agreed Mrs. Tippens, and then she sat down beside her guest's pillow, and tucked the sheet under the tray to keep it steady, and hoped she would relish her breakfast, which, Anne declared "she was sure to do, if only because they were so kind to her."

"We would like to be kind to you," said Mrs. Tippens; adding, so that no more might be said on the subject, "and you slept well?"

"Yes; but isn't it funny, all the earlier part of the night I was dreaming about a woman being murdered. It was talking about old times, and wandering about those ancient places and tombs and monuments, I suppose, made me think of such things. I was quite glad to see the sun shining in at the window when I woke, for oh, the dream did appear just like reality!" And the dreamer paused to drink a little tea, and take a bit of bread and butter, and munch a few leaves of water cress, and taste the delicate slices of ham Dick himself had cut, what he called "Vauxhall fashion," to tempt her cousin's poor appetite, while Mrs. Tippens sat silent, afraid, she could not tell why, of what might be coming.

"Dreams are strange things," proceeded Miss Tippens, after the fashion of a person originating an entirely novel idea, "and mine was a strange dream."

"Your tea will be stone cold, dear," interposed Mrs. Tippens. It was but deferring the evil hour, she felt, yet every moment of delay seemed a moment gained.

"I don't like it very warm," answered the other, "and I want to tell you my dream. I thought I was in a room I had never seen before, with three windows to the street, and one long, narrow window that looked out I didn't know on what. The room was wainscotted about two yards from the floor, well furnished with chairs and tables; I could feel a thick carpet under my feet, and see a glass over the chimney-piece, in which a woman was looking at herself. Oh! Luce, she was the strangest woman I ever beheld, so little, she was forced to stand on a footstool to see herself in the glass; she had a brown face and grey hair, and her dress was unfastened, and a necklace, that sparkled and glittered, clasped her neck, and she pinned a brooch, that shone like fire, in the front of her under bodice; and on a little table beside her lay an open jewel case, in which there were precious stones gleaming like green and yellow stars."

"Do eat your breakfast, Anne, and never mind the dream; you can tell it to me afterwards."

"There isn't much more to tell," answered Anne. "All at once she saw in the glass the door open, and a man come in. With a stifled scream she jumped down from the stool, seized the case, and tried to close her dress up round her throat, and hide the necklace; but he was too quick for her. He said something, I could not hear what; and then, as she cowered down, he caught her and wrenched the case out of her hand, and made a snatch at the necklace just as she flew upon him, with all her fingers bent and uttering the most terrible cries that ever came out of a woman's lips—I think I hear them now; then, in a minute she fell back, and I could see she was only kept from dropping on the floor by the tight grip he had on the necklace. I seemed to know she was being choked, and I tried to call out, but I could not utter a sound. I strove to rush at the man, but my feet felt rooted where I stood; them there came a great darkness like the darkness of a winter's night."

"Let me get you another cup of tea, dear," said Mrs. Tippens, in a voice which shook a little in spite of all her efforts to steady it; "you've let this stand so long it is not fit to drink."

"It is just as I like my tea, thank you," answered Miss Tippens, cheerfully, as she devoted herself to the good things provided. "What do you think of my dream?"

"That I shouldn't have liked to dream it," replied Mrs. Tippens.
"Do let me pour you out some more tea, and then I must run away,
for the first-floor lodgers will be wanting me." Which was a feint on
the part of Mrs. Tippens, who felt she could not bear to hear anything
more at the moment about the little woman with the brown face and
the grey hair, whose portrait she recognised too surely as that of old
Mrs. Jones.

"Though why she can't let us, who never did her any harm, alone, I
can't imagine," considered Mrs. Tippens. "This is a dreadful house—
true enough, there has been murder done in it, and the blood is crying
aloud for vengeance. I wonder where that wicked wretch put her.
Oh ! Mrs Jones, if you'd only tell us where your poor bones are
mouldering, I am sure Dick would have them decently buried, let the
cost be what it might."

The first-floor lodgers were gone, and the rooms scrubbed out before Anne Jane, having dressed and settled up her own bedchamber,
made her appearance in her cousin's parlour; but when she suggested
that they might go upstairs and have a look at the apartments just
vacated, Mrs. Tippens made the excuse that they were not exactly in
order.

"The charwoman is up there still," she exclaimed; "she's making
half-a-day."

"What a wonderfully nice house for Dick to have got," continued
Miss Tippens.

"Yes," answered Dick's wife faintly. There was nothing to be objected to in the size of the house, if only Mrs. Jones could have been
kept out of it !

"If you don't mind my leaving you, Anne, for half an hour, I think
I'll just run out and get a few things we want," she said. "Supposing
anyone should come after the first-floor, Mrs. Burdock can show it."
Which would have been all very well, had not Mrs. Burdock, ten
minutes after Mrs. Tippens' departure, put her head into the parlour to
say that she should like to go home to see to her children's dinners,
and, if it made no difference, she would come back in the afternoon
and wipe over the windows and blacklead the grates. "The rooms are
quite clean and sweet," she added, "if anybody by chance do come to
look at them."

The children were out in the yard playing, the meat was cooking beautifully in the oven, the fruit pudding was boiling gently on the trivet, the potatoes were in the saucepan, ready to be put on the fire at a certain time which Mrs. Tippens had indicated; the street was simmering in the noontide heat of a summer's day, and Anne Jane, making a frock for the baby asleep in its cradle, was thinking Lucy's lines had fallen into very pleasant places, when there came at the front door a knock, which she instinctively understood meant lodgers.

They were two young gentlemen, attracted by the neat appearance of the house, by the snowy curtains in Mrs. Tippens' room, the birdcage hanging in the window, the flowers in bloom, ranged in pots on the sill.

"Could we see the rooms you have to let?" asked the elder, who acted as spokesman.

"Certainly, sir; will you be pleased to walk in?" answered Anne Jane in her best manner; and motioning to the strangers to precede her, she followed them up to the first floor, where she flung wide the door of the principal apartment.

"By Jove!" exclaimed both men, almost simultaneously, "who'd have thought there was such a jolly room in this old house?" and they walked over to one of the windows and looked out into the street, and then turned towards the fireplace, and then——

"Hello! What's the matter?" cried the first speaker, hurrying towards the door, against the lintel of which Mr. Tippens' cousin was leaning, looking more like a corpse than a living woman. "Here, hand over that chair, Hal, I believe she is going to faint."

"No," she gasped; "no—no—I—shall be better—directly."

At that moment Mrs. Tippens, who had heard from a neighbour some gentlemen were gone to look at her rooms, put her key in the lock and came hurrying upstairs. The first glance told her what had happened.

"My cousin is not very strong, sir," she said, in a voice she tried to keep steady, though she was trembling in every limb. "I'll just take her into the parlour, and be with you in a moment, if you please."

"Let me help you," entreated the younger man. "Take my arm, do. —Is she subject to attacks of this sort?" he went on, speaking in a lower tone.

"Not that I know of," was the reply. "Perhaps, sir," suggested Mrs. Tippens, "you would not mind looking over the rooms by yourselves. There is no one in but the children; I scarcely like leaving my cousin alone."

"Is there anything you want—anything I can run out and get for you?" asked the young fellow pleasantly. "Do you think that a little brandy——"

"I have some in the house, thank you, sir," answered Mrs. Tippens; and so at last she got rid of him, and stood looking at Anne Jane, who, leaning back in Mr. Tippens' own particular armchair, looked up at her and murmured, "The room."

"Yes, dear."

"It was the room of my dream."

"I thought as much."

"Did he kill her there?"

"Who's to tell? Nobody knows whether she is alive or dead, for that matter."

Chapter Seven

" No, sir, I won't deceive you. If you are wanting rooms, as you say, for a permanency, and think of buying good furniture that would get knocked about and ruined in moving, and settling down comfortably in the next lodgings you take, you had better not come here."

"Why, are you going to leave the house?"

"My husband is answerable for the rent for nearly two years longer," replied Mrs. Tippens evasively. "No, sir, it is not that; I wish it was."

"Have you any infectious illness in the place?"

"I'd rather have smallpox," broke out Mrs. Tippens, who felt she could endure her trouble no longer in silence. "We might get rid of that, but we can't get rid of old Mrs. Jones."

"Who is she—a lodger?"

"Worse than the worst of lodgers, sir; a lodger can do no more than owe rent, or at the most take things that don't belong to him; but Mrs. Jones pays no rent, and wants to live in every room in the house, and as fast as new lodgers come and we think we are going to be a bit comfortable at last, drives them to give notice. Fever and ague would be small evils in comparison to old Mrs. Jones, and why she torments us so I can't imagine, we never did the woman any injury; and as for her money I am sure if it was lying in bags of gold and silver at my feet I wouldn't touch a coin of it."

The two men stared at each other in amazement, then the elder said solemnly:

"In Heaven's name, *who* is Mrs. Jones?"

"She was the wife of a Doctor Jones, sir. He once rented this house. He and she disappeared the same night, and have never been heard of since."

"But I thought you said she lived here?"

"No, sir; I don't know where she lives, if she is living at all; but this is the way of it, one set of lodgers after another say they are very sorry but they can't stop on account of old Mrs. Jones. They either meet her on the stairs, or she takes a chair at the table when they are having their dinner, or she goes into their bedroom with a light in her hand, and then my cousin must get dreaming about her and, as you saw, was taken bad the moment she crossed the threshold of this room. I am sure, sir, I never did believe in ghosts and suchlike before we came here, but I can't disbelieve now, after what I've heard; and so I tell you not to take the apartments or to go to any expense buying furniture, for you wouldn't stop—I know you wouldn't—a fortnight is the longest anybody ever stays now."

"That settles the matter, we'll come, and we'll stay longer. For my own part I have always rather wanted to see a ghost and——"

"Oh, don't talk that way, please, sir."

"Well, at any rate, we'll pay you for the rooms for a month certain, and if you can do our cooking and make us a little comfortable, we won't quarrel about terms."

"But I don't think you exactly understand, sir."

"Yes I do, and I trust we shall know more about old Mrs. Jones than we do now before we are much older."

"I hope you won't buy good furniture, sir, till you have been here a few days; I can spare enough just to make the place tidy for you to come into." And so it was settled; the young men, after saying they would like to take possession the same evening, put a month's rent and money to provide grocery and so forth into Mrs. Tippens' reluctant hand, and departed.

"Let what will happen, they can't say I did not warn them," thought Mrs. Tippens, as she hurried off to see whether Anne Jane had been able to attend to the potatoes or if they were boiled to pulp.

Meantime the friends, walking along the street together, remarked, "What a strange-looking girl that young woman who so nearly fainted."

"Yes, cataleptic I shouldn't wonder; did you notice what a far-away, unseeing sort of expression there was in her eyes."

"I did; and what a thick white complexion, if I may use the term."

"That is a queer notion about old Mrs. Jones; we must get Mrs. Tippens up to make tea for us some night and hear all the rights of the story."

"And I'll take the liberty of putting fresh locks on the doors."

"You think it is somebody playing tricks, then ?"

"Of course; what else can it be. You don't believe in disembodied spirits taking up their abode in brick and mortar houses, I suppose ?"

It was a strange thing, as Mrs. Tippens often subsequently remarked, that from the time the new lodgers, who were medical students, took possession of the first-floor, people seemed able to stay in the other parts of the house. Where old Mrs. Jones had gone, and what old Mrs. Jones was doing, could only, Mrs. Tippens felt, be matter for conjecture; one comfort, she ceased to roam about the rooms and wander up and down the staircase; there were even times when Mrs. Tippens, passing through the hall, forgot to remember that sudden waft of cold air and the chilly hand laid on the back of her neck; she still—force of habit, perhaps—instinctively refrained from looking round, lest she should encounter the streaming grey hair and dark face and fierce black eyes of old Mrs. Jones; but at the end of a fortnight she began to feel, as she expressed the matter, "quite comfortable and easy in her mind."

She had said something of this sort one evening to her cousin, and was waiting vainly for a reply, when Miss Tippens, without the slightest apparent reason, burst into a despairing fit of tears.

"What, crying ? For the Lord's sake, girl, tell me what you are crying for," exclaimed Mrs. Tippens. "Do, Anne, dear, if you are in any trouble, only trust it to me, and I'll help you all I can, and so will Dick. Who has vexed you ?"

"*It's—old—Mrs.—Jones,*" sobbed Anne Jane. "I have tried hard

for your sake, but I can't bear her any longer; I must go away—I must
—I shall be a raving maniac if I stop in this house much longer. Why
has she fastened on me?" asked Miss Tippens, looking at her relation
with streaming eyes. "Oh, Lucy, why has she left everyone else in the
house to give me no peace of my life—I can't sleep for dreaming of her
—she is at my bedside every night wanting me to do something for her,
or go to some place with her; and then the whole day long I keep
trying to remember what she said and what she wanted, and I can't;
no, Lucy, for no advantage to you, or any other human being, can I
face the horror of her any longer."

At Anne Jane's first words Mrs. Tippens' work dropped from her
hands on to the floor, and during the delivery of this address she remained gazing at the speaker with a sort of fascinated terror; then she
cried out:

"Oh, dear! oh, dear! and just when I thought we were all settling
down so comfortably; what an awful old woman! But do you ever see
her, Anne, except when you are asleep?"

"No, but I feel her round and about me. There's a chilliness blows
on my neck, and a coldness creeps down my spine, and I seem always
to know that there's somebody beside or behind me; it's dreadful—
if it was to go on, I'd rather be dead and out of my misery at
once."

"Suppose I made you up a bed somewhere else," suggested Mrs.
Tippens.

"What would be the good? She's in every room in the house; she's
up and down the stairs, and on the roof, and along the parapet, and——"

"Don't talk about her any more, you'll frighten me," exclaimed
Mrs. Tippens.

"And haven't I been frightened? How would you like to lie in the
dark and know a woman——"

"Mrs. Tippens," called a voice, which made both women jump.

"Lor!" exclaimed Mrs. Tippens, recovering herself, "you needn't
be frightened, Anne, it's only Mr. Maldon—(yes, sir, I'm coming)—I
remember he left word with little Lucy he wanted to see me before he
went out this morning, and what with one thing and another I quite
forgot it." Having tendered which explanation, Mrs. Tippens hurried
to the first floor, leaving Anne Jane sitting with her hands tightly
folded and her great eyes fixed on vacancy, or—old Mrs. Jones.

"Close the door, if you please, Mrs. Tippens," said Mr. Maldon, the elder of her two new lodgers, as, after her apologies for her forgetfulness, the nominal mistress of Dr. Jones' former residence stood waiting to hear what was wanted. "For some days past I have wished to speak to you alone. I only think it right to say——"

"Oh, sir, don't, for mercy's sake, say you've seen old Mrs. Jones *too*."

There was such an agony of entreaty in Mrs. Tippens' voice, the young man, who did not believe in ghosts, and had expressed a wish to see one, might well have been excused smiling, but he did not smile, he only answered :

"No, but I have seen something else."

"What, sir ?"

"Your cousin wandering about the house in her sleep."

"In her sleep ! When, Mr. Maldon ?"

"Well, to go no further back, last night. I followed her up to the top of the house, and she was actually going out on the roof, when I gently took her by the arm and walked her down to her own room again. I am afraid she may do herself a mischief. I was careful not to wake her, but if she should be frightened, and wake suddenly, no one can tell what accident might happen. From the first I thought there was something strange in her appearance, but I should not have imagined she was a sleep-walker."

"And what should you advise me to do, sir?" asked Mrs. Tippens earnestly, for this seemed to her a dreadful thing. For a respectable young woman—and she believed and felt certain Anne Jane to be as respectable a young woman as ever lived, a wise, prudent, sensible, virtuous girl—to go wandering in the middle of the night about a house in which there were lodgers, and be handed down the stairs and back to her own room by any man, young or old, was a matter which appeared in Mrs. Tippens' eyes so preposterous, so dreadful, she could scarcely realise it; she had not courage to inquire the fashion of the costume in which Anne Jane started to make her uncomfortable pilgrimage.

"I should advise you to take your cousin to some good medical man," said Mr. Maldon, answering her spoken question. "There is no doubt she is from some cause thoroughly out of health, but meanwhile I should not say anything to her about this walking in her sleep; only you would do well to take the precaution of locking her door outside at night."

"Oh ! I couldn't do that," answered Mrs. Tippens, "If she were my worst enemy, instead of my husband's first cousin, I couldn't lock her up in a room alone with old Mrs. Jones."

"Oh—old Mrs. Jones !" exclaimed Mr. Maldon.

"Begging your pardon, sir, I don't think you would be right to say that about the worst of sinners, let alone a poor, ill-used lady that, if all accounts be true, led a most miserable life in this very house."

"Yes, yes, that's all very well," interrupted Mr. Maldon, "but don't you see, my good soul, this tendency of your cousin's explains the whole mystery; gets rid, in fact, of Mrs. Jones altogether."

"In what way ?" asked Mrs. Tippens.

"Why, only in one way, of course. Your lodgers had heard the story and thought your cousin walking in her sleep must be old Mrs. Jones."

"Yes, sir, but my cousin never entered these doors till two days before yourself, and for nine months previous to that my lodgers were fainting and flitting on account of the woman who came into their room and met them on the stairs."

"Is that so ?" said Mr. Maldon, in the tone of a man who feels his theory has no more substantial foundation than an air castle.

"Yes, sir, it is quite true," answered Mrs. Tippens, a little triumphantly—since no one likes to be dispossessed of a point. "Anne Jane came up from Brighton the day but one before you took these lodgings. All the same, sir, I don't mind telling you that she can't get rest neither night nor day, because of old Mrs. Jones."

"Dreams about her, eh ?" suggested the medical student with alacrity.

"She has been crying her eyes out just now because she declares the old lady won't let her be. Stands at her bedside every night regular, wanting her to do something Anne Jane spends her days trying to remember."

"Really an interesting case," thought the future medical man, who added aloud: "Well, Mrs. Tippens, I can but repeat my advice, let your cousin see a good doctor, and lock her door on the outside."

"I am sure, sir, I feel very thankful to you," answered Mrs. Tippens, and she went downstairs and tossed up a very pretty little supper for Dick and her cousin, during the course of which meal she announced in a laughing way to her husband that Anne Jane was not very well, and felt a bit nervous, and that she, Luce, meant to sleep with their visitor; which information she accompanied with such sly looks and such a world of meaning in her face, that Tippens, looking up from the crab, cucumber, lettuce, and vinegar he was eating in disastrous quantities, answered shortly:

"All right, old girl."

Consequently, Mrs. Tippens, for once, leaving the custody of her children with Dick, after having cleared away the supper things retired to rest with Miss Tippens.

Mrs. Tippens took the side of the bed next the door (which she locked), and firmly decided she would not go to sleep that night. For about an hour, or an hour and a half, she lay awake, thinking, as she afterwards said, "of all manner of things"; then she "fell over," and did not awaken till the room was full of the light of a summer morning's early dawn.

For a moment she could not remember where she was; then she remembered, and stretching out her hand, found the place her cousin should have occupied empty and cold.

Anne Jane was gone, and Mrs. Tippens, rushing to the door, found it unlocked.

Chapter Eight

Mrs. Tippens, assisted by her husband and Mr. Maldon and his friend Mr. Whipple, and one of the second-floor lodgers, who was out of work, scoured the neighbourhood for Miss Tippens, and scoured it in vain. That young person seemed to have vanished as utterly as old Mrs. Jones. They sought her high, they sought her low; the whole street in confusion; as popular opinion had as yet defined no limit to the powers possessed by Doctor Jones' wife, little doubt existed that Anne Jane had been carried off bodily by the grey-haired lady as an expiation of the sins of the Tippens' family in continuing the tenancy of a house on which it was "well-known a curse rested."

Who had cursed it, on whom it rested, were matters considered quite irrelevant to the general issue. So far sickness had passed over and misfortune shunned the latest dwellers in the haunted dwelling. But now it was felt the day of reckoning had been only deferred in order to inflict a heavier punishment. Old Mrs. Jones was about to vindicate herself as last. And if you don't get out of the place quick," said Mrs. Jubb, who, during the whole of that memorable morning, conducted herself after the manner of some ancient prophetess, "you'll find far worse to follow. I always told you I couldn't sleep in the house if the hall was paved with golden guineas."

"Dick, Dick," cried Mrs. Tippens, "didn't I beg and pray of you long ago to move—that very first night the children saw old Mrs. Jones ?"

But Dick, not being in a fit state of mind either to argue with his wife or endure her reproaches, mounted to the seat of his neat hansom and drove aimlessly about the streets, asking useless questions of persons totally unable to afford the slightest information as to his cousin's whereabouts.

About three o'clock, however, Anne Jane, in person, appeared at her cousin's door, accompanied by a policeman. Early that morning she had been found trying to open the garden gate of a house in the Stratford Road; as, when remonstrated with concerning the impropriety of her conduct, she still continued knocking and pushing the gate, the policeman seized her left arm and told her she couldn't be allowed to make such a noise; then, for the first time, she turned her face towards him, and he saw, as he expressed himself, "there was something stranger about the matter than he thought."

Immediately it dawned upon his understanding that though the woman's eyes were wide open, she did not see him, and that she was not drunk, as he had supposed, but fast asleep.

Therefore he woke her up, and inquired what she was doing there at four o'clock in the morning.

The girl's terror when suddenly recalled to consciousness—she found herself only partially dressed, in a road perfectly unknown to her, held firmly in the grasp of a stalwart policeman was so great as utterly to deprive her of speech. She tried to collect her senses, she strove to ask him how she came there, but no word passed her parched and trembling lips. In a very agony of shame and distress, she allowed herself to be led to the station-house; but there, when addressed by the inspector, she broke into a passion of weeping, which culminated in a fit of violent hysterics, that in turn was succeeded by a sort of wandering the doctor regarded as a precursor of some severe illness. "The girl is quite overwrought," he said; "I wonder who this old Mrs. Jones is she talks so much about."

"Oh, save me from her—oh, Luce!—oh, Dick! don't let her come near me again." At that moment Anne Jane again cried in terror.

"No, she shan't come near you, we won't let her," observed the doctor soothingly; and after a time he managed to give this strange patient a quieting draught.

"Anyone," as Mrs. Tippens observed, when subsequently commenting upon the conduct of the police, "could see Anne Jane was a thoroughly respectable girl, who had been carefully brought up," and accordingly she did not feel so grateful as she ought to have done to the inspector for sending her cousin home in a cab.

"She'll be better with her friends than in a hospital," said the doctor; and accordingly, when she recovered sufficiently to mention Mr. Tippens' address, she was despatched thither under the care of a staid and respectable member of the force.

But nothing could induce her to enter Dick's house, till Mrs. Tippens had solemnly promised at once to go out and find a lodging for her elsewhere.

"If I sleep here again she'll never rest till she has killed me," declared the girl; which utterance seemed so mysterious to the policeman, that, pressing for an explanation, he was told the whole story of "old Mrs. Jones."

"And the young woman solemnly declares," went on the man who repeated the narrative to the inspector, "that Doctor Jones' wife came to her bedside, and bade her get up and dress, and opened the door of the room, and the front door, and made her walk till she was fit to drop through places and streets she had never seen before, till they came to the garden gate of St. Julian's; she passed through that and kept beckoning her to follow—'and I know I tried hard, and then you must have awakened me.'"

"It's a rather unlikely tale altogether," observed the inspector, but still he kept the matter in his mind, and thought it worth while to make a few inquiries and set a detective to work; and had a watch kept on Doctor Schloss, the great German chemist, who lived in a very secluded manner at St. Julian's—the result of all being that one day a policeman appeared at the house, and asking if he could see the doctor, arrested him on the charge of "Wilful Murder."

"But this is absurd," said the great chemist, speaking in very broken English. "Who is it that you make believe I have murdered?"

"Your wife, Zillah Jones," was the answer. Whereupon the doctor shrugged his shoulders and inquired who Zillah Jones might be.

Asked if he would come quietly with the policeman, he laughed, and said, "Oh, yes." Warned that any statement he made would be used as evidence, he laughed again, and observed he had no statement of any kind to make.

On the way he conducted himself, as was remarked, in a very quiet and gentlemanlike manner; and, arrived at his destination, he requested to be allowed to sit down, as he did not feel very well.

"It is a serious charge to bring against an innocent person," he said, still speaking in imperfect English. That was the last sentence he uttered. When he was requested to get up, he did not stir. He was dead —dead as the woman whose remains were found, embalmed in a locked box, in his laboratory at St. Julian's.

No one, however, in the neighbourhood where Doctor Jones once lived believed, or could be persuaded to believe Doctor Schloss and Doctor Jones were one and the same person, or that the embalmed body was that of old Mrs. Jones. Nothing will ever shake the local mind in its conviction that Doctor Jones is still enjoying existence in "foreign parts," or that his wife was buried in the cellar of that old-fashioned house where evil befell all who tried to live.

In proof of which conviction it is still told in bated breath how Anne Jane was never able to go back to service, but was forced eventually to return to her native village, where to this day she earns a modest living with her needle; and how, on the very night of that day when Mr. Tippens removed his family and goods, cabs and horses excepted, to a dwelling he had taken in the next street, where the lodgers accompanied Mrs. Tippens, a passer-by, looking up at the old house, saw something like the figure of a woman, carrying a torch, flit from window to window, and story to story, and ere he had time to think what it meant, beheld flames bursting from every part of the old building.

Before the engines came the fire had got such a mastery it was with difficulty Mr. Tippens' horses were saved, to say nothing of the adjoining houses.

It was indeed a conflagration to be remembered, if for no other reason than that standing on the parapet in the fiercest of the fire a woman, with streaming grey hair, was seen wringing her hands in such an apparent agony of distress that an escape was put up, and one of the brigade nearly lost his life in trying to save her.

At this juncture someone cried out with a loud voice:

"It was a witch the doctor married, and fire alone can destroy her !"

Then for a moment there fell a dead silence upon the assembled crowd, while the dreadful figure was seen running from point to point in a mad effort to escape.

Suddenly the roof crashed in, millions of sparks flew upwards from the burning rafters, there was a roar as if the doors of some mighty furnace had been suddenly opened, a blaze of light shot straight towards the heavens, and when the spectators looked again there was no figure to be seen anywhere, only the bare walls, and red flames rushing through the sashless windows of the house once haunted by "Old Mrs. Jones."

WHY DR. CRAY LEFT
SOUTHAM

"You want to know why I left Southam?" said the Doctor—
meditatively knocking the ashes out of his pipe, preparatory to refilling
it,—he had just come back from the diggings with a nugget big enough
to make him rich, and, if he pleased, an idle man for life—and he was
sitting in Jacob Graham's chambers in Gray's Inn, opposite to his old
friend and schoolfellow—the same unkempt, untrimmed, unconventional Jack Cray, Jacob could remember ever since they went—a pair
of graceless lads—to Todmarsh Grammar School. "You want to
know why I left Southam? Well, I don't mind telling you; in fact, now
I am strong enough to stand an action for libel, I don't mind telling
anybody."

"There was a scandal, then?"

"Not that ever became public, except about myself; but you shall
hear. It was in the spring of 1850, that, investing the small amount of
money my old grandmother left me, I became partner to Dr. Montrose,
of Southam. It was the sweetest place I ever beheld. Green, sloping
meadows, clear streams, wooded heights, picturesque cottages covered
with roses and clematis, old-fashioned houses—where old-fashioned
people lived within their incomes, and saved fortunes for their pretty
daughters—great mansions affected by the nobility and gentry, good
boating, good fishing, good shooting; the very *beau idéal* of a neighbourhood. No wonder Montrose, who was getting into the autumn of
existence, wanted a partner to keep his connection together, to prevent
any outsider taking the cream of a practice which must have grown of
itself, for he could never have made it. I may say, at once, he did not
get that partner in me. We had not been trying to run in harness
together for three months before he told me, as plainly as long habits
of beating about the bush would permit, that either we must separate,
or get in a third partner.

"'The *suaviter in modo*, my good Cray,' he said, 'we want, and we
must have a little more of that. You see what my patients are—now,
don't you?'

"I did. So we got a third partner—a man who knew even less of his profession than Dr. Montrose himself, but who was pronounced by the ladies, charming. The way he placed two fingers on their wrists was in itself a study, and the reverie into which he fell, when the delicate creatures complained of a pain 'just here,' persuaded the patients themselves, and every relation they had in the world, the case was very serious.

"Why," went on Dr. Cray, waxing indignant, "I have known that fellow keep a girl lying on her back for six months, who had no more the matter with her than I have—and yet he was liked, and I was not! To put the matter in plain language, except in desperate cases, there was a beautiful unanimity in preferring my absence to my presence. It was hard, I felt it to be so; for with all my heart and soul I loved my profession, and sympathized with those who really needed such help as I could give them. What I failed to do was, to treat a fair lady's finger-ache as though she had broken every bone in her body; and prescribe for an idle man's imaginary ailments, as if I were not perfectly aware nothing on earth was the matter with him save the lack of some real trouble to occupy his mind—always supposing he had any.

"But when there was anything dangerous in the shape of accident, sickness, or epidemic, Montrose always sent me to the scene of action.

"'Ah! Cray,' he said, 'if you had only a little tact, you might carry all before you.'

"That was after a railway smash, when our list of wounded would not have shamed a battle-field. We did very well out of that, one way or another; but, somehow, though I had all the work, Dr. Montrose got all the credit—and really, and seriously, upon my honour, Graham, he knew no more about medicine than your clerk."

"I want to know why you left Southam," Mr. Graham said; this disparaging reference to his clerk reminding him of his own profession. Why should Dr. Cray suppose Cripps ignorant of medicine? For aught he knew Cripps might have attended all the lectures at St. Bartholomew's!

"I am coming to that, my friend," the Doctor answered. "Only first I must tell you it was after the railway accident he allowed me and Clara to become engaged. She was a dear little thing. I am told she is most happily married, and that her husband is doing wonders as a homœopathist. I was very fond of Clara, and, if it had not been for that little trouble of mine at Southam, I should, perhaps, ere now have moulded myself on the Montrose pattern and become as genial a practitioner as her father."

"For heaven's sake," his friend entreated, "get on."

"What is the hurry?" asked Dr. Cray. "The night is still young, and already I imagine you must feel yourself in possession of the routine of my life at Southam.

"Was the Squire's coachman thrown off the box of the brougham, I attended his broken leg, which was duly charged to the Manor in our bill. Was there fever at the Hall, I, with the help of God, pulled the patients through. When the rector was stricken with cholera, I never left him till I could give good hope to his weeping wife. When my lord put out his shoulder I reduced the dislocation. When—"

"Jack," solemnly interrupted Mr. Graham, "if you do not tell me, and at once, why you left Southam, I shall get up and put your pipe out."

He laughed. Jack Cray was always, except upon some few points, the most goodnatured fellow in all the world.

"Well," he said, "to cut a long story short, my worthy father-in-law who was to be had a good patient at a place called the Chase; a lady, of course—a married lady. Whenever married ladies took to be chronically invalid, we, I speak now in the partnership sense, found them the best patients of all. The name of the lady was Glenalbyn, *née* Frottiss. She was about thirty years of age—old looking for that— plain, not clever, extremely slight and lean, feeble, I should have said, of intellect, but Dr. Montrose maintained, 'a most superior person.'

"Anyhow, she 'enjoyed' bad health; from some cause or other she was eternally wanting the doctor. 'A poor, fragile creature,' said my worthy partner. I would have made her walk five miles a day, when I warrant, she would have been well enough. Glenalbyn (Lord! what a name; I would have split it had I been he, and taken either half) seemed wrapped up in her.

"'Such devotion,' said Dr. Montrose, 'I never witnessed. I never saw a couple so attached, and my experience, Cray,' he added, with tears in his old eyes, 'has been large.'

"As far as the Glenalbyns were concerned I had not the smallest reason to doubt my partner's assertion—neither did I. All I thought was, there could not, judging from the medicine made up, be much of consequence the matter with Mrs. Glenalbyn. Every preparation sent was of the mildest and most rose-water description.

"Digestion out of order, nerves unstrung—nerves unstrung, digestion out of order—that was the way his patient swung backwards and forwards. These symptoms were occasionally varied with a slight cold, earache, pain under her right shoulder; and all the other trivial ailments that afflict the path of those who have nothing in the world to do except get ill, and send for the doctor.

"Montrose was always being sent for to the Chase, and, you may be very sure, he never, when at home or within possible reach, had to be sent for twice. Mrs. Glenalbyn liked him greatly, and Mr. Glenalbyn was wont to say, he did not know what in the world he should do if Dr. Montrose were to leave Southam.

"'He understands my wife's constitution to a nicety,' he generally finished; it being a peculiarity of many persons that they think the constitutions of themselves and families are a sort of special creation.

"However, to sum up the position of affairs in our happy village in the June of 1852, there were three persons resident there perfectly satisfied with each other—Mrs. and Mr. Glenalbyn, and Dr. Montrose.

"Summer outings, which have since then come to be considered an absolute necessity, were not at that time generally common. People who had friends went to visit them; persons who possessed business to see to went and saw to it. Perhaps the same craze for gadding existed, but it was called by another name; the difference might be that families then scattered instead of migrating.

"Anyhow, Dr. Montrose went off to stay with a nephew in Scotland, while his family remained behind. Clara had been away earlier in the year, Mrs. Montrose was going later. Southam was fuller than ever, by reason of the many friends who were stopping on visits at the mansions and old-fashioned houses, but still it seemed to our senior that Perry and I could manage all there was to be done, and he said 'he wanted a change'—I am sure, I did."

"Even though Clara remained?" suggested Mr. Graham.

"Yes. I did not see much of her, and whenever I did, Mrs. Montrose was at our elbow. However, Clara has nothing to do with my story, nothing whatever.

"When Dr. Montrose left, the Glenalbyns were away; but shortly after his departure they returned. Mrs. Glenalbyn had not found the air of the place where they were stopping suit her. Mrs. Glenalbyn 'did not find the air of any place suit her so well as Southam'—Mr. Glenalbyn felt sure 'no air could suit her as well as the air of the Chase.' It is needless to say Southam repeated and approved this opinion. After all, contentment is a virtue!

"The lady had not, however, been long back at the Chase before her nerves and her digestion commenced their old pranks. Montrose was sent for, and being absent, Perry went.

"'A great pity Mrs. Glenalbyn is so delicate,' he said to me, 'delightful woman!' And the mild prescriptions, the pills at night, the draught in the morning, the mixture three times a day, began again, and were duly sent till Mrs. Glenalbyn was pronounced convalescent.

"Just at this time Perry had the misfortune to poison his hand. His was not a constitution to bear anything of the sort with impunity, and though I did my best for, and instead of him, he was at last obliged to knock off work, and go to his mother, who lived in Kent. He sent Southam, in his stead, a raw stripling, just fresh from the examiners, but, upon the whole, I do not think this callow bird did much more harm than Perry himself.

"As a matter-of-course, I could not trust such a mere child with the care of an important patient like Mrs. Glenalbyn, for, although she had no disease, Dr. Montrose chose to believe her delicate, and I did not want the practice to suffer during his absence. In the chapter of accidents, it was thus it chanced that on the next occasion when Dr. Montrose was sent for I repaired to the Chase."

"It is a nice name," observed Mr. Graham.

"Yes, and it is a beautiful place. As I rode up the avenue—bordered by a double row of the most magnificent lime-trees I ever beheld—I could not help thinking about the apparent injustice of conditions in the world—I had stopped to speak a word with poor old Mrs. Jones, suffering from heart complaint, who was labouring away at the washtub, and now I was going to prescribe for a fine lady who had nothing on earth the matter with her. Of course we doctors know—"

"Cray, do please proceed with your story, and defer all reflections till after it is finished," entreated Mr. Graham. "How did you find Mrs. Glenalbyn?"

"As I expected—well enough if she could only have been induced to think so. I had always considered her a plain woman, but she was far plainer than I imagined. When I saw her near, in a good light and without a bonnet, I wondered what in the world Glenalbyn, who was a handsome fellow, could have beheld in her to make him propose.

"If she had been the loveliest creature on the face of the earth, however, he could not have been more attentive to, or seemed more anxious about her.

"'My angel,' he said, leaning over the back of her chair.

"'Darling,' she murmured, rapturously turning a face which might have belonged to a black monkey of an inferior sort, up to his.

"'I shall be in the next room, love, if you want me,' he said.

"'How good you are, dearest!'

"After a little more of this sort of thing he left me alone with my patient. As I knew nothing of her constitution, or, to speak more correctly, of what might be wrong with it, I asked several questions, which she answered satisfactorily. She was not a bad sort of woman I soon discovered—weak, undoubtedly, and crazily fond of her husband, but not selfish or affected. She had no disease, that I could make out, no real ailment. She was sound wind and limb, but no one could have pronounced her strong. Upon the whole I felt more charitably disposed towards Mrs. Glenalbyn than I could have believed possible, seeing she had only about a quarter of an inch of forehead, and might have been mistaken for the 'missing link.' She was certainly a gentlewoman, and seemed amiable and sympathetic. She promised to help poor Mrs. Jones, and begged me not to hesitate to mention any deserving case that came under my notice. As wives go, Glenalbyn might have done worse.

"When I was passing out he intercepted my exit, and insisted I should go into the dining-room and take a glass of wine. Whilst this was in progress he asked anxiously what I thought of his wife. In reply I could but echo Dr. Montrose's words of wisdom—she was not strong, but I could detect no sign of disease; her nervous system was poor, and her digestion weak. I would send something round, and trusted in a few days to find her much better.

"Very courteously Mr. Glenalbyn thanked me, adding some gracious words of compliment concerning my known skill. Altogether I left the house feeling gratified with the manners of its owners. For almost the first time Dr. Montrose and I were at one in our opinions. Husband and wife were undeniably pleasant people."

"Well?" said Mr. Graham, interrogatively, as Dr. Cray paused.

"It was not exactly well," answered the Doctor; "Mrs. Glenalbyn failed to recover under my treatment as rapidly as she had done when Montrose attended her. I wish to conceal nothing, so I must tell you at once I had altered the medicine. I thought that by strengthening her general system I might get her nerves and digestion into such a state that our services could be to a great extent dispensed with, but I soon found that some way or other I had made a mistake in my diagnosis. To be brief the lady got no better.

"'Are you quite sure that you understand my wife's constitution?' asked Mr. Glenalbyn one day, when, meeting him in the avenue, after an unsatisfactory interview with Mrs. Glenalbyn; I was bound to confess the 'improvement slower than I had expected.' 'You must forgive my seeming rudeness in putting the question, Dr. Cray; a husband's anxiety, you know, will supersede politeness—and Dr. Montrose comprehends so perfectly the cause of her slightest ailment.'

"A medical man has to bear a great deal, but though I felt Mr. Glenalbyn had hit me very hard indeed on my most sensitive point, I was forced to confess I did not seem to be so successful in my treatment of the lady as my partner.

"'Do not you think it might be well to call in a further opinion?' suggested Mr. Glenalbyn blandly.

"I answered I should like a further opinion very much indeed, if he was not afraid of causing unnecessary alarm to the patient.

"'Oh! I can manage that,' he answered. 'And I believe, Dr. Cray, there can be no doubt that in any case where there seems the slightest perplexity it is, even in the interest of a medical man himself, better to take a second opinion. Two heads, you know,' he added pleasantly, as if, by an old saw of that kind, he thought to rob his meaning of its sting.

"Dr. Montrose always insisted one of my faults was a conviction I knew my profession more thoroughly than any other person living. If this were so I had now got a nasty fall; and what made it the more aggravating was I had met with it in such a road. It was like a man who after having hunted a bad county gets thrown in a park, through his horse stumbling over a mole-hill."

"Poor Cray!" ejaculated his friend with suspicious gravity; for Graham well remembered how at school Jack had believed no one knew anything except himself.

"Thank heaven, however," went on Dr. Cray, with a visible increase of animation, "I was in no worse case than the London bigwig I met in consultation. That no mistake might be made this time through any hankering after new ideas, when Mr. Glenalbyn asked the name of the physician I considered it would be best to meet, I unhesitatingly mentioned a gentleman in whom Dr. Montrose placed the greatest confidence; by whom, were a stronger expression applicable as regarded my partner, I should say he swore.

"He altered my medicine a little, accommodating it more to the good old Montrose pattern; was most courteous to the lady, encouraging to the gentleman, friendly to myself, and left on good terms with everybody, carrying away with him golden reasons for thinking well of Southam.

"He agreed with me Mrs. Glenalbyn had no disease, and yet, perhaps, for that very reason I began to suspect she must have. If only her nerves and her digestion were out of order, why the deuce should she not get better under treatment that ought to have put her to rights at once? I could discern no disease, yet, for all that, there might be one in progress, one yet not sufficiently developed for science to detect its presence. What could it be? I thought over every possible complaint. I studied my patient's appearance. I troubled myself about her; on my honour, Graham, Mrs. Glenalbyn's case began to haunt me. I never had been so puzzled before in all my life.

"As delicately as I could hint such a thing, I asked her husband if he knew of any secret trouble. He assured me she was as happy as possible. Her mind is a 'clear pool,' he added, 'I know every pebble at the bottom of it.'

"I then tried to ascertain if there were any hereditary disease; but apparently no member of the Frottiss family had ever died from anything save 'accident or old age.'

"'You are vexing yourself too much over what I am sure is really a very simple ailment,' said Mr. Glenalbyn. '*I* am not uneasy now; when Dr. Montrose comes back he will set everything to rights.'

"If such a speech were not enough to drive Montrose's partner to frenzy, I should like to know what you would consider sufficient cause to do so!

"That same afternoon I had to visit a patient residing at some distance from Southam, and, as I returned, the fancy took me to make a slight détour through the woods that rose dark and dense at the back of the Chase. They were no part of that property, and the Southam public was free to wander through them at will; possibly that was the reason the Southam public seemed determined to eschew them altogether. They were the loneliest, loveliest portion of the neighbourhood, and I always chose their green glades when time and opportunity permitted.

'I was walking leisurely along the velvety turf, with my horse's bridle thrown over my arm, when, just before I came to a bridge under which the river meandered gently on its way, I met a Mrs. Coulton—without exception the greatest gossip in England.

"I tried to pass her with a bow, but she would not let me. She forced me to stop while she stood chattering over the affairs of the village. 'What did I think of the rector's sermon on Sunday? How was Mr. Perry? When would Dr. Montrose be back? Why did not Mrs. Montrose and Miss Clara accompany him? Had I heard Miss Mowbray was going to be married—yes, to that tall, dark-looking gentleman who sat at the right-hand corner of the family pew on the previous Sunday.'

"I had nearly cut my way through this barrier of talk, and was on the very point of escape, when she said:—

"'And so I hear poor Mrs. Glenalbyn is worse.'

"'I am not aware that she is worse,' I answered.

"'Oh, indeed! I was told you met a great London physician there the other day, and that his opinion was she would require the most extreme care.'

"'If he made any remark of that sort, he did not make it to me,' was my somewhat incautious reply.

"'Dear, dear! What a place Southam is for magnifying every little bit of news! But then, Dr. Cray, you see people would naturally say if Mrs. Glenalbyn is no worse, why have a great London doctor to see her? Dr. Montrose never needed any other opinion than his own. For my own part I shouldn't wonder if she died; and then all the Southam ladies will be pulling caps for that fine handsome husband of hers. As they walk up the aisle together, sometimes I think, what a contrast!'

"I broke away at last, but after I had crossed the bridge I still heard Mrs. Coulton's stream of talk maundering peaceably along. The river did not ripple more ceaselessly between its banks than Mrs. Coulton's tongue wagged about business with which she had no concern. What was Mrs. Glenalbyn's life or death to her? What right had she to institute comparison between me and Montrose?

"It was late—late for Southam I mean, before I went to bed that night. The day had been hot, and my work heavy, and I was tired, for all of which reasons I fell asleep directly. At the end of about a couple of hours, however, I was awakened suddenly by someone saying in my ear, distinctly, in quite a matter of fact voice,—

"'*Mrs. Glenalbyn is dead.*'

"I started up and looked about me. There was not a soul near. The moon was shining broad and clear into the room, and I could see no creature in it save myself. Nevertheless, I felt quite satisfied some one must have spoken. I was so sure of this I jumped on the floor, and putting my head out of the open window, looked if any messenger were standing on the broad step. No; in the length and breadth of that quiet street there was no living creature, not even a dog. The moonlight lay mellow on the sandy horse-road. The white houses gleamed whiter in its beams. But, look which way I would, not a human being was in sight.

"'What a fool I am,' I thought, and went back to bed again. Still, tired though I was, I could not immediately settle myself to sleep. Mrs. Glenalbyn's case would persist in obtruding itself. Mrs. Glenalbyn's lack of vital power troubled me to such a degree that at last I thought of getting up and dressing myself, and probably I should have done so but that while I was considering the pros and cons of such a course my eyes closed, and without effort I dropped off into dreamland.

"What I dreamt about I have not the slightest recollection. I must have slept and dreamt a long time, for when I again woke, which I did in a state of terrified alarm, the sounds of labour and of life were commencing. It was broad daylight, and a lovely morning.

"But just then I did not notice the beauty of the morning. I was differently engaged. I was wondering who it was that had said in my ear and startled me, '*Look at his eyes! look at his eyes!*' Whose eyes? Why, I knew, I *had* looked at them more than once.

"I could not shake off the influence of this second fright as I had done the first. I dressed, went downstairs, and I took a long solitary walk.

"What did it all mean. In my sleep I knew I could only have been following out to its legitimate end some course of thought I had been pursuing when awake. Hitherto there was a point where I invariably stopped short, where the actual ended, and the vague and unintelligible began. Now I knew where my doubts had all hitherto been tending. I was suspicious of Mr. Glenalbyn—I had felt suspicious of him for weeks.

"Sitting down beside the river, I tried to recall everything I had ever heard concerning that gentleman. There was not much, but I recollected enough to show there might be some ground for my suspicion. Good Heavens! whither was I drifting? Did I really believe the man wanted to be rid of his wife? Did I feel sure he was murdering her before my eyes? I went home and shut myself up. I looked out every book I could find bearing on the points in the case which puzzled me. I suffered nothing to escape my attention likely to elucidate the mystery. I paced my room till I was tired; I thought till I was weary; and at length, when I received an important summons forcing me to go out, I had still to confess myself baffled."

"Did you imagine he was posioning her, then?" asked Mr. Graham, his interest finally aroused.

"Yes—felt sure of it, though there was no poison I was acquainted with that exhibited the symptoms which so puzzled and perplexed me. Needless to say, I went that morning as soon as I could to the Chase. Mrs. Glenalbyn seemed neither better nor worse; but she complained of having passed a bad night, and Mr. Glenalbyn, who was present, asked if I could not give her something to induce sleep.

"I shook my head, and said, perhaps a little foolishly, that what we wanted to get rid of was the cause which prevented her sleeping.

"'It strikes me, Doctor,' he answered, 'you are a little too fond of searching for causes—don't you think that, till you can find them, it might be wiser to deal with effects.'

"'I will send some sedative if you wish me to do so,' I replied, taking no notice of his taunt; but as I walked away from the Chase, I determined I would not send a sedative, and secondly, that before twelve hours had passed I would try to get to know something more of Mr. Glenalbyn's game.

"I could only think of one man in London likely even to be able to help me. If he were alive, I knew I should find him at home, for the simple reason that from year's end to year's end he never went out. He had just enough money to keep a little old-fashioned house, in Westminster, over his head. It was situated near the Horseferry Road. He let off the ground floor to a man who had been forty years clerk in some old bank in the city; he himself occupied the two floors above. He had spent his prime of existence and all his spare cash in purchasing old books, and now in his old age he shut himself up to enjoy their possession.

"I had not seen him for a long time, but I remembered, quite suddenly, he had at one period made poisons his study. He even talked of publishing a book, entitled 'The Poisons of All Times and All Nations.' It had not appeared, however, and I did not think it was likely to appear."

"Why, the title alone," Mr. Graham was beginning, when doctor Cray stopped him—

"I am coming to the gist of my story now—let me finish. The same day I ran up to London and found Mr. Ordford in cap, slippers and dressing gown. The place might have been cleaner, and so might he for that matter, but I gave little heed at the moment to externals. Time was of value to me. If things at the Chase were as I suspected, not an hour ought to be lost. He was very glad to see me, and offered, in an old-fashioned way, 'such hospitality as his poor house boasted,' but I told him I could not stop—that I had come to him for help. In ten minutes I had told my story, described the symptoms, and asked if in his researches he had come on any poison in use amongst the Hindoos or North American Indians likely to reduce the vital power as I had seen. Ordford had studied medicine, and though some reason —laziness, I suspect—prevented his following it as a profession, he was as well able to follow what I said as the first doctor in London might have been.

"When I had done he rose, and, unlocking a cupboard, produced a manuscript book covered only with brown paper. There were about a hundred such on the shelf piled one above the other. On the outside of each was pasted a piece of white paper. That he first brought out was labeled—

'POISONS IN USE AMONGST THE NATIVES OF INDIA.'

"Opening the folio and running his finger down the index, which was singularly clear and copious he asked, 'What reason have you for thinking your man has resorted to India for his materials?'

"I had no better reason to give than that his father was long stationed in India, he himself was born there, and I vaguely recollected hearing something about when he was 'amongst the Indians.'

"'Ah! that would not be the Hindoos,' said Mr. Ordford. 'There is nothing in this volume to help us. Let us try another,' and he produced a second manuscript book labelled—

POISONS IN USE AMONGST THE DIFFERENT TRIBES
OF NORTH AMERICAN INDIANS.

"I never saw anything so full as that old man's repertory. I will not say every poison on earth was to be found mentioned there; but it seemed to me an almost exhaustive analysis of a subject which has never yet received sufficient attention. The symptoms—the result—the antidote, if any—the mode of use—everything you could speak of almost, was written down in a clerkly hand, with a conciseness and brevity that seemed to me amazing.

"'There is nothing to help us here either,' he said, after he had referred to several books and examined many papers. 'Shall we try Italy?'

"We tried Italy with the same result.

"'What shall we do now?' he asked .'We are just about as wise as when we started.'

"I felt woefully disappointed. 'Have you no recollection at all,' I inquired, 'of hearing anything or reading of some simple subtle poison, chemistry cannot trace, medicine cannot combat?'

"He smiled, and laid his hand on his manuscript treasures, as he answered, 'Why these are full of such. Chemistry as a rule could not detect them—as yet science cannot combat them. In most cases the antidote, provided by nature for the bane she provides likewise, is known to man, but not to civilized man. Why, our own fields and hedgerows produce the most dangerous poisons, and to how many of them can we point the antidote? And yet there can be no question they grow almost side by side. If you see a nettle, be sure a dock is not far distant, and if we only were wise enough to know, we should be able to place our hand as instantly on the herb from which virtue may be distilled, as on that containing the deadliest poison.'

"'Look here,' he added, and producing another book he placed it before me. This contains a list of poisonous plants growing in the three kingdoms—plants fatal to man or cattle, or both. Here is a harmless-looking weed,* which did a good deal of mischief in the middle ages. Ah!—'

"He pushed back his cap, he drew a long breath, he turned towards me, and then with his forefinger pointed to the manuscript.

"'There you have it,' he said, 'there you have your mysterious illness, your "symptoms which baffle the most skilful leeches," your method of preparation, your mode of administration, the time it takes to kill by almost imperceptible degrees, and the antidote,' and Mr. Ordford folded up his spectacles, put them in their case, took out his box, refreshed himself with a pinch of snuff, and felt like Sir Christopher Wren when he saw from London Bridge that the lantern spire of St. Dunstan's in the East defied the fury of the gale, and that his faith was justified.

"'My dear Ordford!' was all I could say for a minute.

"'What are you going to do now?' he asked.

"'I don't know,' I answered. 'First tell me where I can get this herb—this antidote—I do not know it even by name.'

"'It was freely grown in English gardens in the time of Gerard,' he replied; 'now it has fallen almost out of cultivation, but it can still, no doubt, be procured.'

"'Where, for Heaven's sake?' I asked.

"'In Covent Garden, I daresay.'

"I could not get it in Covent Garden, however, but was there told where it might be kept, and being fortunate enough to secure a small portion I hastened back to Southam.

"Already I had matured a plan of action—already I was taking the

* For obvious reasons the author refrains from giving either the common or botanical name.

first step in a course which compelled me to leave my partner, my promised wife, give up my professional prospects, and start for the diggings. In wild haste I decocted the antidote, scented it with poppies, labelled it 'Sedative draught,' and rode over myself with it to the Chase. Mr. Glenalbyn was absent, and not expected back till late. So much the better.

"Next morning found me again at the Chase. Mrs. Glenalbyn had slept a little, and said she thought the draught had done her good.

"'I know you do not like opiates, Doctor,' said Mr. Glenalbyn, who came into the room at this juncture, 'but you see I was right. If you think well, she might have another draught to-night—a little stronger.'

"I saw what his drift was, but only answered,—

"'I should like to leave one night between.'

"After I had said 'Good morning' to my patient, Mr. Glenalbyn, as usual, came down the staircase with me. Instead of going to the hall-door, as he expected, I asked if I could speak to him for a minute.

"'Certainly,' he answered, looking a little surprised; 'you don't think my wife worse, do you, Doctor?'

"'I do not consider her worse this morning,' I replied, 'but, looking back over a week, I cannot blind myself to the fact that she is not making the progress she ought. Has she any friends, that in case of—of—'

"'Good Heavens!' he cried, 'you don't mean to imply that there is *danger!*'

"'I am not at all satisfied,' I said. 'I have never clearly understood what was the matter; I only see that, from whatever cause, Mrs. Glenalbyn is losing strength daily; and, though the end may be long deferred, still if some change does not soon—'

"I stopped. I had been looking him straight in the face, and saw his eyes flash with a momentary delight, which brought again the sleeping horror to my mind. I felt I turned colour—I felt the expression of my face change—but evidently he misunderstood the cause of my emotion, for he exclaimed,—

"'Well, rest assured of one thing, Dr. Cray. *Whatever* may happen I shall not blame you. So far as you could, you have done your best—'

"'God knows I have!' I interrupted.

"'And though I may foolishly have imagined Dr. Montrose, had he been here at first, might have done more—'

"'He could not,' I interposed.

"'However that may be, you have done your utmost to save her. Do I understand you to say—I am so stunned with the suddenness of the blow—there is *no* hope?'

"'While there is life there is hope,' I replied; 'but still, unless some great alteration takes place—'

"'Quite so—quite so; I comprehend,' and he turned his head aside as if struggling to conceal the agony of his feelings; then, after a pause 'Her poor father—and—mother, wrapped up in her—only daughter—only—child. Do you think I had better telegraph for them?'

"'There is no actual necessity for such haste as that, I should hope,' I answered, well on my guard to avoid exciting his suspicion.

"'Still it might be more satisfactory. And you do not think you will send her another sleeping draught?'

"'Not to-night. I mean to try altering the medicine a little, and may look in again this evening.'

"'Do so—do so, by all means; and—Cray—if I have seemed at all to question your skill, forgive me; my anxiety has made me occasionally scarcely know what I have been saying.'

"'All now depends on the father,' I thought, after I had left Mr. Glenalbyn, his eyes a shade too near together, with a glitter in them which was not agreeable to contemplate.

"Alas! next morning when the father came I saw he was a degree more feeble mentally than his daughter. If anything depended on him she was a dead woman; but Mrs. Frottiss was a different sort of person altogether—strong, sharp, brisk, decided—to her I determined to appeal.

"She took me apart from the others, and asked me many questions. She grew so earnest in her maternal trouble and anxiety, that at last she put her hand on my arm and led me through the open window.

"'I can't understand it at all, Doctor Cray,' she said, and her voice never faltered, though her eyes were full of tears; 'it seems so sudden—so inexplicable. What is my daughter dying of, Doctor? Oh! pray, pray be frank!'

"Instantly I took my resolution. 'Mrs. Frottiss,' I said, 'I can't tell you here. I want to speak to you alone. Can you make any excuse to come into Southam this afternoon, and call on me. I have something to say which is most important, but—'

"She looked at me keenly, then—,

"'You don't want Glenalbyn to know.'

"I inclined my head.

"She was a wise woman, but she had not grasped the truth, yet.

"Three hours later she was sitting in my room—Mr. Glenalbyn's carriage waited outside my door, Mr. Glenalbyn's horses were impatiently pawing the ground.

"'I will come direct to the point,' I began. 'Has Mr. Glenalbyn any interest in your daughter's life?'

"'No more than in her death,' answered the old lady. 'She inherited a large fortune from her godmother—she ran away with her husband, there were no settlements; he has everything now, and when she dies he will have everything just the same.'

"Then I told her. I began at the beginning, and traced every step of the way. I gave the antidote into her hands and begged her to see it was taken. I said I knew it was not too late to save her daughter's life, but unless she could remove her entirely from the Chase, I failed to see how Mrs. Glenalbyn's safety was to be ensured.

"'Would she consult Mr. Frottiss,' I suggested.

"'Not of the slightest use,' she answered. 'See, Doctor Cray, are you willing to repeat what you have told me, in Mr. Glenalbyn's presence?'

"For a moment I hesitated, but after that I said, 'Yes, I am.'

"'Then I shall telegraph for our solicitor as I return to the Chase.'"

"What was the result," inquired Mr. Graham curiously.

"Such a scene as I trust I may never be present at again. I told my story, and I believe if Mr. Glenalbyn could have killed me on the spot, I should not be talking to you now. He vowed and protested—he stormed and raved. He said I was an ignorant impostor, who desiring to escape the consequences of my own want of knowledge, had devised this vile plan of fixing guilt on a husband who only loved his wife too much.

"Like a rock the solicitor stood firm.

"'All we want,' he said, 'is to remove Mrs. Glenalbyn; we shall take no further steps.'

"'Because you cannot,' interrupted Mr. Glenalbyn.

"We shall remove Mrs. Glenalbyn to her father's, where I trust she may recover her health—we desire no scandal—we claim no portion of her fortune.'"

"You got her away, I suppose, on those terms?" said Mr. Graham. "Did she recover?"

"Oh, yes, she recovered," answered Doctor Cray, with a grim smile.

"And—"

"The first thing she did was to rejoin her husband! and her next to state publicly I had tried to sow disunion between them. Such is Woman's Devotion!

"Husband and wife and Doctor Montrose and Perry all joined forces against me. A party was formed, I found it useless to resist, and that was the reason I left Southam."

"And is Mrs. Glenalbyn still living?"

"No; she died the victim of bronchitis—at least so it was reported. It is possible she succumbed to Montrose and the malady. I don't think Glenalbyn was to blame that time."

"He got all her money, I suppose?"

"Every farthing. He is married again, and still lives at the Chase. He put up a monument, with a most touching inscription to his wife's memory, in Southam Church."

"What is Ordford doing?"

"I do not know; for one thing—he is dead."

"And his manuscripts?"

"He died without a will, and the heir-at-law sold them for waste paper."

"And you, Jack, do you propose to take up doctoring again?"

"No—I mean to follow Ordford's example, and write a History of Poisons."

"Oh!" said Mr. Graham, and it would have been difficult to add anything to the significance of that interjection as uttered by the barrister.

CONN KILREA

Chapter One

EVER since morning, when the early post brought him a letter, Private Conway Kilray had been in low spirits; not by any means an unusual occurrence, for no man of his regiment could remember ever seeing him in good, but on the evening of the 14th December, 1892, he seemed to have sounded even a lower depth of depression than that wherein he usually dwelt.

He was young—not eight and twenty—fairly good looking, healthy, in full enjoyment of such faculties, bodily and mental, as God gives to most men, and yet possessed by a demon of melancholy, discontent, or unavailing repentance, that made him a mystery to his comrades and the dullest companion possible.

All the men among whom his lot was cast had tried to pierce the mail of his reserve, and retired worsted, feeling as though they had struck against something tougher than chain armour.

They could not make him out; he was always willing to help, always ready to do a good turn, always civil and quiet spoken, but always also grievously depressed, weighed down by some sin or wrong or trouble which lay heavy at his heart.

When, on the evening of that 14th December, he entered the barrack library at Weyport, the gloom of his expression so awed the few soldiers present that no one spoke while he passed to a desk, followed by a wiry Scotch terrier, who, being indeed nobody's dog, but only a poor stray, had conceived a fancy for the silent, lonely man.

Private Kilray seemed to have brought a blight into the room with him, which hushed the light chatter of those who were playing cards, and caused others who had selected reading as an amusing way of killing time, to glance constantly at the man who sat writing, cloaked with some strange gloom they could not understand, while the dog lay at his feet silent and self-contained also.

A few of those present winked at each other, or shook their heads gravely, but neither action was of any real import, for they knew nothing of what had put one life out of joint, whether murder, burglary, highway robbery, or forgery.

Some who had once been priviliged to see Kilray in a passion held that the first-named crime had driven him into the army, but the most general belief, founded perhaps on his bold and dashing caligraphy, was that signing a name not his own would eventually be found sufficient to account for much that puzzled them.

"Depend upon it, he took to gambling, and then used his pen once too often," said the oracle of "The Light Bays," when Kilray first joined. "He is Irish, yet he enlisted in England, as if there were not always regiments enough stationed in his own country, any one of which might have served his turn. No; we'll hear more about him after a while, and then the whole thing will be plain as a pikestaff."

At the end of eighteen months, however, things were as dark as at first. No inquiries had been made for Conway Kilray. No friend or foe had asked whether he were living or dead. A few letters arrived, which he answered and posted himself. When first he came among the Light Bays, a report soon got about that he knew more concerning horses than the riding master himself, who was asserted to have said he had nothing to teach the young recruit except how to trot.

Private Kilray had found that piece of learning difficult exceedingly, as most good riders do, but he set his teeth and curbed his temper, and ere very long could trot with the best. For the rest he groomed a horse excellently well; no one found any fault with him, no one said a word against him, but yet he was not popular. He walked a living enigma among his fellows, never making merry, never laughing nor joking, never talking part in any buffoonery nor more sober enjoyment. He was sufficient unto himself, which it may here be said is a peculiarity society—any society, whether high or low—cannot forgive, and naturally, since it is unpleasant to be continually getting figurative slaps in the face in return for well-meant civility.

On the evening when this story opens Private Kilray had not advanced at all in favour of his comrades, rather the reverse, as he had chosen to keep himself to himself. They, after some attempts at friend-liness, held aloof, and looked at him as he sat at his desk with a certain amount of curiosity and dislike.

Never heeding them, he wrote on, filling sheet after sheet, which he blotted hastily, folded without once glancing over, and placed in a directed and stamped envelope. Then he pushed the letter from him, and, resting his elbow on the desk, leaned his head upon his hand as though tired.

He sat so long thus that a man who was reading close by suspended his occupation in order to watch him. While he was doing so he became aware of a singular change in Kilray's manner. At first while engaged in thinking out some evidently unpleasant subject he kept his eyes dreamily fixed on a corner of the room near at hand which lay in shadow.

After a time, however, he lifted his head and peered into the darkness, as though he saw something he could not quite understand.

Involuntarily the man who was watching turned to see what his comrade was looking at, but failed to discern any object.

He had withdrawn his attention only for a moment, yet when he glanced again at Kilray he perceived his attitude was totally changed.

Both his hands firmly clenched were on the desk, he was sitting bolt upright, his eyes, filled with an expression of incredulous horror, were fixed on something he perceived looming out of the darkness.

He was white as death—he who was never known to fear—and a sort of grey shade came over his face, as with a shudder he rose and tried to pull himself together.

Then, for the first time, the other noticed that Kilray's terrier was looking into the corner also, very hair on his body standing more upright than ever.

"Hillo! have you seen a ghost, old man?" asked a new-comer who had just lounged up to the little group.

Startled by the question, Kilray turned swiftly round as if to resent it. Instantly recollecting himself, however, he laconically answered "yes," picked up his letter, and strode out into the night, followed by his dog.

Chapter Two

INSTINCTIVELY choosing the least frequented road, Private Kilray, feeling like one in a nightmare, walked on till he reached the seashore, and heard the waves washing in over a sandy beach.

It was a dark night—lit not by moon or star—but none too dark for a man, whose whole mind was filled by thoughts of eternity, to wrestle with the terror of that awful warning which had so lately, as he believed, been delivered to him.

Before he began to write he would have told any one, and according to his then belief, truly, that he felt his life not worth living, that there was little pleasant in the past to look back upon, and nothing in the future to look forward to; but now, when it seemed his time was come, he could have prayed for more years to be given unto him—years, whether joyful or sorrowful, that he might live and not go to the grave while it was yet noon.

The love of life is a thanksgiving to God. Which amongst us, having some jewel of price received from some earthly friend, decries its value? If we met with such an ingrate, we should write him down accordingly, and what must we say of the man who fails in his heart of hearts to praise God for placing him in a land overflowing with beauty, rich with colour, fragrant with perfume? And why? Because he has to work for his day's wage of things good and fair and sweet; he is discontented because he wants to choose his wage rather than accept that his Maker bestows!

Standing by the seashore, with the night wind fanning his face, with the waves' sobbing music sounding in his ears, with heaven's canopy above him and the dear earth beneath his feet, some dim understanding came to Private Kilray that he had been a very churl—that he had not made the best of life; that like a child in a temper he had refused to smile when Nature was putting out her loveliest playthings for his delight, and turned his back on man's more clumsy efforts to please and befriend him.

Ah, if he could only have seen sooner—if sight had not come so late! And then and there he bared his soul before God, and talked with the Almighty as he might aforetime have talked with man.

He had thought in the first bitterness of his anguish, he, who was done with life, to tear his letter to bits, and cast it to the winds; but his heart failed him now. That letter lay close to his bosom, close and warm like some throbbing human heart, and he could not fling it to the mercy of the elements as a thing of no account.

It is a sore trial to have to die, but it is a worse trial to die hard, with an angry and rebellious spirit, with a hand which refuses to take its loving Lord's as guide through the awful darkness of that valley which, willing or unwilling, our feet must tread!

Through the darkness the truth of this came home to one who felt himself standing on the very border of that unseen land whither he was journeying.

"Dear God," he cried in his agony, where there was no one save God to hear, where the night winds alone stirred, and only sea-birds and the waves broke the stillness, "dear God, forgive my sins, and grant me courage when Thy appointed time comes, to give my soul into Thy holy keeping, bravely and without fear, for Christ's sake— Amen." And he fell down beside a piece of rock, and covered his face, even though it was night, and dark, and arose comforted!

After a while, hearing some clock strike, he retraced his steps to the barracks, posting that letter by the way. His comrades, who were all acquainted with the fact that Kilray had actually seen a ghost, presumably of some one whose death he would ere long have to answer for, spoke to him with a strange reserve, which did not affect the young man at all.

He knew what they did not know. He was attended to the barrack-room by a face never seen since early childhood, which he had quite forgotten till it looked solemnly at him from out of the darkness of that unlighted corner.

The ghastly inheritance of an old family hovered over his bed, and caused foreboding dreams the while he slept uneasily, surrounded by the careless, the indifferent, the sorrowful, the struggling, the bad and the good till getting-up time came, and awoke with its noisy bustling, memories he would have fain forgotten for a little longer.

It was afternoon before he could snatch a minute in which to write another letter as short as the first had been long.

"DEAREST KATHLEEN" (he said)

"I have bad news for you, love; and yet, perhaps, it is the best I could have to tell you, because it points to the cutting of many a difficulty—to the ending of all anxiety.

"*I have seen Lord Yiewsley. You know what that means,* so I need add no more. I will meet you when and where you appoint to say good-bye. Do not grieve, dear. Fate has settled matters better for us than we could have done for ourselves. God bless you, my faithful darling.

"Ever in this world and in the next, your devoted lover,
                                                    " Conn.

"If I wrote a word yesterday that caused you annoyance, forgive me. I hadn't seen *him* then, though the envelope was scarcely closed before he appeared. I thought at one time of tearing up the sheets, but could not—my last love letter! Oh, sweet! pardon all the pain I have given you—I, who would have died to save you sorrow."

As the day wore on, as the twilight faded and merged into the gloom of evening, the restlessness which had, nearly twenty-four hours previously, driven him out through the night to the sad seashore, returned with greater intensity. He could not sit still. He felt like one who, having received sudden marching orders, wants to utilize every moment of the brief time left at his command; who tries to pack, to purchase, to make arrangements, to go and bid farewell, to be at home when some one dear calls, to clasp hands in a parting that may be eternal, to read letters, to write them, to make his will, to speak the tender words which always sound so inadequate. He felt all this; and over and above and beyond he longed for the touch of humanity, to hear the sound of a mortal voice bringing his trouble within the range of possibility. Death and dying in a natural way would have been bad enough, but to have to depart, he knew not how, at the beckoning of a ghostly finger, at the wordless bidding of one from out the world of spirits, added a new horror to the gruesome mandate. He must speak or he should go mad. So, as a sort of forlorn hope, he betook him to the chaplain, though, indeed, he knew rather less of that reverend gentleman than he did of his commanding officer.

At that moment, however, he was not thinking much of incongruities of rank or inequalities of station. He felt only intent on getting a straightforward answer to a question which was troubling him; therefore, when once he found himself in the clergyman's presence, and taken a chair, having been politely bidden to sit, he said—

"I am distressed in mind, sir; so I thought I would come round to you."

"It is my earnest desire that all who are distressed in mind or uneasy in conscience should bring their perplexities and burdensome sins to me, that I may tell them where to find relief," was the answer.

"You are very kind;" and the pair looked at each other.

"Not at all; I am only doing my duty," said the chaplain, graciously, though he did not quite like or understand his visitor.

If it be true that there is no bar to human progress like a theory, it is equally true that a foregone conclusion destroys human usefulness.

Mr. Pellock had accepted the charge of military souls without the faintest idea of what those souls were like. All he felt sure about was that they were wrong in the lump, and he dealt with them accordingly. They were given to drunkenness, brawling, folly, and many other sins—that is, whole regiments, excepting here and there a picked saint, a brand plucked from the burning, who believed in Mr. Pellock, in his sermons, his ministrations, his exhortations, his rebukes. If ever there was a square peg fitted painfully into a round hole that peg was the Reverend Carus Pellock. Of the British soldier, save as a good fighting creature, he had not the smallest opinion. He said sadly that he knew poor Tommy Atkins too well, but there were officers, old and young, who inclined to the belief he knew him too little. However this might be, Mr. Pellock did not think much either of the raw recruit or the finished warrior.

"A soldier disheartened him," he was wont to declare in moments of sadness, when the result of all his efforts seemed about as satisfactory as making ropes from sea-sand. That he might be saved seemed to Mr. Pellock possible, but only through a miracle. Nevertheless, the chaplain tried hard to do his duty, preached at, and to, and over the heads of his people, and was always courteous in a highly dignified sort of way.

He did not like any one presuming on his affability though, and doubted whether Private Kilray had a proper appreciation of the gulf which yawned between a simple unit in her Majesty's famous regiment, The Light Bays, and the man who had been good enough to undertake the charge of all the Light Bays' souls.

For this reason he answered "not at all," politely, yet with a certain frigid restraint, which failed to produce the desired effect.

"You remember, sir, perhaps, preaching a sermon about angels some little time since."

Remember! as if the Rev. Carus Pellock ever forgot the matter of his sermons. "Really," he thought, "this is very remarkable—very gratifying to find one of the rank and file so appreciative! But he is Irish evidently from his accent, and the Irish are more open to impressions than the English. I must know more of this poor fellow," all of which pleasant music Mr. Pellock played to himself the while he answered—

"You are quite right. I rejoice to find you were so attentive."

"In that sermon you said the angels were always with us."

"Just so, just so," purred the chaplain, feeling like a cat whose back is being stroked gently.

"And I suppose you believe what you said?"

Here was a question to be put to a clergyman wont to talk about angels and archangels familiarly, as though he had been brought up amongst them!

"I should certainly not preach anything I did not believe implicitly," he answered in such a crushing tone that his visitor, humbly apologetic, replied—

"No, sir, I feel certain of that; but it is hard to understand. That was all I meant, I assure you; I intended no offence."

"It is very odd," thought the chaplain, appeased, "but this private speaks almost like a gentleman." Then he said aloud—

"Many things in which we believe most firmly are difficult to understand."

"No one knows that better than I," was the answer so sadly spoken Mr. Pellock felt constrained to reply—

"Only tell me your doubts, and I will try to help you to overcome them."

"I don't doubt; I only wish I could," was the unexpected rejoinder. "You preached another sermon, sir, on All Saints' Eve," continued Private Kilray, before the clergyman could interpose. "I remember it particularly, because in certain districts in Ireland All Saints' Eve is kept with religious observance."

"Very proper, very proper indeed," said Mr. Pellock, who had not the faintest idea what the observance was, and felt more convinced than ever the Irish must be a charming people to work among.

"And if I did not greatly misunderstand," went on Private Kilray, as though he had not heard the chaplain's approving remark, "you are of opinion it is not possible for departed spirits to return to earth."

"I do not imagine I said impossible—only that such reappearances have never taken place," answered the chaplain, immensely interested

—so greatly interested that he scarcely noticed the wording of Private Kilray's criticism.

"Never taken place!" repeated that person; "think a moment—only think."

Mr. Pellock did not need to think, and recovered his mistake by a clever flank movement.

"Nearly two thousand years have elapsed," he said reverently, "since the Divine reappearance, to which, no doubt, you allude. It was miraculous, and we have no right to quote it as a precedent. What I spoke against, and always shall consider my duty to speak against, are the legendary stories inspired by superstitious fear, and the wicked and pernicious falsehoods continually poured forth from the press, more especially at Christmas—Christmas of all times!"

"But if those legends and what you call falsehoods are true, or at least have a substratum of truth? Dead men did appear to living men once—take the case of Samuel, for instance—why should they not do so now?"

"Idle inquiries are always profitless," was the reply. "Surely it is enough for us to know, that though all things are possible, as a matter of fact the dead do *not* now return. Tell me the sin or sorrow that is troubling you, and I will do my best to advise and console, but I must decline to discuss abstract questions."

"Then, if I were to tell you that no later than last night I saw one risen from the dead, what should you say?"

"I should say you need either a confessor or a doctor."

"In other words, that I am either criminal or mad; but you mistake, sir; the man whom I saw was done to death more than a hundred years before I came into the world, and during the whole of that time he has appeared to every member of my family previous to his or her decease. He came to me because I have been thankless and foolish, and did not value the gift of life; and now I want to live—I want to live!"

"You want a doctor, your hands twitch, your cheeks are flushed, your lips parched—you are in an overwrought and highly nervous condition. Go to a doctor, and repeat to him what you have told me. He will know how to deal with your complaint. You ought to see him soon, so I won't keep you longer now, but I should like on a future day to have some more talk with you."

Hearing this broad hint, Private Kilray rose at once and said, in his best soldier manner—

"I thank you, sir, for your kindness; good night." Then, after saluting, he went out.

"Clear case of mania," thought Mr. Pellock. "Religious mania!— worst form of all. An interesting case." After which, the conversation having suggested an idea to him, he turned to his desk and wrote—

"On the fleshy walls of our earthly tenements a mysterious hand is always writing the solemn warning, 'This night thy soul shall be required of thee.' Let us take heed that we do not neglect it," with which burst of eloquence he concluded a sermon on the following Sunday—a sermon no single person present understood, for Private Kilray, who might have hazarded a wide conjecture as to its meaning, was not amongst the audience.

Chapter Three

No. Private Kilray, doubtless to his great disadvantage, did not hear Mr. Pellock's famous sermon on the text, "Now, the king's countenance changed, and his thoughts troubled him," which was long remembered among the "Light Bays" by reason or its utter irrelevance to any subject likely to touch or interest that gallant corps.

He was gone on leave. After his interview with the chaplain, he did not seek medical advice; rather, when the proper time came, went to bed feeling sorely depressed, not merely on account of the many things he had from boyhood left undone which he ought to have done, and the many more things he had done which he ought not to have done, but also by reason of the utter impossibility he had always experienced of getting any one to understand him—except Kathleen. She was the one sweet exception in a bitter world, and he lay awake a long time, wondering whether there could be anywhere on earth so brave, so patient, so wise, so dear a girl as Kathleen Mawson, once in her little way an heiress, now a homeless orphan, companion to Mrs. FitzDonnell, widow of Admiral Burke FitzDonnell, who wrote his name large on the naval history of England? Yes, she was living with that lady in Lowndes Square, and had told him no further back than the previous morning that Mrs. FitzDonnell would not let a private soldier inside her door, not even if that private were her own son. On reading which statement, Private Kilray waxed exceeding wroth, and, not waiting to consider whether there might not be some faint rhyme or reason, or sense, or expediency or anything save prejudice in the amiable old lady's objection to receive such a visitor, delivered his soul of a passionate tirade against a state of society which had compelled him to accept her Majesty's shilling, and Miss Mawson a salary.

This was the letter on which he had been engaged while Lord Yiewsley, dead and buried for a century and a half, or thereabouts, was stealing back from wherever he had gone to, in order that he might frighten one of his enemy's descendants almost out of his wits.

In this amiable intention he succeeded, for Private Kilray, who would have gone into battle with a light heart, was quite demoralized by the sight of that apparition which came he knew not whence, and went he knew not where.

When quite a child, living with his mother on a lonely seashore, he had one night sprung up out of his sleep uttering fearful shrieks and earnest entreaties for his nurse "to take that man away," which shrieks and entreaties were remembered when news arrived of his father's death.

Gossips then shook their heads, and observed, "Ay, *he* has not forgotten; *he'll* come, as he promised he would, till there is not one of the stock left to die," which, indeed, had been his lordship's threat. In local opinion this threat received remarkable confirmation from the fact that his enemy's family went on steadily disappearing from the face of the earth. In the ordinary course of events they ought to have multiplied exceedingly, whereas there were now left of an old family but three men and two women.

For which reason it seemed likely Lord Yiewsley's self-imposed task would soon be completed.

The morning's post following his interview with Mr. Pellock might have brought an answer to Private Kilray's letter full of love for Kathleen, and brimful of anger against every one else, but it did not, and the unhappy young man felt glad to think his darling, having received that despairing second epistle, would not now write to chide him for his first, but despatch instead a tender missive breathing forgiveness, sorrow, pity—

As it is always the unexpected which happens, however, the letter—one of two which reached him in the afternoon—proved quite different from what he had expected.

"You silly, silly Conn," began his fair, "are you the only one of your name left? Is it because you consider yourself such a great personage that you imagine you must take precedence of the rest of your family? If you did see Lord Yiewsley, which I do not for a moment believe, having, as you know, always considered that story on all fours with the mourning coach, the drummer boy, the ghostly funeral procession, the white bird, the wailing banshees, and other cheerful omens proudly claimed by various families, you may live to be ninety notwithstanding. Do try to put away such silly fancies, dear boy. No, I will not meet you anywhere to say good-bye, but I am going to Weyport to bid you hope very much.

"I took courage to-day, and told Mrs. FitzDonnell our story, and what a foolish wrong-headed person my Conn is, prone to give way to little tempers, prone to spoiling his life because the moon won't come down to him, honourable darling living, for all that.

"And she? Well, she said, 'I should like to see this strange creature, so we will take a train for Weyport one day before Christmas, and put up at "The Sussex," which I know well, and your Conn shall come to us there, and we must think what can be done for him, the poor hotheaded young fellow.' There, Sir, is not that better than seeing a hundred Lord Yiewsleys? I feel wild with happiness, for Mrs. Fitz-Donnell would not even half promise anything she was not able to fulfil.

> 'Ever yours,
> "KATHLEEN.

"I do hope you will get this *soon*."

It was a well-meant, nice letter—Kathleen all over—affectionate, encouraging, sensible from beginning to end; but Private Kilray derived no comfort from it.

He knew that he had seen Lord Yiewsley, and though that defunct nobleman's visits could not be considered agreeable, still, had they ceased, every member of the young soldier's family would have felt as though some order had been taken from the Kilreas. People who have never owned a banshee, or a white bird, or a phantom drummer, or even a modest mouse, would probably fail to understand either the pride or the fear of possession, but the pride and the fear are both very strong for all that.

Had Miss Mawson been so fortunate as to be able to claim an ancestor who killed his man in the year 1640, she would have cherished his memory just as fondly as anybody else, and respected the family ghost his sin created very much indeed.

Still there was some truth in what she said. Though bad luck had pursued him through life, the summons might not have been specially meant for Private Kilray. His aunts now were getting on into years; one was nearly sixty; perhaps she would like to die; she always said she wished to do so; but, no, he would not think of such a thing; the lot had fallen on him, and he must meet his fate like a man.

While these thoughts and many more were passing through his mind, the second letter lay still unopened. It was disagreeably suggestive of a bill, and though Private Kilray was to die so soon—Lord Yiewsley's shade never gave his victims longer than a fortnight—he did not care to open that business-like envelope, on which one postmark (Dublin) stood out with painful distinctiveness. Others— London, for instance—were but faintly stamped, while Dublin blackly pointed its accusing finger at a young man never backward in the former days about getting into debt.

How had any creditor discovered his whereabouts? and he turned the letter over gingerly.

If a man were going to the scaffold it would give him a shock to be presented with "my little bill, sir," on the way. Humanity to its latest breath retains an insuperable objection to such ghastly reminders of happy times departed, and it was some little while before Private Kilray, taking his courage in his hand, tore open the well-gummed envelope, which he found to contain a letter, a memorandum, and a banker's draft.

The memorandum said—

"—— Street, Dublin,
"15th December, 1892.

"DEAR SIR,
    "By request of Mrs. Kilrea, we beg to enclose draft at sight for ten pounds, and remain your obedient servants,
                    "KAVANAGH, RUTLAND & CO., LTD."

There are few things capable of producing a more sudden transformation scene than a cheque or its equivalent. Who has not seen sunshine instantly take the place of shade on the receipt of a remittance; the life and joyousness of summer succeed to the cold dullness of winter when, after weeks of shortness, an empty purse is again relined with crisp bank notes? But as every rule has its exception, that ten-pound draft, which, after a fashion, was a fortune to one of her Majesty's rank and file, caused, when he read the sealed letter which accompanied it, an expression of pained grief and anxiety to overspread his countenance.

> "Moyle Abbey, Moyle,
> "14th December, 1892.
>
> "MY DEAR GRANDSON" (so ran the epistle),
>
> "Directly you receive this I want you, if possible, to come over here. Your grandfather is very ill, and *has asked for you*, and I do hope will not have to ask long in vain. Perhaps he was too hasty; but remember, Conn, you were hasty also when you ought to have remembered he was an old man who had been very kind to you. How could you leave us for eighteen months without knowledge of your whereabouts? But for Kathleen Mawson I should not even now know where to address this letter. With it Messrs. Kavanagh will enclose ten pounds, as you may be without ready money. COME AT ONCE.
>
> "Your affectionate grandmother,
>
> "MARY KILREA."

The young man hardly read this letter—rather his eyes galloped over it.

"My God! it is he then; the dear old man," he muttered, as he glanced up at the clock. "I shall have time to do it if I get leave," he thought; "and if I don't get leave I will take it."

Having swiftly decided which point, he rushed off in search of his No. 1, who, yielding to the urgency of his entreaties, forthwith accompanied him to his section officer, who in turn took him into the presence of a commanding officer named Captain Dace.

Now, Captain Dace was just going out, and, not feeling pleased at the detention, sharply refused Private Kilray's request.

He felt that if he granted leave about Christmas time to every man whose father, or grandfather, or sisters, or uncles, or other relatives were ill, he would soon have no men left, and said so in remarkably terse and forcible language.

Every one, however, knew that Captain Dace's bark was worse than his bite, and the section officer therefore ventured to remind him that Private Kilray had never asked for leave before.

"Well, he has made up for it now; a whole fortnight, no less!"

"I mightn't want so long," said the applicant in a hoarse whisper.

"Such perpetual applications really cannot be entertained," returned Captain Dace, brusquely, though touched by something in the private's tone. "If it had been your father, now"—relenting—"but a grandfather!"

"He was a father to me when my own died. If you would just glance over this letter, captain, perhaps—"

It was all said in little jerks by one evidently striving hard not to break down while the letter got into the officer's hands, that gentleman himself scarcely knew how.

Much inclined to return it, he nevertheless looked at the written sheet, on the top of which was printed "Moyle Abbey."

Why, he knew Moyle Abbey—at least, where it was. He had once been staying with a friend who lived a few miles from it—about eight— and what are eight miles in one of the wildest parts of Ireland, where gentlemen's seats are few and far between, the roads perfect, the horses almost thoroughbred?

He had heard of Moyle Abbey, and the family that lived there, and thought of all this while he read, and the fashion of his face changed.

"Do you mean to say you are one of the Kilreas, of Moyle Abbey?"

"Yes," answered the young man softly, as though confessing some sin.

"And enlisted under the name Kilray"—with the accent well on the first syllable, whereas the accent in Kilrea was, the speaker knew, laid on the last.

"No, I gave my right name, 'Conn Kilrea,' but the sergeant thought he knew better how to spell and pronounce the word than I—that is all."

"But how the—"

Captain Dace got no further in that sentence, and his private, though he was perfectly aware of the nature of the question left unfinished, made no reply.

"I suppose you are the heir?" were the next words spoken.

"No—Major Kilrea, of the Rushers," a regiment so called because of the wild way in which officers and men had once charged and turned the fortunes of war when defeat seemed inevitable.

"The Rushers, eh?" commented Captain Dace. "Well"—looking at his watch—"you have just an hour before the express for London. You can catch the mail train to Holyhead. I hope you will find your grandfather better," with which words the interview ended, and Private Kilray left his chief, accompanied by the section officer, who felt deeply convinced men may, and often do, even nowadays entertain angels unawares.

Chapter Four

As the Irish mail sped across England, Conn Kilrea thought concerning his past and future as he had never done before, even while the dread of death lay sore upon him. His own death would have ended the business, written "Finis" to the uncompleted volume, once containing so many hopes, latterly only soiled and blotted by fears, but with the belief that the doom he had shrank from was transferred to another, something for which he could find no name began to struggle within him, and fight with his worse self for mastery.

Looking back, he knew he had been his own most bitter foe—that it was his indifference, his indolence, his love of pleasure, his uncontrolled jealousy, his bursts of passion, which gave a handle to the enemy, while grieving the hearts and wounding the pride of those who loved him best.

He had been given his chance, and neglected it, he bitterly confessed. He thought of his schoolboy days, when he would not learn; of his college career, when he only laughed at opportunity, casting each as it came aside for the sake of some rowdy party or foolish escapade. He had taken life as a jest, and feasted and made merry till the hour of reckoning came, when, solemnly convinced the world was all wrong, or at least Conn Kilrea the only right person in it, he cast himself adrift from old ties, and took refuge amongst those who were but as his father's "hired servants."

Then, instead of making the best of a bad business, as even in the ranks a man may, he had allowed a very demon of sullenness to gain possession of him, and repelled the well-meant, though rough attempt at kindness of those who would have tried to make his life better. Voluntarily he had thrown himself out of the rank in which he had been born, and then he resented the fact that people did not know by intuition he was a prince in disguise.

"A prince," indeed! Nay, rather a humble dependent, who had not been grateful for the money spent, for the money given, for shelter, food, clothing; who had never earned a single penny till he enlisted in the "Light Bays."

He saw it all at last. While the train swept through the night he recalled the story of his life from youth to manhood, and found it wanting.

"God helping me, I'll try to mend my ways now," he thought, "but it's too late to please the dear old man—too late, too late!"

At the very time all this passed through Conn Kilrea's mind, and he was inaudibly uttering his own heartfelt self-condemnation, another man, who had far more reason than his prodigal cousin to love the owner of Moyle Abbey, stood in a brilliant ballroom, waiting and watching for the arrival of one he believed was not indifferent to him.

At last she entered—his fair, his queen. The expectant lover's pulse beat a little faster as he advanced to meet a portly lady, magnificently dressed, glittering with jewels, handsome, self-possessed, a thorough woman of society, and one well able to hold her own in it.

"Ah, Major Kilrea," she said, "we did not expect to see you here to-night."

"Why not?" he asked gallantly, in a tone addressed more to the daughter than the mother.

"Because I thought you would be in Ireland."

"I go to Ireland by the early morning mail."

"Oh!" she returned; and he knew instantly why her manner had changed.

"I was so grieved to hear of Mr. Kilrea's illness," Mrs. Gerrard went on, after an almost imperceptible pause.

"Yes, but I trust it is not serious," rejoined Mr. Kilrea's grandson. "He has had similar attacks before." And then Mrs. and Miss Gerard were swept away, and their friend the handsome major was left to his own reflections.

"Just my luck," he thought, "my cursed luck."

Quite an hour elapsed before Miss Gerard could give him the waltz she had promised a week previously.

"You do not blame me for coming here to-night," he said tenderly, as they stopped for a moment.

"Oh no," she returned with a cool ease, which showed she would at some future time be as good a society woman as her mother; "every one must in such matters judge for himself."

"You speak as though I ought to have gone"—reproachfully.

"I should have gone, but, as I said this moment, no one can judge for another."

The game was up. He felt he had lost her and her fortune as certainly as though a thousand tongues had proclaimed the fact.

"Are you rested? Shall we take another turn?" he asked, and it was not till they paused again that Major Kilrea inquired, "From whom did you hear of my grandfather's illness?"

"From Admiral Gerard, who was saying also how sorry he had been to learn his old comrade's son was in the Light Bays, and only a private. He thought something ought to be done for him."

She spoke quite calmly and distinctly, as if talking about some common matter, but the officer felt there was a sting in every word.

"Conn is an odd fellow, and it is hard to know what to do for him. He has never written me a line since he enlisted."

"Perhaps he expected a line from you," she answered. "I hope you will have a good passage, and find Mr. Kilrea better," she added, as another partner came forward. "Good-bye," and so left him to consider the irony of fate.

This was what was going on a few miles out of London while the Irish express dashed through Wales. The wind had risen, and howled mournfully among the hills.

"Doesn't omen well," said one of Conn's fellow-passengers, and the omen was fulfilled.

But after an awful passage the young man stepped ashore, hurried up to Dublin, and without stopping to eat or drink, crossed the city, and took train for Moyle.

A groom stood outside the station holding two horses. It was like a dream. Conn Kilray had not thought to come home thus or ever!

"How is my grandfather?" he asked the man.

"Very bad, sir; but he'll be better for the sight of you!"

They rode on fast, and in less than an hour Conn was pressing the sick man's hand, but could not speak because of tears which were choking him.

"I thought Leo would have been here by now," said old Mr. Kilrea, feebly.

"I am sure he will come as soon as he can get away," answered the young man, stinting his grief.

"Can that be Conn who spoke?" thought Mrs. Kilrea—Conn who for years had never uttered a word concerning his cousin without an accent of irritation.

Yes, it was Conn—Conn also who sat up with his grandfather, watched him as a mother might a child, raised him tenderly, and twenty-four hours later broke the news just received by telegram that the reason why Major Kilrea did not come was because he had met with an accident!

Before very long they were obliged to tell the old man that accident was death. He had been pitched from his dogcart while driving a friend home from the ball at Stanmore, and killed on the spot.

Said the friend before the coroner: "He drove so recklessly, I wonder I am alive to tell the tale. The horse bolted; we ran into a market van, were both shot out; Major Kilrea was dead when picked up."

The catastrophe affected Mr. Kilrea less than might have been expected. He had heard something about his heir's proceedings, which, perhaps, reconciled him to that heir's premature death. Besides, he himself was old, and felt life very sweet.

"It was not for me then," he muttered, "not for me; poor Leo," and forthwith began to get better.

But Conn took his cousin's fate greatly to heart, and won golden opinions by the humility with which he assumed his new honours, and his gentle forbearance and kindness to all with whom he came in contact.

"The Light Bays must be a gran' corps for training a man," said the old butler to the old cook at Moyle when the spring had come and flowers were blooming, "for it's not Conn Kilrea they've sent back to us, but a saint. He has never rapped out an oath, nor knocked down a single one, nor run over man or woman, child or pig, since he came home! Instead of the biggest divil ever stepped, anybody might think he'd been brought up in a convent—among the holy nuns. Milk is strong compared with him, and if he only holds on as he's doing he'll be the best Kilrea ever owned Moyle Abbey, and there never was to say a bad one yet!"

From which it would seem that Lord Yiewsley's visit had been productive of good, though neither Mrs. Kilrea senior nor junior will permit that nobleman's name to be mentioned in the house.

DIARMID CHITTOCK'S STORY

Chapter One

Since the beginning of this century civilization has advanced by such leaps and bounds that we may well ask how much further it can go.

In less than a hundred years we have on the sea learnt how to dispense with sails, and on land to travel at a speed which would have appalled our forefathers. Like Ariel, we have put a girdle round the world, so that messages can be flashed from earth's remotest corner in a few hours. All the luxuries of the East are brought to our doors. The cottager now possesses a more comfortable house than kings in the old days dreamt of. And yet the curious outcome of all this civilization, all this luxury, all this comfort, is that the natural man—the strongest, bravest, staunchest, most masculine man, the man to whom one's heart turns instinctively— seems continually trying to escape from their trammels.

In the earlier stages of civilization he liked to dance and attend mild parties, to don gorgeous dress, and, with a similarly minded friend, to lounge up and down Bond Street; but now all these things are to him pain and weariness.

By preference he wears a tweed suit and a pot hat, he shirks afternoon tea, and hostesses are at their wits' end to find a sufficient number of partners for their "pretty girls."

Girls themselves have for the most part now to do the love-making, and often fail to do it successfully, while the "natural" man is considering how he can best get away to tempt the ocean, to shoot big game, to explore strange lands, where civilization was never so much as heard of, and camp out, and eat rough food, and lead as wild and savage a life as possible.

It is rare, on the other hand, for women to seek seclusion from the world nowadays.

When they do, it is, as a rule, in company with their fellows, especially their fellows of the male persuasion. With them they will for a time gladly chase the wild deer and follow the roe, climb cliffs, and scale mountains; but they have no fancy for the lonely days and nights men not merely endure but love, which is probably only another proof that Mohammedans are right when they say women are not possessed of souls.

It is perhaps the terrible thoughts that dwell in many a male soul which drive modern men out into desolate lands, as the unimaginable terrors of morbid or stricken consciences drove of old both saints and sinners into hermits' cells and awful fastnesses, such as we can at this time of the world only faintly realize.

However this may be, and perhaps a mere teller of stories has no right even to conjecture, it is certain that in the year of our Lord 1883, Mr. Cyril Danson, well known in London society, felt a consuming desire to change his surroundings.

He was sick of them—sick of the men, more sick of the women; sick of the talk, sick of the streets, sick of the newspapers, sick of everything!

In modern society he was one of those individuals who seem to hang between heaven and hell. He was not rich enough to hunt with the hounds or poor enough to run with the hare. He came of good people, and was possessed of an independent income, which he lacked the business ability necessary to increase; he was not a director on the board of any company; it had never occurred to him to speculate; he did not feel inclined to go in for mines, or horses, or gambling, or concessions, or politics—in a word, he was only an honest English gentleman who held strictly by his own notions of honour and had grown tired of everything, merely because the one flower he fancied in that garden of beauty, "London in the season," was plucked by a newly made lord with a fabulous rent-roll.

He had known and loved her a long time, and thought she loved him.

In the slang of to-day he was "hit very hard"—hit so hard that at first his brain reeled under the blow.

After the lapse of a few weeks, however, he was able to see things in their true proportions and to feel the lady had been a very happy loss; but "going out into the wilderness" was a fancy which nevertheless came to him and stayed with him, and, unlike his faithful love, refused to leave him.

Yes, he would go into the wilderness—he quite made up his mind on that point—but then a very pertinent question arose, viz. "Into what wilderness should he go?"

It was impossible for him to seek his desert in Africa, or India, or even America.

He had enough money to live at home quietly like a gentleman, but he did not possess such means as would enable him to start as a modern apostle. Things have changed a good deal since St. Paul's time, besides which the Apostle of the Gentiles throughout his Epistles merely indicates that his expenses were not extravagant, and never tells us the amount to which they totted up.

Mr. Danson could have wished to go round the world—to visit stray groups of almost unknown islands, to spend a summer at the South Pole, to make his way across the interior of Africa, to see Siberia; but as it was necessary to stint his desires and keep them low like a weaned child, he decided to shake the London dust off his feet, and, taking only his soul for companion, talk confidentially with that too long neglected friend, conscience, when they reached some "void place" situated in Wales, Scotland, or—Blackstone Castle, Chittock's place.

Ah! a capital thought. Chittock's house was no doubt vacant, for Chittock nearly three years before, very hard hit himself, had tried whether the wilderness of London could not minister to a mind diseased as well as any other desert.

Mr. Danson knew Blackstone Castle well. In the days of his early youth he had spent a month there so pleasantly that the memory remained with him like some sweet tune heard of yore.

No lonelier or lovelier place than Blackstone Castle could well be imagined. It stood on a cliff from which, to the nearest continent, stretched straight as a crow could fly a thousand miles of sea.

There was excellent shooting in the neighbourhood, to say nothing of lake and river fishing, a sandy beach, great stretches of bog land, mountains covered with purple heather, and deep wide valleys, where Fin M'Coul and his children might have been playing "bowls" for centuries with huge fragments of granite for balls.

Yes, Blackstone Castle, situated almost at the world's end, was, if still lacking a tenant, precisely the hermit's cell he desired to find, and, having made up his mind on this point, he repaired to the "Cashel Club," where he thought he should probably meet his man.

As it happened, he did meet him on the threshold, and they walked into St. James' Park together, Mr. Danson, though "down," looking much as usual, but Mr. Chittock, after nearly three years' experience of the great city, appearing so little the better for such a decided change, his companion felt shocked to notice the alteration a comparatively short time had wrought.

Formerly he had been a fine, handsome, jovial fellow, with a hearty ring in his cheerful voice and a kind word for every one.

Now he was thin, haggard, dull, with a far-off sad expression in his blue eyes, seemingly twenty years older than his actual age.

LOVE serves her votaries many a strange trick. She strips the flesh off one, and plumps another up like a Christmas turkey!

In a very few words Mr. Danson explained what he wanted, and in an even shorter sentence Mr. Chittock told him the house had only been let one season for the shooting, and was at that moment empty, and quite at his service.

"Of course," he went on after an instant's pause, "I shall be charmed if you will take the place, but it is desolation made visible. It is twelve miles from anywhere. Personally, I would not go back again and live in my old house for any consideration. Had you not better think twice about the matter?"

Mr. Danson would not think twice. He was done up; he craved for quiet; he was tired of people; he desired utter solitude.

"Cannot you compass that in London?" asked Mr. Chittock, with a grave, curious smile.

"No—I must get quite away," was the answer.

"Is it so bad as that?"

"So bad as that! Just as you, Chittock, found it necessary to leave Ireland, so I feel I cannot stop in London. It is not that I am heart-broken," he added, moved by some impulse he was unable to resist, "but I want to get to some out-of-the-way place where people won't look as if they saw "JILTED" printed in big type all over me."

Mr. Chittock nodded. Though he had not been jilted, he understood.

"I want to change my life, too," went on Mr. Danson, a little ashamed of his outburst. "I could wish to be of a little use in the world —to know I had made a few persons the happier. If I were to die to-morrow not a creature, except perhaps my man, would be sorry. Did I only possess an estate like yours, even! But such good things are not for poor men."

Mr. Chittock walked on for about a dozen paces as though he did not hear—or, hearing, failed to understand. Then he said in those slow, melancholy tones, which contrasted so forcibly with his former utterances—

"Things are changed as well as myself, and you might have Blackstone at a very low figure. I do not intend, however, to take any man in, unless indeed a millionaire, such as your lost love's lord," he added, with a forced laugh. "Go and try how you like living in my old barrack all alone; then if, after a fair trial, you still desire to buy, I will meet you more than half-way."

Something he could not comprehend in Mr. Chittock's voice and manner struck Mr. Danson with a strange surprise, but he only answered—

"All right, old fellow, state your figure. Let the lawyers put all shipshape, and if I can be your man I will—anyhow, I'll take the place for a twelvemonth. By-the-by—"

"By-the-by what?"

"Did your young woman marry a lord?"

"Certainly not."

"Did she marry anybody, then, or what is she doing?"

"She never married at all, and is governessing I believe."

"She prefered governessing?"

"Not very complimentary to me," returned Mr. Chittock, "but a fact. And I loved her, Danson. She had no fortune; I wanted none, I only wanted her, and her father and mother wished her to marry me, but she wouldn't," he added with a sort of gasp. "There is something about me women don't like, I suppose. Anyhow, she would have nothing to do with me—not at any price."

"Poor old chap! Was she very pretty?"

"I think not—I do not know. She was pretty enough for me, and I loved her. Do not let us talk about it any more."

Mr. Danson asked no further questions. Here was a trouble deeper than any he had felt—a trouble he failed exactly to understand, and one with which he knew he lacked all right to intermeddle.

"My dear Chittock, I wish I could bring you balm of Gilead," he said earnestly.

"If you could I am sure you would," was the answer, "but not a man living can do that—there is no balm for me anywhere."

Chapter Two

DESPITE its pretentious name, Blackstone Castle was really a rather modest mansion. A few crumbling walls and a ruined tower adjacent to the house bore picturesque testimony to the fact that some sort of fortress had in old, old days occupied its site; but the modern Blackstone Castle was merely a square, roomy country mansion, big enough to hold a large family of small sons and daughters when young, and welcome plenty of high-spirited, laughing, joyous guests when the little people grew old enough to think of love-making—of marriage and giving in marriage!

It was in his " calf days "—which are, after all, the sweetest, pleasantest, most innocent days man can ever know, full of the fresh immaturity of morning and the happy, half-conscious expectation of a glorious noon to come—that Mr. Danson had been made "free" of Blackstone Castle, where he accompanied Diarmid Chittock when both of the young fellows were leaving school.

For ever the recollection of old Mr. Chittock standing on the great doorstep and welcoming first his grandson's friend and then, well-nigh with tears, his grandson, remained in Mr. Danson's memory.

Stalwart fellow as he was, his own eyes filled when he beheld once again the well-remembered place where that gracious, old-world man could never welcome friend nor grandson more.

A splendid old man—one of the best breed of gentry this world ever saw, and which it is unlikely the world will ever see again, belonging as it did to an impossible-to-return, long gone-by—a gone-by it is well never can return, but which was a magnificent painting nevertheless, full of gorgeous colouring and soft tender tints, deep shadows, and wrongs, alas! unimaginable.

As he entered the spacious hall—architectural grandeur was at one time a thing no good house in Ireland ever wanted—Mr. Danson felt himself to be a very fortunate hermit, for while seeking solitude it was borne in upon him he need be no anchorite. His own man stood there to wait on him, just as if he had only stepped across Pall Mall; his horses were in the stables; his servants in the kitchen; certainly the rooms lacked all modern æsthetic refinement, but Mr. Danson was weary of æsthetic refinement as well as of many other things.

He knew he was not in the van of civilization, and he did not wish to be; nevertheless, on the other hand, he had not dropped quite to the rear. It was early summer; and while he smoked a quiet cigar after dinner he looked out over thousands of miles of ocean, and felt as if some soft hand were being laid on his heart and drawing something of its bitterness away.

That night, wearied with his journey, and believing he had reached a desired goal, he slept, lulled by the gentle murmur of Atlantic waves, the deep restful sleep of youth.

Next day the rector called, next day the priest, the third the doctor.

The wilderness was not so absolutely desolate as he had intended, but still three visitors in seventy-two hours could not be regarded as exactly a "rush" of society. Besides they were, each in his way, all interesting men, who had something to tell and were willing to hear.

Before the week was over, Mr. Danson had quite settled down to the routine of a dull country life. He who had squirmed at afternoon teas, and garden parties, and days up the river, and four-in-hand expeditions to whatever race might be on; who had objected to assist at the laying of foundation-stones, to hearing of speeches, to receptions to dinners, to balls; who had grown to detest with a deadly detestation London gossip and even London itself,—found himself taking an interest in the post, and walking down to the village each morning for his daily paper, returning the mail-car driver's salute with ceremonious civility and chattering to the local shopkeeper in the most affable manner possible.

So far as we have ever been told, saints and sinners who in the early days went out into the wilderness of this wicked world did none of these things; but, then, history is silent on many of those subjects about which we should all, no doubt, like to hear a great deal. Distance probably lends a considerable amount of enchantment to the holy men of old. Near at hand they were presumably much like their descendants. They could not have been considering their shortcomings, and contemplating the mysteries of life and death, day and night for forty years. Possibly, among those of the number who were sincere, their voluntary withdrawal from the world was only an attempt to coax back the mental strength of which a too long sojourn in it had temporarily bereft them—just as Nature taught Mr. Danson he ought to leave

London and talk quietly with the wise old mother of us all if he wished ever again to have a sane mind located in a sound body. Her remedies are of the simplest; and quite unconsciously this man, who had been turning night into day, burning his candle at both ends, working harder than any horse in a mill, was taking them regularly.

The solitude could not be considered perfect; but though, properly speaking, it was out of character for him to take an interest in the rector's college reminiscences, in the priest's stories, or the doctor's recollections of Ballyragshanan dispensary, the hermit's cell he had chosen answered its purpose admirably, and

> "He ate and drank and slept—what then?
> He ate and drank and slept again.

And there were times when he actually wondered why he had come to the "back of beyond," and fancied it must have been for pleasure!

The face of his false lady-love and her wealthy lord soon grew faded and blurred like shadowy old photographs. He could read their names in the *Times* and never turn a hair. That great stretch of sand, that vast expanse of ocean, became pleasanter day by day, and he began to like his "constitutional" beside the Atlantic as he had once never thought to like anything except the "sweet shady side of Pall Mall."

"Each morning when returning home with my paper" (posted to him regularly from London), Mr. Danson said one day to the constabulary officer, with whom he was on particularly good terms. "I meet a girl—not tall, not pretty, not striking-looking, but yet a girl who attracts me, because she has the quietest, saddest expression I ever saw on a woman's face. You can tell me who she is, no doubt?"

"Dressed in black? Steps out, too?"

"Yes, and walks well."

"That is Miss Oona Rosterne."

"Miss—?" suggested Cyril Danson, puzzled.

"Oona Rosterne," repeated Mr. Melsham, "the daughter of my predecessor, who disappeared."

"Good heavens! I thought that poor lady was a governess somewhere."

"So she is—daily governess at Fort Cloyne. Walks three miles out and three miles in—hail, shine, or snow—five times a week. If she would leave her mother she might get a large salary, for she can teach everything. As it is, the Mustos pay her fifty pounds a year, which is thought unbounded wealth hereabouts."

"Was any trace of her father ever discovered?"

"Not a trace."

"How very strange!"

"Why strange? There are bogs enough about here to engulf a whole army, let alone one inspector."

"Do you mean that he lost his way?"

"Lost his way on a starlight night! Why, he knew every inch of the country," scoffed Mr. Melsham. "No; some one knocked him over quietly and put him where he will, maybe, be dug up a couple of hundred years hence."

'I thought people imagined he had left the country.'

"People over the Channel might, but not a soul about here did. He was over head and ears in debt, to be sure; but a man needs money when starting on foreign travel, and Rosterne never had any. Then he loved both wife and daughter after his fashion, and nobody was pressing for payment, because it was well known Miss Oona had but to say 'Yes,' and Chittock would have found every penny that was needed to rid her father of debt.—No; the whole business is a mystery. One day, perhaps, when the fellow who did away with him is dying, or some one who knows gets tired of keeping the secret, we may hear more about the matter; but the likelihood is, not a soul now living will ever learn what it was happened between seven p.m., when he left Letterpass to walk home, and the next morning, when he had not got home. He was seen about two miles from Letterpass striking down to the shore, but never after by any one we can trace." A blank ensues. "That is the whole story."

"It is a terrible story. If his body had been found, dead or alive—"

"But it was not, you see. No wonder Miss Oona looks as she does. Yes"—reflectively—"she walks three Irish miles out and three Irish miles in, five days a week, hail, rain, or shine, and her grandmother was an O'Considine, too!"

"Oh! was she?" said Mr. Danson, who had not the faintest idea the O'Considines had ever been reckoned grand people—in fact, had never even heard of them till that moment.

"Indeed she was," replied Mr. Melsham, who received the remark as a tribute of respect to the great house mentioned. "Her grandfather was about the last of the race—the last, that is, who could and did stick to the estate—drove his four-in-hand, kept open house, and never wanted for anything as long as there was a shot in the locker or an acre of land to be mortgaged."

Though Mr. Danson as yet knew but little of the "first gem of the sea," it seemed to him this had been the practice of many excellent Irish gentleman, and one apparently that had secured for them the esteem of their contemporaries and even the admiration of posterity. Right royally they had lived on their capital while it lasted.

And for those who came after?

Why, those who came after have ever since been paying for the piper's merry tune, to which men and women danced such joyous measures in the old days departed.

It was less, however, with those old days Mr. Danson occupied his mind the while he strolled leisurely towards Blackstone Castle than with that girl who walked thirty miles each week and toiled all day, instructing, probably, many young ideas how to shoot, in order to add fifty pounds a year to her mother's income.

And all the while there was a man in London breaking his heart because this sad-faced governess would have nothing to do with him; and Blackstone Castle remained without a mistress, who would have lacked no manner of good things had she married its owner. Mr. Danson's soul yearned over the pair; he longed to bring them to-gether and make them happy—ay, even in spite of themselves.

Certainly a remarkable-looking girl, not strictly pretty, perhaps, but a girl not easily to be forgotten for all that. Though Mr. Danson had not spoken to her, he knew those dark grey eyes, that curious melan-choly expression, that sensitive, troubled mouth, would never pass quite out of his recollection.

Of course it was the knowledge that she ought to become Chittock's wife which attracted and riveted his attention.

Without some interest, he told himself, he would never have looked at her twice, and it was a long time before he remembered he had looked at her more than twice before he learned she was *the* woman of Chittock's life.

It would be an excellent work, he decided, to make the divided pair one, to bridge the river of their unhappiness, and bring about a happy reconciliation.

He could do this, he felt confident, and then he remembered that Mr. Musto had called a week previously, while the new tenant of Blackstone Castle was exploring the Blackstone caves, and that his visit ought to be returned.

When people have an object in view they can take very prompt action. Accordingly Mr. Danson, having an end to gain, decided to ride over to Fort Cloyne that very afternoon.

Only to meet with a check, however. Mr. and Mrs. Musto, he was informed, had left the same morning for Switzerland, and would be absent for two months, or perhaps longer.

Two months! For the second time that year life stretched before Mr. Danson as a perfect blank.

Foiled both in love and friendship, what could he do?

Why, get acquainted with Mrs. Rosterne. How stupid not to have thought sooner of that simple plan!

"Gorey," he said, pulling up his horse to a walk, and beckoning the man so called, who was at once his own groom and Mr. Chittock's foster-brother, to come beside him, "I was talking to Mr. Melsham this morning about Captain Rosterne's extraordinary disappearance."

An English servant, had such a piece of information been vouchsafed to him, would have answered vaguely and discreetly, "Yes, sir;" but Gorey replied after a different fashion—

"Mr. Melsham was not here then, sir. He only came when Inspector Hume left."

"And who was Inspector Hume?" asked Mr. Danson, as utterly ignorant of the whole affair as any one could be.

"Just about as sharp and clever a gentleman as any poor fellow in trouble would wish *not* to meet."

"Meaning, I suppose, any one who had stolen a sheep or killed a landlord?"

"Or done anything else your honour pleases to think of."

This was a nice way of putting things! As if his honour was pleased with or had a love for people who stole sheep, or shot a landlord, or did "anything else."

And yet Mr. Danson felt convinced Gorey could only be considered a willing, faithful, honest, capable servant, and a law-abiding man. Such was the character Mr. Chittock had given him, and such, it may at once be said, was the character he deserved, with higher praise to the back of it.

"I suppose Mr. Hume inquired into the whole matter?"

"He did, sir. He was at it day and night, after a manner of speaking. I don't think he had right rest all the time he was there, or the master either, for Mr. Hume was for ever at the castle."

"And he never got a clue?"

"Not a one of any good at all. He went here and went there, but the end was the same as the beginning."

"And what is your own notion, Gorey? Come, now, what do you think became of Captain Rosterne—where did he go? or if he did not go, where was he taken?"

The afternoon sun was blazing into Mr. Danson's eyes while he asked this question, and he might, he thought, have been in error. Nevertheless, he could not shake off the impression that just for one moment the guard of Gorey's impassive face changed, that his eyes flickered, as one may say, and the muscles of his mouth twitched.

The whole thing was instantaneous and perfectly incapable of description—a little transformation scene Mr. Danson felt rather than saw—for the sun, as has been said, was in his eyes and blinding him, and when Gorey spoke his voice was calm and natural.

"Indeed, sir, I couldn't say. I don't know where he would want to go away from wife and child; and though he wasn't too well liked, I am very sure nobody ever wished him enough ill to put a bullet in his heart."

"Oh! he wasn't well liked, then," said Mr. Danson, who felt at the moment as if he were a second Columbus.

"He wasn't hated, sir, if that is what you are thinking about," returned Gorey in a moment, taking all the wind out of Mr. Danson's sails; "for he never did any man a serious wrong, so far as I heard. He was just, and often and often stood up for the poor when they had no other to speak for them. But still and for all that he wasn't liked. He had come from nothing, yet still took a heap on him. Many a one such as him does that."

"He was bumptious, in fact?" suggested Mr. Danson.

"People about here said he was an arbitrary gentleman," said Gorey, substituting what he considered, and what was, a better word. "No man had a keener notion of justice, no man was civiller. If a beggar touched his hat to him, up went his stick or umbrella or finger in return. He had the best of manners, sir; but yet there are those that feel good manners and the height of justice are not a patch on the love of God. And he had no love of God or of God's creatures."

"That is a hard saying, Gorey," remarked Mr. Danson, impressed in spite of himself.

"It's true, your honour, for all that. Now I'll tell you. Supposing he was driving on his car and he saw a string of loaden carts on the wrong side of the road, where it was not metalled, he'd whistle them all to get out of the way—ay, and if they didn't, summon them. And all the same, I've seen her Grace the Duchess when she was driving her pair of cobs sign to the men to make no shift and walk her own horses over the stones, and was there a soul in the barony did not say, God bless her!"

"Still, in Captain Rosterne's position he might have thought it his duty to see that the rule of the road was observed."

"Maybe, sir; but the Almighty is much easier with those who go a bit wrong than he was. Still, though nobody much cared for him, I never heard a man, woman, or child that hadn't the soft word for him when he forgot to come back—ay, and the wet eye too for the wife and child he left lamenting."

"And what did chance to the unhappy man, Gorey?"

"Not a one was able to say, sir—not a one. Pat Harrigan met him on the shore road walking home, but he never got home, poor gentleman."

"He did not drink?"

"No, sir, not to say drink; he took his glass like anybody else, but it was never said that he took a glass too much."

"Or gamble?"

"He might a little, but not beyond the common."

Mr. Danson wondered what "the common" might be, but held his tongue. So far he had not made a single point. Of course, if Gorey knew nothing, there could be nothing to tell. If, on the other hand, he suspected foul play, it was quite evident he did not intend to share that suspicion with any one.

Moreover, the man had been questioned and cross-questioned, and no doubt Mr. Chittock and he had talked the matter over exhaustively. The probability was he really had not a word to say, and yet Mr. Danson could not feel satisfied concerning that strange flicker.

"Mr. Chittock must have taken the affair terribly to heart," he observed at last.

"He did so, sir; he never to say has been the same man since—and small wonder. There was no one in these parts he was as intimate with as the Captain; he'd have been his son if all had gone as it might have done."

It was all very well to speak to Gorey about Captain Rosterne's disappearance, but Mr. Danson felt he could not let a servant talk concerning Captain Rosterne's daughter.

It seemed to him dreadful that such a girl should be the subject of common gossip. He would have set her on a pedestal high above the reach of vulgar tongues, which looked very much as if Mr. Danson had conceived a marvellously high opinion of his friend's wife that was, he hoped, to be.

Very possibly he thought Captain Rosterne had for reasons of his own left the country. Some painful scandal, some terrible misfortune, might be at the bottom of the mystery, which he had better not try to search out further.

But it could do no harm to try and bring the divided pair together again, and, full of this intention, he proceeded at a good round trot to Blackstone Castle, followed by Gorey, who had dropped behind to a respectful distance.

Chapter Three

MR. DANSON did not owe the rector a visit, but he thought he would walk down to the village and call on the rector's sister, a lady of uncertain age, though certainly not under fifty, who always amused Mr. Danson immensely. Her one great desire, poor soul, was to see London; her one great regret that her brother's lines had been cast in such a primitive parish as Lisnabeg.

"Ah, if he were only in or near London now," she said, "where he could mix with men of his own calibre!"

It had never occurred to Mr. Danson that the rector's intellectual capacities were so great he could hope only to meet with one equally mighty among the most cultured classes in a great city; but it would

have needed a much harder heart than that which beat in the Englishman's breast even to hint that Miss Heath perhaps overrated her
brother's abilities. He contented himself with remarking, therefore—

"Sometimes London proves a little disappointing."

"But why? How can it? Is not all the THOUGHT of the world there?"

"Much of it, certainly; but a person may live a long time in London
without meeting with a vast amount of thought, or any indeed," he
added.

"I scarcely understand how that can be at the fountain-head of
everything."

"True; but if you consider the fountain-head has a population
almost equal to that of Ireland, you will understand many of the
inhabitants have to remain at a considerable distance from the well."

"Ah! that wouldn't be the case with Phil; he could make his way to
the centre at once."

"I am sure he would, whenever he was known," answered Mr.
Danson heartily.

And then Miss Heath went on to tell him how he could not conceive
—he who had so recently left "the thought of the whole world, and
still felt its invigorating breeze fanning his cheek"—how deadly dull
their village really was.

"You have not to *live* in it, Mr. Danson," she went on; "you can
leave it whenever you like—run over to London or Paris, or New
York, for that matter; but we who, fettered by pecuniary trammels, are
compelled to tread the same monotonous round week after week and
year after year, alone understand its weariness."

Mr. Danson thought he had felt the full weariness of fashionable
London's monotonous round; but that was a subject on which he did
not care to enter, so he seized the opportunity presented of saying—

"The Mustos have taken wing, I find. I rode over to-day, only to
hear they left this morning for Switzerland."

"Oh, yes," answered Miss Heath, "and will be away for two
months. They always start in this sudden fashion, just as the whim
seizes them. We shall miss them very much, because, though they are
not exactly—well, you know they are not of the old gentry—"

"I suppose the old gentry were new once also. Everything must
have a beginning," suggested Mr. Danson.

"Quite so; and, as I was about to add, the Mustos are kindness itself—hospitable, charitable, and considerate. Why, the very carriage that took them to the station called on its way back for Mrs. Rosterne."

"Why for Mrs. Rosterne?" asked Mr. Danson.

"Because she and her daughter always stay at Fort Cloyne when Mr. and Mrs. Musto are absent. They are quite members of the family, I assure you. Mrs. Musto says she has never an anxious thought concerning the children when Oona Rosterne is in the house with them."

"Miss Rosterne must be a very exceptional young lady," Mr. Danson forced himself to say, though he felt that day had been but a series of disappointments.

"Indeed she is. My brother says another girl like her could not be found in the three kingdoms, and he ought to know, because he prepared her for confirmation. Still I feel myself I never can forgive Oona the way in which she treated poor Mr. Chittock."

"But I always understood—and remember, no one can feel more sorry for Chittock than I—that she was straightforward from the first—told him plainly she had no love to give him," answered Mr. Danson, eagerly.

"And what right had a chit like Oona to set herself up against those older and wiser than she was?" asked Miss Heath. "Look what a match it would have been for her—the salvation, after a fashion, of her heartbroken, overworked father; a husband she could have led about with a string; a home for her mother; the best of marriages any girl need have desired. But no; my lady had her own fancies, and would pay heed neither to father nor mother, lover nor friend. When I was young, Mr. Danson, girls took advice; Oona would take none, and you see the result."

"But still, if she could not care for Chittock—" pleaded Mr. Danson.

"Could not care, indeed!" repeated Miss Heath. "I have no patience with such nonsense. What was there about the dear kind fellow to dislike?"

"I cannot tell you, Miss Heath. I always liked him, and my dearest wish is to see him married to Miss Rosterne."

"Then you may give it up, Mr. Danson. So long as the sea ebbs and flows she will have nothing to do with him. Sorrow has not taught her; poverty has not changed her. Since her father's death—for no one believes the poor man is alive—she has been more set against Mr. Chittock than ever. Would you believe it?—he wanted to allow Mrs.

Rosterne an annuity, and the foolish girl wouldn't let her mother take a penny. What do you think of that in one so young? For Oona can't be reckoned old even now, though she is nearly three and twenty. I call that young even for a governess."

"If she did not care for Chittock, I think she was right."

"But why did not she care for him? A man who was, as one may say, a specimen man—quiet and well-living, good to look at, and pleasant to listen to—a man who could not drink if he wished, because a glass of punch got into his head at once. Mrs. Rosterne told me the only reason Oona ever gave for saying 'no' was that she felt afraid of his temper; but, then, what is a husband who has no temper? and his was just a flash and over. It's a saint, I suppose, she's expecting to get, and I wish she may succeed."

"Is there some suitor, then, Miss Rosterne favours?"

"I'd like to have seen the man except Diarmid Chittock dare look at, much less speak to her, when her father was alive. And who do you think she'd take up with would throw a thought her way now? No, she's let her chance slip—a grand chance, too. She'll never get another, so she'll just have to go on drudging through life. I am sorry for her, but she wouldn't take advice. You are not going yet, though, Mr. Danson, surely? You would stop till my brother comes in? He won't be long."

No, Mr. Danson was much obliged, but he must get home; in fact, he had only called to bid a short good-bye. He intended to walk through Connemara. He wished to see that part of Ireland particularly, and might probably include in his programme Killarney and the Golden Mountains.

"Tired of Blackstone Castle already," decided Miss Heath, as she watched him walking fast towards that desirable residence. "Well, it's natural—no one can say it is not."

Chapter Four

FASHIONS change, but not to such extent as many people imagine. A stout pair of walking-shoes now represents the picturesque sandal of old, and a well-made knapsack serves the pedestrian's purpose much better than any wallet ever did that of pilgrim; while the modern tourist is, seen from an artistic point of view, most distinctly merely an improved copy of the long-bearded, not over-clean, very often extremely lazy, peripatetic gentleman who formerly made a living by piously doing nothing.

The same restlessness that drove the devotee into void places and caused him to make his home among the graves now sends his smart, well-set-up, well-dressed, but much happier nineteenth-century proto-type to scale mountains, to stem rivers, to cross oceans, and to live in unfamiliar countries.

There is, to put the matter in a sentence, as much human nature running loose about the world now as there was nineteen hundred years since, or, for the matter of that, as when, nearly forty centuries ago, Abraham "sat in the tent door in the heat of the day."

It was the human nature in Mr. Danson that made him tell Miss Heath he intended to walk through Connemara—an idea which had never entered his mind till the rector's sister drove him to the verge of desperation by speaking with the voice of the world concerning Oona Rosterne.

He felt he could not endure to hear Chittock's dear love gossiped about in such fashion, and that he could still less endure waiting two long months before it would be possible to make Mrs. Rosterne's acquaintance.

Therefore he resolved to go away, and he did; clad in a serviceable suit of frieze, well shod, admirably financed, he tramped from Castlebar to Galway by zigzag routes, which enabled him to see every place of interest in the county; then he took train to Dublin, and returned to Blackstone Castle. He only remained there, however, long enough to find matters were going on as usual, and that likewise, as usual, Time was sitting on the cliff with folded wings brooding over Mr. Rosterne's disappearance perhaps, but more possibly brooding over nothing.

Having satisfied himself on these points, he went away again, first to Dublin, where, chancing to pick up LeFanu's "House by the Church-yard," he explored Chapelizod reverently and with a deep feeling of sadness, thinking all the while Chittock's future wife ought to be a second Lilian. Then through the too little-known County Wicklow, and afterwards to beautiful Killarney. From thence he bent his vagrant steps to the Golden Mountains, and finally made his way back to

Blackstone Castle, firmly convinced Ireland was the loveliest country on earth.

Nature seemed a pleasant change to this man, who had lived so much in society and been disappointed by it. Perhaps if he had lived as long with Nature she would have disappointed him also cruelly. Who can say?

When he last left Blackstone Castle, sea and land and sky lay bathed in mellow sunshine. It was the "Green Isle's" golden season, when grain, ready for the sickle, and bound by the reaper into sheaves, was to be seen on every hillside; when the mountains looked purple, clad as they were with heather in full flower; and the Atlantic rippled in over a shell-strewn shore, quietly, as though storms and tempests had never ruffled its peace.

When he returned, the whole landscape was changed. Stern mountains looked darkly away to a swelling sea trying in vain to calm itself after wild Equinoctial gales. Afar out the white seahorses were chasing each other like living things, while on the sunken rocks nearer at hand wild billows expended their fury by dashing over them in showers of spray; black and green, crested as if with snow, they rushed to their doom, succeeding each other with the solemn regularity of an advancing army.

Above, a grey sky kept mournful watch over the scene of desolation.

"Could anything be grander?" though Mr. Danson, as he walked along the cliffs and surveyed the mighty panorama spread below. "What a magnificent country, what a glorious land!"

He was in excellent spirits—in such spirits as would have caused him to look favourably on even a much humbler picture.

The Mustos were at Fort Cloyne, and Mr. Musto at once hastened to Blackstone Castle, and gratified the new tenant by asking him to join their houseparty before it broke up.

"Just a few crack shots," he said; "men who enjoy a country like this, and never mind how long or how far they have to tramp after their game. Do come. We shall be so glad, though we have no inducement to offer beyond good sport. There are only four lady guests— two old friends of my wife, and Mrs. and Miss Rosterne. You have heard of the latter, I dare say?—Yes. Poor Chittock—such a pity! We may expect you, then, to-morrow?"

Mr. Danson said yes, saw his guest off, and then in a state of great exultation took his way along that high path which commanded so fine a prospect.

All things seemed possible to him then. He could see, he could talk to the girl Chittock loved so well. He would be his friend's ambassador, find out where the trouble lay, and put everything that was wrong right.

As a rule, people who essay meddling in the affairs of others make great mistakes. Perhaps the mere fact of adventuring on such delicate ground proves their unfitness for the self-imposed task. But Mr. Danson knew no fear. The cause was so good, his own intentions so excellent, that success must ensue; and it was, therefore, with a light heart he sat down to dinner next evening, having on his right hand Mrs. Musto and on his left Mrs. Rosterne. Obliquely across the table he saw Miss Rosterne, who looked as though she would have been much happier anywhere else.

The dinner was rather a success. People talked freely, and when the ladies left the room and the gentleman drew closer together, Mr. Danson felt he had assisted at many far more stupid entertainments when the London season was in full swing, in the days before he determined to give up this world's pomps and adopt the *rôle* of hermit.

Later on in the drawing-room, after some of the elder ladies had played and sung, a veteran colonel entreating Miss Oona, whom he seemed to know very well indeed, for one Irish ballad, "If it must be only one, my dear," Mr. Chittock's obstinate fair, after a few preliminary notes of introduction, began—

"Ah! 'tis all but a dream at the best;" and immediately a hush fell on every one present, which lasted till the spell of Miss Rosterne's voice was broken by—utter silence.

The song itself is not specially pathetic, and yet the listeners did not at first seem inclined to speak.

"Isn't she wonderful?" at last Mrs. Musto asked Cyril Danson almost in a whisper; but the gentleman could only look an answer, because the charm of the girl's rare voice held him dumb.

When at length he sought his room, he did it with the feeling that Chittock's infatuation was justified. Nevertheless he fell asleep while endeavouring to discover wherein the secret of Miss Rosterne's curious fascination lay. She was not handsome or beautiful, or even strictly pretty. She had no becks and nods and wreathed smiles for the outside world; she spread no lures to attract; her singing even lacked the little artifices with which quite legitimately many a woman tries to win admiration. No; he could not tell how or why it was she touched all the hidden fountains of his heart and drew virtue from them, only he knew her voice haunted his dreams, that he heard it during the course of an exhaustive conversation with her concerning Mr. Chittock—a conversation that removed all misapprehensions, put all mistakes right!

When he awoke he could not, however, at all remember the arguments he had used, the misconceptions he had explained away. He only knew he had seen those strangely pathetic eyes uplifting to his, and heard that low rich voice assuring him, "I always loved Diarmid—always, from the time I was a little girl."

Which was well enough as a dream. In waking life, however, Mr. Danson found at the end of seven pleasant days he had not advanced one step. With the other ladies he soon became on terms of friendly intimacy, but with Oona his progress was absolutely *nil*.

She did not repulse or snub him, it is true, but the masterly inactivity she displayed repelled his advances more effectually than any open antagonism could have done.

"I am afraid Miss Rosterne dislikes me," said Mr. Chittock's friend to Mrs. Musto on the day when his visit was to terminate.

"Do you think so?" returned the lady.

"Yes, I do—or rather I am sure she does," he answered, "and I cannot imagine the reason, for I have always endeavoured to conciliate her."

"Yes," said Mrs. Musto.

"Cannot you help me to solve the enigma?" he asked. "Ladies understand each other so much better than we do. I most earnestly wish to be on friendly terms with her, for poor Chittock's sake."

"I imagine that is where the trouble lies."

"I beg your pardon—I fear I am very dense."

"You are thoroughly kind. Still, if you will forgive me for saying so, you made a mistake when you took Miss Heath into your confidence."

"Miss Heath!" Mr. Danson repeated, mystified; "when did I take her into confidence?"

"You told her the dearest wish of your heart was to see Mr. Chittock and Miss Rosterne man and wife."

"Did I? Very possibly. I do not remember using such a phrase, but the matter has lain very close to my heart, and Miss Heath and I talked about the trouble once."

"Precisely, and poor dear Miss Heath is a sad gossip. She does not mean to make mischief, but she is always repeating things that vex people, and I have no doubt what you said in such good faith has been told to Miss Rosterne with the inevitable additions, so that it hurt her very much."

"I am extremely sorry. What can I do to repair my blunder?"

"Nothing much, I fear; but I should certainly refrain from speaking of Mr. Chittock's rejected suit to any one except myself. I except myself," she added, with a pleasant little laugh, "because I am quite on Oona's side. I consider she was right; every one else believes she was wrong."

"But why do you consider she was right, Mrs. Musto?"

"Because she did not love the man."

"And why did she not love him?"

"That is a question I am unable to answer positively, but I think because she knew him too well, and also because he wooed her after a somewhat masterful fashion—took too much for granted, in fact. Till she refused his hand, not once or twice or thrice, Mr. Chittock's opinion of himself was exactly the opinion of every one about here—namely, that he had but to ask and have. Now, to a girl brought up in the way Oona Rosterne was, that seemed utterly intolerable. Perhaps you do not know how she was brought up, Mr. Danson?"

"I do not," he answered humbly.

"Well, I will tell you. It seems to me a strangely pathetic story. Up to her ninth year she was just Oona Rosterne, which meant she was Oona anybody. Then Sir Thomas Glanmyre died in India, and his widow, an O'Considine, returned to Ireland and bethought her of the relative who had married Mr., or, as the people hereabouts always called him, Captain Rosterne. She came down here, took a fancy to the little girl, and adopted her. From that day, for seven years Oona lived amid luxury, saw only people moving in good society, was taught by the best masters and mistresses, and grew to be, to all intents and purposes, a child of the upper ten thousand."

"Naturally."

"Lady Glanmyre resided for the most part in Paris," continued Mrs. Musto, "and only occasionally came to Ireland. It was always understood she would provide for Oona, but a short time before her death the bank in which her husband had invested his money failed, with the result that everything went except Lady Glanmyre's pension.

"The shock killed her. She left her young relative what she could—her jewellery, plate, furniture—but after the debts were paid only a mere trifle remained, which Captain Rosterne promptly spent.

"Then Mr. Chittock appeared on the scene, and the girl would have none of him. Between her and her father there were several disagreements. Oona felt he was wanting to sell her, and Mr. Chittock's very kindness about money estranged her more from him.

"After Mr. Rosterne's death or disappearance, over head and ears in debt, very angry letters from Mr. Chittock, written evidently under great irritation, were found among the missing man's papers, refusing to lend any more money, and asking why he should be expected to do so. They were disagreeable letters—letters which Mr. Rosterne ought to have burnt at once, but which he did not, and Oona saw them, and the iron entered into her very soul, so Mrs. Rosterne told me.

"I have only given you a mere sketch. You can fill in the details for yourself, and when you have done so, you will understand why the way to make Miss Rosterne dislike you is to plead Mr. Chittock's cause."

Mr. Danson remained silent for a minute.

"Still I believe, if she could see poor Chittock now," he began at last.

"It would make no difference whatever," interrupted Mrs. Musto. "I spoke to her once—only once—on the subject, and gathered nothing could reconcile her to the idea of marrying him. 'And believe me, Mrs. Musto,' she said 'no one wishes less to marry me now than Mr. Chittock; we quite understand each other.' What she meant I do not know; but I suppose even a devoted lover may weary of a hopeless pursuit. At all events, what I have told you—in strict confidence—is absolutely correct. If you want Miss Rosterne to treat you more graciously, you must try to be less Mr. Chittock's friend."

"I can't be that," said Mr. Danson.

"Ah well, then, I am afraid the case is hopeless," answered Mrs. Musto.

But when she came to think matters over, she did not feel quite certain on that point.

Like a wise woman, however, she said nothing.

Chapter Five

FINDING his scheme for making Mr. Chittock happy was impracticable, Cyril Danson began to consider that a winter enlivened only by an occasional visit to Fort Cloyne and a continual prospect of the Atlantic might, to use Miss Heath's expression, prove "monotonous," and accordingly, following Mr. Musto's excellent example, he wrote to a few men he knew would enjoy the wild sport, the desolate country, and the utter liberty of the life he could offer—for a time.

He was right—each and all, they accepted his invitation. At the moment they were unfortunately engaged; but the moment they had, to quote one Curled Darling's expression, "done their time," he might depend on receiving a wire.

"It will be very jolly. Thank you, old fellow. It is good of you, who are off the treadmill, to remember those who are less lucky. We shall like to see your bogs and climb your mountains."

So said the Curled Darling afore mentioned, and so in effect said the others.

Then, for the first time, Mr. Danson took an exhaustive survey of Blackstone Castle, and considered its capabilities.

"I will change my quarters, and sleep in the oak room as soon as it can be got ready, Chenery," he said.

"Yes, sir," answered Chenery, who was that servant Mr. Danson had referred to as the only person likely to miss him. Then, after an almost imperceptible pause, "Gorey says the oak chamber is very cold indeed."

"Possibly—but I like cold. And, Chenery, you had better have the dining-room put in order."

"Yes, sir." And Chenery turned, as if to commence operations forthwith.

If such were ever his intention, he must have changed his mind very speedily, for ere reaching the door he stopped to observe—

"Beg pardon, sir, but Gorey says the wind is amazing blusterous in the dining-room, which is like a barrack in the winter-time."

"Can you remember anything else Gorey has been pleased to remark?" asked Mr. Danson.

"Well, no, sir, not at the moment, except that the library and the bedroom you occupy at present are the only two comfortable apartments in the house when stormy weather prevails, as it generally does in these parts from September to April."

In spite of himself Mr. Danson could not help smiling, even while he said—

"You are becoming demoralized, Chenery, I am afraid. Do precisely what I have ordered, without any further reference to Gorey's opinions."

"Yes, sir," replied Chenery meekly, and departed.

But for the fact that he had so peremptorily signified his determination to be master in Blackstone Castle while he rented it, Mr. Danson might within a week have returned to his former sleeping apartment.

Each room in a house, whether the house chance to be in a town or country, has its own peculiar set of noises; and Mr. Danson, who had occupied as many rooms in different houses as most men, was perfectly aware of this fact. Nevertheless, all previous experience proved quite insufficient to account for the sounds appertaining to the oak chamber.

They were always varying, yet scarcely with the variation which might well belong to the same family. Such unaccountable noises he had never heard before anywhere; but then he recollected he had never previously slept on the top of a rock within sound of any ocean's roar.

At last, unable longer to refrain from speech, he said to Gorey one morning—

"I did not know there was any right of way up those steps from the beach."

"No more there is, sir; but maybe once in a while some poor fellow does make so free as to take them as a short cut. It was done in the old gentleman's time now and again, and neither he nor Mr. Diarmid made any disturbance more than a shake of the head or 'I can't let this go on.'"

"Oh!" returned Mr. Danson, drawing a long breath. "And when all that is settled," he went on, as if talking to himself, "what I should like to know is why any one thinks fit to tramp up those steps in the dead of night."

"Indeed it would be hard to tell, your honour, for the way is none too safe, even in the daytime," Gorey made answer, though the question had not been addressed to him.

"I wonder sometimes," observed Mr. Danson, looking speculatively in the man's face, "whether you are very simple or very wise?"

"It would not be becoming in me, sir, to say," replied the groom modestly, "though there have been some thought I knew as much about horses as any man in the country. Colonel Jerome, that took Blackstone Castle after the master went away, was that well pleased with my handling of his mare—who had, saving your presence, a devil of a temper—he wanted me to go with him to Worcestershire, and offered me good wages too."

"Why did you not take his offer, then?" asked Mr. Danson.

"I can give you no better reason, sir, than that I thought I would rather stay here."

"Which, I suppose, was reason enough for you?"

"It was, your honour, and that's why I didn't go."

There ensued a short pause, during the continuance of which Mr. Danson considered the position, and Mr. Chittock's foster-brother stood at ease.

"Gorey," began his latest employer at length.

"Yes, sir!"

"I wish very much you would answer me one question straight-forwardly—if you can?"

"You may depend I'll do my uttermost, your honour," answered the man, unconscious, apparently, of the slur cast on his veracity.

"Then tell me who you suppose would wish to come up those steps after dark, to say nothing of midnight."

"If I was never to speak another word, I don't know sir. At this time of the year there is hardly a man, unless among the gentry, out of his bed after nine o'clock, unless it might be a constable or a gauger."

"Why, there's no smuggling here?"

"Not this many a year; but then there would be, the gaugers say, if it wasn't for them."

"And do you mean to tell me any exciseman would risk his neck up those steps in such pitchdark nights as we have been treated to of late?"

"Indeed, it is hard to say where they wouldn't go, for they are just like cats, and have as many lives. You see, sir, it is not so much smuggling they are keen on now as illicit stills. They got up a story once about there being a still in the dungeons of the old castle."

"And was there?"

"They never found one, or any dungeons either. All the same, everybody round these parts believes the ruins are like a rabbit warren, and just burrowed with secret passages."

"And what is your notion, Gorey?"

"I have none, sir; strange things were done in the old times, Mr. Diarmid always did say. But I know I've heard old people sit and tell a parcel of nonsense over the fire till young girls and boys, for that matter, were afraid to turn their heads for fear of what might be standing behind them."

"But not merely do I hear the sounds mentioned on the steps, but there are the strangest noises in the dining room."

"It is all according to the wind, sir, as I made bold to tell Chenery. The east side of Blackstone Castle isn't fit to live in the whole winter through. Colonel Jerome said he'd as soon try to sleep on the seashore; and indeed, Mr. Danson, if you'd take the lower path any evening after dusk, when the wind sets from the north-east, not even blowing a gale, but just a moderate breeze, you would wonder what could be going on out in the Atlantic. My old grandmother used to say it was the dead—drowned people, I mean—talking to each other, and making ready for the company the coming storm would send them. I'll take your honour down any night you like, and you can hear for yourself."

"Thank you; I hear quite enough above," returned Mr. Danson, coldly. And he went away feeling very doubtful concerning Mr. Daniel Gorey's strict adherence to truth.

When once a man gives imagination the rein, whether in the matter of love, hope, suspicion, jealousy, or any other master passion, it would be difficult to say where that artful sprite will take him. He may only pause to look at a glorious sunset, and behold, before the pomp of gold and crimson is chased away by clouds of darkness, fancy will have taken him round the world, and shown him such marvels as in his sober moments he never could have so much as thought of.

It was thus with Mr. Danson; from the moment when he saw, or believed he saw, that flicker in Gorey's expression he began to mistrust the man, and every word he spoke subsequently seemed confirmation that the truth was not in him.

His answers to questions were always shifty, Mr. Danson considered, and hitherto that gentleman could not understand the reason. Now a light broke upon him—Gorey was engaged in some unlawful enterprise. Gorey wished to keep Blackstone Castle empty. The presence of any stranger interfered with his illegal operations. Possibly the excise officers were not far wrong when they suspected the existence of an illicit still on the premises, and who would be better able to baffle all search for it than a man who had known from childhood the house, the ruins, the caves, the coast, and every inch of country? Imagination had already taken Mr. Danson on a wild chase, but it was inevitable but that fancy should lead him still further. Evidently, Gorey knew something about Captain Rosterne's disappearance. What more likely than that the unfortunate inspector had come across the potheen manufacturers and been done to death lest his revelations should stop their trade?

From all he, Mr. Danson, had heard, Captain Rosterne was a man who would have died sooner than make terms with such people, and very probably—nay, very certainly—Gorey knew the whole of the circumstances.

So far, Mr. Chittock's tenant did not suppose that Gorey assisted at Captain Rosterne's murder, or was even present at it, but who could tell the length to which imagination might yet take him? Once a man lets that jade get the bit between her teeth, he might as well be mounted on the Phoul-a-Phooka.

Three mornings later, Gorey asked his employer if he could "spare a minute," and Mr. Danson reluctantly intimating it might be possible for him to do so, the groom led him to the top of that rude flight of steps which gave access to the beach.

"I know now," said Gorey, "what it was your honour heard. It was that"—and he pointed to an upright piece of iron, to which was fitted a sort of broken wheel, which revolved when caught by the wind, and gave forth a sound as if of many feet hurrying up a stone staircase.

"D'ye hear, sir? Wait a minute, and the wind'll be on it again."

"Oh!" exclaimed Mr. Danson, thereby freezing the glow of Gorey's enthusiasm. "And how did that invention come there?"

"No man now living could tell, I am thinking," was the reply. "It's bedded in the solid rock, and that is all time has left of it, but I said to myself I'll never rest till I find out the English for those steps, for I couldn't make head nor tail of the constant running up and down you said you heard."

"Oh!" exclaimed Mr. Danson, again giving the iron wheel, which would have served well to frighten birds, a careless touch with his stick, when clatter, clatter, clatter, clang it went as if a dozen men in hobnailed boots were running post-haste over the stones.

"Bring round the dog-cart in half an hour; I shall want you to go with me to Letterpass," he said, in that peremptory-courteous, pleasant English way Gorey had learnt to know and dread.

It was disappointing, the groom felt; but, then, he knew Mr. Danson had long lost confidence in him.

And he was quite right. Since the hour when he, in the dazzling sunlight, first fancied Gorey's face changed for an instant, the Englishman had not felt at ease concerning Mr. Chittock's foster-brother.

To use a lovely phrase, he "misdoubted" him, which involves a hard ordeal for the misdoubted man or woman to pass through.

The conclusion Mr. Danson had come to was this: "When first one sees the Irish, they seem quite open and above board; they charm by their apparent frankness, and are cheerful to a fault, if cheerfulness ever can be called a fault. As day after day passes, however, the reverse of the shield presents itself, and they show themselves in their true colours —shifty, plausible, false, unreliable, but pleasant—to a certain point," he mentally finished, "though there is no more reliance to be placed on them than in their climate."

Poor climate! Poor Ireland! Poor Irish! Poor Gorey!

And yet Mr. Danson's feelings were natural enough. He had come to Ireland carrying his heart in his hand, and that hand open.

He had come prepared to like, prepared to give, wishful to make those he came in contact with happy, desirous most of all to remove a load of care from Mr. Chittock; and of the two persons he thought could best have helped him to compass the last wish, one coldly thwarted his endeavours, while the other evaded his most simple question.

Often he marvelled why he remained amid such unsatisfactory surroundings. But Mrs. Musto did not wonder; *she knew!*

There is no truer saying than that "it never rains but it pours," and accordingly the post-bag one morning rained such a number of coming guests that Mr. Danson for the moment felt appalled.

Not merely did the three men he had invited herald their early arrival, but two out of the number proposed to bring a friend with him. "Adson wants to see your cell so awfully," said one; "may I bring him?" "Mayford, who is the best fellow on earth, has never been in Ireland; can you take him in? If not, wire at once."

Mr. Danson telegraphed that he would be glad to see them all, and then set Chenery to work to make things ready for the expected guests. Immediately the whole economy of Blackstone Castle underwent a change—fires blazed in hitherto unoccupied apartments, the house-maid looked up her stores of linen, and asked for assistance. The cook told Chenery she must have more pots and pans, and a woman in to help. Chenery himself had to report an absence of sufficient glass and crockery ware. Gorey spent his time scouring the country in order to bespeak provisions and "making ready" for the moment when he should receive orders to "meet the train" at Letterpass, while to Mr. Danson the bustle and excitement proved delightful after six months' absence from the hurly-burly, and diverted his attention completely from the noise of mysterious footsteps and the strange wailing sounds that rendered the dining-room well-nigh uninhabitable.

The dining-room at that time really was in the possession of Chenery, who served his master's meals in the library, and was making many changes which cost little more than a good deal of personal trouble, in the apartments devoted to the reception of company.

Chenery was in his element. His master gave him *carte blanche*, and he had men up from the village to shake, and clean, and hammer, and tack, as well as arrange goods ordered down from Dublin; and, in short, as the cook joyously expressed herself, "It is like the good old times come again, God bless them!" while Gorey said, though not audibly, "He'll have something now to take his mind off Captain Rosterne and the din there is about the place sometimes. Lord send these gentleman may entice him back with them to where he came from!"

Charlie Langley, the curled darling, dreaded by fashionable mothers, beloved of daughters, a sad, unscrupulous detrimental who danced like an angel and was a very bad boy without a bit of harm in him, was the first to arrive at Blackstone Castle.

He appeared one afternoon carrying a modest portmanteau, which, he explained, had, with himself, been "tooled over from Letterpass by a delightful old Presbyterian minister who might have drawn up the Westminster Confession of Faith. He traveled in the compartment with me from Rathstewart, and we got into friendly relations immediately. I told him where I was going, and he told me the distance.

"'Which I must tramp, I suppose?' I said, 'for Mr. Danson doesn't know I am coming by this train.'

"'You needn't do that,' replied Martin Luther, 'for if you don't object to an old-fashioned gig, I can give you a lift.'

"I told him if there were one conveyance I loved more than another it was a gig of the pre-Adamite build; and then he said he liked young people with no nonsense about them, and that he knew you very well."

"I am afraid I have not the honour of the gentleman's acquaintance," interposed Mr. Danson.

"By sight, by sight, my arrogant friend," exclaimed Mr. Langley. "He lives at Cloyne Vale, and has seen you riding over to Fort Cloyne; pray, observe how pat I have your heathenish names already. My divine proceeded to say you were a fine-looking man; 'would make three of you,' he remarked so disparagingly that I felt constrained to answer, 'I know I am very small, but indeed I am very good.'

"He shook his head as if he did not believe my assurance, but only looked at me as a father might at a naughty child, more in sorrow than in anger, and we parted on the best terms. I said I would do myself the honour of calling on him, and I want you to ask him up here."

"Very well," agreed Mr. Danson; "only, Langley, there is one warning I must give you—the Irish do not like chaff."

"I don't know about chaff," returned Mr. Langley, gaily, "but they will like *me*."

Chapter Six

THE fulfilment justified Mr. Langley's prediction. Before the week was out he had conquered the village. No one could be said to have a chance beside him. All the children, and they were many; all the dogs, likewise numerous; all the beggars, ditto, adored the lively young

Englishman. Old women rose up and called him blessed. Men would have risked breaking their necks at his bidding. He knew every one— the rector and the baker, the publican and the sinner, the doctor and his patient. Miss Heath was his sworn ally. Mr. Danson discovered him on one knee holding her worsted while she wound. Mr. and Mrs. Musto and the little Mustos were enchanted with the new-comer, while he walked in and out of Mrs. Rosterne's cottage as though an inmate of the house, and Miss Rosterne, whom he dubbed the "blessed damosel," was actually seen to laugh at one of what Mr. Danson in his inmost heart called Langley's senseless sallies.

It was then a sword pierced Mr. Danson's soul; then for the first time he asked himself a very serious question; then he began to understand what his feelings had always been towards the girl who held him at such a distance! "And who now encourages that mountebank?" he reflected most unjustly, for Miss Rosterne did not encourage, only laughed, and that but once, as she might at the gambols of a frolicsome child. Then her face grew grave again as was its wont.

How tired Mr. Danson soon felt of his visitors it would be difficult to tell. Their talk, their jokes, their liveliness, jarred upon him like merriment in church. What a roystering set they were to bring to a hermit's cell! How could he ever return to a world of which they were rather favourable representatives?

For they all could but be considered kindly, honourable men, who were doing nothing wrong except enjoying themselves thoroughly; who would have been quite as ready to condole with the sorrowful as they were to rejoice in their own youth.

"Jolly companions every one," they tramped across bogs and over heather; they walked long miles; they never grumbled if rain swept down upon their devoted heads; they were charmed with the scenery, delighted with the people; vowed they would ask nothing better than to spend years in Blackstone Castle, and voted their host by acclamation the best fellow living!

They sat up late and rose early; walked and rode when the weather proved propitious; lounged, chatted, and played billiards when it was wet; after dinner they amused themselves with cards, smoked cigars, and drank punch, which the doctor brewed scientifically; they made themselves as contented and happy as children; they declared they would never have such a good time again; and who could say they were mistaken? Christmas—a green Christmas—came and passed; and then one night the storm-fiends, which had been laid to rest for a long time, were let loose in their power and might. Through all the hours of darkness there raged a furious gale from the north-east, and when morning came Mr. Danson saw "what he had never seen."

"The wild waves tossing their foam to the stormy sky"—earth and heaven seeming to meet, giant billows madly chasing each other and rushing in-shore as if steadily purposed to sweep over and destroy the land.

He stood looking out on the magnificient spectacle in absorbed admiration till he suddenly remembered this was the wind which, according to Gorey, rendered the dining-room as well as his own sleeping apartment unfit for human habitation.

Well, he knew what the night had been to him, and he regretted not having told Chenery to lay breakfast in the library.

"Danson," shouted Mr. Langley up the wide staircase as soon as his host appeared, "have you a cell underneath the dining-room where you keep all the winds that blow? I never heard such a din. Do make haste; the noise is glorious—better by far than anything I ever heard at sea. Just listen;" and he held his friend on the threshold while what one of the others called "an infernal row" broke on his ears and fairly appalled him.

"No one could stand this," Mr. Danson said at last; "let us go into the library."

"No, no, I wouldn't miss the fun for anything," declared Mr. Langley; "all the powers of hell seem to be warring against us. Talk of the Swine's Gun! Not to be compared with the concerted music at Blackstone Castle!"

"But what in the name of everything wonderful is it?" asked Mr. Tankerton.

"The cry of the wind," answered Mr. Danson, feebly.

"Have you heard anything like this before?"

"No, but Gorey warned me this room was unfit for occupation during the winter."

"I am going to occupy it, for one," said Mr. Langley, seating himself at the table. "Here, who will have toast?"

"I will have potato cake—a good thing, and one I shall probably never taste again," answered Mr. Adson.

"The strangest part of the affair to me is that, spite of the saturnalia somebody is holding, the house still stands. It does not even rock," contributed Mr. Mayford to the conversation.

"I do not profess to understand or explain the noises about Blackstone Castle," said Mr. Danson. "They seem to have been here before I came."

"After breakfast I shall make it my business to understand them," declared Mr. Langley, attacking a huge sirloin.

"Gorey knows more about Blackstone than any one else," remarked Mr. Danson, not without a feeling of grim satisfaction at the idea of pitting the wits of his guest and his groom against each other.

"Then Gorey shall share his knowledge with me," was the confident reply.

Mr. Danson went to the sideboard and helped himself to fried cod.

The luncheon hour arrived and found Mr. Langley comparatively silent. Yes, he had talked to Gorey. "Yes," in answer to pressing questions, Gorey had personally conducted him to that unsafe, rocky staircase leading to the beach, where his hat was blown off instantly, and he had to hold his hair tight lest that should follow also.

Gorey seemed favourably impressed with the devil's own triangles, which were making the most awful clatter he, the Curled Darling, ever heard.

Gorey had offered to take him that evening, after dark, to a place where he would be able to hear quite distinctly the dead talking to the dead, but Mr. Langley had refused the charming invitation.

He did not care for great sensations. He told Gorey, he said, he was young and easily frightened, and liked his bed; so if Gorey of his kindness, instead of dragging him miles along the seashore, would come in and tuck him up and sing him to sleep, and remain beside him during the night lest he should wake up and be terrified at finding himself "all his lone"—a delightful Hibernian phrase—he would feel much more grateful than if taken to the grandest ghost-party ever given by the Atlantic.

"Gorey tells me he knows a lot of ballads," finished Mr. Langley, "so I intend to make arrangements for a musical evening when next Danson and his rough team are invited to Fort Cloyne."

"Of which I will give you due notice, and hope you may enjoy your sing-song," said Mr. Danson.

"I only wish the blessed damosel would come up and assist," remarked Mr. Langley.

"I should love to hear her rare voice mingling with Gorey's in 'Fight on, ye brave heroes, fight on,'" said Munro. "I can just fancy how she would give that line."

"Miss Rosterne has endured a great trial, and I think we ought to respect her sorrow," remarked Mr. Danson, severely.

"I respect Miss Rosterne. She seems to me the pluckiest girl I ever met." answered Mr. Langley. "But concerning her 'trial' I am not quite so sure. At one *coup* it rid her of an unwelcome lover and a father who, if all accounts be true, was the most undesirable of 'stern parients.'"

No one, replied. Mr. Danson did not care to do so, and the other men were not sufficiently interested.

"One thing I do like about Gorey," resumed Mr. Langley, "is that he has the most loyal regard for my 'dear damosel.' He says if she and the master, meaning Mr. Chittock, could have 'sorted matters,' it would have been the making of Blackstone Castle and all these parts."

"Very likely," assented Mr. Danson. "Judging from appearances, Blackstone Castle as well as poor Chittock want some one badly to 'make them.'"

"The whole business seems to me so unaccountable!" observed Mr. Tankerton. "I always thought any girl would marry any man if only he were rich enough."

Mr. Danson winced, but said nothing. Mr. Tankerton remembered and stopped—too late.

Mr. Langley hummed, "I am a loyal subject, brave as any in this nation," and remarked calmly, "Gorey has certainly a great repertory."

Chapter Seven

The storm had sobbed itself to rest. Worn out, the Atlantic lay almost calm under a cold winter sky; the dead were quiet in their ocean graves, or at least no sound of their terrible discourse broke the evening stillness; while Peace seemed for a time at least to have taken up her abode among the headlands of that iron-bound coast.

"But this weather is a delusion," said the doctor, who, at the earnest desire of Mr. Charles Langley, had, with the priest and Mr. Melsham, been invited to relieve the monotony of Blackstone Castle, and was in the act as he spoke of mixing that famous brew which was known and esteemed within a circuit of fifteen miles—"a complete delusion; it is not going to last. I saw three gulls to-day on the Cronan Bog, and we know what that means. Eh, Father John?"

"It means mischief," answered the other. "Are you sure they were gulls?"

"Quite; I was close to them, and I thought to myself, 'There is a fine storm brewing up at the North Pole, and it'll be here before Mr. Langley bids us good-bye.'"

"How jolly!" exclaimed that gentleman.

"You would not think it jolly if you were out on the Atlantic with only a plank between you and eternity," observed the priest, gravely.

"Pooh!" was the reply; "what is between us and eternity sitting in this room? After all, by land or by water, it is but a step from the world we know to the world we don't know."

"It is a very serious one, my young friend."

Mr. Langley did not answer, and as no other person spoke for a few seconds, there ensued a brief silence, which was at last broken by the irrepressible Charlie.

"I am sorely vexed that duty calls," he began. "I don't remember ever being so sorry to leave a place in my life. When I am back in London I shall always be thinking of this grim old spot—the lonely mountains, the stretch of sad seashore, and the 'wild waves raging high.' And one was able to enjoy it in peace and comfort," he added, throwing up his arms and laying his head on his hands, clasped lazily behind, "because there were no women to spoil the fun."

"Hear him!" exclaimed Mr. Tankerton. "Why, the fellow is never happy unless he is making love to half a dozen girls."

"I don't like the sport, though—I don't, upon my word. When a man gets to my age—there is nothing to laugh at," he added, as his friends grinned in mockery—"when a man gets to my age he begins to tire of all that sort of thing. Wherever I went since the 1st August last there were women, women, women—women, old and young, plain and pretty, women who rode, women who drove, shot, fished,

stalked, swam, handled an oar, danced, dressed, spouted on platforms
—and never left one a moment in peace. I don't know what the world
is coming to—petticoats here, petticoats there, petticoats everywhere.
Enough to make a man go hang himself!"

The last word was barely spoken before there echoed through the
room a long, wailing sigh—a sigh as if some one's suffering heart were
being literally rent in twain.

"Heaven preserve us!" said the priest.

"What the —— is that!" exclaimed the doctor, with such an excess
of profane expression that Father John crossed himself, the while Mr.
Melsham sprang to his feet—an example followed, indeed, by every
person present.

"Was any one in the room trying to play a bad practical joke?"
asked Mr. Adson, sternly. "Good Lord! the house must be coming
down," he suddenly added, as a tremendous crash, followed by the
sound of bitter gasping sobs, struck consternation into all present.

Mr. Langley was the first to recover his composure.

"Faith, Danson," he said, "all the winds of heaven were bad
enough, but this is worse. There must be something very wrong
somewhere, and you ought to see about it."

"Gorey warned me this room was uninhabitable during the winter,"
said Mr. Danson, trying to speak calmly, though a terrible idea had
come into his mind—viz. that Captain Rosterne still lived, and was
dragging out a miserable existence in some dungeon known only to
his captors.

It was an absurd idea—one he would have felt ashamed to mention.
Yet the mystery of the inspector's disappearance, the crumbling ruins
of the old castle, the utter desolation of the new building, the unearthly
sounds, the weird stories he had listened to concerning the unquiet
dead, had prepared his mind to receive any impression, no matter how
wild and impossible.

"It must have grown uninhabitable very lately, then," said the
doctor, in answer to Mr. Danson's remark, "for many a pleasant
evening I have spent here, both in storm and shine, and never heard a
sound except of the wind or the rain beating against the glass."

"If I had not gone into the cellars and found them as quiet as family
vaults, I'd have sworn there must be one beneath this room, where Mr.
Danson kept a few Atlantic tempests for his own especial benefit,"

remarked Mr. Langley. "Just hark! Can Gorey's drowned have come on shore to hold their revel?"

The party had not resumed their chairs, and stood looking stupidly at each other and into the dark corners which the fire and lamplight failed to penetrate.

"I think there is something very suspicious about all this," said Mr. Melsham, speaking for the first time.

The priest's lips moved, though no word was audible. The doctor's glance wandered along the east wall with a curious intentness.

"I wonder——" he began at last.

"What do you wonder?" asked Mr. Melsham.

"Well, there used to be a door behind where that sideboard now stands. It has been papered over, and I was wondering—but that is all nonsense. Old Mr. Chittock was in the habit of opening it often enough, and I never heard an uncanny sound."

"Where did the door lead to?"

"To the island of Madeira—in other words, to a small cellar where the old gentleman kept some marvellous wine he produced on special occasions only."

"We will find that door," said Mr. Langley. "Tankerton, Adson, Mayford, bear a hand. Here you are," he cried, tapping the wall, from which a heavy sideboard had been dragged. "Has anybody a knife?" And, one being forthcoming, in a trice the canvas over which the paper had been hung was cut away, and some light boarding stood revealed.

"That covers the door," said the doctor, oracularly.

"We will soon get to that," declared Mr. Melsham, ripping off a length of the match-boarding. "There it is, right enough. We must have the rest of this woodwork down, though."

"I was here for a month when a lad," observed Mr. Danson, puzzled, "but I never remember noticing that door."

"A screen always stood in front of it," said the doctor; "besides, you were not a wine-bibber in those days, I suppose, and if you had been, Mr. Chittock would scarcely have produced his old Madeira for a boy's benefit."

"Here we are then," interrupted Mr. Langley, "face to face with a locked door, and a deuce of a wind blowing through the keyhole. How it moans, like a lost soul in torment! Who keeps the key?"

"Gorey, I conclude. Let us have him in."

And Gorey accordingly was summoned.

As he saluted the company, his eye caught the gaping rent in the paper, and his attitude instantly stiffened.

"Where is the key of that door, Gorey?" asked Mr. Danson.

"I never had it, sir."

"Fetch an axe, then."

"What for, your honour—if I may make so free?"

"To get into the cellar beyond."

"Begging your pardon, I can't do that, sir."

"Why not?"

"Because I am Mr. Chittock's servant before I am yours, and I dursn't break any lock in this house without his authority."

"There is something in that," muttered Mr. Melsham.

"Of course, if you take that line, Gorey, there is nothing more to be said," returned Mr. Danson.

"But I am sure Mr. Chittock would not object," urged Mr. Langley. "Now, seriously, Gorey, do you believe he would wish any gentleman to sit over a cauldron bubbling such infernal noises as we have been listening to for the last half-hour?"

"I do not suppose he would, sir; but, all the same, there are plenty of other rooms in the house, and it is not likely he would be best pleased to see his proprety wrecked this way. If Mr. Danson will get my master's leave, I'll try to knock down the castle, if that is all."

"You need say no more; you can go," remarked Mr. Danson, coldly.

"Might I speak one word, sir, first?" pleaded the man. "It doesn't take long for a letter to travel from here to London, and maybe you'd be glad afterwards to think you hadn't destroyed the place."

"You had better leave the room," repeated Mr. Danson, more than ever determined not to be thwarted, and Gorey reluctantly departed.

What did Mr. Chittock's friend expect?

If the truth must be told, he had been straining his ears to catch a cry for help, a word of thankfulness, passionate entreaties for release, and instead there came at intervals only that strange sobbing, that pathetic, long-drawn sigh.

"It is just the wind that's rising," said the doctor, "but where it comes from is beyond me. The house was as tight as a drum in the old days."

"What are we going to do now?" asked Mr. Danson, though indeed he knew perfectly what he meant to do. "What should you advise, Mr. Melsham?"

"I can scarcely advise," was the reply. "The way that fellow put the matter seems to me right enough. You are not the owner of this house, and it is a risky thing to burst open any place the rightful possessor has locked up. There may be wine in that cellar, or whisky, or—or anything, and indeed I think if I were in your place—"

"You'd see the matter through," finished Mr. Langley.

"No, nothing of the sort. I should communicate with Mr. Chittock."

"Well, it is of no use writing till to-morrow, so meantime I vote we have some punch," cried the young misogamist. "Let me carry the flowing bowl, Danson; the doctor's brew will taste better in the library. Follow, gentleman all, please. We are going to make a night of it."

Despite this assurance, however, the village guests were walking sedately home when the church clock struck eleven, and gravely opining something had given way in the cellar which ought to be seen to. But it could only be considered right and proper in the first instance to communicate with Mr. Chittock, who would probably come over.

"It is a deuced awkward thing to tamper with locks and bolts," declared Mr. Melsham. "No, it would not have done to break in that door. Put it to yourself, Father John."

"I should not stand anything in my house being meddled with," declared that worthy.

"And I am sure you wouldn't, doctor?"

"No. All the same, I'd like to see the inside of that old cellar. It is built with slabs, which formed part of the original castle, and which look on the outside just like rough pieces of rock flung together anyhow."

"I suppose there is some foundation for that legend about a secret passage?" said Mr. Melsham, tentatively.

"There may be. Listen to the 'sea's trouble,' as the poor people about here call it, which always seems to me the saddest, most impressive sound on earth," and the doctor stood still while he spoke. "It is like a deep grief which no words could tell; a lost soul might make such a lament."

"Well I know it," capped the priest. "Many a night when I have been coming home from some far-away cabin where my help was needed I have wondered what sore trouble the great deep was trying to express, for hers is an awful wail!"

"Let us get on," said Mr. Melsham impatiently, "and leave the ocean to manage its own affairs. What a chilly night!"

Whether Mr. Danson found the night chilly or not has never been recorded. One thing only is certain—it seemed very long.

Disturbed by doubt, distracted by conjecture, he sought rest and did not find it. When utterly exhausted he fell into an uneasy slumber, it was but to go over all the old weary ground again.

Ceaselessly Mr. Chittock, Captain Rosterne, Gorey, and Blackstone Castle, with its mysterious noises and various unknown passages, flitted across the field of his dream-seeing eyes.

The real and the imaginary mingled together in such awful fashion that he felt glad when the first faint streak of dawn declared that the time of dreams was over, and the period for action close at hand.

More than once during the passage of an apparently endless night he had, moved by some impulse he could not analyze, risen and bent his steps to that room which, he felt assured, held the key to his perplexity.

Well, if it did contain anything in the shape of a mystery, ere many hours passed the doubts which had taken his mind captive would be either justified or laid to rest.

After the departure of Doctor Gage, and his friends, it had been decided at a council composed of the Blackstone Castle house-party at all hazards to force an entrance into what Mr. Langley styled the "mysterious cave." "And I will go down to the village quite early to-morrow morning," proceeded that young gentleman, "and get a couple of stalwart fellows, armed with picks and crowbars," which promise he fulfilled so admirably that even before Mr. Danson left his sleeping apartment he heard sounds in the dining-room betokening preparations were being made for the siege.

On the landing he came face to face with Gorey, who looked as if he had not slept for a month.

"I beg pardon, sir, for making so free to ask," began the groom, "but is it true you are going to batter in the cellar door without writing to Mr. Chittock?"

"Quite true," answered Mr. Danson.

"I suppose, then, it is no use my saying a word more?"

"Of no use whatever, unless you give me some good reason for staying my hand. What is the secret you are trying to keep, Gorey?"

"What secret could there be, your honour?"

"That is precisely what I want to know."

"If you were away on a journey, sir, you would not be best pleased to find when you came home we had picked the lock of your dressing-box."

"I will account to Mr. Chittock for my present action, but not to any one else," replied Mr. Chittock's friend, passing Gorey with a gesture of dismissal.

"I hope you'll never rue this morning's work, sir," said Gorey, in a voice which struck Mr. Danson unpleasantly even while he replied—

"I must take my chance of that."

"What am I to do? what am I to do at all?" muttered the groom, as he turned despairingly to leave.

Mr. Danson could not catch the words, but he heard the pitiful sorrow in their tone, and saw the blank hopelessness written on the man's face.

"Gorey," he said, retracing his steps so as to speak without being overheard.

"Yes, sir."

"Is there any place you would like to go—never mind where—but should you like to go?"

"What for would I want to go away from Blackstone Castle?"

"You alone can tell that. Understand, however, if you do, I will give you ten pounds. That would take you a long distance."

"It would, and thank you kindly; but I have no conceit to leave Blackstone Castle. There is only one thing," he added, "that your honour could do for me this morning, and that is, send word to my master about what you have in your mind."

"Unless you give me some better reason than I have yet heard I need not trouble your master."

For a moment Gorey hesitated—then, "I can't do that, sir," he said.

"Very well;" and Mr. Danson walked into the dining-room and closed the door.

Already the men had turned back the carpet prior to commencing operations.

"It will be a tough job," remarked Mr. Langley. "Hillo! where is Gorey off to in such a hurry?"

Mr. Danson turned to one of the windows in time to see Mr. Chittock's foster-brother running down the castle slope as fast as his legs would take him.

"He has gone," thought the Englishman, relieved.

But Gorey had not gone far. Ere he reached the village he slackened his speed, and walked sedately enough up to the door of Mrs. Rostern's cottage, where he asked if he could see Miss Oona for a minute, and then, when she came into her narrow hall, if he could speak a word with her alone.

"Certainly," said the girl, taking him into a little drawing-room not much larger than a band-box.

"Are you in trouble? Is there anything I can do for you?" she asked.

"Yes, miss, in sore trouble, and I want you to write a line of a telegraphed message for me."

"Of course," producing a slip of paper and a pencil. "What am I to say?"

"It is for Mr. Chittock, miss."

"Oh! And what am I to write?"

"Mr. Danson is breaking open the door that was papered up in the dining-room—the door leading into the old cellar."

Gorey stopped. Miss Rosterne was looking at him with a sort of questioning horror—not writing, but resting her elbows on the table and holding the pencil between her fingers.

"For the Lord's sake, put down what I tell you," gasped Gorey.

She did not answer. She sat like one deaf, slowly twirling the pencil round and round, round and round.

"You never were hard, Miss Oona. Write, and God'll reward you. *It's a man's life,*" he added hoarsely.

Still she did not speak or move, save to twirl that pencil slowly, slowly round.

"I thought you'd have done it; I never deemed you would deny me; but I can't be wasting my time here," he went on in an access of passionate disappointment. "I'll go to the Church minister or the doctor. I'll find somebody that'll do that much for me;" and he was rushing out of the room, when the girl said—

"Stop, Dan, I will do what you ask. It was not that—no, it was not that."

"I spoke too sudden, but there's no time to spare," Gorey was beginning, with a quick revulsion of feeling, when she made a sign for him to remain silent, while she wrote rapidly without waiting for any dictation.

"Will this do?" she asked, when she had finished reading the message aloud.

"Yes."

"Then go back to the castle and I will send the telegram from Terrig. Leave all to me. *I promise you*," she finished, seeing his hesitation.

And Gorey went out and made his way back to Blackstone by various lonely paths, crying like a child.

Nothing had happened during his absence. When he returned, the lock was still intact, Chenery told him, and the hinges had not given. Sitting on some trusses of straw, he trembled in his stable, as even there he heard the thud of the pickaxe, the grind of the crowbar. A mist lay over the Atlantic. The morning was warm and lowering, the gulls were flying inland, and the ocean's lament sounded mournful as some wild death keen; but Gorey did not see shore or sea or sky, or aught save the interior of that vault, which, during the passage of the last few years, he had often longed to enter.

Suddenly there came one tremendous crash and then silence. He knew what had happened, and instinctively rose to his feet, placing a hand on one of the stalls to steady himself.

"Why, Gorey, I thought you were out," cried Mr. Langley, jubilantly rushing in. "We are through, and I have come for the stable lantern."

"I will bring it in, your honour," answered the man in a dull, slow voice.

"Come along then. Never mind stopping to light it; we can do that ourselves."

Like one walking in some horrible nightmare, Gorey followed the lively young fellow across the yard, through the back passages, into the front hall and the dining-room beyond, where they were met by a rush of strangely chill air, and a sound as of the wash and sob of many waters against the rocks.

In a moment Mr. Langley had taken the lantern out of his hand, lighted it, and disappeared through the gaping doorway into the cavernous darkness beyond.

Every man present followed him save Gorey, who stood by the threshold waiting.

There was a noise as if of the crunching of glass underfoot, then ensued a pause while one stopped apparently to pick up something.

"Why, it is a spoon," said Mr. Tankerton, which remark caused a laugh that awoke every unearthly echo in the place.

Still, with Mr. Langley as leader, the search-party went forward, squeezing into a passage beyond the cellar, the door opening into which stood ajar.

No one spoke. The darkness and the mystery seemed to daunt even Mr. Langley. Gorey strained his ears to listen. All at once a voice said, "What is this?" then, "My God!"

The long strain was over. The worst had come. Sight and hearing deserted Gorey, and for the first time in his life he fell back in a dead faint.

When he came to himself he was lying on a sofa in the dining-room, where many people were standing around.

Mr. Langley chafed his left hand, while Dr. Burke felt his right pulse, and as from a great distance came the sound of Mr. Melsham's voice speaking earnestly to Mr. Danson.

"Quiet, gentleman, if you please," said the doctor. "He is regaining consciousness."

Immediately a dead silence ensued, a silence broken at last by Gorey, who, struggling to a sitting position, exclaimed—

"*I done it. Take me where you please.*"

About the time he made this statement a gentleman resident in London sat in a pleasant room overlooking Holland Park busily engaged in finishing his correspondence for the day.

For more than an hour he wrote on steadily, but at length he laid down his pen, closed and sealed the last envelope, then placed that letter with others in a conspicuous position. He seemed weary. A glass of water stood beside him. Into this he poured a few drops of something which diffused a strange yet not unpleasant odour through the room, and immediately drained the tumbler. After doing so he laid his head back and died. The man was Diarmid Chittock, and the liquid poison.

Conclusion

NEARLY twenty years have come and gone since that grey morning on which the house-party at Blackstone Castle passed gaily into the mysterious darkness of Madeira Island to find a corpse. Yet the story of Mr. Chittock's crime, and of his foster-brother's loyal attempt to take the burden and the punishment on his own shoulders, remains fresh in the memory of Lisnabeg as the green grass growing on Captain Rosterne's grave.

Mr. Chittock's heir-at-law now resides at the castle. He has blocked up the passage leading from the caves to the cellar. He and his friends have drank all the old Madeira. There are boys and girls in the familiar rooms, young men and maidens tread the cliffs and uneven steps, but the tale of their relative's sin and sorrow means nothing to them save that it gave to their father a property he might never otherwise have owned.

On a fair estate in Hampshire Cyril Danson lives the quiet, happy life of an English country gentleman.

Not alone, however. After long and patient wooing he won for his wife the girl who "walked three miles Irish out, and three in, five days a week, and she an O'Considine," and is the angel of the fair home.

Gorey says there "never was her like for goodness," and declares the master is not far behind. Yet, though he is happy enough and well-to-do, his heart clings with fond faithfulness to the memory of that poor sinner who received his death-warrant when the telegram carried by Oona Rosterne to Terrig reached its destination.

And yet she had hoped to save him—she did all she could to save him!

A TERRIBLE VENGEANCE

Chapter One

VERY STRANGE

Round Dockett Point and over Dumsey Deep the water-lilies were blooming as luxuriantly as though the silver Thames had been the blue Mummel Lake.

It was the time for them. The hawthorn had long ceased to scent the air; the wild roses had shed their delicate leaves; the buttercups and cardamoms and dog-daises that had dotted the meadows were garnered into hay. The world in early August needed a fresh and special beauty, and here it was floating in its matchless green bark on the bosom of the waters.

If those fair flowers, like their German sisters, ever at nightfall assumed mortal form, who was there to tell of such vagaries? Even when the moon is at her full there are few who care to cross Chertsey Mead, or face the lonely Stabbery.

Hard would it be, indeed, so near life, railways, civilization, and London, to find a more lonely stretch of country, when twilight visits the landscape and darkness comes brooding down over the Surrey and Middlesex shores, than the path which winds along the river from Shepperton Lock to Chertsey Bridge. At high noon for months together it is desolate beyond description—silent, save for the rippling and sobbing of the currents, the wash of the stream, the swaying of the osiers, the trembling of an aspen, the rustle of the withies, or the noise made by a bird, or rat, or stoat, startled by the sound of unwonted footsteps. In the warm summer nights also, when tired holiday-makers are sleeping soundly, when men stretched on the green sward outside their white tents are smoking, and talking, and planning excursions for the morrow; when in country houses young people are playing and singing, dancing or walking up and down terraces over-looking well-kept lawns, where the evening air is laden with delicious perfumes— there falls on that almost uninhabited mile or two of riverside a stillness which may be felt, which the belated traveller is loth to disturb even by the dip of his oars as he drifts down with the current past objects that seem to him unreal as fragments of a dream.

It had been a wet summer—a bad summer for the hotels. There had been some fine days, but not many together. The weather could not be depended upon. It was not a season in which young ladies were to be met about the reaches of the Upper Thames, disporting themselves in marvellous dresses, and more marvellous headgear, unfurling brilliant parasols, canoeing in appropriate attire, giving life and colour to the streets of old-world villages, and causing many of their inhabitants to consider what a very strange sort of town it must be in which such extraordinarily-robed persons habitually reside.

Nothing of the sort was to be seen that summer, even as high as Hampton. Excursions were limited to one day; there were few tents, few people camping-out, not many staying at the hotels; yet it was, perhaps for that reason, an enjoyable summer to those who were not afraid of a little, or rather a great deal, of rain, who liked a village inn all the better for not being crowded, and who were not heart-broken because their women-folk for once found it impossible to accompany them.

Unless a man boldly decides to outrage the proprieties and decencies of life, and go off by himself to take his pleasure selfishly alone, there is in a fine summer no door of escape open to him. There was a time—a happy time—when a husband was not expected to sign away his holidays in the marriage articles. But what boots it to talk of that remote past now? Everything is against the father of a family at present. Unless the weather help him, what friend has he? and the weather does not often in these latter days prove a friend.

In that summer, however, with which this story deals, the stars in their courses fought for many an oppressed paterfamilias. Any curious inquirer might then have walked ankle-deep in mud from Penton Hook to East Molesey, and not met a man, harnessed like a beast of burden, towing all his belongings up stream, or beheld him rowing against wind and tide as though he were a galley-slave chained to the oar, striving all the while to look as though enjoying the fun.

Materfamilias found it too wet to patronize the Thames. Her dear little children also were conspicuous by their absence. Charming young ladies were rarely to be seen—indeed, the skies were so treacherous that it would have been a mere tempting of Providence to risk a pretty dress on the water; for which sufficient reasons furnished houses remained unlet, and lodgings were left empty; taverns and hotels welcomed visitors instead of treating them scurvily; and the river, with its green banks and its leafy aits, its white swans, its water-lilies, its purple loosestrife, its reeds, its rushes, its weeping willows, its quiet backwaters, was delightful.

One evening two men stood just outside the door of the Ship, Lower Halliford, looking idly at the water, as it flowed by more rapidly than is usually the case in August. Both were dressed in suits of serviceable dark grey tweed; both wore round hats; both evidently belonged to that class which resembles the flowers of the field but in the one respect that it toils not, neither does it spin; both looked intensely bored; both were of rather a good appearance.

The elder, who was about thirty, had dark hair, sleepy brown eyes, and a straight capable nose; a heavy moustache almost concealed his mouth, but his chin was firm and well cut. About him there was an indescribable something calculated to excite attention, but nothing in his expression to attract or repel. No one looking at him could have said offhand, "I think that is a pleasant fellow," or "I am sure that man could make himself confoundedly disagreeable."

His face revealed as little as the covers of a book. It might contain interesting matter, or there might be nothing underneath save the merest commonplace. So far as it conveyed an idea at all, it was that of indolence. Every movement of his body suggested laziness; but it would have been extremely hard to say how far that laziness went. Mental energy and physical inactivity walk oftener hand in hand than the world suspects, and mental energy can on occasion make an indolent man active, while mere brute strength can never confer intellect on one who lacks brains.

In every respect the younger stranger was the opposite of his companion. Fair, blue-eyed, light-haired, with soft moustache and tenderly cared-for whiskers, he looked exactly what he was—a very shallow, kindly, good fellow, who did not trouble himself with searching into the depths of things, who took the world as it was, who did not go out to meet trouble, who loved his species, women included, in an honest way; who liked amusement, athletic sports of all sorts—dancing, riding, rowing, shooting; who had not one regret, save that hours in a Government office were so confoundedly long, "eating the best part out of a day, by Jove;" no cause for discontent, save that he had very little money, and into whose mind it had on the afternoon in question been forcibly borne that his friend was a trifle heavy—"carries too many guns," he considered—and not exactly the man to enjoy a modest dinner at Lower Halliford."

For which cause, perhaps, he felt rather relieved when his friend refused to partake of any meal.

"I wish you could have stayed," said the younger, with that earnest and not quite insincere hospitality people always assume when they feel a departing guest is not to be overpersuaded to stay.

"So do I," replied the other. "I should have liked to stop with *you*, and I should have liked to stay here. There is a sleepy dullness about the place which exactly suits my present mood, but I must get back to town. I promised Travers to look in at his chambers this evening, and to-morrow as I told you, I am due in Norfolk."

"What will you do, then, till train-time? There is nothing up from here till nearly seven. Come on the river for an hour with me."

"Thank you, no. I think I will walk over to Staines."

"Staines! Why Staines in heaven's name?"

"Because I am in the humour for a walk—a long, lonely walk; because a demon has taken possession of me I wish to exorcise; because there are plenty of trains from Staines; because I am weary of the Thames Valley line, and any other reason you like. I can give you none better than I have done."

"At least let me row you part of the way."

"Again thank you, no. The eccentricities of the Thames are not new to me. With the best intentions, you would land me at Laleham when I should be on my (rail) way to London. My dear Dick, step into that boat your soul has been hankering after for the past half-hour, and leave me to return to town according to my own fancy."

"I don't half like this," said genial Dick. "Ah! here comes a pretty girl—look."

Thus entreated, the elder man turned his head and saw a young girl, accompanied by a young man, coming along the road, which leads from Walton Lane to Shepperton.

She was very pretty, of the sparkling order of beauty, with dark eyes, rather heavy eye-brows, dark thick hair, a ravishing fringe, a delicious hat, a coquettish dress, and shoes which by pretty gestures she seemed to be explaining to her companion were many—very many—sizes too large for her. Spite of her beauty, spite of her dress, spite of her shoes so much too large for her, it needed but a glance from one conversant with subtle social distinctions to tell that she was not quite her "young man's" equal.

For, in the parlance of Betsy Jane, as her "young man" she evidently regarded him, and as her young man he regarded himself. There could be no doubt about the matter. He was over head and ears in love with her; he was ready to quarrel—indeed, had quarrelled with father, mother, sister, brother on her account. He loved her unreasonably—he loved her miserably, distractedly; except at odd intervals, he was not in the least happy with her. She flouted, she tormented, she maddened him; but then, after having nearly driven him to the verge of distraction, she would repent sweetly, and make up for all previous short-comings by a few brief minutes of tender affection. If quarrelling be really the renewal of love, theirs had been renewed once a day at all events, and frequently much oftener.

Yes, she was a pretty girl, a bewitching girl, and arrant flirt, a scarcely well-behaved coquette; for as she passed the two friends she threw a glance at them, one arch, piquant, inviting glance, of which many would instantly have availed themselves, venturing the consequences certain to be dealt out by her companion, who, catching the look, drew closer to her side, not too well pleased, apparently. Spite of a little opposition, he drew her hand through his arm, and walked on with an air of possession infinitely amusing to onlookers, and plainly distasteful to his lady-love.

"A clear case of spoons," remarked the younger of the two visitors, looking after the pair.

"Poor devil!" said the other compassionately.

His friend laughed, and observed mockingly paraphrasing a very different speech,—

"But for the grace of God, there goes Paul Murray."

"You may strike out the 'but,'" replied the person so addressed, "for that is the very road Paul Murray is going, and soon."

"You are not serious!" asked the other doubtfully.

"Am I not? I am though, though not with such a vixen as I dare swear that little baggage is. I told you I was due to-morrow in Norfolk. But see, they are turning back; let us go inside."

"All right," agreed the other, following his companion into the hall. "This is a great surprise to me, Murray: I never imagined you were engaged."

"I am not engaged yet, though no doubt I shall soon be," answered the reluctant lover. "My grandmother and the lady's father have arranged the match. The lady does not object, I believe, and who am I, Savill, that I should refuse good looks, a good fortune, and a good temper?"

"You do not speak as though you liked the proposed bride, nevertheless," said Mr. Savill dubiously.

"I do not dislike her, I only hate having to marry her. Can't you understand that a man wants to pick a wife for himself—that the one girl he fancies seems worth ten thousand of a girl anybody else fancies? But I am so situated—Hang it, Dick! what are you staring at that dark-eyed witch for?"

"Because it is so funny. She is making him take a boat at the steps, and he does not want to do it. Kindly observe his face."

"What is his face to me?" retorted Mr. Murray savagely.

"Not much, I daresay, but it is a good deal to him. It is black as thunder, and hers is not much lighter. What a neat ankle, and how you like to show it, my dear. Well, there is no harm in a pretty ankle or a pretty foot either, and you have both. One would not wish one's wife to have a hoof like an elephant. What sort of feet has your destined maiden, Paul?"

"I never noticed."

"That looks deucedly bad," said the younger man, shaking his head.

"I know, however, she has a pure, sweet face," observed Mr. Murray gloomily.

"No one could truthfully make the same statement about our young friend's little lady," remarked Mr. Savill, still gazing at the girl, who was seating herself in the stern. "A termagant, I'll be bound, if ever there was one. Wishes to go up stream, no doubt because he wishes to go down. Any caprice about the Norfolk 'fair'?"

"Not much, I think. She is good, Dick—too good for me," replied the other, sauntering out again.

"That is what we always say about the things we do not know. And so your grandmother has made up the match?"

"Yes: there is money, and the old lady loves money. She says she wants to see me settled—talks of buying me an estate. She will have to do something, because I am sure the stern parent on the other side would not allow his daughter to marry on expectations. The one drop of comfort in the arrangement is that my aged relative will have to come down, and pretty smartly too. I would wed Hecate, to end this state of bondage, which I have not courage to flee from myself. Dick, how I envy you who have no dead person's shoes to wait for!"

"You need not envy me," returned Dick, with conviction, "a poor unlucky devil chained to a desk. There is scarce a day of my life I fail to curse the service, the office, and Fate—"

"Curse no more, then," said the other; "rather go down on your knees and thank Heaven you have, without any merit of your own, a provision for life. I wish Fate or anybody had coached me into the Civil Service—apprenticed me to a trade—sent me to sea—made me enlist, instead of leaving me at the mercy of an old lady who knows neither justice nor reason—who won't let me do anything for myself, and won't do anything for me—who ought to have been dead long ago, but who never means to die—"

"And who often gives you in one cheque as much as the whole of my annual salary," added the other quietly.

"But you know you will have your yearly salary as long as you live. I never know whether I shall have another cheque."

"It won't do, my friend," answered Dick Savill; "you feel quite certain you can get money when you want it."

"I feel certain of no such thing," was the reply. "If I once offended her—" he stopped, and then went on: "And perhaps when I have spent twenty years in trying to humour such caprices as surely woman never had before, I shall wake one morning to find she has left every penny to the Asylum for Idiots."

"Why do you not pluck up courage, and strike out some line for yourself?"

"Too late, Dick, too late. Ten years ago I might have tried to make a fortune for myself, but I can't do that now. As I have waited so long, I must wait a little longer. At thirty a man can't take pick in hand and try to clear a road to fortune."

"Then you had better marry the Norfolk young lady."

"I am steadily determined to do so. I am going down with the firm intention of asking her."

"And do you think she will have you?"

"I think so. I feel sure she will. And she is a nice girl—the sort I would like for a wife, if she had not been thrust upon me."

Mr. Savill stood silent for a moment, with his hands plunged deep in his pockets.

"Then when I see you next?" he said tentatively.

"I shall be engaged, most likely—possibly even married," finished the other, with as much hurry as his manner was capable of. "And now jump into your boat, and I will go on my way to—Staines—"

"I wish you would change your mind, and have some dinner."

"I can't; it is impossible. You see I have so many things to do and to think of. Good-bye, Dick. Don't upset yourself—go down stream, and don't get into mischief with those dark eyes you admired so much just now."

"Make your mind easy about that," returned the other, colouring, however, a little as he spoke. "Good-bye, Murray. I wish you well through the campaign." And so, after a hearty hand-shake, they parted, one to walk away from Halliford, and past Shepperton Church, and across Shepperton Range, and the other, of course, to row up stream, through Shepperton Lock, and on past Dockett Point.

In the grey of the summer's dawn, Mr. Murray awoke next morning from a terrible dream. He had kept his appointment with Mr. Travers and a select party, played heavily, drank deeply, and reached home between one and two, not much the better for his trip to Lower Halliford, his walk, and his carouse.

Champagne, followed by neat brandy, is not perhaps the best thing to insure a quiet night's rest; but Mr. Murray had often enjoyed sound repose after similar libations; and it was, therefore, all the more unpleasant that in the grey dawn he should wake suddenly from a dream, in which he thought some one was trying to crush his head with a heavy weight.

Even when he had struggled from sleep, it seemed to him that a wet dead hand lay across his eyes, and pressed them so hard he could not move the lids. Under the weight he lay powerless, while a damp, ice-cold hand felt burning into his brain, if such a contradictory expression may be permitted.

The perspiration was pouring from him; he felt the drops falling on his throat, and trickling down his neck; he might have been lying in a bath, instead of on his own bed, and it was with a cry of horror he at last flung the hand aside, and, sitting up, looked around the room, into which the twilight of morning was mysteriously stealing.

Then, trembling in every limb, he lay down again, and fell into another sleep, from which he did not awake till aroused by broad daylight and his valet.

"You told me to call you in good time, sir," said the man.

"Ah, yes, so I did," yawned Mr. Murray. "What a bore! I will get up directly. You can go, Davis. I will ring if I want you."

Davis was standing, as his master spoke, looking down at the floor. "Yes, sir." he answered, after the fashion of a man who has something on his mind,—and went.

He had not, however, got to the bottom of the first flight when peal after peal summoned him back.

Mr. Murray was out of bed, and in the middle of the room, the ghastly pallor of his face brought into full prominence by the crimson dressing-gown he had thrown round him on rising.

"What is that?" he asked. "What the in world is that, Davis?" and he pointed to the carpet, which was covered, Mrs. Murray being an old-fashioned lady, with strips of white drugget.

"I am sure I do not know, sir," answered Davis. "I noticed it the moment I came into the room. Looks as if some one with wet feet had been walking round and round the bed."

It certainly did. Round and round, to and fro, backwards and forwards, the feet seemed to have gone and come, leaving a distinct mark wherever they pressed.

"The print is that of a rare small foot, too," observed Davis, who really seemed half stupefied with astonishment.

"But who would have dared—" began Mr. Murray.

"No one in this house," declared Davis stoutly. "It is not the mark of a boy or woman inside these doors;" and then the master and the man looked at each other for an instant with grave suspicion.

But for that second they kept their eyes thus occupied; then, as by common consent, they dropped their glances to the floor. "My God!" exclaimed Davis. "Where have the footprints gone?"

He might well ask. The drugget, but a moment before wet and stained by the passage and repassage of those small restless feet, was now smooth and white, as when first sent forth from the bleach-green. On its polished surface there could not be discerned a speck or mark.

Chapter Two

WHERE IS LUCY?

In the valley of the Thames early hours are the rule. There the days have an unaccountable way of lengthening themselves out which makes it prudent, as well as pleasant, to utilize all the night in preparing for a longer morrow.

For this reason, when eleven o'clock p.m. strikes, it usually finds Church Street, Walton, as quiet as its adjacent graveyard, which lies still and solemn under the shadow of the old grey tower hard by that ancient vicarage which contains so beautiful a staircase.

About the time when Mr. Travers' friends were beginning their evening, when talk had abated and play was suggested, the silence of Church Street was broken and many a sleeper aroused by a continuous knocking at the door of a house as venerable as any in that part of Walton. Rap—rap—rap—rap awoke the echoes of the old-world village street, and at length brought to the window a young man, who, flinging up the sash, inquired,—

"Who is there?"

"Where is Lucy? What have you done with my girl?" answered a strained woman's voice from out the darkness of that summer night.

"Lucy?" repeated the young man; "is not she at home?"

"No; I have never set eyes on her since you went out together."

"Why, we parted hours ago. Wait a moment, Mrs. Heath; I will be down directly."

No need to tell the poor woman to "wait." She stood on the step, crying softly and wringing her hands till the door opened, and the same young fellow who with the pretty girl had taken boat opposite the Ship Hotel bade her "Come in."

Awakened from some pleasant dream, spite of all the trouble and hurry of that unexpected summons, there still shone the light of a reflected sunshine in his eyes and the flush of happy sleep on his cheek. He scarcely understood yet what had happened, but when he saw Mrs. Heath's tear-stained face, comprehension came to him, and he said abruptly,—

"Do you mean that she has never returned home?"

"Never!"

They were in the parlour by this time, and looking at each other by the light of one poor candle which he had set down on the table.

"Why, I left her," he said, "I left her long before seven."

"Where?"

"Just beyond Dockett Point. She would not let me row her back. I do not know what was the matter with her, but nothing I did seemed right."

"Had you any quarrel?" asked Mrs. Heath anxiously.

"Yes, we had; we were quarrelling all the time—at least she was with me; and at last she made me put her ashore, which I did sorely against my will."

"What had you done to my girl, then?"

"I prayed of her to marry me—no great insult, surely, but she took it as one. I would rather not talk of what she answered. Where can she be? Do you think she can have gone to her aunt's?"

"If so, she will be back by the last train. Let us get home as fast as possible. I never thought of that. Poor child! she will go out of her mind if she finds nobody to let her in. You will come with me. O, if she is not there, what shall I do—what ever shall I do?"

The young man had taken his hat, and was holding the door open for Mrs. Heath to pass out.

"You must try not to fret yourself," he said gently, yet with a strange repression in his voice. "Very likely she may stay at her aunt's all night."

"And leave me in misery, not knowing where she is? Oh, Mr. Grantley, I could never believe that."

Mr. Grantley's heart was very hot within him; but he could not tell the poor mother he believed that when Lucy's temper was up she would think of no human being but herself.

"Won't you take my arm, Mrs. Heath?" he asked with tender pity. After all, though everything was over between him and Lucy, her mother could not be held accountable for their quarrel; and he had loved the girl with all the romantic fervour of love's young dream.

"I can walk faster without it, thank you," Mrs. Heath answered. "But Mr. Grantley, whatever you and Lucy fell out over, you'll forget it, won't you? It isn't in you to be hard on anybody, and she's only a spoiled child. I never had but the one, and I humoured her too much; and if she is wayward, it is all my own fault—all my own."

"In case she does not return by this train," said the young man, wisely ignoring Mrs. Heath's inquiry, "had I not better telegraph to her aunt directly the office opens?"

"I will be on my way to London long before that," was the reply. "But what makes you think she won't come? Surely you don't imagine she has done anything rash?"

"What do you mean by rash?" he asked evasively.

"Made away with herself."

"*That!*" he exclaimed. "No, I feel very sure she has done nothing of the sort."

"But she might have felt sorry when you left her—vexed for having angered you—heartbroken when she saw you leave her."

"Believe me, she was not vexed or sorry or heartbroken; she was only glad to know she had done with me," he answered bitterly.

"What has come to you, Mr. Grantley?" said Mrs. Heath, in wonder. "I never heard you speak the same before."

"Perhaps not; I never felt the same before. It is best to be plain with you," he went on. "All is at an end between us; and that is what your daughter has long been trying for."

"How can you say that, and she so fond of you?"

"She has not been fond of me for many a day. The man she wants to marry is not a poor fellow like myself, but one who can give her carriages and horses, and a fine house, and as much dress as she cares to buy."

"But where could she ever find a husband able to do that?"

"I do not know, Mrs. Heath. All I do know is that she considers I am no match for her; and now my eyes are opened, I see she was not a wife for me. We should never have known a day's happiness."

It was too dark to see his face, but his changed voice and words and manner told Lucy's mother the kindly lad, who a couple of years before came courting her pretty daughter, and offended all his friends for her sake, was gone away for ever. It was a man who walked by her side—who had eaten of the fruit of the tree, and had learned to be as a god, knowing good from evil.

"Well, well," she said brokenly, "you are the best judge, I suppose; but O, my child, my child!"

She was so blinded with tears she stumbled, and must have fallen had he not caught and prevented her. Then he drew her hand within his arm, and said,—

"I am so grieved for you. I never received anything but kindness from you."

"And indeed," she sobbed, "you never were anything except good to me. I always knew we couldn't be considered your equals, and I often had my doubts whether it was right to let you come backwards and forwards as I did, parting you from all belonging to you. But I thought, when your mother saw Lucy's pretty face—for it is pretty, Mr. Grantley—'

"There never was a prettier," assented the young man, though, now his eyes were opened, he knew Lucy's beauty would scarcely have recommended her to any sensible woman.

"I hoped she might take to her, and I'd never have intruded. And I was so proud and happy, and fond of you—I was indeed; and I used to consider how, when you came down, I could have some little thing you fancied. But that's all over now. And I don't blame you; only my heart is sore and troubled about my foolish girl."

They were on Walton Bridge by this time, and the night air blew cold and raw down the river, and made Mrs. Heath shiver.

"I wonder where Lucy is," she murmured, "and what she'd think if she knew her mother was walking through the night in an agony about her? Where was it you said you left her?"

"Between Dockett Point and Chertsey. I shouldn't have left her had she not insisted on my doing so."

"Isn't that the train?" asked Mrs. Heath, stopping suddenly short and listening intently.

"Yes; it is just leaving Sunbury Station. Do not hurry; we have plenty of time."

They had: they were at Lucy's home, one of the small houses situated between Battlecreese Hill and the Red Lion in Lower Halliford before a single passenger came along The Green, or out of Nannygoat Lane.

"My heart misgives me that she has not come down," said Mrs. Heath.

"Shall I go up to meet her?" asked the young man; and almost before the mother feverishly assented, he was striding through the summer night to Shepperton Station, where he found the lights extinguished and every door closed.

Chapter Three

POOR MRS. HEATH

By noon the next day every one in Shepperton and Lower Halliford knew Lucy Heath was "missing."

Her mother had been up to Putney, but Lucy was not with her aunt, who lived not very far from the Bridge on the Fulham side, and who, having married a fruiterer and worked up a very good business, was inclined to take such bustling and practical views of life and its concerns as rather dismayed her sister-in-law, who had spent so many years in the remote country, and then so many other years in quiet Shepperton, that Mrs. Pointer's talk flurried her almost as much as the noise of London, which often maddens middle-aged and elderly folk happily unaccustomed to its roar.

Girt about with a checked apron which lovingly enfolded a goodly portion of her comfortable figure, Mrs. Pointer received her early visitor with the sportive remark, "Why, it's never Martha Heath! Come along in; a sight of you is good for sore eyes."

But Mrs. Heath repelled all such humorous observations, and chilled those suggestions of hospitality the Pointers were never backward in making by asking in a low choked voice,—

"Is Lucy here?"

"Lor! whatever put such a funny notion into your head?"

"Ah! I see she is," trying to smile. "After all, she spent the night with you."

"Did what?" exclaimed Mrs. Pointer. "Spent the night—was that what you said? No, nor the day either, for this year nearly. Why, for the last four months she hasn't set foot across that doorstep, unless it might be to buy some cherries, or pears, or apples, or grapes, or such-like, and then she came in with more air than any lady; and after paying her money and getting her goods went out again, just as if I hadn't been her father's sister and Pointer my husband. But there! for any sake, woman, don't look like that! Come into the parlour and tell me what is wrong. You never mean she has gone away and left you?"

Poor Mrs. Heath was perfectly incapable at that moment of saying what she did mean. Seated on a stool, and holding fast by the edge of the counter for fear of falling, the shop and its contents, the early busses, the people going along the pavement, the tradesmen's carts, the private carriages, were, as in some terrible nightmare, gyrating before her eyes. She could not speak, she could scarcely think, until that wild whirligig came to a stand. For a minute or two even Mrs. Pointer seemed multiplied by fifty; while her checked apron, the bananas suspended from hooks, the baskets of fruit, the pine-apples, the melons, the tomatoes, and the cob-nuts appeared and disappeared, only to reappear and disappear like the riders in a maddening giddy-go-round.

"Give me a drop of water," she said at last; and when the water was brought she drank a little and poured some on her handkerchief and dabbed her face, and finally suffered herself to be escorted into the parlour, where she told her tale, interrupted by many sobs. It would have been unchristian in Mrs. Pointer to exult; but it was only human to remember she had remarked to Pointer, in that terrible spirit of prophecy bestowed for some inscrutable reason on dear friends and close relations, she knew some such trouble must befall her sister-in-law.

"You made an idol of that girl, Martha," she went on, "and now it is coming home to you. I am sure it was only last August as ever was that Pointer—But here he is, and he will talk to you himself."

Which Mr. Pointer did, being very fond of the sound of his own foolish voice. He stated how bad a thing it was for people to be above their station or to bring children up above that rank of life in which it had pleased God to place them. He quoted many pleasing saws uttered by his father and grandfather; remarked that as folks sowed they were bound to reap; reminded Mrs. Heath they had the word of Scripture for the fact—than, which, parenthetically, no fact could be truer, as he knew—that a man might not gather grapes from thorns or even figs from thistles. Further he went on to observe generally—the observation having a particular reference to Lucy—that it did not do to judge things by their looks. Over and over again salesmen had tried to "shove off a lot of foreign fruit on him, but he wasn't a young bird to be taken in by that chaff." No; what he looked to was quality; it was what his customers expected from him, and what he could honestly declare his customers got. He was a plain man, and he thought honesty was the best policy. So as Mrs. Heath had seen fit to come to them in her trouble he would tell her what he thought, without beating about the bush. He believed Lucy had "gone off."

"But where?" asked poor Mrs. Heath.

"That I am not wise enough to say; but you'll find she's gone off. Girls in her station don't sport chains and bracelets and brooches for nothing—"

"But they did not cost many shillings," interposed the mother.

"She might tell you that," observed Mrs. Pointer, with a world of meaning.

"To say nothing," went on Mr. Pointer, "of grey gloves she could not abear to be touched. One day she walked in when I was behind the counter, and, not knowing she had been raised to the peerage, I shook hands with her as a matter of course; but when I saw the young lady look at her glove as if I had dirtied it, I said 'O, I beg your pardon, miss'—jocularly, you know. 'They soil so easily,' she lisped."

"I haven't patience with such ways!" interpolated Mrs. Pointer, without any lisp at all. "Yes, it's hard for you, Martha, but you may depend Pointer's right. Indeed, I expected how it would be long ago. Young women who are walking in the straight road don't dress as Lucy dressed, or dare their innocent little cousins to call them by their Christian names in the street. Since the Spring, and long before, Pointer and me has been sure Lucy was up to no good."

"And you held your tongues and never said a word to me!" retorted Mrs. Heath, goaded and driven to desperation.

"Much use it would have been saying any word to you," answered Mrs. Pointer. "When you told me about young Grantley, and I bid you be careful, how did you take my advice? Why, you blared out at me, went on as if I knew nothing and had never been anywhere. What I told you then, though, I tell you now: young Grantleys, the sons of rectors and the grandsons of colonels, don't come after farmer's daughters with any honest purpose."

"Yet young Grantley asked her last evening to fix a day for their marriage," said Mrs. Heath, with a little triumph.

"O, I daresay!" scoffed Mrs. Pointer.

"Talk is cheap," observed Mr. Pointer.

"Some folks have more of it than money," supplemented his wife.

"They have been, as I understand, keeping company for some time now," said the fruiterer, with what he deemed a telling and judicial calmness. "So if he asked her to name the day, why did she not name it?"

"I do not know. I have never seen her since."

"O, then you had only his word about the matter," summed up Mr. Pointer. "Just as I thought—just as I thought."

"What did you think?" inquired the poor troubled mother.

"Why, that she has gone off with this Mr. Grantley."

"Ah, you don't know Mr. Grantley, or you wouldn't say such a thing."

"It is true," observed Mr. Pointer, "that I do not know the gentleman, and, I may add, I do not want to know him; but speaking as a person acquainted with the world—"

"I'll be getting home," interrupted Mrs. Heath. "Most likely my girl is there waiting for me, and a fine laugh she will have against her poor old mother for being in such a taking. Yes, Lucy will have the breakfast ready. No, thank you; I'll not wait to take anything. There will be a train back presently; and besides, to tell you the truth, food would choke me till I sit down again with my girl, and then I won't be able to eat for joy."

Husband and wife looked at each other as Mrs. Heath spoke, and for the moment a deep pity pierced the hard crust of their worldly egotism.

"Wait a minute," cried Mrs. Pointer, "and I'll put on my bonnet and go with you."

"No," interrupted Mr. Pointer, instantly seizing his wife's idea, and appropriating it as his own. "I am the proper person to see this affair out. There is not much doing, and if there were, I would leave everything to obtain justice for your niece. After all, however wrong she may have gone, she is your niece, Maria."

With which exceedingly nasty remark, which held a whole volume of unpleasant meaning as to what Mrs. Pointer might expect from that relationship in the future, Mr. Pointer took Mrs. Heath by the arm, and piloted her out into the street, and finally to Lower Halliford, where the missing Lucy was not, and where no tidings of her had come.

Chapter Four

MR. GAGE ON PORTENTS

ABOUT the time when poor distraught Mrs. Heath, having managed to elude the vigilance of that cleverest of men, Maria Pointer's husband, had run out of her small house, and was enlisting the sympathies of gossip-loving Shepperton in Lucy's disappearance, Mr. Paul Murray arrived at Liverpool Street Station, where his luggage and his valet awaited him.

"Get tickets, Davis," he said; "I have run it rather close;" and he walked towards Smith's stall, while his man went into the booking-office.

As he was about to descend the stairs, Davis became aware of a very singular fact. Looking down the steps, he saw precisely the same marks that had amazed him so short a time previously, being printed hurriedly off by a pair of invisible feet, which ran to the bottom and then flew as if in the wildest haste to the spot where Mr. Murray stood.

"I am not dreaming, am I?" thought the man; and he shut his eyes and opened them again.

The footprints were all gone!

At that moment his master turned from the bookstall and proceeded towards the train. A porter opened the door of a smoking carriage, but Murray shook his head and passed on. Mr. Davis, once more looking to the ground, saw that those feet belonging to no mortal body were still following. There were not very many passengers, and it was quite plain to him that wherever his master went, the quick, wet prints went too. Even on the step of the compartment Mr. Murray eventually selected the man beheld a mark, as though some one had sprung in after him. He secured the door, and then walked away, to find a place for himself, marvelling in a dazed state of mind what it all meant; indeed, he felt so much dazed that, after he had found a seat to his mind, he did not immediately notice an old acquaintance in the opposite corner, who affably inquired,—

"And how is Mr. Davis?"

Thus addressed, Mr. Davis started from his reverie, and exclaimed, "Why, bless my soul, Gage, who'd have thought of seeing you here?" after which exchange of courtesies the pair shook hands gravely and settled down to converse.

Mr. Davis explained that he was going down with his governor to Norwich; and Mr. Gage stated that he and the old general had been staying at Thorpe, and were on their way to Lowestoft. Mr. Gage and his old general had also just returned from paying a round of visits in the West of England. "Pleasant enough, but slow," finished the gentleman's gentleman. "After all, in the season or out of it, there is no place like London."

With this opinion Mr. Davis quite agreed, and said he only wished he had never to leave it, adding,—

"We have not been away before for a long time; and we should not be going where we are now bound if we had not to humour some fancy of our grandmother's."

"Deuced rough on a man having to humour a grandmother's fancy," remarked Mr. Gage.

"No female ought to be left the control of money," said Mr. Davis with conviction. "See what the consequences have been in this case— Mrs. Murray outlived her son, who had to ask her for every shilling he wanted, and she is so tough she may see the last of her grandson."

"That is very likely," agreed the other. "He looks awfully bad."

"You saw him just now, I suppose?"

"No; but I saw him last night at Chertsey Station, and I could but notice the change in his appearance."

For a minute Mr. Davis remained silent. "Chertsey Station!" What could his master have been doing at Chertsey? That was a question he would have to put to himself again, and answer for himself at some convenient time; meanwhile he only answered,—

"Yes, I observe an alteration in him myself. Anything fresh in the paper?"

"No," answered Mr. Gage, handing his friend over the *Daily News*—the print he affected: "everything is as dull as ditchwater."

For many a mile Davis read or affected to read; then he laid the paper aside, and after passing his case, well filled with a tithe levied on Mr. Murray's finest cigars, to Gage, began solemnly,—

"I am going to ask you a curious question, Robert, as from man to man."

"Ask on," said Mr. Gage, striking a match.

"Do you believe in warnings?"

The old General's gentleman burst out laughing. He was so tickled that he let his match drop from his fingers unapplied.

"I am afraid most of us have to believe in them, whether we like it or not," he answered, when he could speak. "Has there been some little difference between you and your governor, then?"

"You mistake," was the reply. "I did not mean warnings in the sense of notice, but warnings as warnings, you understand."

"Bother me if I do! Yes, now I take you. Do I believe in 'coming events casting shadows before,' as some one puts it? Has any shadow of a coming event been cast across you?"

"No, nor across anybody, so far as I know; but I've been thinking the matter over lately, and wondering if there can be any truth in such notions."

"What notions?"

"Why, that there are signs and suchlike sent when trouble is coming to any one."

"You may depend it is right enough that signs and tokens are sent. Almost every good family has its special warning: one has its mouse, another its black dog, a third its white bird, a fourth its drummer-boy, and so on. There is no getting over facts, even if you don't understand them."

"Well, it is very hard to believe."

"There wouldn't be much merit in believing if everything were as plain as a pikestaff. You know what the Scotch minister said to his boy: 'The very devils believe and tremble.' You wouldn't be worse than a devil, would you?"

"Has any sign ever appeared to you?" asked Davis.

"Not exactly; but lots of people have told me they have to them; for instance, old Seal, who drove the Dowager Countess of Ongar till the day of her death, used to make our hair stand on end talking about phantom carriages that drove away one after another from the door of Hainault House, and wakened every soul on the premises, night after night till the old Earl died. It took twelve clergymen to lay the spirit."

"I wonder one wasn't enough!" ejaculated Davis.

"There may have been twelve spirits, for all I know," returned Gage, rather puzzled by this view of the question; "but anyhow, there were twelve clergymen, with the bishop in his lawn sleeves chief among them. And I once lived with a young lady's-maid, who told me when she was a girl she made her home with her father's parents. On a winter's night, after everybody else had gone to bed, she sat up to make some girdle-bread—that is a sort of bread the people in Ireland, where she came from, bake over the fire on a round iron plate; with plenty of butter it is not bad eating. Well, as I was saying, she was quite alone; she had taken all the bread off, and was setting it up on edge to cool, supporting one piece against the other, two and two, when on the table where she was putting the cakes she saw one drop of blood fall, and then another, and then another, like the beginning of a shower.

"She looked to the ceiling, but could see nothing, and still the drops kept on falling slowly, slowly; and then she knew something had gone wrong with one dear to her; and she put a shawl over her head, and without saying a word to anybody, went through the loneliness and darkness of night all by herself to her father's."

"She must have been a courageous girl," remarked Mr. Davis.

"She was, and I liked her well. But to the point. When she reached her destination she found her youngest brother dead. Now what do you make of that?"

"It's strange, but I suppose he would have died all the same if she had not seen the blood-drops, and I can't see any good seeing them did her. If she had reached her father's in time to bid brother good-bye, there would have been some sense in such a sign. As it is, it seems to me a lot of trouble thrown away."

Mr. Gage shook his head.

"What a sceptic you are, Davis! But there! London makes sceptics of the best of us. If you had spent a winter, as I did once, in the Highlands of Scotland, or heard the Banshee wailing for the General's nephew in the county of Mayo, you wouldn't have asked what was the use of second sight or Banshees. You would just have stood and trembled as I did many and many a time."

"I might," said Davis doubtfully, wondering what his friend would have thought of those wet little footprints. "Hillo, here's Peterborough! Hadn't we better stretch our legs? and a glass of something would be acceptable."

Of that glass, however, Mr. Davis was not destined to partake.

"If one of you is Murray's man," said the guard as they jumped out, "he wants you."

"I'll be back in a minute," observed Mr. Murray's man to his friend, and hastened off.

But he was not back in a minute; on the contrary, he never returned at all.

Chapter Five

KISS ME

THE first glance in his master's face filled Davis with a vague alarm. Gage's talk had produced an effect quite out of proportion to its merit, and a cold terror struck to the valet's heart as he thought there might, spite of his lofty scepticism, be something after all in the mouse, and the bird, and the drummer-boy, in the black dog, and the phantom carriages, and the spirits it required the united exertions of twelve clergymen (with the bishop in lawn sleeves among them) to lay; in Highland second sight and Irish Banshees; and in little feet paddling round and about a man's bed and following wherever he went. What awful disaster could those footprints portend? Would the train be smashed up? Did any river lie before them? and if so, was the sign vouchsafed as a warning that they were likely to die by drowning? All these thoughts, and many more, passed through Davis' mind as he stood looking at his master's pallid face and waiting for him to speak.

"I wish you to come in here," said Mr. Murray after a pause, and with a manifest effort. "I am not quite well."

"Can I get you anything, sir?" asked the valet. "Will you not wait and go by another train?"

"No; I shall be better presently; only I do not like being alone."

Davis opened the door and entered the compartment. As he did so, he could not refrain from glancing at the floor, to see if those strange footsteps had been running races there.

"What are you looking for?" asked Mr. Murray irritably. "Have you dropped anything?"

"No, sir; O, no! I was only considering where I should be most out of the way."

"There," answered his master, indicating a seat next the window, and at the same time moving to one on the further side of the carriage. "Let no one get in; say I am ill—mad; that I have scarlet fever—the plague—what you please." And with this wide permission Mr. Murray laid his legs across the opposite cushion, wrapped one rug round his shoulders and another round his body, turned his head aside, and went to sleep or seemed to do so.

"If he is going to die, I hope it will be considered in my wages, but I am afraid it won't. Perhaps it is the old lady; but that would be too good fortune," reflected Davis; and then he fell "a-thinkynge, a-thinkynge," principally of Gage's many suggestions and those mysterious footprints, for which he kept at intervals furtively looking. But they did not appear; and at last the valet, worn out with vain conjections, dropped into a pleasant doze, from which he did not awake till they were nearing Norwich.

"We will go to an hotel till I find out what Mrs. Murray's plans are," said that lady's grandson when he found himself on the platform; and as if they had been only waiting this piece of information, two small invisible feet instantly skipped out of the compartment they had just vacated, and walked after Mr. Murray, leaving visible marks at every step.

"Great heavens! what is the meaning of this?" mentally asked Davis, surprised by fright after twenty prayerless and scheming years into an exclamation which almost did duty for a prayer. For a moment he felt sick with terror; then clutching his courage with the energy of desperation, he remembered that though wet footprints might mean death and destruction to the Murrays, his own ancestral annals held no record of such a portent.

Neither did the Murrays', so far as he was aware, but then he was aware of very little about that family. If the Irish girl Gage spoke of was informed by drops of blood that her brother lay dead, why should not Mr. Murray be made aware, through the token of these pattering footsteps, that he would very soon succeed to a large fortune?

Then any little extra attention Mr. Davis showed his master *now* would be remembered in his wages.

It was certainly unpleasant to know these damp feet had come down from London, and were going to the hotel with them; but "needs must" with a certain driver, and if portents and signs and warnings were made worth his while, Mr. Davis conceived there might be advantages connected with them.

Accordingly, when addressing Mr. Murray, his valet's voice assumed a more deferential tone than ever, and his manner became so respectfully tender, that onlookers rashly imagined the ideal master and the faithful servant of fiction had at last come in the flesh to Norwich. Davis' conduct was, indeed, perfect: devoted without being intrusive, he smoothed away all obstacles which could be smoothed, and even, by dint of a judicious two minutes alone with the doctor for whom he sent, managed the introduction of a useful sedative in some medicine, which the label stated was to be taken every four hours.

He saw to Mr. Murray's rooms and Mr. Murray's light repast, and then he waited on Mr. Murray's grandmother, and managed that lady so adroitly, she at length forgave the offender for having caught a chill.

"Your master is always doing foolish things," she said. "It would have been much better had he remained even for a day or two in London rather than risk being laid up. However, you must nurse him carefully, and try to get him well enough to dine at Losdale Court on Monday. Fortunately to-morrow is Sunday, and he can take complete rest. Now Davis, remember I trust to you."

"I will do my best, ma'am," Davis said humbly, and went back to tell his master the interview had gone off without any disaster.

Then, after partaking of some mild refreshment, he repaired to bed in a dressing-room opening off Mr. Murray's apartment, so that he might be within call and close at hand to administer those doses which were to be taken at intervals of four hours.

"I feel better to-night," said Mr. Murray last thing.

"It is this beautiful air, sir," answered Davis, who knew it was the sedative. "I hope you will be quite well in the morning."

But spite of the air, in the grey dawn Mr. Murray had again a dreadful dream—a worse dream than that which laid its heavy hand on him in London. He thought he was by the riverside beyond Dockett Point—beyond where the water-lilies grow. To his right was a little grove of old and twisted willows guarding a dell strewed in dry seasons with the leaves of many autumns, but, in his dream, wet and sodden by reason of heavy rain. There in June wild roses bloomed; there in winter hips and haws shone ruddy against the snow. To his left flowed a turbid river—turbid with floods that had troubled its peace. On the other bank lay a stagnant length of Surrey, while close at hand the Middlesex portion of Chertsey Mead stretched in a hopeless flat on to the bridge, just visible in the early twilight of a summer's evening that had followed after a dull lowering day.

From out of the gathering gloom there advanced walking perilously near to Dumsey Deep, a solitary female figure, who, when they met, said, "So you've come at last;" after which night seemed to close around him, silence for a space to lay its hands upon him.

About the same time Davis was seeing visions also. He had lain long awake, trying to evolve order out of the day's chaos, but in vain. The stillness fretted him; the idea that even then those mysterious feet might in the darkness be printing their impress about his master's bed irritated his brain. Twice he got up to give that medicine ordered to be taken every four hours, but finding on each occasion Mr. Murray sleeping quietly, he forbore to arouse him.

He heard hour after hour chime, and it was not till the first hint of dawn that he fell into a deep slumber. Then he dreamt about the subject nearest his heart—a public house.

He thought he had saved or gained enough to buy a roadside inn on which he had long cast eyes of affectionate regard—not in London, but not too far out: a delightful inn, where holiday-makers always stopped for refreshment, and sometimes for the day; an inn with a pretty old-fashioned garden filled with fruit trees and vegetables, with a grass-plot around which were erected little arbours, where people could have tea or stronger stimulants; a skittle-ground, where men could soon make themselves very thirsty; and many other advantages tedious to mention. He had the purchase-money in his pocket, and, having paid a deposit, was proceeding to settle the affair, merely diverging from his way to call on a young widow he meant to make Mrs. Davis—a charming woman, who, having stood behind a bar before, seemed the very person to make the Wheatsheaf a triumphant success. He was talking to her sensibly, when suddenly she amazed him by saying, in a sharp, hurried voice. "Kiss me, kiss me, kiss me!" three times over.

The request seemed so strange that he stood astounded, and then awoke to hear the same words repeated.

"Kiss me, kiss me, kiss me!" some one said distinctly in Mr. Murray's room, the door of which stood open, and then all was quiet.

Only half awake, Davis sprang from his bed and walked across the floor, conceiving, so far as his brain was in a state to conceive anything, that his senses were playing him some trick.

"You won't?" said the voice again, in a tone which rooted him to the spot where he stood; "and yet, as we are never to meet again, you might *Kiss me once*," the voice added caressingly, "*only once more.*"

"Who the deuce has he got with him now?" thought Davis; but almost before the question was shaped in his mind there came a choked, gasping cry of "Unloose me, tigress, devil!" followed by a sound of desperate wrestling for life.

In a second, Davis was in the room. Through the white blinds light enough penetrated to show Mr. Murray in the grip apparently of some invisible antagonist, who seemed to be strangling him.

To and fro from side to side the man and the unseen phantom went swaying in that awful struggle. Short and fast came Mr. Murray's breath, while, making one supreme effort, he flung his opponent from him and sank back across the bed exhausted.

Wiping the moisture from his forehead, Davis, trembling in every limb, advanced to where his master lay, and found *he was fast asleep!*

Mr. Murray's eyes were wide open, and he did not stir hand or foot while the man covered him up as well as he was able, and then looked timidly around, dreading to see the second actor in the scene just ended.

"I can't stand much more of this," Davis exclaimed, and the sound of his own voice made him start.

There was brandy in the room which had been left over-night, and the man poured himself out and swallowed a glass of the liquor. He ventured to lift the blind and look at the floor, which was wet, as though buckets of water had been thrown over it, while the prints of little feet were everywhere.

Mr. Davis took another glass of brandy. *That* had not been watered.

"Well, this is a start!" he said in his own simple phraseology. "I wonder what the governor has been up to?"

For it was now borne in upon the valet's understanding that this warning was no shadow of any event to come, but the tell-tale ghost of some tragedy which could never be undone.

Chapter Six

FOUND DROWNED

AFTER such a dreadful experience it might have been imagined that Mr. Murray would be very ill indeed; but what we expect rarely comes to pass, and though during the whole of Sunday and Monday Davis felt, as he expressed the matter, "awfully shaky," his master appeared well and in fair spirits.

He went to the Cathedral, and no attendant footsteps dogged him. On Monday he accompanied his grandmother to Losdale Court, where he behaved so admirably as to please even the lady on whose favour his income depended. He removed to a furnished house Mrs. Murray had taken, and prepared to carry out her wishes. Day succeeded day and night to night, but neither by day nor night did Davis hear the sound of any ghostly voices or trace the print of any phantom foot.

Could it be that nothing more was to come of it—that the mystery was never to be elucidated but fade away as the marks of dainty feet had vanished from floor, pavement, steps, and platform?

The valet did not believe it; behind those signs made by nothing human lay some secret well worth knowing, but it had never been possible to know much about Mr. Murray.

"He was so little of a gentleman" that he had no pleasant, careless ways. He did not leave his letters lying loose for all the world to read. He did not tear up papers, and toss them into a waste-paper basket. He had the nastiest practice of locking up and burning; and though it was Mr. Davis's commendable custom to collect and preserve unconsidered odds and ends as his master occasionally left in his pockets, these, after all, were trifles light as air.

Nevertheless, as a straw shows how the wind blows, so that chance remark anent Chertsey Station made by Gage promised to provide a string on which to thread various little beads in Davis' possession.

The man took them out and looked at them: a woman's fall—white tulle, with black spots, smelling strongly of tobacco-smoke and musk; a receipt for a bracelet, purchased from an obscure jeweller; a Chertsey Lock ticket; and the return half of a first-class ticket from Shepperton to Waterloo, stamped with the date of the day before they left London.

At these treasures Davis looked long and earnestly.

"We shall see," he remarked as he put them up again; "there I think the scent lies hot."

It could not escape the notice of so astute a servant that his master was unduly anxious for a sight of the London papers, and that he glanced through them eagerly for something he apparently failed to find—more, that he always laid the print aside with a sigh of relief. Politics did not seem to trouble him, or any public burning question.

"He has some burning question of his own," thought the valet, though he mentally phrased his notion in different words.

Matters went on thus for a whole week. The doctor came and went and wrote prescriptions, for Mr. Murray either was still ailing or chose to appear so. Davis caught a word or two which had reference to the patient's heart, and some shock. Then he considered that awful night, and wondered how he, who "was in his sober senses, and wide awake, and staring," had lived through it.

"My heart, and a good many other things, will have to be considered," he said to himself. No wages could pay for what has been put upon me this week past. I wonder whether I ought to speak to Mr. Murray now?"

Undecided on this point, he was still considering it when he called his master on the following Sunday morning. The first glance at the stained and polished floor decided him. Literally it was interlaced with footprints. The man's hand shook as he drew up the blind, but he kept his eyes turned on Mr. Murray while he waited for orders, and walked out of the room when dismissed as though such marks had been matters of customary occurrence in a nineteenth century bedroom.

No bell summoned him back on this occasion. Instead of asking for information, Mr. Murray dropped into a chair and nerved himself to defy the inevitable.

Once again there came a pause. For three days nothing occurred; but on the fourth a newspaper and a letter arrived, both of which Davis inspected curiously. They were addressed in Mr. Savill's handwriting, and they bore the postmark "SHEPPERTON."

The newspaper was enclosed in an ungummed wrapper, tied round with a piece of string. After a moment's reflection Davis cut that string, spread out the print, and beheld a column marked at top with three blue crosses, containing the account of an inquest held at the King's Head on a body found on the previous Sunday morning, close by the "Tumbling Bay."

It was that of a young lady who had been missing since the previous Friday week, and could only be identified by the clothes.

Her mother, who, in giving evidence, frequently broke down, told how her daughter on the evening in question went out for a walk and never returned. She did not wish to go, because her boots were being mended, and her shoes were too large. No doubt they had dropped off. She had very small feet, and it was not always possible to get shoes to fit them. She was engaged to be married to the gentleman with whom she went out. He told her they had quarrelled. She did not believe he could have anything to do with her child's death; but she did not know what to think. It had been said her girl was keeping company with somebody else, but that could not be true. Her girl was a good girl.

Yes; she had found a bracelet hidden away among her girl's clothes, and she could not say how she got the seven golden sovereigns that were in the purse, or the locket taken off the body; but her girl was a good girl, and she did not know whatever she would do without her, for Lucy was all she had.

Walter Grantley was next examined, after being warned that anything he said might be used against him.

Though evidently much affected, he gave his evidence in a clear and straightforward manner. He was a clerk in the War Office. He had, against the wishes of all his friends, engaged himself to the deceased, who, after having some time professed much affection, had latterly treated him with great coldness. On the evening in question she reluctantly came out with him for a walk; but after they passed the Ship she insisted he should take a boat. They turned and got into a boat. He wanted to go down the river, because there was no lock before Sunbury. She declared if he would not row her up the river, she would go home.

They went up the river, quarrelling all the way. There had been so much of this sort of thing that after they passed through Shepperton Lock he tried to bring matters to a conclusion, and asked her to name a day for their marriage. She scoffed at him and asked if he thought she meant to marry a man on such a trumpery salary. Then she insisted he should land her; and after a good deal of argument he did land her; and rowed back alone to Halliford. He knew no more.

Richard Savill deposed he took a boat at Lower Halliford directly after the last witness, with whom he was not aquainted, and rowed up towards Chertsey, passing Mr. Grantley and Miss Heath, who were evidently quarrelling. He went as far as Dumsey Deep, where, finding the stream most heavily against him, he turned, and on his way back saw the young lady walking slowly along the bank. At Shepperton Lock he and Mr. Grantley exchanged a few words, and rowed down to Halliford almost side by side. They bade each other good-evening, and Mr. Grantley walked off in the direction of Walton where it was proved by other witnesses he arrived at eight o'clock, and did not go out again till ten, when he went to bed.

All efforts to trace what had become of the unfortunate girl proved unavailing, till a young man named Lemson discovered the body on the previous Sunday morning close by the Tumbling Bay. The coroner wished to adjourn the inquest, in hopes some further light might be thrown on such a mysterious occurrence; but the jury protested so strongly against any proceeding of the sort, that they were directed to return an open verdict.

No one could dispute that the girl had been "found drowned," or that there was "no evidence to explain how she came to be drowned."

At the close of the proceedings, said the local paper, an affecting incident occurred. The mother wished the seven pounds to be given to the man "who brought her child home," but the man refused to accept a penny. The mother said she would never touch it, when a relation stepped forward and offered to take charge of it for her.

The local paper contained also a leader on the tragedy, in the course of which it remarked how exceedingly fortunate it was that Mr. Savill chanced to be staying at the Ship Hotel, so well known to boating-men, and that he happened to go up the river and see the poor young lady after Mr. Grantley left her, as otherwise the latter gentle-man might have found himself in a most unpleasant position. He was much to be pitied, and the leader-writer felt confident that every one who read the evidence would sympathize with him. It was evident the inquiry had failed to solve the mystery connected with Miss Heath's untimely fate, but it was still competent to pursue the matter if any fresh facts transpired.

"I must get to know more about all this," thought Davis as he refolded and tied up the paper.

Chapter Seven

DAVIS SPEAKS

IF there be any truth in old saws, Mr. Murray's wooing was a very happy one. Certainly it was very speedy. By the end of October he and Miss Ketterick were engaged, and before Christmas the family lawyers had their hands full drawing settlements and preparing deeds. Mrs. Murray disliked letting any money slip out of her own control, but she had gone too far to recede, and Mr. Ketterick was not a man who would have tolerated any proceeding of the sort.

Perfectly straightforward himself, he compelled straightforwardness in others, and Mrs. Murray was obliged to adhere to the terms proposed when nothing seemed to her less probable than that the marriage she wished ever would take place. As for the bridegroom, he won golden opinions from Mr. Ketterick. Beyond the income to be insured to his wife and himself, he asked for nothing. Further he objected to nothing. Never before, surely, had man been so easily satisfied.

"All I have ever wanted," he said, "was some settled income, so that I might not feel completely dependent on my grandmother. That will now be secured, and I am quite satisfied."

He deferred to Mr. Ketterick's opinions and wishes. He made no stipulations.

"You are giving me a great prize," he told the delighted father, "of which I am not worthy, but I will try to make her happy."

And the gentle girl was happy: no tenderer or more devoted lover could the proudest beauty have desired. With truth he told her he "counted the days till she should be his." For he felt secure when by her side. The footsteps had never followed him to Losdale Court. Just in the place that of all others he would have expected them to come, he failed to see that tiny print. There were times when he even forgot it for a season; when he did remember it, he believed, with the faith born of hope, that he should never see it again.

"I wonder he has the conscience," muttered Mr. Davis one morning, as he looked after the engaged pair. The valet had the strictest ideas concerning the rule conscience should hold over the doings of other folks, and some pleasingly lax notions about the sacrifices conscience had a right to demand from himself. "I suppose he thinks he is safe now that those feet are snugly tucked up in holy ground," proceeded Davis, who, being superstitious, faithfully subscribed to all the old formulæ. "Ah! he doesn't know what I know—yet;" which last word, uttered with much gusto, indicated a most unpleasant quarter of an hour in store at some future period for Mr. Murray.

It came one evening a week before his marriage. He was in London, in his grandmother's house, writing to the girl he had grown to love with the great, entire, remorseful love of his life, when Davis, respectful as ever, appeared, and asked if he might speak a word. Mr. Murray involuntarily put his letter beneath some blotting-paper, and, folding his hands over both, answered, unconscious of what was to follow, "Certainly."

Davis had come up with his statement at full-cock, and fired at once.

"I have been a faithful servant to you, sir."

Mr. Murray lifted his eyes and looked at him. Then he knew what was coming. "I have never found fault with you, Davis," he said, after an almost imperceptible pause.

"No, sir, you have been a good master—a master I am sure no servant who knew his place could find a fault with."

If he had owned an easy mind and the smallest sense of humour— neither of which possessions then belonged to Mr. Murray—he might have felt enchanted with such a complete turning of the tables; but as matters stood, he could only answer, "Good master as I have been, I suppose you wish to leave my service. Am I right, Davis?"

"Well, sir, you are right and you are wrong. I do not want to leave your service just yet. It may not be quite convenient to you for me to go now; only I want to come to an understanding."

"About what?" Mr. Murray asked, quite calmly, though he could feel his heart thumping hard against his ribs, and that peculiar choking sensation which is the warning of what in such cases must come some day.

"Will you cast your mind back, sir, to a morning in last August, when you called my attention to some extraordinary footprints on the floor of your room?"

"I remember the morning," said Mr. Murray, that choking sensation seeming to suffocate him. "Pray go on."

If Davis had not been master of the position, this indifference would have daunted him; as it was, he again touched the trigger, and fired this: "*I know all!*"

Mr. Murray's answer did not come so quick this time. The waters had gone over his head, and for a minute he felt as a man might if suddenly flung into a raging sea, and battling for his life. He was battling for his life with a wildly leaping heart. The noise of a hundred billows seemed dashing on his brain. Then the tempest lulled, the roaring torrent was stayed, and then he said interrogatively, "Yes?"

The prints of those phantom feet had not amazed Davis more than did his master's coolness.

"You might ha' knocked me down with a feather," he stated, when subsequently relating this interview. "I always knew he was a queer customer, but I never knew how queer till then."

"Yes?" said Mr. Murray, which reply quite disconcerted his valet.

"I wouldn't have seen what I have seen, sir," he remarked, "not for a king's ransom."

"No?"

"No, sir, and that is the truth. What we both saw has been with me at bed and at board, as the saying is, ever since. When I shut my eyes I still feel those wet feet dabbling about the room; and in the bright sunshine I can't help shuddering, because there seems to be a cold mist creeping over me."

"Are you not a little imaginative, Davis?" asked his master, himself repressing a shudder.

"No, sir, I am not; no man can be that about which his own eyes have seen and his own ears have heard; and I have heard and seen what

I can never forget, and what nothing could pay me for going through."

"Nevertheless?" suggested Mr. Murray.

"I don't know whether I am doing right in holding my tongue, in being so faithful, sir; but I can't help it. I took to you from the first, and I wouldn't bring harm on you if any act of mine could keep it from you. When one made the remark to me awhile ago it was a strange thing to see a gentleman attended by a pair of wet footprints, I said they were a sign in your family that some great event was about to happen."

"Did you say so?"

"I did, sir, Lord forgive me!" answered Davis, with unblushing mendacity. "I have gone through more than will ever be known over this affair, which has shook me, Mr. Murray. I am not the man I was before ghosts took to following me, and getting into trains without paying any fare, and waking me in the middle of the night, and rousing me out of my warm bed to see sights I would not have believed I could have seen if anybody had sworn it to me. I have aged twenty-five years since last August—my nerves are destroyed; and so, sir, before you got married, I thought I would make bold to ask what I am to do with a constitution broken in your service and hardly a penny put by;" and, almost out of breath with his pathetic statement, Davis stopped and waited for an answer.

With a curiously hunted expression in them, Mr. Murray raised his eyes and looked at Davis.

"You have thought over all this," he said. "How much do you assess them at?"

"I scarcely comprehend, sir—assess what at?"

"Your broken constitution and the five-and-twenty years you say you have aged."

His master's face was so gravely serious that Davis could take the question neither as a jest nor a sneer. It was a request to fix a price, and he did so.

"Well, sir," he answered, "I have thought it all over. In the night-watches, when I could get no rest, I lay and reflected what I ought to do. I want to act fair. I have no wish to drive a hard bargain with you, and, on the other hand, I don't think I would be doing justice by a man that has worked hard if I let myself be sold for nothing. So, sir, to cut a long story short, I am willing to take two thousand pounds."

"And where do you imagine I am to get two thousand pounds?"

Mr. Davis modestly intimated he knew his place better than to presume to have any notion, but no doubt Mr. Murray could raise that sum easily enough.

"If I could raise such a sum for you, do you not think I should have raised it for myself long ago?"

Davis answered that he did; but, if he might make free to say so, times were changed.

"They are, they are indeed," said Mr. Murray bitterly; and then there was silence.

Davis knocked the conversational ball the next time.

"I am in no particular hurry, sir," he said. "So, long as we understand one another I can wait till you come back from Italy, and have got the handling of some cash of your own. I daresay even then you won't be able to pay me off all at once; but if you would insure your life—"

"I can't insure my life: I have tried, and been refused."

Again there ensued a silence, which Davis broke once more.

"Well, sir," he began, "I'll chance that. If you will give me a line of writing about what you owe me, and make a sort of a will, saying I am to get two thousand, I'll hold my tongue about what's gone and past. And I would not be fretting, sir, if I was you: things are quiet now, and, please God, you might never have any more trouble."

Mr. Davis, in view of his two thousand pounds, his widow, and his wayside public, felt disposed to take an optimistic view of even his master's position; but Mr. Murray's thoughts were of a different hue. "If I do have any more," he considered, "I shall go mad;" a conclusion which seemed likely enough to follow upon even the memory of those phantom feet coming dabbling out of an unseen world to follow him with their accursed print in this.

Davis was not going abroad with the happy pair. For sufficient reason Mr. Murray had decided to leave him behind, and Mrs. Murray, ever alive to her own convenience, instantly engaged him to stay on with her as butler, her own being under notice to leave.

Thus, in a semi-official capacity, Davis witnessed the wedding, which people considered a splendid affair.

What Davis thought of it can never be known, because when he left Losdale Church his face was whiter than the bride's dress; and after the newly-wedded couple started on the first stage of their life-journey he went to his room, and stayed in it till his services were required.

"There is no money would pay me for what I've seen," he remarked to himself. "I went too cheap. But when once I handle the cash I'll try never to come anigh him or them again."

What was he referring to? Just this. As the bridal group moved to the vestry he saw, if no one else did, those wet, wet feet softly and swiftly threading their way round the bridesmaids and the groomsman, in front of the relations, before Mrs. Murray herself, and hurry on to keep step with the just wed pair.

For the last time the young wife signed her maiden name. Friends crowded around, uttering congratulations, and still through the throng those unnoticed feet kept walking in and out, round and round, backward and forward, as a dog threads its way through the people at a fair. Down the aisle, under the sweeping dresses of the ladies, past courtly gentlemen, Davis saw those awful feet running gleefully till they came up with bride and bridegroom.

"She is going abroad with them," thought the man; and then for a moment he felt as if could endure the ghastly vision no longer, but must faint dead away. "It is a vile shame," he reflected, "to drag an innocent girl into such a whirlpool;" and all the time over the church step the feet were dancing merrily.

The clerk and the verger noticed them at last.

"I wonder who has been here with wet feet?" said the clerk; and the verger wonderingly answered he did not know.

Davis could have told him, had he been willing to speak or capable of speech.

Conclusion

HE'D HAVE SEEN ME RIGHTED

IT was August once again—August, fine, warm, and sunshiny—just one year after that damp afternoon on which Paul Murray and his friend stood in front of the Ship at Lower Halliford. No lack of visitors that season. Hotels were full, and furnished houses at a premium. The hearts of lodging-house keepers were glad. Ladies arrayed in rainbow hues flashed about the quiet village streets; boatmen reaped a golden harvest; all sorts of crafts swarmed on the river. Men in flannels gallantly towed their feminine belongings up against a languidly flowing stream. Pater and materfamilias, and all the olive branches, big and little, were to be met on the Thames, and on the banks of Thames, from Richmond to Staines, and even higher still. The lilies growing around Dockett Point floated with their pure cups wide open to the sun; no close folding of the white wax-leaves around the golden centre that season. Beside the water purple loosestrife grew in great clumps of brilliant colour dazzling to the sight. It was, in fact, a glorious August, in which pleasure-seekers could idle and sun themselves and get tanned to an almost perfect brown without the slightest trouble.

During the past twelvemonth local tradition had tried hard to add another ghost at Dumsey Deep to that already established in the adjoining Stabbery; but the unshrinking brightness of that glorious summer checked belief in it for the time. No doubts when the dull autumn days came again, and the long winter nights, full of awful possibilities, folded water and land in fog and darkness, a figure dressed in grey silk and black velvet fichu, with a natty grey hat trimmed with black and white feathers on its phantom head, with small feet covered by the thinnest of openwork stockings, from which the shoes, so much too large, had dropped long ago, would reappear once more, to the terror of all who heard, but for the time being, snugly tucked up in holy ground the girl whose heart had rejoiced in her beauty, her youth, her admirers, and her finery, was lying quite still and quiet, with closed eyes, and ears that heard neither the church bells nor the splash of oars nor the murmur of human voices.

Others, too, were missing from—though not missed by—Shepperton (the Thames villages miss no human being so long as other human beings, with plenty of money, come down by rail, boat, or carriage to supply his place). Paul Murray, Dick Savill, and Walter Grantley were absent. Mrs. Heath, too, had gone, a tottering, heartbroken woman, to Mr. Pointer's, where she was most miserable, but where she and her small possessions were taken remarkably good care of.

"Only a year agone," she said one day, "my girl was with me. In the morning she wore her pretty cambric with pink spots; and in the afternoon, that grey silk in which she was buried—for we durst not change a thread, but just wrapped a winding-sheet round what was left. O! Lucy, Lucy, Lucy! to think I bore you for that!" and then she wept softly, and nobody heeded or tried to console her, for "what," as Mrs. Pointer wisely said, "was the use of fretting over a daughter dead a twelvemonth, and never much of a comfort neither?"

Mr. Richard Savill was still "grinding away," to quote his expression. Walter Grantley had departed, so reported his friends, for the diamond-fields; his enemies improved on this by carelessly answering,—

"Grantley! O, he's gone to the devil;" which latter statement could not have been quite true, since he has been back in England for a long time, and is now quite well to do and reconciled to his family.

As for Paul Murray, there had been all sorts of rumours floating about concerning him.

The honeymoon had been unduly protracted; from place to place the married pair wandered—never resting, never staying; alas! for him there was no rest—there could be none here.

It mattered not where he went—east, west, south, or north—those noiseless wet feet followed; no train was swift enough to outstrip them; no boat could cut the water fast enough to leave them behind; they tracked him with dogged persistence; they were with him sleeping, walking, eating, drinking, praying—for Paul Murray in those days often prayed after a desperate heathenish fashion—and yet the plague was not stayed; the accursed thing still dogged him like a Fate.

After a while people began to be shy of him, because the footsteps were no more intermittent; they were always where he was. Did he enter a cathedral, they accompanied him; did he walk solitary through the woods or pace the lake-side, or wander by the sea, they were ever and always with the unhappy man.

They were worse than any evil conscience, because conscience often sleeps, and they from the day of his marriage never did. They had waited for that—waited till he should raise the cup of happiness to his lips, in order to fill it with gall—waited till his wife's dream of bliss was perfect, and then wake her to the knowledge of some horror more agonizing than death.

There were times when he left his young wife for days and days, and went, like those possessed of old, into the wilderness, seeking rest and finding none; for no legion of demons could have cursed a man's life more than those wet feet, which printed marks on Paul Murray's heart that might have been branded by red-hot irons.

All that had gone before was as nothing to the trouble of having involved another in the horrible mystery of his own life—and that other a gentle, innocent, loving creature he might just as well have killed as married.

He did not know what to do. His brain was on fire; he had lost all hold upon himself, all grip over his mind. On the sea of life he tossed like a ship without a rudder, one minute taking a resolve to shoot himself, the next turning his steps to seek some priest, and confess the whole matter fully and freely, and, before he had walked a dozen yards, determining to go away into some savage and desolate land, where those horrible feet might, if they pleased, follow him to his grave.

By degrees this was the plan which took firm root in his dazed brain; and accordingly one morning he started for England, leaving a note in which he asked his wife to follow him. He never meant to see her sweet face again, and he never did. He had determined to go to his father-in-law and confess to him; and accordingly, on the anniversary of Lucy's death, he found himself at Losdale Court, where vague rumours of some unaccountable trouble had preceded him.

Mr. Ketterick was brooding over these rumours in his library, when, as if in answer to his thoughts, the servant announced Mr. Murray.

"Good God!" exclaimed the older man, shocked by the white, haggard face before him, "what is wrong?"

"I have been ill," was the reply.

"Where is your wife?"

"She is following me. She will be here in a day or so."

"Why did you not travel together?"

"That is what I have come to tell you."

Then he suddenly stopped and put his hand to his heart. He had voluntarily come up for execution, and now his courage failed him. His manhood was gone, his nerves unstrung. He was but a poor, weak, wasted creature, worn out by the ceaseless torment of those haunting feet, which, however, since he turned his steps to England had never followed him. Why had he travelled to Losdale Court? Might he not have crossed the ocean and effaced himself in the Far West, without telling his story at all?

Just as he had laid down the revolver, just as he had turned from the priest's door, so now he felt he could not say that which he had come determined to say.

"I have walked too far," he said, after a pause. "I cannot talk just yet. Will you leave me for half an hour? No; I don't want anything, thank you—except to be quiet." Quiet!—ah, heavens!

After a little he rose and passed out on to the terrace. Around there was beauty and peace and sunshine. He—he—was the only jarring element, and even on him there seemed falling a numbed sensation which for the time being simulated rest.

He left the terrace and crossed the lawn till he came to a great cedar tree, under which there was a seat, where he could sit a short time before leaving the Court.

Yes, he would go away and make no sign. Dreamily he thought of the wild lone lands beyond the sea, where there would be none to ask whence he came or marvel about the curse which followed him. Over the boundless prairie, up the mountain heights, let those feet pursue him if they would. Away from his fellows he could bear his burden. He would confess to no man—only to God, who knew his sin and sorrow; only to his Maker, who might have pity on the work of his hands, and some day bid that relentless avenger be still.

No, he would take no man into his confidence; and even as he so decided, the brightness of the day seemed to be clouded over, warmth was exchanged for a deadly chill, a horror of darkness seemed thrown like a pall over him, and a rushing sound as of many waters filled his ears.

An hour later, when Mr. Ketterick sought his son-in-law, he found him lying on the ground, which was wet and trampled, as though by hundreds of little feet.

His shouts brought help, and Paul Murray was carried into the house, where they laid him on a couch and piled rugs and blankets over his shivering body.

"Fetch a doctor at once," said Mr. Ketterick.

"And a clergyman," added the housekeeper.

"No, a magistrate," cried the sick man, in a loud voice.

They had thought him insensible, and, startled, looked at each other. After that he spoke no more, but turned his head away from them and lay quiet.

The doctor was the first to arrive. With quick alertness he stepped across the room, pulled aside the coverings, and took the patient's hand; then after gently moving the averted face, he said solemnly, like a man whose occupation has gone,—

"I can do nothing here; he is dead."

It was true. Whatever his secret, Paul Murray carried it with him to a country further distant than the lone land where he had thought to hide his misery.

"It is of no use talking to me," said Mr. Davis, when subsequently telling his story. "If Mr. Murray had been a gentleman as was a gentleman, he'd have seen me righted, dead or not. *She* was able to come back—at least, her feet were; and he could have done the same if he'd liked. It was as bad as swindling not making a fresh will after he was married. How was I to know that will would turn out so much waste paper? And then when I asked for my own, Mrs. Murray dismissed me without a character, and Mr. Ketterick's lawyers won't give me anything either; so a lot I've made by being a faithful servant, and I'd have all servants take warning by me."

Mr. Davis is his own servant now, and a very bad master he finds himself.

A BIBLIOGRAPHY OF
MRS. J. H. RIDDELL

MRS. RIDDELL's fiction has become quite rare. There does not seem to be a library in the world that contains a full set of all her published books, in any edition, let alone first editions. The British Museum is lacking many titles, while the Library of Congress in Washington is lamentably weak. Even the remarkable Sadleir Collection, which contained first editions of all LeFanu, Braddon, and Wood, held only a handful of Mrs. Riddell's works.

The following bibliography is basically a revision of the pioneer list prepared by S. M. Ellis in his *Wilkie Collins, LeFanu and Others* (London, 1931). Some dates have been changed; a few new works have been added; more information has been gathered on certain titles; and new pseudonyms used by Mrs. Riddell have been identified. Mrs. Riddell's first book, *Zuriel's Grandchild*, has finally been located bibliographically, and is no longer to be considered a ghost book.

The books listed below are first editions, although in many cases periodical publication preceded the books. Unless otherwise indicated, all items were published as "by Mrs. J. H. Riddell" and issued in London. Reissues of the earlier, pseudonymous books were accredited to Mrs. Riddell after she started using her own name.

The full designations of the publishers are: T. C. Newby, 30, Welbeck Street, Cavendish Square; Smith, Elder and Co., 65, Cornhill (later 15, Waterloo Place); Charles J. Skeet, 10, King William Street, Charing Cross; Tinsley Brothers, 18, Catherine Street, Strand; F. Enos Arnold, St. James's Magazine Office, Strand; George Routledge and Sons, Broadway, Ludgate Hill; Chatto and Windus, Piccadilly; Richard Bentley and Son; Society for Promoting Christian Knowledge, Northumberland Avenue; Ward and Downey, 12, York Street, Covent Garden; William Heinemann; F. V. White and Co., 31, Southampton Street (later 14, Bedford Place), Strand; Remington and Company, 15, King Street, Covent Garden; Hutchinson and Co., 34, Paternoster Row; Downey and Co., Ltd., 12, York Street, Covent Garden.

Books

1. *Zuriel's Grandchild. A Novel* by R. V. Sparling (3 vols., Newby, 1856). This first edition may be lost. No copies are known to survive and the only record of it is under the author's pseudonym in the *English Catalogue*. It was republished under Mrs. Riddell's name in 1873 as *Joy after Sorrow*.

2. *The Ruling Passion* by Rainey Hawthorne (3 vols., Bentley, 1857).

3. *The Rich Husband* by The Author of The Ruling Passion (3 vols., Skeet, 1858).

4. *The Moors and the Fens* by F. G. Trafford (3 vols., Smith, Elder, 1858).

5. *Too Much Alone* by F. G. Trafford (3 vols., Skeet, 1860).

6. *City and Suburb* by F. G. Trafford (3 vols., Skeet, 1861).

7. *The World in the Church* by F. G. Trafford (3 vols., Skeet, 1862).

8. *George Geith of Fen Court. A Novel* by F. G. Trafford (3 vols., Tinsley, 1864).

9. *Maxwell Drewitt. A Novel* by F. G. Trafford (3 vols., Tinsley, 1865).

10. *Phemie Keller. A Novel* by F. G. Trafford (3 vols., Tinsley, 1866). S. M. Ellis considered the possibility of an 1865 edition, but none has been located.

11. *The Race for Wealth. A Novel* (3 vols., Tinsley, 1866). Beginning with this book Mrs. J. H. Riddell is accredited as author on title pages.

12. *Far above Rubies* (3 vols., Tinsley, 1867).

13. *My First Love* (St. James's Christmas Box, 1869). Republished with sequel, *My Last Love*, as a separate book, Hutchinson, 1891.

14. *Austin Friars. A Novel* (3 vols., Tinsley, 1870).

15. *Long Ago* (F. Enos Arnold, 1870). The Sadleir Collection contains Part One only, which is all that is recorded. It was probably the St. James's Christmas Box for 1870.

16. *A Life's Assize. A Novel* (3 vols., Tinsley, 1871).

17. *The Earl's Promise. A Novel* (3 vols., Tinsley, 1873).

18. *Home, Sweet Home. A Novel* (3 vols., Tinsley, 1873).

19. *Fairy Water: A Christmas Story* (*Routledge's Christmas Annual*, 1873).

20. *Mortomley's Estate. A Novel* (3 vols., Tinsley, 1874).

21. *Frank Sinclair's Wife and Other Stories* (3 vols., Tinsley, 1874).
22. *The Uninhabited House* (*Routledge's Christmas Annual*, 1875).
23. *Above Suspicion. A Novel* (3 vols., Tinsley, 1876).
24. *Her Mother's Darling. A Novel* (3 vols., Tinsley, 1877).
25. *The Haunted River. A Christmas Story* (*Routledge's Christmas Annual*, 1877). *The Haunted River* and *The Uninhabited House* were published together by Routledge, 1883.
26. *The Disappearance of Mr. Jeremiah Redworth* (*Routledge's Christmas Annual*, 1878).
27. *The Mystery in Palace Gardens. A Novel* (3 vols., Bentley, 1880).
28. *Alaric Spenceley, or, A High Ideal* (3 vols., Skeet, 1881).
29. *The Senior Partner. A Novel* (3 vols., Bentley, 1881).
30. *Daisies and Buttercups. A Novel* (3 vols., Bentley, 1882).
31. *The Prince of Wales's Garden Party and Other Stories* (Chatto and Windus, 1882).
32. *Weird Stories* (Hogg, 1882).
33. *A Struggle for Fame. A Novel* (3 vols., Bentley, 1883).
34. *Susan Drummond. A Novel* (3 vols., Bentley, 1884).
35. *Berna Boyle. A Love Story of the County Down* (3 vols., Bentley, 1884).
36. *Mitre Court. A Tale of the Great City* (3 vols., Bentley, 1885).
37. *For Dick's Sake* (S.P.C.K., 1886). Paperback, in Penny Library of Fiction series.
38. *Miss Gascoyne. A Novel* (Ward and Downey, 1887).
39. *The Government Official* (3 vols., Bentley, 1887). A collaboration with Arthur H. Norway, published anonymously.
40. *Idle Tales* (Ward and Downey, 1888). The story "Only a Lost Letter" from *Idle Tales* was printed in America in dime-novel format under the title "A Lost Letter," sometimes as the title member of collections.
41. *The Nun's Curse. A Novel* (3 vols., Ward and Downey, 1888).
42. *Princess Sunshine and Other Stories* (2 vols., Ward and Downey, 1889).
43. *A Mad Tour, or A Journey Undertaken in an Insane Moment through Central Europe on Foot* (Bentley, 1891). A travel account of a trip taken by Mrs. Riddell and A. H. Norway through the Black Forest.
44. *The Head of the Firm. A Novel* (3 vols., Heinemann, 1892).

45. *The Rusty Sword, or Thereby Hangs a Tale* (S.P.C.K., 1893).
46. *A Silent Tragedy. A Novel* (F. V. White, 1893).
47. *The Banshee's Warning and Other Tales* (Remington, 1894).
48. *Did He Deserve It?* (Downey, 1897).
49. *A Rich Man's Daughter* (F. V. White, 1897). This is the earliest
    known British edition, but the American Book Co. edition,
    New York, carries an 1895 copyright notice.
50. *Handsome Phil and Other Stories* (F. V. White, 1899).
51. *The Footfall of Fate* (F. V. White, 1900).
52. *Poor Fellow!* (F. V. White, 1902).

Miscellaneous and Uncollected Material

"The Miseries of Christmas." Essay in *Routledge's Christmas Annual*
    (1867).
"A Strange Christmas Game." Short story in *Novels, Tales, and
    Poetry by The Author of "Guy Livingstone," etc. etc.* Routledge
    (1868?)
"Couleur de Rose." Short story in *Novels, Tales, and Poetry by
    The Author of "Guy Livingstone," etc. etc.* Routledge (1868?)
How to Spend a Month in Ireland by Sir Cusack P. Roney. New edition
    revised by Mrs. J. H. Riddell, Chatto and Windus, 1872. A
    Baedeker-like guidebook.
"The Curate of Lowood." Short story in *Proverb Stories for Boys and
    Girls*, Office of London Society, 1882.

Supposititious and Possibly Spurious Work

Michael Gargrave's Harvest by Mrs. J. H. Riddell. Seaside Library
    #445, New York, 1878. Known from listings, but not located. It
    seems to be a long short story or a short novel. This may be a
    printing of a periodical piece that has not been observed else-
    where, or it may be spurious. American publishers were not
    always too scrupulous, and attributed anonymous works to
    authors with reputation, to increase sales.
Ruthvens. The Estes and Lauriat (Boston, Mass.) edition of *Too Much
    Alone* lists *Ruthvens* on the title page as a work of Mrs. Riddell's.
    This is probably a reference to *City and Suburb*, but no record of
    such an edition has been found.

SOURCES

THE STORIES in this volume have been taken from the following sources:

"Nut Bush Farm," "The Open Door," "The Old House in Vauxhall Walk," "Sandy the Tinker," "Old Mrs. Jones" and "Walnut-Tree House" from *Weird Stories* by Mrs. J. H. Riddell.

"A Strange Christmas Game" from *Novels, Tales, and Poetry by The Author of "Guy Livingstone,"* etc. etc.

"Forewarned, Forearmed" and "Hertford O'Donnell's Warning" from *Frank Sinclair's Wife and Other Stories* by Mrs. J. H. Riddell.

"The Last of Squire Ennismore" from *Idle Tales* by Mrs. J. H. Riddell.

"A Terrible Vengeance" and "Why Dr. Cray Left Southam" from *Princess Sunshine and Other Stories* by Mrs. J. H. Riddell.

"Diarmid Chittock's Story" from *The Lady of the House*, October through December, 1894.

"Conn Kilrea" from *Handsome Phil and Other Stories* by Mrs. J. H. Riddell.

A CATALOGUE OF SELECTED DOVER BOOKS
IN ALL FIELDS OF INTEREST

A CATALOGUE OF SELECTED DOVER BOOKS
IN ALL FIELDS OF INTEREST

LEATHER TOOLING AND CARVING, Chris H. Groneman. One of few books concentrating on tooling and carving, with complete instructions and grid designs for 39 projects ranging from bookmarks to bags. 148 illustrations. 111pp. 7⅞ x 10.
23061-9 Pa. $2.50

THE CODEX NUTTALL, A PICTURE MANUSCRIPT FROM ANCIENT MEXICO, as first edited by Zelia Nuttall. Only inexpensive edition, in full color, of a pre-Columbian Mexican (Mixtec) book. 88 color plates show kings, gods, heroes, temples, sacrifices. New explanatory, historical introduction by Arthur G. Miller. 96pp. 11⅜ x 8½.
23168-2 Pa. $7.50

AMERICAN PRIMITIVE PAINTING, Jean Lipman. Classic collection of an enduring American tradition. 109 plates, 8 in full color—portraits, landscapes, Biblical and historical scenes, etc., showing family groups, farm life, and so on. 80pp. of lucid text. 8⅜ x 11¼.
22815-0 Pa. $4.00

WILL BRADLEY: HIS GRAPHIC ART, edited by Clarence P. Hornung. Striking collection of work by foremost practitioner of Art Nouveau in America: posters, cover designs, sample pages, advertisements, other illustrations. 97 plates, including 8 in full color and 19 in two colors. 97pp. 9⅜ x 12¼.
20701-3 Pa. $4.00
22120-2 Clothbd. $10.00

THE UNDERGROUND SKETCHBOOK OF JAN FAUST, Jan Faust. 101 bitter, horrifying, black-humorous, penetrating sketches on sex, war, greed, various liberations, etc. Sometimes sexual, but not pornographic. Not for prudish. 101pp. 6½ x 9¼.
22740-5 Pa. $1.50

THE GIBSON GIRL AND HER AMERICA, Charles Dana Gibson. 155 finest drawings of effervescent world of 1900-1910: the Gibson Girl and her loves, amusements, adventures, Mr. Pipp, etc. Selected by E. Gillon; introduction by Henry Pitz. 144pp. 8¼ x 11⅜.
21986-0 Pa. $3.50

STAINED GLASS CRAFT, J.A.F. Divine, G. Blachford. One of the very few books that tell the beginner exactly what he needs to know: planning cuts, making shapes, avoiding design weaknesses, fitting glass, etc. 93 illustrations. 115pp.
22812-6 Pa. $1.50

CREATIVE LITHOGRAPHY AND HOW TO DO IT, Grant Arnold. Lithography as art form: working directly on stone, transfer of drawings, lithotint, mezzotint, color printing; also metal plates. Detailed, thorough. 27 illustrations. 214pp.
21208-4 Pa. $3.00

DESIGN MOTIFS OF ANCIENT MEXICO, Jorge Enciso. Vigorous, powerful ceramic stamp impressions — Maya, Aztec, Toltec, Olmec. Serpents, gods, priests, dancers, etc. 153pp. 6⅛ x 9¼. 20084-1 Pa. $2.50

AMERICAN INDIAN DESIGN AND DECORATION, Leroy Appleton. Full text, plus more than 700 precise drawings of Inca, Maya, Aztec, Pueblo, Plains, NW Coast basketry, sculpture, painting, pottery, sand paintings, metal, etc. 4 plates in color. 279pp. 8⅜ x 11¼. 22704-9 Pa. $4.50

CHINESE LATTICE DESIGNS, Daniel S. Dye. Incredibly beautiful geometric designs: circles, voluted, simple dissections, etc. Inexhaustible source of ideas, motifs. 1239 illustrations. 469pp. 6⅛ x 9¼. 23096-1 Pa. $5.00

JAPANESE DESIGN MOTIFS, Matsuya Co. Mon, or heraldic designs. Over 4000 typical, beautiful designs: birds, animals, flowers, swords, fans, geometric; all beautifully stylized. 213pp. 11⅜ x 8¼. 22874-6 Pa. $5.00

PERSPECTIVE, Jan Vredeman de Vries. 73 perspective plates from 1604 edition; buildings, townscapes, stairways, fantastic scenes. Remarkable for beauty, surrealistic atmosphere; real eye-catchers. Introduction by Adolf Placzek. 74pp. 11⅜ x 8¼. 20186-4 Pa. $2.75

EARLY AMERICAN DESIGN MOTIFS. Suzanne E. Chapman. 497 motifs, designs, from painting on wood, ceramics, appliqué, glassware, samplers, metal work, etc. Florals, landscapes, birds and animals, geometrics, letters, etc. Inexhaustible. Enlarged edition. 138pp. 8⅜ x 11¼. 22985-8 Pa. $3.50
23084-8 Clothbd. $7.95

VICTORIAN STENCILS FOR DESIGN AND DECORATION, edited by E.V. Gillon, Jr. 113 wonderful ornate Victorian pieces from German sources; florals, geometrics; borders, corner pieces; bird motifs, etc. 64pp. 9⅜ x 12¼. 21995-X Pa. $2.75

ART NOUVEAU: AN ANTHOLOGY OF DESIGN AND ILLUSTRATION FROM THE STUDIO, edited by E.V. Gillon, Jr. Graphic arts: book jackets, posters, engravings, illustrations, decorations; Crane, Beardsley, Bradley and many others. Inexhaustible. 92pp. 8⅛ x 11. 22388-4 Pa. $2.50

ORIGINAL ART DECO DESIGNS, William Rowe. First-rate, highly imaginative modern Art Deco frames, borders, compositions, alphabets, florals, insectals, Wurlitzer-types, etc. Much finest modern Art Deco. 80 plates, 8 in color. 8⅜ x 11¼. 22567-4 Pa. $3.00

HANDBOOK OF DESIGNS AND DEVICES, Clarence P. Hornung. Over 1800 basic geometric designs based on circle, triangle, square, scroll, cross, etc. Largest such collection in existence. 261pp. 20125-2 Pa. $2.50

150 MASTERPIECES OF DRAWING, edited by Anthony Toney. 150 plates, early 15th century to end of 18th century; Rembrandt, Michelangelo, Dürer, Fragonard, Watteau, Wouwerman, many others. 150pp. 8⅜ x 11¼. 21032-4 Pa. $3.50

THE GOLDEN AGE OF THE POSTER, Hayward and Blanche Cirker. 70 extraordinary posters in full colors, from Maîtres de l'Affiche, Mucha, Lautrec, Bradley, Cheret, Beardsley, many others. 9⅜ x 12¼. 22753-7 Pa. $4.95
21718-3 Clothbd. $7.95

SIMPLICISSIMUS, selection, translations and text by Stanley Appelbaum. 180 satirical drawings, 16 in full color, from the famous German weekly magazine in the years 1896 to 1926. 24 artists included: Grosz, Kley, Pascin, Kubin, Kollwitz, plus Heine, Thöny, Bruno Paul, others. 172pp. 8½ x 12¼. 23098-8 Pa. $5.00
23099-6 Clothbd. $10.00

THE EARLY WORK OF AUBREY BEARDSLEY, Aubrey Beardsley. 157 plates, 2 in color: Manon Lescaut, Madame Bovary, Morte d'Arthur, Salome, other. Introduction by H. Marillier. 175pp. 8½ x 11. 21816-3 Pa. $3.50

THE LATER WORK OF AUBREY BEARDSLEY, Aubrey Beardsley. Exotic masterpieces of full maturity: Venus and Tannhäuser, Lysistrata, Rape of the Lock, Volpone, Savoy material, etc. 174 plates, 2 in color. 176pp. 8½ x 11. 21817-1 Pa. $4.00

DRAWINGS OF WILLIAM BLAKE, William Blake. 92 plates from Book of Job, Divine Comedy, Paradise Lost, visionary heads, mythological figures, Laocoön, etc. Selection, introduction, commentary by Sir Geoffrey Keynes. 178pp. 8½ x 11. 22303-5 Pa. $3.50

LONDON: A PILGRIMAGE, Gustave Doré, Blanchard Jerrold. Squalor, riches, misery, beauty of mid-Victorian metropolis; 55 wonderful plates, 125 other illustrations, full social, cultural text by Jerrold. 191pp. of text. 8⅛ x 11. 22306-X Pa. $5.00

THE COMPLETE WOODCUTS OF ALBRECHT DÜRER, edited by Dr. W. Kurth. 346 in all: Old Testament, St. Jerome, Passion, Life of Virgin, Apocalypse, many others. Introduction by Campbell Dodgson. 285pp. 8½ x 12¼. 21097-9 Pa. $6.00

THE DISASTERS OF WAR, Francisco Goya. 83 etchings record horrors of Napoleonic wars in Spain and war in general. Reprint of 1st edition, plus 3 additional plates. Introduction by Philip Hofer. 97pp. 9⅜ x 8¼. 21872-4 Pa. $3.00

ENGRAVINGS OF HOGARTH, William Hogarth. 101 of Hogarth's greatest works: Rake's Progress, Harlot's Progress, Illustrations for Hudibras, Midnight Modern Conversation, Before and After, Beer Street and Gin Lane, many more. Full commentary. 256pp. 11 x 14. 22479-1 Pa. $7.00
23023-6 Clothbd. $13.50

PRIMITIVE ART, Franz Boas. Great anthropologist on ceramics, textiles, wood, stone, metal, etc.; patterns, technology, symbols, styles. All areas, but fullest on Northwest Coast Indians. 350 illustrations. 378pp. 20025-6 Pa. $3.50

MOTHER GOOSE'S MELODIES. Facsimile of fabulously rare Munroe and Francis "copyright 1833" Boston edition. Familiar and unusual rhymes, wonderful old woodcut illustrations. Edited by E.F. Bleiler. 128pp. 4½ x 6⅜. 22577-1 Pa. $1.00

MOTHER GOOSE IN HIEROGLYPHICS. Favorite nursery rhymes presented in rebus form for children. Fascinating 1849 edition reproduced in toto, with key. Introduction by E.F. Bleiler. About 400 woodcuts. 64pp. 6⅞ x 5¼. 20745-5 Pa. $1.00

PETER PIPER'S PRACTICAL PRINCIPLES OF PLAIN & PERFECT PRONUNCIATION. Alliterative jingles and tongue-twisters. Reproduction in full of 1830 first American edition. 25 spirited woodcuts. 32pp. 4½ x 6⅜. 22560-7 Pa. $1.00

MARMADUKE MULTIPLY'S MERRY METHOD OF MAKING MINOR MATHEMATICIANS. Fellow to Peter Piper, it teaches multiplication table by catchy rhymes and woodcuts. 1841 Munroe & Francis edition. Edited by E.F. Bleiler. 103pp. 4⅝ x 6.
22773-1 Pa. $1.25
20171-6 Clothbd. $3.00

THE NIGHT BEFORE CHRISTMAS, Clement Moore. Full text, and woodcuts from original 1848 book. Also critical, historical material. 19 illustrations. 40pp. 4⅝ x 6. 22797-9 Pa. $1.00

THE KING OF THE GOLDEN RIVER, John Ruskin. Victorian children's classic of three brothers, their attempts to reach the Golden River, what becomes of them. Facsimile of original 1889 edition. 22 illustrations. 56pp. 4⅝ x 6⅜.
20066-3 Pa. $1.25

DREAMS OF THE RAREBIT FIEND, Winsor McCay. Pioneer cartoon strip, unexcelled for beauty, imagination, in 60 full sequences. Incredible technical virtuosity, wonderful visual wit. Historical introduction. 62pp. 8⅜ x 11¼. 21347-1 Pa. $2.50

THE KATZENJAMMER KIDS, Rudolf Dirks. In full color, 14 strips from 1906-7; full of imagination, characteristic humor. Classic of great historical importance. Introduction by August Derleth. 32pp. 9¼ x 12¼. 23005-8 Pa. $2.00

LITTLE ORPHAN ANNIE AND LITTLE ORPHAN ANNIE IN COSMIC CITY, Harold Gray. Two great sequences from the early strips: our curly-haired heroine defends the Warbucks' financial empire and, then, takes on meanie Phineas P. Pinchpenny. Leapin' lizards! 178pp. 6⅛ x 8⅜. 23107-0 Pa. $2.00

WHEN A FELLER NEEDS A FRIEND, Clare Briggs. 122 cartoons by one of the greatest newspaper cartoonists of the early 20th century — about growing up, making a living, family life, daily frustrations and occasional triumphs. 121pp. 8½ x 9½.
23148-8 Pa. $2.50

THE BEST OF GLUYAS WILLIAMS. 100 drawings by one of America's finest cartoonists: The Day a Cake of Ivory Soap Sank at Proctor & Gamble's, At the Life Insurance Agents' Banquet, and many other gems from the 20's and 30's. 118pp. 8⅜ x 11¼. 22737-5 Pa. $2.50

THE BEST DR. THORNDYKE DETECTIVE STORIES, R. Austin Freeman. The Case of Oscar Brodski, The Moabite Cipher, and 5 other favorites featuring the great scientific detective, plus his long-believed-lost first adventure — 31 New Inn — reprinted here for the first time. Edited by E.F. Bleiler. USO 20388-3 Pa. $3.00

BEST "THINKING MACHINE" DETECTIVE STORIES, Jacques Futrelle. The Problem of Cell 13 and 11 other stories about Prof. Augustus S.F.X. Van Dusen, including two "lost" stories. First reprinting of several. Edited by E.F. Bleiler. 241pp. 20537-1 Pa. $3.00

UNCLE SILAS, J. Sheridan LeFanu. Victorian Gothic mystery novel, considered by many best of period, even better than Collins or Dickens. Wonderful psychological terror. Introduction by Frederick Shroyer. 436pp. 21715-9 Pa. $4.00

BEST DR. POGGIOLI DETECTIVE STORIES, T.S. Stribling. 15 best stories from EQMM and The Saint offer new adventures in Mexico, Florida, Tennessee hills as Poggioli unravels mysteries and combats Count Jalacki. 217pp. 23227-1 Pa. $3.00

EIGHT DIME NOVELS, selected with an introduction by E.F. Bleiler. Adventures of Old King Brady, Frank James, Nick Carter, Deadwood Dick, Buffalo Bill, The Steam Man, Frank Merriwell, and Horatio Alger — 1877 to 1905. Important, entertaining popular literature in facsimile reprint, with original covers. 190pp. 9 x 12. 22975-0 Pa. $3.50

ALICE'S ADVENTURES UNDER GROUND, Lewis Carroll. Facsimile of ms. Carroll gave Alice Liddell in 1864. Different in many ways from final Alice. Handlettered, illustrated by Carroll. Introduction by Martin Gardner. 128pp. 21482-6 Pa. $1.50

ALICE IN WONDERLAND COLORING BOOK, Lewis Carroll. Pictures by John Tenniel. Large-size versions of the famous illustrations of Alice, Cheshire Cat, Mad Hatter and all the others, waiting for your crayons. Abridged text. 36 illustrations. 64pp. 8¼ x 11. 22853-3 Pa. $1.50

AVENTURES D'ALICE AU PAYS DES MERVEILLES, Lewis Carroll. Bué's translation of "Alice" into French, supervised by Carroll himself. Novel way to learn language. (No English text.) 42 Tenniel illustrations. 196pp. 22836-3 Pa. $2.50

MYTHS AND FOLK TALES OF IRELAND, Jeremiah Curtin. 11 stories that are Irish versions of European fairy tales and 9 stories from the Fenian cycle — 20 tales of legend and magic that comprise an essential work in the history of folklore. 256pp. 22430-9 Pa. $3.00

EAST O' THE SUN AND WEST O' THE MOON, George W. Dasent. Only full edition of favorite, wonderful Norwegian fairytales — Why the Sea is Salt, Boots and the Troll, etc. — with 77 illustrations by Kittelsen & Werenskiöld. 418pp. 22521-6 Pa. $4.00

PERRAULT'S FAIRY TALES, Charles Perrault and Gustave Doré. Original versions of Cinderella, Sleeping Beauty, Little Red Riding Hood, etc. in best translation, with 34 wonderful illustrations by Gustave Doré. 117pp. 8⅛ x 11. 22311-6 Pa. $2.50

EARLY NEW ENGLAND GRAVESTONE RUBBINGS, Edmund V. Gillon, Jr. 43 photographs, 226 rubbings show heavily symbolic, macabre, sometimes humorous primitive American art. Up to early 19th century. 207pp. 8⅜ x 11¼.
21380-3 Pa. $4.00

L.J.M. DAGUERRE: THE HISTORY OF THE DIORAMA AND THE DAGUERREOTYPE, Helmut and Alison Gernsheim. Definitive account. Early history, life and work of Daguerre; discovery of daguerreotype process; diffusion abroad; other early photography. 124 illustrations. 226pp. 6⅙ x 9¼.
22290-X Pa. $4.00

PHOTOGRAPHY AND THE AMERICAN SCENE, Robert Taft. The basic book on American photography as art, recording form, 1839-1889. Development, influence on society, great photographers, types (portraits, war, frontier, etc.), whatever else needed. Inexhaustible. Illustrated with 322 early photos, daguerreotypes, tintypes, stereo slides, etc. 546pp. 6⅛ x 9¼.
21201-7 Pa. $5.95

PHOTOGRAPHIC SKETCHBOOK OF THE CIVIL WAR, Alexander Gardner. Reproduction of 1866 volume with 100 on-the-field photographs: Manassas, Lincoln on battlefield, slave pens, etc. Introduction by E.F. Bleiler. 224pp. 10¾ x 9.
22731-6 Pa. $5.00

THE MOVIES: A PICTURE QUIZ BOOK, Stanley Appelbaum & Hayward Cirker. Match stars with their movies, name actors and actresses, test your movie skill with 241 stills from 236 great movies, 1902-1959. Indexes of performers and films. 128pp. 8⅜ x 9¼.
20222-4 Pa. $2.50

THE TALKIES, Richard Griffith. Anthology of features, articles from Photoplay, 1928-1940, reproduced complete. Stars, famous movies, technical features, fabulous ads, etc.; Garbo, Chaplin, King Kong, Lubitsch, etc. 4 color plates, scores of illustrations. 327pp. 8⅜ x 11¼.
22762-6 Pa. $6.95

THE MOVIE MUSICAL FROM VITAPHONE TO "42ND STREET," edited by Miles Kreuger. Relive the rise of the movie musical as reported in the pages of Photoplay magazine (1926-1933): every movie review, cast list, ad, and record review; every significant feature article, production still, biography, forecast, and gossip story. Profusely illustrated. 367pp. 8⅜ x 11¼.
23154-2 Pa. $6.95

JOHANN SEBASTIAN BACH, Philipp Spitta. Great classic of biography, musical commentary, with hundreds of pieces analyzed. Also good for Bach's contemporaries. 450 musical examples. Total of 1799pp.
EUK 22278-0, 22279-9 Clothbd., Two vol. set $25.00

BEETHOVEN AND HIS NINE SYMPHONIES, Sir George Grove. Thorough history, analysis, commentary on symphonies and some related pieces. For either beginner or advanced student. 436 musical passages. 407pp.
20334-4 Pa. $4.00

MOZART AND HIS PIANO CONCERTOS, Cuthbert Girdlestone. The only full-length study. Detailed analyses of all 21 concertos, sources; 417 musical examples. 509pp.
21271-8 Pa. $4.50

THE FITZWILLIAM VIRGINAL BOOK, edited by J. Fuller Maitland, W.B. Squire. Famous early 17th century collection of keyboard music, 300 works by Morley, Byrd, Bull, Gibbons, etc. Modern notation. Total of 938pp. 8⅜ x 11.
ECE 21068-5, 21069-3 Pa., Two vol. set $14.00

COMPLETE STRING QUARTETS, Wolfgang A. Mozart. Breitkopf and Härtel edition. All 23 string quartets plus alternate slow movement to K156. Study score. 277pp. 9⅜ x 12¼. 22372-8 Pa. $6.00

COMPLETE SONG CYCLES, Franz Schubert. Complete piano, vocal music of Die Schöne Müllerin, Die Winterreise, Schwanengesang. Also Drinker English singing translations. Breitkopf and Härtel edition. 217pp. 9⅜ x 12¼.
22649-2 Pa. $4.50

THE COMPLETE PRELUDES AND ETUDES FOR PIANOFORTE SOLO, Alexander Scriabin. All the preludes and etudes including many perfectly spun miniatures. Edited by K.N. Igumnov and Y.I. Mil'shteyn. 250pp. 9 x 12. 22919-X Pa. $5.00

TRISTAN UND ISOLDE, Richard Wagner. Full orchestral score with complete instrumentation. Do not confuse with piano reduction. Commentary by Felix Mottl, great Wagnerian conductor and scholar. Study score. 655pp. 8⅛ x 11.
22915-7 Pa. $10.00

FAVORITE SONGS OF THE NINETIES, ed. Robert Fremont. Full reproduction, including covers, of 88 favorites: Ta-Ra-Ra-Boom-De-Aye, The Band Played On, Bird in a Gilded Cage, Under the Bamboo Tree, After the Ball, etc. 401pp. 9 x 12.
EBE 21536-9 Pa. $6.95

SOUSA'S GREAT MARCHES IN PIANO TRANSCRIPTION: ORIGINAL SHEET MUSIC OF 23 WORKS, John Philip Sousa. Selected by Lester S. Levy. Playing edition includes: The Stars and Stripes Forever, The Thunderer, The Gladiator, King Cotton, Washington Post, much more. 24 illustrations. 111pp. 9 x 12.
USO 23132-1 Pa. $3.50

CLASSIC PIANO RAGS, selected with an introduction by Rudi Blesh. Best ragtime music (1897-1922) by Scott Joplin, James Scott, Joseph F. Lamb, Tom Turpin, 9 others. Printed from best original sheet music, plus covers. 364pp. 9 x 12.
EBE 20469-3 Pa. $6.95

ANALYSIS OF CHINESE CHARACTERS, C.D. Wilder, J.H. Ingram. 1000 most important characters analyzed according to primitives, phonetics, historical development. Traditional method offers mnemonic aid to beginner, intermediate student of Chinese, Japanese. 365pp. 23045-7 Pa. $4.00

MODERN CHINESE: A BASIC COURSE, Faculty of Peking University. Self study, classroom course in modern Mandarin. Records contain phonetics, vocabulary, sentences, lessons. 249 page book contains all recorded text, translations, grammar, vocabulary, exercises. Best course on market. 3 12" 33⅓ monaural records, book, album. 98832-5 Set $12.50

MANUAL OF THE TREES OF NORTH AMERICA, Charles S. Sargent. The basic survey of every native tree and tree-like shrub, 717 species in all. Extremely full descriptions, information on habitat, growth, locales, economics, etc. Necessary to every serious tree lover. Over 100 finding keys. 783 illustrations. Total of 986pp.
20277-1, 20278-X Pa., Two vol. set $8.00

BIRDS OF THE NEW YORK AREA, John Bull. Indispensable guide to more than 400 species within a hundred-mile radius of Manhattan. Information on range, status, breeding, migration, distribution trends, etc. Foreword by Roger Tory Peterson. 17 drawings; maps. 540pp. 23222-0 Pa. $6.00

THE SEA-BEACH AT EBB-TIDE, Augusta Foote Arnold. Identify hundreds of marine plants and animals: algae, seaweeds, squids, crabs, corals, etc. Descriptions cover food, life cycle, size, shape, habitat. Over 600 drawings. 490pp.
21949-6 Pa. $5.00

THE MOTH BOOK, William J. Holland. Identify more than 2,000 moths of North America. General information, precise species descriptions. 623 illustrations plus 48 color plates show almost all species, full size. 1968 edition. Still the basic book. Total of 551pp. 6½ x 9¼. 21948-8 Pa. $6.00

AN INTRODUCTION TO THE REPTILES AND AMPHIBIANS OF THE UNITED STATES, Percy A. Morris. All lizards, crocodiles, turtles, snakes, toads, frogs; life history, identification, habits, suitability as pets, etc. Non-technical, but sound and broad. 130 photos. 253pp. 22982-3 Pa. $3.00

OLD NEW YORK IN EARLY PHOTOGRAPHS, edited by Mary Black. Your only chance to see New York City as it was 1853-1906, through 196 wonderful photographs from N.Y. Historical Society. Great Blizzard, Lincoln's funeral procession, great buildings. 228pp. 9 x 12. 22907-6 Pa. $6.00

THE AMERICAN REVOLUTION, A PICTURE SOURCEBOOK, John Grafton. Wonderful Bicentennial picture source, with 411 illustrations (contemporary and 19th century) showing battles, personalities, maps, events, flags, posters, soldier's life, ships, etc. all captioned and explained. A wonderful browsing book, supplement to other historical reading. 160pp. 9 x 12. 23226-3 Pa. $4.00

PERSONAL NARRATIVE OF A PILGRIMAGE TO AL-MADINAH AND MECCAH, Richard Burton. Great travel classic by remarkably colorful personality. Burton, disguised as a Moroccan, visited sacred shrines of Islam, narrowly escaping death. Wonderful observations of Islamic life, customs, personalities. 47 illustrations. Total of 959pp. 21217-3, 21218-1 Pa., Two vol. set $10.00

INCIDENTS OF TRAVEL IN CENTRAL AMERICA, CHIAPAS, AND YUCATAN, John L. Stephens. Almost single-handed discovery of Maya culture; exploration of ruined cities, monuments, temples; customs of Indians. 115 drawings. 892pp.
22404-X, 22405-8 Pa., Two vol. set $8.00

CONSTRUCTION OF AMERICAN FURNITURE TREASURES, Lester Margon. 344 detail drawings, complete text on constructing exact reproductions of 38 early American masterpieces: Hepplewhite sideboard, Duncan Phyfe drop-leaf table, mantel clock, gate-leg dining table, Pa. German cupboard, more. 38 plates. 54 photographs. 168pp. 8⅜ x 11¼.   23056-2 Pa. $4.00

JEWELRY MAKING AND DESIGN, Augustus F. Rose, Antonio Cirino. Professional secrets revealed in thorough, practical guide: tools, materials, processes; rings, brooches, chains, cast pieces, enamelling, setting stones, etc. Do not confuse with skimpy introductions: beginner can use, professional can learn from it. Over 200 illustrations. 306pp.   21750-7 Pa. $3.00

METALWORK AND ENAMELLING, Herbert Maryon. Generally conceded best all-around book. Countless trade secrets: materials, tools, soldering, filigree, setting, inlay, niello, repoussé, casting, polishing, etc. For beginner or expert. Author was foremost British expert. 330 illustrations. 335pp.   22702-2 Pa. $3.50

WEAVING WITH FOOT-POWER LOOMS, Edward F. Worst. Setting up a loom, beginning to weave, constructing equipment, using dyes, more, plus over 285 drafts of traditional patterns including Colonial and Swedish weaves. More than 200 other figures. For beginning and advanced. 275pp. 8¾ x 6⅜.   23064-3 Pa. $4.00

WEAVING A NAVAJO BLANKET, Gladys A. Reichard. Foremost anthropologist studied under Navajo women, reveals every step in process from wool, dyeing, spinning, setting up loom, designing, weaving. Much history, symbolism. With this book you could make one yourself. 97 illustrations. 222pp.   22992-0 Pa. $3.00

NATURAL DYES AND HOME DYEING, Rita J. Adrosko. Use natural ingredients: bark, flowers, leaves, lichens, insects etc. Over 135 specific recipes from historical sources for cotton, wool, other fabrics. Genuine premodern handicrafts. 12 illustrations. 160pp.   22688-3 Pa. $2.00

THE HAND DECORATION OF FABRICS, Francis J. Kafka. Outstanding, profusely illustrated guide to stenciling, batik, block printing, tie dyeing, freehand painting, silk screen printing, and novelty decoration. 356 illustrations. 198pp. 6 x 9.
                                                          21401-X Pa. $3.00

THOMAS NAST: CARTOONS AND ILLUSTRATIONS, with text by Thomas Nast St. Hill. Father of American political cartooning. Cartoons that destroyed Tweed Ring; inflation, free love, church and state; original Republican elephant and Democratic donkey; Santa Claus; more. 117 illustrations. 146pp. 9 x 12.
                                                          22983-1 Pa. $4.00
                                                          23067-8 Clothbd. $8.50

FREDERIC REMINGTON: 173 DRAWINGS AND ILLUSTRATIONS. Most famous of the Western artists, most responsible for our myths about the American West in its untamed days. Complete reprinting of *Drawings of Frederic Remington* (1897), plus other selections. 4 additional drawings in color on covers. 140pp. 9 x 12.
                                                          20714-5 Pa. $3.95

HOW TO SOLVE CHESS PROBLEMS, Kenneth S. Howard. Practical suggestions on problem solving for very beginners. 58 two-move problems, 46 3-movers, 8 4-movers for practice, plus hints. 171pp. 20748-X Pa. $2.00

A GUIDE TO FAIRY CHESS, Anthony Dickins. 3-D chess, 4-D chess, chess on a cylindrical board, reflecting pieces that bounce off edges, cooperative chess, retrograde chess, maximummers, much more. Most based on work of great Dawson. Full handbook, 100 problems. 66pp. 7⅞ x 10¾. 22687-5 Pa. $2.00

WIN AT BACKGAMMON, Millard Hopper. Best opening moves, running game, blocking game, back game, tables of odds, etc. Hopper makes the game clear enough for anyone to play, and win. 43 diagrams. 111pp. 22894-0 Pa. $1.50

BIDDING A BRIDGE HAND, Terence Reese. Master player "thinks out loud" the binding of 75 hands that defy point count systems. Organized by bidding problem—no-fit situations, overbidding, underbidding, cueing your defense, etc. 254pp. EBE 22830-4 Pa. $2.50

THE PRECISION BIDDING SYSTEM IN BRIDGE, C.C. Wei, edited by Alan Truscott. Inventor of precision bidding presents average hands and hands from actual play, including games from 1969 Bermuda Bowl where system emerged. 114 exercises. 116pp. 21171-1 Pa. $1.75

LEARN MAGIC, Henry Hay. 20 simple, easy-to-follow lessons on magic for the new magician: illusions, card tricks, silks, sleights of hand, coin manipulations, escapes, and more —all with a minimum amount of equipment. Final chapter explains the great stage illusions. 92 illustrations. 285pp. 21238-6 Pa. $2.95

THE NEW MAGICIAN'S MANUAL, Walter B. Gibson. Step-by-step instructions and clear illustrations guide the novice in mastering 36 tricks; much equipment supplied on 16 pages of cut-out materials. 36 additional tricks. 64 illustrations. 159pp. 6⅝ x 10. 23113-5 Pa. $3.00

PROFESSIONAL MAGIC FOR AMATEURS, Walter B. Gibson. 50 easy, effective tricks used by professionals —cards, string, tumblers, handkerchiefs, mental magic, etc. 63 illustrations. 223pp. 23012-0 Pa. $2.50

CARD MANIPULATIONS, Jean Hugard. Very rich collection of manipulations; has taught thousands of fine magicians tricks that are really workable, eye-catching. Easily followed, serious work. Over 200 illustrations. 163pp. 20539-8 Pa. $2.00

ABBOTT'S ENCYCLOPEDIA OF ROPE TRICKS FOR MAGICIANS, Stewart James. Complete reference book for amateur and professional magicians containing more than 150 tricks involving knots, penetrations, cut and restored rope, etc. 510 illustrations. Reprint of 3rd edition. 400pp. 23206-9 Pa. $3.50

THE SECRETS OF HOUDINI, J.C. Cannell. Classic study of Houdini's incredible magic, exposing closely-kept professional secrets and revealing, in general terms, the whole art of stage magic. 67 illustrations. 279pp. 22913-0 Pa. $2.50

THE MAGIC MOVING PICTURE BOOK, Bliss, Sands & Co. The pictures in this book move! Volcanoes erupt, a house burns, a serpentine dancer wiggles her way through a number. By using a specially ruled acetate screen provided, you can obtain these and 15 other startling effects. Originally "The Motograph Moving Picture Book." 32pp. 8¼ x 11. 23224-7 Pa. $1.75

STRING FIGURES AND HOW TO MAKE THEM, Caroline F. Jayne. Fullest, clearest instructions on string figures from around world: Eskimo, Navajo, Lapp, Europe, more. Cats cradle, moving spear, lightning, stars. Introduction by A.C. Haddon. 950 illustrations. 407pp. 20152-X Pa. $3.00

PAPER FOLDING FOR BEGINNERS, William D. Murray and Francis J. Rigney. Clearest book on market for making origami sail boats, roosters, frogs that move legs, cups, bonbon boxes. 40 projects. More than 275 illustrations. Photographs. 94pp. 20713-7 Pa. $1.25

INDIAN SIGN LANGUAGE, William Tomkins. Over 525 signs developed by Sioux, Blackfoot, Cheyenne, Arapahoe and other tribes. Written instructions and diagrams: how to make words, construct sentences. Also 290 pictographs of Sioux and Ojibway tribes. 111pp. 6⅛ x 9¼. 22029-X Pa. $1.50

BOOMERANGS: HOW TO MAKE AND THROW THEM, Bernard S. Mason. Easy to make and throw, dozens of designs: cross-stick, pinwheel, boomabird, tumblestick, Australian curved stick boomerang. Complete throwing instructions. All safe. 99pp. 23028-7 Pa. $1.50

25 KITES THAT FLY, Leslie Hunt. Full, easy to follow instructions for kites made from inexpensive materials. Many novelties. Reeling, raising, designing your own. 70 illustrations. 110pp. 22550-X Pa. $1.25

TRICKS AND GAMES ON THE POOL TABLE, Fred Herrmann. 79 tricks and games, some solitaires, some for 2 or more players, some competitive; mystifying shots and throws, unusual carom, tricks involving cork, coins, a hat, more. 77 figures. 95pp. 21814-7 Pa. $1.25

WOODCRAFT AND CAMPING, Bernard S. Mason. How to make a quick emergency shelter, select woods that will burn immediately, make do with limited supplies, etc. Also making many things out of wood, rawhide, bark, at camp. Formerly titled Woodcraft. 295 illustrations. 580pp. 21951-8 Pa. $4.00

AN INTRODUCTION TO CHESS MOVES AND TACTICS SIMPLY EXPLAINED, Leonard Barden. Informal intermediate introduction: reasons for moves, tactics, openings, traps, positional play, endgame. Isolates patterns. 102pp. USO 21210-6 Pa. $1.35

LASKER'S MANUAL OF CHESS, Dr. Emanuel Lasker. Great world champion offers very thorough coverage of all aspects of chess. Combinations, position play, openings, endgame, aesthetics of chess, philosophy of struggle, much more. Filled with analyzed games. 390pp. 20640-8 Pa. $3.50

SLEEPING BEAUTY, illustrated by Arthur Rackham. Perhaps the fullest, most delightful version ever, told by C.S. Evans. Rackham's best work. 49 illustrations. 110pp. 7⅞ x 10¾.   22756-1 Pa. $2.00

THE WONDERFUL WIZARD OF OZ, L. Frank Baum. Facsimile in full color of America's finest children's classic. Introduction by Martin Gardner. 143 illustrations by W.W. Denslow. 267pp.   20691-2 Pa. $2.50

GOOPS AND HOW TO BE THEM, Gelett Burgess. Classic tongue-in-cheek masquerading as etiquette book. 87 verses, 170 cartoons as Goops demonstrate virtues of table manners, neatness, courtesy, more. 88pp. 6½ x 9¼.
                                                                22233-0 Pa. $1.50

THE BROWNIES, THEIR BOOK, Palmer Cox. Small as mice, cunning as foxes, exuberant, mischievous, Brownies go to zoo, toy shop, seashore, circus, more. 24 verse adventures. 266 illustrations. 144pp. 6⅝ x 9¼.   21265-3 Pa. $1.75

BILLY WHISKERS: THE AUTOBIOGRAPHY OF A GOAT, Frances Trego Montgomery. Escapades of that rambunctious goat. Favorite from turn of the century America. 24 illustrations. 259pp.   22345-0 Pa. $2.75

THE ROCKET BOOK, Peter Newell. Fritz, janitor's kid, sets off rocket in basement of apartment house; an ingenious hole punched through every page traces course of rocket. 22 duotone drawings, verses. 48pp. 6⅞ x 8⅜.   22044-3 Pa. $1.50

PECK'S BAD BOY AND HIS PA, George W. Peck. Complete double-volume of great American childhood classic. Hennery's ingenious pranks against outraged pomposity of pa and the grocery man. 97 illustrations. Introduction by E.F. Bleiler. 347pp.   20497-9 Pa. $2.50

THE TALE OF PETER RABBIT, Beatrix Potter. The inimitable Peter's terrifying adventure in Mr. McGregor's garden, with all 27 wonderful, full-color Potter illustrations. 55pp. 4¼ x 5½.   USO 22827-4 Pa. $1.00

THE TALE OF MRS. TIGGY-WINKLE, Beatrix Potter. Your child will love this story about a very special hedgehog and all 27 wonderful, full-color Potter illustrations. 57pp. 4¼ x 5½.   USO 20546-0 Pa. $1.00

THE TALE OF BENJAMIN BUNNY, Beatrix Potter. Peter Rabbit's cousin coaxes him back into Mr. McGregor's garden for a whole new set of ·dventures. A favorite with children. All 27 full-color illustrations. 59pp. 4¼ x 5½.
                                                                USO 21102-9 Pa. $1.00

THE MERRY ADVENTURES OF ROBIN HOOD, Howard Pyle. Facsimile of original (1883) edition, finest modern version of English outlaw's adventures. 23 illustrations by Pyle. 296pp. 6½ x 9¼.   22043-5 Pa. $2.75

TWO LITTLE SAVAGES, Ernest Thompson Seton. Adventures of two boys who lived as Indians; explaining Indian ways, woodlore, pioneer methods. 293 illustrations. 286pp.   20985-7 Pa. $3.00

HOUDINI ON MAGIC, Harold Houdini. Edited by Walter Gibson, Morris N. Young. How he escaped; exposés of fake spiritualists; instructions for eye-catching tricks; other fascinating material by and about greatest magician. 155 illustrations. 280pp. 20384-0 Pa. $2.50

HANDBOOK OF THE NUTRITIONAL CONTENTS OF FOOD, U.S. Dept. of Agriculture. Largest, most detailed source of food nutrition information ever prepared. Two mammoth tables: one measuring nutrients in 100 grams of edible portion; the other, in edible portion of 1 pound as purchased. Originally titled Composition of Foods. 190pp. 9 x 12. 21342-0 Pa. $4.00

COMPLETE GUIDE TO HOME CANNING, PRESERVING AND FREEZING, U.S. Dept. of Agriculture. Seven basic manuals with full instructions for jams and jellies; pickles and relishes; canning fruits, vegetables, meat; freezing anything. Really good recipes, exact instructions for optimal results. Save a fortune in food. 156 illustrations. 214pp. 6⅛ x 9¼. 22911-4 Pa. $2.50

THE BREAD TRAY, Louis P. De Gouy. Nearly every bread the cook could buy or make: bread sticks of Italy, fruit breads of Greece, glazed rolls of Vienna, everything from corn pone to croissants. Over 500 recipes altogether. including buns, rolls, muffins, scones, and more. 463pp. 23000-7 Pa. $3.50

CREATIVE HAMBURGER COOKERY, Louis P. De Gouy. 182 unusual recipes for casseroles, meat loaves and hamburgers that turn inexpensive ground meat into memorable main dishes: Arizona chili burgers, burger tamale pie, burger stew, burger corn loaf, burger wine loaf, and more. 120pp. 23001-5 Pa. $1.75

LONG ISLAND SEAFOOD COOKBOOK, J. George Frederick and Jean Joyce. Probably the best American seafood cookbook. Hundreds of recipes. 40 gourmet sauces, 123 recipes using oysters alone! All varieties of fish and seafood amply represented. 324pp. 22677-8 Pa. $3.00

THE EPICUREAN: A COMPLETE TREATISE OF ANALYTICAL AND PRACTICAL STUDIES IN THE CULINARY ART, Charles Ranhofer. Great modern classic. 3,500 recipes from master chef of Delmonico's, turn-of-the-century America's best restaurant. Also explained, many techniques known only to professional chefs. 775 illustrations. 1183pp. 6⅝ x 10. 22680-8 Clothbd. $17.50

THE AMERICAN WINE COOK BOOK, Ted Hatch. Over 700 recipes: old favorites livened up with wine plus many more: Czech fish soup, quince soup, sauce Perigueux, shrimp shortcake, filets Stroganoff, cordon bleu goulash, jambonneau, wine fruit cake, more. 314pp. 22796-0 Pa. $2.50

DELICIOUS VEGETARIAN COOKING, Ivan Baker. Close to 500 delicious and varied recipes: soups, main course dishes (pea, bean, lentil, cheese, vegetable, pasta, and egg dishes), savories, stews, whole-wheat breads and cakes, more. 168pp.
USO 22834-7 Pa. $1.75

COOKIES FROM MANY LANDS, Josephine Perry. Crullers, oatmeal cookies, chaux au chocolate, English tea cakes, mandel kuchen, Sacher torte, Danish puff pastry, Swedish cookies — a mouth-watering collection of 223 recipes. 157pp.
22832-0 Pa. $2.00

ROSE RECIPES, Eleanour S. Rohde. How to make sauces, jellies, tarts, salads, potpourris, sweet bags, pomanders, perfumes from garden roses; all exact recipes. Century old favorites. 95pp.
22957-2 Pa. $1.25

"OSCAR" OF THE WALDORF'S COOKBOOK, Oscar Tschirky. Famous American chef reveals 3455 recipes that made Waldorf great; cream of French, German, American cooking, in all categories. Full instructions, easy home use. 1896 edition. 907pp. 6⅝ x 9⅜.
20790-0 Clothbd. $15.00

JAMS AND JELLIES, May Byron. Over 500 old-time recipes for delicious jams, jellies, marmalades, preserves, and many other items. Probably the largest jam and jelly book in print. Originally titled May Byron's Jam Book. 276pp.
USO 23130-5 Pa. $3.00

MUSHROOM RECIPES, André L. Simon. 110 recipes for everyday and special cooking. Champignons à la grecque, sole bonne femme, chicken liver croustades, more; 9 basic sauces, 13 ways of cooking mushrooms. 54pp.
USO 20913-X Pa. $1.25

FAVORITE SWEDISH RECIPES, edited by Sam Widenfelt. Prepared in Sweden, offers wonderful, clearly explained Swedish dishes: appetizers, meats, pastry and cookies, other categories. Suitable for American kitchen. 90 photos. 157pp.
23156-9 Pa. $2.00

THE BUCKEYE COOKBOOK, Buckeye Publishing Company. Over 1,000 easy-to-follow, traditional recipes from the American Midwest: bread (100 recipes alone), meat, game, jam, candy, cake, ice cream, and many other categories of cooking. 64 illustrations. From 1883 enlarged edition. 416pp.
23218-2 Pa. $4.00

TWENTY-TWO AUTHENTIC BANQUETS FROM INDIA, Robert H. Christie. Complete, easy-to-do recipes for almost 200 authentic Indian dishes assembled in 22 banquets. Arranged by region. Selected from Banquets of the Nations. 192pp.
23200-X Pa. $2.50

Prices subject to change without notice.
Available at your book dealer or write for free catalogue to Dept. GI, Dover Publications, Inc., 180 Varick St., N.Y., N.Y. 10014. Dover publishes more than 150 books each year on science, elementary and advanced mathematics, biology, music, art, literary history, social sciences and other areas.